# TALES OF MENDELE THE BOOK PEDDLER

THE LIBRARY OF YIDDISH CLASSICS
IS SPONSORED BY THE FUND FOR THE
TRANSLATION OF JEWISH LITERATURE

Series editor: Ruth R. Wisse

LIBRARY OF YIDDISH CLASSICS

# TALES OF MENDELE THE BOOK PEDDLER

## FISHKE THE LAME AND BENJAMIN THE THIRD

### S. Y. Abramovitsh

(MENDELE MOYKHER SFORIM)

**Edited by Dan Miron and Ken Frieden**

INTRODUCTION BY DAN MIRON
TRANSLATIONS BY TED GORELICK
AND HILLEL HALKIN

SCHOCKEN BOOKS / NEW YORK

All rights reserved under International and Pan-American
Copyright Conventions. Published in the United States by
Schocken Books Inc., New York, and simultaneously in Canada
by Random House of Canada Limited, Toronto. Distributed by
Pantheon Books, a division of Random House, Inc., New York.

Library of Congress Cataloging-in-Publication Data

Mendele Moykher Sforim, 1835–1917.
[Fishke der krumer. English]
Tales of Mendele the Book Peddler: Fishke the Lame and Benjamin
the Third / S. Y. Abramovitsh (Mendele Moykher Sforim); edited by
Dan Miron and Ken Frieden; introduction by Dan Miron; translations
by Ted Gorelick and Hillel Halkin.
p. cm. — (Library of Yiddish classics)
ISBN 0-8052-4136-1
I. Mendele Moykher Sforim, 1835–1917. II. Miron, Dan.
III. Frieden, Ken, 1955– . IV. Mendele Moykher Sforim,
1835–1917. Kitsur mas‘ ot Binyamin ha-shelishi. English. V. Title.
VI. Series.
PJ5129.A2F513 1996
839'.0933—dc20        95-38178
CIP

*Book design by Chris Welch*

Manufactured in the United States of America
2   4   6   8   9   7   5   3   1

# CONTENTS

# INTRODUCTION

## I

FOR A CENTURY S. Y. ABRAMOVITSH (1835–1917), popularly known by the name of his fictional persona, Mendele Moykher Sforim (Mendele the Book Peddler), has been acknowledged not only as the founding father of modern Jewish prose fiction in both Yiddish and Hebrew but also as a literary master of international significance, a writer whose work represents one of the most distinctive, poignant, and universally meaningful expressions of the Jewish imagination. Within the particular framework of the history of both modern Yiddish and modern Hebrew literature, Abramovitsh has been hailed as a towering innovator who freed these literatures from the strictures of the belated Jewish "Age of Reason," the Haskalah, or Jewish Enlightenment, which began in the last decades of the eighteenth century and lingered throughout the better part of the nineteenth. Having done so, he propelled these literatures—artistically, stylistically, and ideationally—directly into modernity. Of course, he himself was born into that same Haskalah environment, both as an intellectual and as a writer, and in some ways retained throughout his long career some of its characteristic imprint. He managed, however, to transcend its limitations, to lead a host of younger writers toward freer and more accommodating artistic and ideological surroundings. In this way, he directly contributed to the historical coming-of-age of modern writing in both Yiddish and Hebrew.

As an artist of universal stature Abramovitsh gained distinction by projecting—for the first time in modern literature—the historical presence and unique lifestyle of the traditional premodern Eastern European Jewish community as a total, complex, and aesthetically balanced and self-contained "world." If the civilization of the Jewish shtetl became a source of meaningful images for modern European intellectuals and artists, it was Abramovitsh who formed the conceptual and aesthetic terms that made this possible. He was the first modern Jewish artist who learned how to balance his own modernity, and that of the culture he represented, with the traditionalism of an essentially medieval civilization without destroying the spirit of that civilization and without betraying his own commitment as a modernist to the norms of European humanism. He subjected the shtetl to a scathing exposé and presented its traditional culture as deeply flawed; and yet he also managed, as an artist, not to remain at a distance from the object of his aesthetic exploration and to allow the shtetl to speak for itself, to use its own authentic voice, to project its own inherent priorities, values, and fantasies. In all of this he was the trailblazer for all of the modern Jewish artists who found in the image of the shtetl a metaphor, ethnically distinct and historically focused but also of suprahistorical and universal significance, representing the human condition at large as well. Thus, Abramovitsh is the spiritual father not only of internationally renowned writers such as Sholem Aleichem, I. L. Peretz, S. Y. Agnon, and I. B. Singer but also of artists working in other media, such as the painters Marc Chagall, El (Eliezer) Lissitzky, and I. B. Ryback and the great Yiddish stage actors Shloyme Mikhoels and Maurice Schwartz. No wonder that with such an achievement, perfected throughout the course of an arduous career encompassing more than a half century, Abramovitsh has become something of a cult figure as the "grandfather" of modern Jewish literature, the first of its "classics," and the quintessential modern Jewish artist.

## II

This recognition, however, did not come to Abramovitsh early or easily. When his unique contribution was first acknowledged by people like Sholem Aleichem or the historian Simon Dubnov, in the late 1880s, he had already published an early version of all but one of his major works. He could already look back—not without some frustration—to three decades of literary labor. By no means could he consider himself, at that point in his career, a happy and fulfilled person.

Born in 1835 in the tiny provincial Belorussian town of Kapulye into a middle-class shtetl family, Abramovitsh lost all familial support and status at the age of fifteen when his father died and his consequently impoverished mother remarried. This was the first of several calamities he suffered during the first fifty years of his life. Abramovitsh was left to fend for himself and after spending two or three years at various *ye-*

*shivas,* as a poor student, dependent on charity, he decided to make the long, adventuresome, and perilous trek south, to the Ukraine. Within the Jewish linguistic and cultural geography of Eastern Europe, Belorussia formed a part of "Lithuania," the center of Jewish learning and traditional scholastic prowess. However, Lithuanian Jewry underwent a continuous process of pauperization throughout the first half of the nineteenth century, and young scholars like Abramovitsh, without a future in their hometowns, emigrated to the relatively more prosperous, but intellectually more impoverished, southern communities, offering their services as tutors and teachers and seeking sustenance and social support. Abramovitsh found both in the Volhynian communities, first in Kamieniec-Podolsk (1853–58) and then in Berdichev (1858–68), in the form of marriages into middle-class families and through the guidance and friendship of some local exponents of the Haskalah. For a short while, he served as a teacher in a "modern" Jewish school, supervised by the Russian authorities; most of the time, however, the support of his father-in-law allowed him to devote himself to secular learning and soon enough (from 1857 on) to writing and publishing as well. His first, miserable marriage to a mentally unbalanced young woman had to be dissolved. The second match, to the "educated" daughter of a Berdichev notary (during their courtship Abramovitsh wrote letters to her in faltering Russian), was happier and lasted the rest of his life. For a full decade, this marriage enabled him to lead a life free from financial worries and dedicated to literary and intellectual pursuits.

Berdichev, a relatively large urban center that served as the capital of Jewish commerce in the Ukraine, had its intellectual circle as well as a small literary community. Here, young Abramovitsh could truly develop as a writer and a thinker. He

read, wrote, became acquainted with the "enlightened" people of the town, and engaged in communal and charitable
activities. What interested him most were the classics of
eighteenth-century German rationalist philosophy, nineteenth-
century Russian "progressive" literary criticism, and, above
all, popular science, which he absorbed from German biology, chemistry, and physics textbooks. His central project was
to assemble a large compendium of science textbooks, beginning with a zoology textbook, which he adapted from the
German. In 1862 he also published the first part of a Hebrew
novel. Somewhat earlier, in 1860, he had made a name for
himself as a literary critic, creating a "scandal" by attacking a
literary miscellany of an older fellow-*maskil*. He also became
known as a journalist and a writer of essays, focusing on current Jewish affairs, particularly the problems of education.
Moving from one genre to another, he achieved prominence
in none.

Two important qualities characterized his work. First,
Abramovitsh proved to be an innovator and a pioneer from
the very beginning of his writing career. When he wrote his
"notorious" critical essay in 1860, "professional" Hebrew literary criticism was yet to be invented. Along with his rival
and enemy A. A. Kovner and his fellow Kapulyer A. J. Pa-
perna, Abramovitsh became one of the founding fathers of
this genre in Hebrew. The same is true of his role as the author of the 1862 novel *Limdu hetev* (Learn to do good). As a
novel which focused on contemporary Jewish life in Eastern
Europe, it had but one predecessor, A. Mapu's then as-yet-
unfinished *Ayit tsavua* (The hypocrite). Applying the language
to brand-new ends, Abramovitsh had to adapt stiff, pseudobiblical Hebrew to the representation of contemporary Jewish affairs, and create from scratch the vocabulary needed for
scientific textbooks. Second, Abramovitsh's efforts were in-

formed by a central idea: his goal was to orient the mind of Hebrew readers, particularly the younger ones, toward "reality" by distancing them from the world of abstraction and mystification and making them encounter "things as they are." Then, as later, Abramovitsh believed this was a moral necessity. Thus, he adapted texts dealing with biology and chemistry not merely to introduce his readers to the rudiments of scientific knowledge but also to strengthen their moral equilibrium and mental clarity. The novel was meant to present an encounter with social reality, just as the science textbooks offered a close-up view of the material-biological sphere. In his literary criticism Abramovitsh attacked a literature which he thought did not relate to reality and was immersed in its own flowery verbosity.

Of course, there was nothing particularly original in all of this. The Haskalah literature as a whole based itself on the premise that the Jews, caught within the "dreams" of their old, and by then archaic, cultural traditions of legal exegesis and kabbalistic mysticism, had to be awakened, jolted if necessary, into facing up to present social and cultural realities. They had to shake off their ostensible inertia and actively join the progressive European community of the nineteenth century. After Alexander II, the great liberator-czar, ascended the Russian throne in 1856, the literature of the Hebrew Enlightenment reverberated with Y. L. Gordon's cry, "Awake, my people!" In this climate, Abramovitsh's ardent faith in the transforming power of "education" was hardly original. What was relatively new about his definition of the "reality" principle was the very concrete and literal identification of the "real" with one's immediate material, biological, and social surroundings. Although "progressive" Russian and German thinkers had insisted on this identification for some time and Abramovitsh had found it in Russian literary criticism, which he read avidly, the idea was still quite new in the essentially idealistic milieu of the Hebrew Enlightenment.

## III

In 1864, Abramovitsh's radical allegiance to the "reality" principle led him into a literary experiment far riskier than anything he had attempted before: the writing of a short novel in Yiddish, entitled *Dos kleyne mentshele* (The little man). In Eastern Europe, the language of the Jewish masses was Yiddish; in order to spread their ideas, local exponents of the Haskalah had to address their intended audience in its own spoken medium. Most Jewish men used some Hebrew for liturgical purposes, but only a scholarly minority knew the language well enough to read a Hebrew literature which presumably was written for their benefit. Women understood Yiddish only. Clearly, the "simple" people and the female readership could be reached only through Yiddish. The leaders of the Hasidic movement had understood this well enough to develop a hagiographic and homiletic literature in Yiddish as well as in Hebrew; only their more abstract theological and kabbalistic treatises did they publish exclusively in Hebrew. Faced with the growing popularity of Hasidism, adherents of the Haskalah had to acknowledge a need for popular Yiddish literature through which their ideals could be propagated. However, despite their many attempts to initiate such a literature, by the end of the first half of the nineteenth century it barely existed. There were many reasons for this failure, beginning with a deep-seated "objection" to Yiddish on the part of the *maskilim*. Most of them violently despised the language, which, besides offending them linguistically and aesthetically as a "hodgepodge jargon," symbolized to them Jewish sepa-

rateness, that inbred solipsistic Jewish self-sufficiency rendering Jews "a nation unto itself" in the midst of their host nations. While Hebrew served as the vehicle of the authentic
Jewish tradition embodied in the Bible, in the liturgy, and in
religious ritual, and thus had to be preserved and developed
as the core of Jewish identity, Yiddish allegedly presented
nothing more than a stubborn vestige of medieval particular-
ism, an unwillingness on the part of its speakers to engage in
a cultural dialogue with the non-Jewish environment. As
such, Yiddish formed a barrier which had to be removed and
eliminated rather than preserved. Because of this attitude, by
the beginning of the 1860s, Eastern Europe contained no
more than two "professional" *maskilic* Yiddish writers. One,
Yisroel Aksenfeld, a novelist and playwright, could get
scarcely any of his work into print. The other, A. M. Dik, the
author of many popular novellas and homiletic tales, was despised as a two-penny raconteur for female audiences. Yiddish
literature as an institution was still nonexistent.

Driven by the inner logic of realism, Abramovitsh moved
into the neglected domain of Yiddish writing. The launching
in 1863 of *Kol mevasser* (The herald), a weekly Yiddish magazine with a *maskilic* orientation—an admission that Yiddish
was required—served as an additional source of motivation,
as did perhaps his personal acquaintance with Y. M. Lifshits, a
fellow resident of Berdichev and a very rare bird among the
*maskilim* in his authentic dedication and devotion to colloquial
Yiddish. However, Abramovitsh knew that by succumbing to
the Yiddish "itch" he was crossing a cultural boundary. He
therefore took every precaution to hide his authorship and
published *The Little Man* anonymously in *Kol mevasser*, presenting the narrative to the readers of the magazine as an authentic written confession and will of a real person who, before
he died, had entrusted a real local book peddler, Mendele,

with the task of making the document publicly known. As he was to divulge later, Abramovitsh initially viewed his Yiddish writing as a kind of transgression, as if he had developed an illicit affair with a mistress whom he visited secretly and shamefully enjoyed; eventually, this "mistress" would become the mother of some of his literary offspring.[1] Obviously, Hebrew was meant to remain the legitimate, acknowledged spouse and Abramovitsh's Hebrew publications were regarded as his own legitimate "progeny." The Yiddish "bastards" were to be tended by Mendele Moykher Sforim—a mask, a fiction, a spokesman, and a cover. Abramovitsh himself would deny paternity.

Clearly, Abramovitsh was increasingly "seduced" by his Yiddish mistress. For one thing, *The Little Man* as it appeared in the magazine in installments and also a short time later in book form (1865) scored a great hit and proved to be one of the few really popular successes that Abramovitsh was ever to enjoy. This warm reception contrasted favorably with the very limited response to his Hebrew works, even to his first completed Hebrew novel, *Ha'oves vehabonim* (The fathers and the sons, 1868). Then, too, working with the flowing, malleable, and lively spoken idiom released Abramovitsh's artistic passion. How difficult and frustrating it must have been to return from the lovely mistress to dour cohabitation with a stiff and stilted "spouse": the writing of fiction without real passion usually yields very poor results.

And then there was an additional consideration. Hebrew literature of the Haskalah had traditionally cast its lot with the Jewish mercantile middle class. While waiting for good tidings from enlightened emperors such as the Austro-Hungarian Joseph II or the Russian Alexander II, the Hebrew Enlighteners relied on the expanding class of Jewish large- and small-scale entrepreneurs participating in one way or another in the development of capitalism in Eastern Europe. These people, in constant contact with non-Jews, had, in order to conduct their business affairs successfully, to think and behave rationally and realistically. Thus, they would form the sociocultural vanguard and the source from which rationality, good order, and liberal attitudes would spread and influence the Jewish population as a whole. Some *maskilim* genuinely empathized with the lot of the lower classes, the artisans, the servants, the pauperized hawkers and penny-merchants. They were fully aware that these people were not only poor, hungry, and ignorant but also brutalized, manipulated, and exploited in various ways. They blamed the Hasidic leaders for squeezing their last pennies from these people; they exposed a communal leadership which handed over the children of the poor into military service in place of the children of the rich. None of them, however, addressed the poor directly. No one considered that the poor were possessed of a presence of mind sufficient to "receive the light."

Abramovitsh shared these attitudes. For instance, when he became socially active around 1864, his mission was to help members of the Berdichev commercial middle class who had suffered financial losses as a result of the Polish rebellion of 1863. Abramovitsh maintained that cheap credit, if made available to these people, would prevent their proletarization. The truly destitute were beyond help and doomed anyhow. Characteristically, Abramovitsh's early Hebrew novel, *The Fathers and The Sons,* focuses on a family melodrama in which a middle-class merchant, a follower of Hasidism, learns through a crisis—both familial and financial—that the future belongs to the younger generation allied with the forces of the Enlightenment. However, Abramovitsh's view of the middle class was changing. He realized that when it came to protecting its own interests, the middle class cared little about

morality or even good sense and the "enlightened" among
them gladly cooperated with the "benighted" at the expense of
the poor.

Thus, Abramovitsh gradually cut himself off from the
socio-ideological moorings and the traditional attitudes of the
Hebrew Enlightenment and this was undoubtedly connected
with his switch to Yiddish; for as a popular Yiddish writer he
was now bonding with the poorer people, who were among
his most enthusiastic readers. By writing his fiction in Yiddish
instead of Hebrew, he not only was replacing one language
with another and one narrative order (authorial, all-knowing,
objective) with another (colloquial, monologic, subjective),
but was also discovering new issues and new protagonists. He
turned his back on both the fathers, the middle-class merchants, and the children, the heroic young scholars and beautiful, long-suffering young women, who as followers of the
Enlightenment clashed with their parents. Instead, he became
interested in helpless and ignorant characters such as Hershele of *Dos vintshfingerl* (The magic ring, first version 1865),
a poor shtetl kid left to fend for himself in a larger commercial town and all but lost when a benevolent and enlightened
businessman with German connections takes pity on him; or
Fishke of *Fishke der krumer* (Fishke the lame, first version
1869), an ignorant, simpleminded cripple who much more
than his "betters" knows how to respond to the call of human
emotion. In his first play, *Di takse* (The tax, 1869),
Abramovitsh settled accounts with the Jewish middle class
and with the communal leaders of Berdichev, whom he portrayed as bloodthirsty predators preying on the poor. The
melodrama, which presents a divided community, one part
haggard, pale, bloodless, and naive and the other red, padded
with flesh, seething with cunning and malevolence, gave
much offense. Abramovitsh often repeated the claim that it

triggered his departure from Berdichev because threats were made against his life and the well-being of his family.

We need not accept this as a historical truth; Abramovitsh actually left Berdichev and settled in Zhitomir a few months *before* the publicaton of *The Tax*. In fact, this move was occasioned by far more serious circumstances. His father-in-law, whose business had been deteriorating for some time, died in 1868, leaving his family very little. Suddenly, Abramovitsh found himself in a situation similar to the one he faced in the wake of his own father's death. But this time he was thirty-three years old and financially responsible for a large and growing family. The Volhynian town of Zhitomir housed one of the two government-sponsored rabbinical seminaries in czarist Russia, an institution that ordained crown rabbis to serve in an official administrative capacity within the Jewish community, rather than as experts in Jewish rabbinic law. Abramovitsh saw no reason why, with his erudition, knowledge of Russian, and long list of publications, he might not complete the required course of study, be ordained as a crown rabbi, and thus support his family. He was accepted and in a short time completed his studies. Despite his ordination, however, he was unable to find a position. He would remain in Zhitomir for the next twelve years (1869–81) in great financial straits.

## IV

The 1870s were the most trying years in Abramovitsh's life. Financially, he could never make ends meet; literature—Yiddish or Hebrew—could not put food on the table of a large household. He hoped for public assistance, in recognition of the publication of the third volume of his zoology textbook in

1872, but was disappointed. After the demise of *Kol mevasser,*
he dreamed of editing his own Yiddish weekly. He scored one
more hit with his brilliant allegorical novel *Di klyatshe* (The
nag, 1873), popular particularly among the better-educated
shtetl readership, who debated the meaning of the work and
attempted to decipher its allegorical symbols. However, even
this triumph could not save him from having to waste a great
deal of time on hack jobs, such as publishing calendars (Jewish merchant counterparts of farmers' almanacs). He stopped
writing belles-lettres in any language but Yiddish, and despite
the fact that he continued to publish important essays quite
regularly in Hebrew periodicals, his career as a Hebrew
writer seemed to have run aground. Toward the end of the
decade he was hit by personal catastrophes—a death in the
family and the conversion to Christianity of his son, in exile as
a result of having been charged with revolutionary activity.
These events paralyzed him as a writer for the next five years
(1879–84).

Despite these hardships, it was in the 1870s that Abramovitsh developed as an original thinker and brilliant artist. As a
thinker, he had finally wrenched himself out of the habitual
concerns of the Haskalah, with its view of education as the
panacea for all human and, particularly, for Jewish ills. He
began to pay attention to the dynamics of the historical
process and the development of historical legacies. He came
to understand, for instance, that anti-Semitism was not
merely a dying ember left over from the Middle Ages or a justified reaction to the refusal of the Jews to become "European." Rather, it was an entrenched mental attitude nourished
by religion, myth, irrational fear, and sheer brutality, which
had to be acknowledged as an integral part of European society. As such, it showed no signs of petering out but rather
changed its outward form and ideology, seeping into various

"modern" and even liberal views and attitudes. He also revised his understanding of the Jewish past, summarized in *The
Nag* and in his long allegorical poem, *Yudl* (1875), as something that could not simply be wiped out by "education." In
fact, it served to foster an identity, a "character," an essence
which, for all its flaws, would remain at the core of the Jewish
people. These new insights found their first fresh and exciting
expression in *The Nag*, where a comic or a tragicomic reversal
of roles reflects the far-reaching changes in the author's attitude. Isrolik, the *maskil* rationalist educator, loses his mental
equilibrium in an unsuccessful attempt to matriculate in a
Russian university as a medical student. Significantly, his
stumbling blocks prove to be Russian history, literature, and
folklore, that is, his inability to grasp the real historical identity and psychomythical legacy of the host nation with which
he wants his own nation to fraternize. Thus, the rationalist
unable to face the irrational loses his reason, and as a madman
encounters what his mind had previously refused to recognize: the essence of his own historical identity and that of his
people, personified by a miserable, hungry, and beleaguered
nag. He approaches it patronizingly and offers the cure prescribed by the Enlightenment: self-improvement by means of
education. But the nag is not convinced. Low-spirited and
submissive as she is, she trusts her own long history of experience of persecution and subtly resists Isrolik's exhortations.
As the story unfolds, the nag, although far from accepting Isrolik's "solutions," gradually overcomes her suspicions and resistance and waxes more intimate and frank with him. How
can a hungry and sick creature be expected to improve itself
through education? she asks. Is the stipulation that help to the
needy should depend on self-improvement through education
realistic, fair, or morally tenable? Her negative answer—"No

dancing before feeding"—is devastatingly logical on both moral and practical levels.

Isrolik the educator is reduced to a humble student and the ignorant nag becomes his teacher. Their encounter opens up a series of intellectual perspectives: the nature of sanity and insanity, the function of the irrational, the power of poetry and emotive language, the aridity of reason unless it is supported by sensibility and true emotion, the "truth" inherent in folklore and myth, even the dangers of industrial pollution, which metaphorically represents the moral threat and challenge of modern industrialism. In this masterpiece, which is the closest thing in the Jewish literary tradition to Swift's *Gulliver's Travels*, Abramovitsh abandoned the threadbare Enlightenment triad—rationality, education, and optimistic faith in the liberal ideal—and grappled with issues of universal and national significance which the Haskalah had never faced before. He did not sever his ties with the Enlightenment, but gave it a new definition which vastly broadened and deepened the intellectual perspective and the sheer perceptiveness indicated by the term. Thus, when in 1878 Abramovitsh published his most caustic and devastating *maskilic* satire, *Kitser masoes Binyomin hashlishi* (The brief travels of Benjamin the Third), he pushed his Haskalah critique of Jewish life virtually to the point where in a few years hence, under the impact of the 1881–82 pogroms, it would be replaced by Jewish nationalism in general and by Zionism in particular. Leaving aside the issues of ignorance, superstition, archaic educational methods, and so on, he focused on issues pertaining to the *political* identity of the Jews: issues of Jewish power and powerlessness, Jewish political passivity against the backdrop of a politically hyperactive modern Europe, Jewish yearning for political independence and sovereignty—all of these before

Zionism was officially born. The question posed by Abramovitsh was whether a Jewish political awakening was possible
or whether it was bound to result in a mere caricature, as the
genre of *Masoes Binyomin,* the mock-epic, indicated.

# V

In 1881, in the midst of a harrowing familial and personal crisis, Abramovitsh was invited to serve as the principal or superintendent of a new school founded and maintained by the
Jewish community of Odessa. The position ensured him the
financial stability he had been seeking for years and he gladly
accepted, moving with his family to the southern seaport
where he was to remain for the rest of his long life (except for
three years in the wake of the 1905 pogroms, which he spent
in Geneva).

Like the city itself, the Odessa Jewish community was
young, commercially active, affluent, unburdened by tradition, and relatively modern in its Jewish outlook. Having
barely shaken off its frontier-town ambience, Odessa housed
a Jewish community founded by adventurers—contractors,
merchants, and entrepreneurs—who had left their Jewish
families and their Jewish piety back home in the little towns
dotting the Pale. Gradually, the community assumed the religious and cultural patterns of behavior imported by immi-
grant Galician merchants, Germanized and acculturated in
their hometown of Brody, an Enlightenment outpost in the
Austro-Hungarian empire. Soon, Odessa could boast of a Re-
form synagogue and a German, university-trained rabbi. On
the other hand, the city never quite lost its slightly seedy, low-
brow, "Wild West" quality, which it imparted to its own
unique brand of modern Jewish culture; in the infamous tav-

erns of Odessa the foundations of Yiddish vaudeville were laid. Beginning in the 1870s, Odessa would become the crucible for the creation of a modern Jewish literary culture as well; in the 1880s it would become one of the organizational and spiritual centers for the emerging Zionist movement. Here a new Russian-Jewish *Wissenschaft des Judentums* was created by the historian Simon Dubnov, and a modern Hebrew humanism by the preeminent Zionist philosopher Ahad Ha'am (Asher Ginzberg). During the last two decades of the nineteenth century, Odessa played host to a variety of Russian-Jewish thinkers, artists, publicists, and litterateurs, collectively known as *Khakhmey Odessa* (the sages of Odessa), and it was here that Abramovitsh would find his intellectual and spiritual niche.

As the locus of cultural experimentation, Odessa quite naturally became the place where experiments in Jewish education were first tried—for example, attempts to modernize traditional biblical and Talmudic study and teaching very young children "Hebrew in Hebrew." Hence the appeal to a self-proclaimed modernist and innovator such as Abramovitsh to assume the role of principal in the modernized communal *talmud toyre*. His new duties as both teacher and administrator were numerous and time-consuming. But the move successfully revived Abramovitsh's literary talents. He was quickly absorbed into the nationalist intellectual circle of Jewish writers, scholars, and cultural activists. The invigorating atmosphere whetted his literary appetite and he soon began writing and publishing again, starting with his second melodrama, *Der priziv* (The military draft, 1884), and then moving on to the grand project of refashioning and completely rewriting all of his major works. Actually, he had already conceived of the project in the 1870s as the accelerated process of his artistic development made his earlier works seem

primitive and skeletal. In 1879 he published a greatly expanded, fleshed-out, and reworked version of *The Little Man*.
Now, in the mid-1880s, he proceeded to rewrite *Fishke the
Lame* and *The Magic Ring*. These new versions of the old stories were suddenly in great demand by the new literary editors of the day, such as Sholem Aleichem, and triggered an
enthusiastic critical response from famous Odessa intellectuals such as Dubnov and M. Morgulis. Indeed, within less than
a decade an almost miraculous change in his professional and
literary status took place.

The event that precipitated this change was the rise of the
new Jewish nationalism, in the course of which the status of
Yiddish underwent a transformation. Together with the realization that the hope for Jewish emancipation in a progres-
sively liberalized czarist empire was a mere pipe dream and
had to be replaced with a plan for "auto-emancipation," a
more comprehensive intellectual reorientation sent members
of the Russian-Jewish intelligentsia "back to the people," to
the Yiddish-speaking masses. Although still despised by committed Hebraists, Yiddish was suddenly given pride of place
as a national asset. Just as suddenly, people began to discover a
need for and the actual existence of a modern literature in
Yiddish. Clearly, if such a literature existed, Abramovitsh
would be one of its mainstays. His experiments in writing a
new kind of modern Jewish narrative in colloquial Yiddish
were now hailed as "classics," cornerstones of a new cultural
institution. *Fishke the Lame,* for example, was held up by
Sholem Aleichem as a shining model for younger writers who
were exploring the possibilities inherent in a "Jewish novel."

On top of this new popularity as the "grandfather of Yiddish literature," an appellation invented by Sholem Aleichem,
Abramovitsh returned to writing Hebrew fiction in 1886,
catching something of the Hebraic-Zionist mood then cur-

rent in Odessa. Throughout the late 1880s and early 1890s, he produced a series of brilliant short stories and novellas in Hebrew, in which the hot issues of the age of the new Jewish nationalism were shrewdly and sensitively scrutinized. Soon after, he expanded the project of rewriting his entire oeuvre to include the Hebrew versions of his works as well. Almost immediately he was hailed as the greatest contemporary writer of Hebrew prose fiction; for in reverting to Hebrew he would not relinquish the warmth, fluidity, and pungency to which he had become accustomed in his Yiddish writing. With consummate skill, he devised a new narrative Hebrew idiom in which various historical layers of the language—biblical, post-biblical, midrashic, and rabbinic—were dextrously blended, allowing for a syntactic freedom, richness of vocabulary, variety of nuance, idiomatic pungency, parodic wit, and sheer descriptive accuracy which had never before existed in modern Hebrew. This, in itself, was acknowledged—particularly by younger writers who readily availed themselves of the successful formula—as a contribution of historic import.

Abramovitsh never became a full-fledged Zionist, and indeed in his short stories of the late 1880s and early 1890s he often made Zionist activism the object of his satire. Nevertheless, he was now as fully acceptable to Zionists as he was to Yiddishists, Jewish socialists, and the prophets of a Jewish aesthetic renaissance. It was generally recognized that as early as the 1870s he had thoroughly grappled with the basic issues of the new Jewish nationalism. For that as well as for his artistic achievement he was viewed as a figure of national stature. Over time, his Odessa home became a literary court of sorts and was duly frequented by the local Jewish intellectuals and aspiring young writers who arrived in town and were quick to pay homage to "the grandfather." Abramovitsh developed a royal, sometimes despotic manner and thoroughly enjoyed a prestige which in the 1890s was rivaled only by the charisma of Ahad Ha'am and in the first decade of the twentieth century by the magnetism of the young Hayim Nahman Bialik.

As a fabulist, Abramovitsh did not possess a very strong and fertile imaginative capacity, so from the second half of the 1890s he settled down to a regimen of daily toil which was increasingly channeled in the direction of rewriting, with less and less effort devoted to new creations. For many years he worked on his last major novel, the autobiographical *Shloyme reb khayims* (Shloyme, the son of Reb Khayim), which he composed in Yiddish and in Hebrew simultaneously; the title of the Hebrew version was *Bayamim hahem* (In days of old). The better part of his remarkable energy was invested in endless preparation of the definitive collected editions of his oeuvre in both languages. Finally, when he was seventy-five, both editions appeared, Hebrew in 1910 and Yiddish in 1911. The occasion was celebrated with great pomp and press coverage befitting a royal fete.

# VI

Having thus far told the story of Abramovitsh's trial, struggle, and final triumph, we should now ponder once again the significance of his achievement. We more or less know how and why he eventually won universal recognition in his own lifetime during the quarter-century which preceded the first World War. The question now before us is what merit or merits of Abramovitsh's work served to ensure that he would continue to be held in high esteem throughout the twentieth century, to our own day. His ardent admirers hailed—in the 1920s and 1930s, for instance—from Jewish cultural circles as inimical to each other as the Yiddish Marxist establishment in the U.S.S.R. and the Zionist centers of Jerusalem and Tel Aviv. When an author is so highly respected by critics deeply entangled on all sides in ideological rivalry, he must surely possess an enduring appeal independent of ephemeral cultural circumstances. What is the essence or the nature of this appeal, and is it still operative in our own day?

Since the beginning of the twentieth century, a rich and extensive corpus of critical writing in Yiddish, Hebrew, and other languages has accumulated around the work of Abramovitsh. While "Mendele literature" is by no means unanimous, it offers four major answers to our question, answers which represent not only shifts in emphasis but also genuine disagreements.

The first of these—by the early Mendele critics whose views and conceptions had crystallized before World War I—pertains to Abramovitsh's artistic manner, particularly to his method of mimetic representation. Simply put, these critics believed that Abramovitsh's great achievement inhered in his realistic rendering of objects, situations, and social settings. They called him the first modern Jewish writer both in Yiddish and in Hebrew who accurately and poignantly described what his eye saw and his ear heard. A face, a place, a landscape, the commotion of a fair, the dialogue and body language of vendors in the market, and so on—the vibrant realism of Abramovitsh's descriptions supposedly "caught" all of these in their full bloom. We may take the ability to convey verisimilitude almost for granted in the work of a writer of realist fiction. We need to remember, however, that to the turn-of-the-century Hebrew and Yiddish critics, realist prose fiction in the manner of Turgenev or Tolstoy was the highest achievement to which a literature could aspire. Moreover, these critics attributed to mimetic realism a "national" significance. In extolling Abramovitsh's descriptive realism, they were not only praising an aesthetic virtue. After all, modern Jewish literature and culture as a whole were supposed to tear the Jews away from the world of ritual, mystical faith, and legal abstractions and make them face up to "reality"—particularly material and biological reality. Here was a writer who, instead of losing himself in wordy approximations, would awaken in the reader's soul the dormant sense of the concrete, the sense that the world actually existed. Was this not a feat worthy of the highest praise?

The second answer, an extension of the first and likewise formulated and asserted by the earliest Hebrew and Yiddish critics, pertained not to Abramovitsh's mimetic technique but to the subjects which this technique helped to re-create. Abramovitsh was not merely a great realist technician; he also deserved high praise for what he chose to describe—namely, the physical and social totality of traditional pre-urban Jewish life in the nineteenth-century czarist empire. In his five or six short novels and a dozen short stories and novellas, he was said to have captured every aspect of the shtetl: economic circumstances, social stratification, every ethnographic detail, specification of habitat, garments and accessories, rituals, holidays, intellectual pursuits, matrimonial relationships, the experience of childhood, adolescence, adulthood, old age, and much more. Moreover, although Abramovitsh was not credited with a firm grasp of psychological realism and was not deemed able to convey the nuances of an individual psychic life, he was said to have populated his work with a vast array of Jewish "types" and "characters"—men, women, children, representatives of the various classes and professions, and so on. Thus, his work was celebrated by David Frishman, the most important Hebrew-Yiddish critic of his day, as the best "panoramic" representation of the historical reality of the shtetl:

He [Abramovitsh] encompassed the entire spectrum of
Jewish life in the alleys of the small towns of Russia in the
first half of the preceding century, developing it into a
fully detailed picture . . . If, let us assume, a deluge comes
inundating and washing away from the face of the earth
the Jewish ghetto and the life which it contains, not leaving
behind so much as a trace, a sign, except by sheer luck,
Mendele's [Abramovitsh's] four major works, *Fishke the
Lame, The [Brief] Travels of Benjamin the Third, The Magic Ring*
and *Shloyme, the Son of Reb Khayim,* as well as two or three
shorter works—then I doubt not that with these spared,
the future scholar would be able to reconstruct the entire
map of Jewish *shtetl* life in Russia in the first half of the
nineteenth century in such a manner that not even one iota
would be left out.[2]

Abramovitsh was thus "the painter of the convocation of Israel," warts and all. The Jewish people were in the throes of
an alarmingly quick metamorphosis. If the past was not to be
lost and the continuity of the national self-image was to be
maintained, a vast task of artistic preservation was called for;
Abramovitsh was seen as the true custodian of national memory and the authority on shtetl civilization. True, he was often
bitterly critical of this civilization, but contemporary readers
and critics, themselves modern Jews, had more or less dis-
tanced themselves from their traditional origins and needed
both a justification for this and the nostalgic reassurance that
the past was still available to them—at least in the form of a
literary reconstruction. Abramovitsh's lifework satisfied both
of these needs and was therefore canonized as the very core
of a new Jewish literature, the most "Jewish" prose fiction in
existence. It was deemed essentially "Jewish" because of its
strict focus on one subject—Jewish communal life—and
something supposedly "Jewish" about its narrative manner. By

the latter claim, the critics meant to justify Abramovitsh's digressive and sometimes quite arbitrary fabulae or compositional patterns, which did not follow the structural norms of the contemporary psychological novel. As the quintessential Jewish artist, Abramovitsh was to be allowed his digressive, meandering plot lines in the name of Jewish authenticity.

# VII

With the third answer our attention shifts from representational art to the realm of ideas. Critics of a somewhat later period, themselves often committed to complex and demanding ideologies, turned their attention toward Abramovitsh's contribution to what Yosef Hayim Brenner called *ha'arakhat atsmenu,* or national self-criticism. What was of crucial importance was not the mere "description" of the traditional Jewish way of life in the works of Abramovitsh but the moral evaluation of that way of life as it reverberated through the description.

The Hebrew novelist and essayist Y. H. Brenner, the intellectual leader of the second aliyah, who wrote his essay on Abramovitsh in Palestine while it was cut off from the rest of the Jewish world by World War I, admired his predecessor not because he had overcome Haskalah ideology to become "the painter of the convocation of Israel" but rather because he saw through its limitations and broadened it in a way which placed its essential liberating truth at the core of real national self-criticism. Like his contemporary the poet Y. L. Gordon, Abramovitsh went beyond the favorite butts of *maskilic* satire: the ignorance of the Jewish masses, their inability or unwillingness to communicate with the non-Jewish environment, and their archaic, irrelevant educational system. Both writers

understood that these superficial deformities were not at the
root of the inability of the Jewish people to come to grips
with the challenges of modern times. Other, more inherent
and fundamental realities, with deep roots in Jewish history,
were to blame. Gordon identified these with the Jewish inherent tendency, already in evidence even before the destruction of the independent Jewish commonwealth, to embrace a
heightened spirituality as a way of evading the responsibilities
of real life. Abramovitsh pointed to a similar, although not entirely identical, fatal flaw in the traditional role of the Jew as
mediator and purveyor rather than as true creator. Instead of
producing the necessities of human survival, the Jews sold
them. The fact that this role had been forced upon them by
others and that their survival as a nation depended on their
acceptance of this role and their success in living up to it was,
to Brenner, irrelevant because he did not attribute any moral
value to survival per se. Whether the Jews willed this historical role for themselves or simply learned to live with it, it vitiated their existence. The corruption triggered by the loss of
direct contact with the primary "labor of life" penetrated
everywhere, contaminating not only the Jewish economy but
also other areas presumably detached from the economy, such
as sexuality (which waxed "mercantile," as a series of business
transactions), as well as spiritual and religious life. The unique
intellectual and artistic contribution of Abramovitsh lay in his
keen sensitivity to the processes and routes of this subtle
seepage. He was able to detect signs of this contamination
everywhere, no matter how faint and imperceptible to others. Hence, he was to be considered the actual founding father of modern Jewish moral self-consciousness. His great
contribution consisted not of a quantitatively maximized,
objective-descriptive "coverage" of traditional Jewish life, but
rather of a qualitative analytical-subjective exposure of Jew-

ish life, both traditional *and* modern. Of course, to Brenner, the Europeanization of the Jews, even their complete assimilation into the non-Jewish national society, would not serve to rectify that which was originally problematic. Only a revolutionary reversal of roles, a return to primal productivity attempted in Palestine by a small group of Zionist pioneers, could achieve this.[3]

From an altogether different angle, Marxist and socialist critics, active in the Soviet Union up to the 1940s, when Soviet-Jewish cultural life was brutally destroyed, arrived at conclusions parallel to those of Brenner. The role of "their" Abramovitsh in the development of modern Jewish self-consciousness was based upon his pioneering insights into the real meaning of class struggle within the traditional Jewish community. Exploitation, brutalization, and manipulation of the Jewish poor by their rich "brethren" had been exposed earlier by the "democratic" exponents of the Haskalah. According to them, only Abramovitsh, through his brilliant satirical representations, had shown how Jewish medievalism as a whole, and the mentality and behavioral patterns that went with it, not only depended on this exploitation but also confirmed and justified it. This medievalism of the shtetl was seen not as a mere antiquated remnant of tradition with which the Jews refused to part; on the contrary, it represented a dynamic social force necessitated by the course of the class struggle: the Jewish masses had to be kept ignorant and superstitious, cut off from any kind of comprehension of the reality which rendered them its victims, immersed in mystical faith and controlled by rabbis and *tsaddikim* in order to maintain the social hierarchy. Above all else, the Jews had to be kept in complete ignorance of the meaning of history and historical change; this preemptive task was successfully accomplished by promoting the concept of a separate Jewish "sacred history" which reduced all historical processes and vicissitudes to a single repeating pattern: sin, punishment by exile, persecutions, *gezerot* (evil decrees), brief temporary moments of reprieve bestowed by a merciful God due to the intercession of saintly religious leaders and miracle workers, and, of course, the ever-present but always deferred expectation of imminent messianic redemption. From the perspective of these critics, Abramovitsh saw through the lie of Jewish spirituality; Jewish "sacred history" was a myth, upheld and sanctified for dubious "unholy" purposes. His main contribution was thus located in his "radical" phase, in the 1870s. In the 1880s, he suffered a certain diminution of insight because of the pernicious influence of "reactionary" Jewish nationalism in general and the even more reactionary Hebraism of his Odessa friends. However, even in the 1880s and 1890s Abramovitsh remained the keen social observer par excellence, always going beyond the facade of position and attitude to read the secret text containing the real agenda of those who sported attitudes as pretexts for their self-serving rationalizations.[4]

Marxist critics, often marshaling an impressive body of literary evidence in support of their position, also insisted upon presenting Abramovitsh outside the confines of his image as an exclusively "Jewish" artist. Naturally, an artist who understood the cultural and psychological dynamics of class struggle so well had to realize the universal, supranational implications of the conflicts which he studied and portrayed. Thus, these critics presented him as a typical European "bourgeois intellectual" who, while not of the working class, understood its historical role very well and even identified with it. They compared Abramovitsh's work to that of bourgeois writers who were active when their societies were undergoing the early and more "progressive" phases of capitalism,

such as English and French novelists of the eighteenth century. With these critics, Mendele scholarship began to be conducted along comparative lines for the first time, integrating
his achievement within a comprehensive view of the development of the European novel.


# VIII

The fourth answer is essentially linguistic; however, it was put
forward throughout the development of Mendele literature
not only by linguists or by people who were professionally
trained to deal with issues of language but also by literary
critics, ideologues, and cultural activists. In modern Jewish
literature, language has hardly ever been regarded solely as a
means of articulation, a communicative system only. It was
seen also, and perhaps primarily, as the declaration of a cultural credo and an ideological commitment. The writer's
choice of language or languages as well as his handling of language were examined and judged as acts of faith. Both Yiddish
and Hebrew critics and scholars insisted on designating
Abramovitsh the "inventor" or one of the founders of the nor-
mative literary idiom in both languages. This characterization
served to underscore not only the author's stylistic gifts but
also his prominence as a national cultural figure, a trailblazer
who explored and cultivated the ground upon which the bas-
tions of a new Jewish civilization would be erected.

As far as Abramovitsh's Yiddish works are concerned, this
Herculean task was allegedly carried out by means of a conscious process of fashioning out of a spoken idiom an elegant
and disciplined literary language. To do this, he had to overcome a crippling dichotomy faced by every contemporary
writer of Yiddish. On the one hand, a writer who meant to

convey to his readers modern ideas and concepts could resort to a "high" literary Yiddish based on a thorough Germanization of grammar, syntax, and vocabulary of the Eastern European spoken dialects. This was deemed as the only possible way of rendering Yiddish grammatical and *salonfähig* and of equipping it with a modern vocabulary. This option, however, while it was taken up by the majority of Yiddish writers, particularly by those in the better-educated north, demanded a high price of artificiality, pompousness, and the loss of idiomatic vigor. On the other hand, the writer could reproduce by strict imitation actual Yiddish speech—as was done by a minority of writers, particularly of southern origin, most notably by Isroel Aksenfeld. However, the price involved in this choice was also prohibitive, limiting the writer to one specific dialect, the idiosyncrasies and localisms of which were often hardly comprehensible two hundred miles away, and to dialogue spoken by folksy "simple" people about mundane matters. It could hardly serve the writer if and when he wanted to enable his characters to think, imagine, or indulge in subtle thoughts or emotions. Imitation almost invariably produced a text which was essentially parodic. Liveliness and idiomatic pungency were purchased at the price of depth, subtlety, and interiority. Abramovitsh was successful in transcending the schism between "high" and "low" Yiddish; as a *litvak* who emigrated to the Ukrainian south he decided to straddle both. He would abide by the southern norm of colloquial and idiomatic language while at the same time he would search for ways to overcome motley dialecticism and to broaden the expressional scope of imitated speech. He accomplished the former by systematically weeding out localisms as well as strengthening common linguistic features, such as the Hebrew component of the Yiddish language, and blending a variety of dialects. The latter he achieved through a most skillful creation of a style which was "ideally" colloquial but which was actually more complex, subtle, and disciplined than any version of spoken Yiddish.

From the 1880s on, as we have noted, Abramovitsh performed a similarly heroic feat in Hebrew. He was in many ways not only the "inventor" of modern pre–Israeli Hebrew prose but also the bridge builder who helped modern Hebrew to overcome its initial aphasic biblical regression. Under his tutelage, the language, acknowledging all of its various historical layers, became a Hebrew of the Jewish present.

Each of the four answers we have summarized represents an authentic and significant response to Abramovitsh and an important legitimation of the greatness of his achievement. All of them reflect both the specific concerns and biases of various critics working in different times and places and important aspects of Abramovitsh's work. In the history of modern Jewish culture the perfection of a mimetic-realistic representational technique in Yiddish and Hebrew is certainly an artistic triumph, and the "invention" of modern Hebrew and Yiddish prose is a feat of tremendous significance. But are these historical reasons sufficient for us today, to compel us once again to immerse ourselves in the works of Abramovitsh and enable us to enjoy them for their literary qualities? As for Abramovitsh's contribution to the development of modern Jewish self-criticism, we cannot help but wonder if such self-criticism is still either valid or relevant even in its historical context; can this devastating evaluation of the shtetl civilization withstand close historical scrutiny? Can it be upheld as ideologically and emotionally tenable after this civilization was so horribly and unspeakably annihilated? Do we still dare to take seriously the messages that were so close to the hearts of Brenner and the Soviet Marxist critics, particularly since the latter supported a brutal totalitarian regime which played

an important role in wiping out traditional Jewish life in Eastern Europe, the very thing that was the subject of their
scathing critique?

Other aspects of the four answers strike us now as somewhat off the mark or simply wrong. For example, Abramovitsh certainly created very lively descriptions which, in part,
were strikingly "lifelike." However, these descriptions were
also informed by blatantly antirealistic principles, such as caricature, extreme synecdochic reduction—people being identified with their noses, for instance—as well as figurative
bestialization of human beings, a strong penchant for the
grotesque and the bizarre.[5] A passionate moralist and satirist
above all else, Abramovitsh did not indulge in "pure" mimetic
descriptivism—description for description's sake—as he was
said to have done. Also as a wit, an *eiron,* an artist committed
to subversion, he did not invest all of his creative energies in
sheer duplication of the surface of "things as they were."

As a matter of fact, all of the "classical" answers that we
have delineated above—with the exception of the linguistic
one—are the source of serious and harmful misunderstand-
ings in the development of the Mendele literature. After
World War II and the Holocaust, critics expecting Abramovitsh to fulfill a national agenda found themselves bitterly disappointed. Was the image preserved in his work really the
full, definitive historical summation of a world now lost but
continually mourned and idealized? The Yiddish poet and
critic Yankev Glatshteyn wondered, as he browsed through
*Fishke the Lame:* How could this story about beggars, cripples,
criminals, lost children, "cholera weddings" conducted in
cemeteries, petty cunning, fraud, and sweaty, brutal sexuality
represent the totality of the essence of traditional Jewish life?
Where was the spirituality, the learning, the creativity, the intimacy, the sense of mutual responsibility, even common de-

cency which made the shtetl experience what it had been?[6]
The Hebrew critic Avraham Kariv made lists of Mendele la-
cunae, that is, he listed institutions and phenomena which
were not covered by Abramovitsh, and concluded that "the
painter of the convocation of Israel" had "forgotten" to include in his densely populated canvas anything which might
have redeemed the ugly picture. He did this, Kariv charged,
because, like Brenner, his admirer, he had been infected with
*Selbsthass,* the modern Jewish neurosis par excellence.[7] Obviously, these charges represent an overreaction to false critical notions rather than to Abramovitsh's works per se.
Abramovitsh had never promised or even intended to incor-
porate in his *Fishke* the reified essence of Jewish life. This does
not mean that the chaotic world he created in this work was
not informed by significant and original insights into the dynamics of human behavior in general and of Jewish behavior
in particular. The fact that Abramovitsh did not pay close attention to the institutions and the theology of the Hasidic
movement or to those of the Lithuanian *musar* movement
does not mean that he had nothing important to say about a
life conditioned and guided by religious faith.

In short, some of the classical arguments with which the
Mendele criticism justified and rationalized its admiration of
Abramovitsh and its evaluation of his major works need to be
altogether replaced, or at the very least to be subjected to a
thorough reassessment. At least two major components of
the Mendele world—the Jewish space created in it and the
figure of Mendele the Book Peddler himself—clearly need to
be redefined and reinterpreted. The balance of this introduction is devoted to such an interpretation.

# IX

Let us first pose the question that still concerns contemporary readers who might turn to Abramovitsh, as they turn to other classic Yiddish and Hebrew writers, such as Sholem Aleichem, I. L. Peretz, or S. Y. Agnon, with the hope of communicating through them with their shtetl roots. Such use of literature is not only possible and legitimate but actually unavoidable. We certainly read literature in order to immerse ourselves in a world to which we might be drawn. The question remains, however: How can we do this without losing sight of the literary, imaginary, suprahistorical, and idiosyncratic nature of the world that literature creates, rather than "preserves," for us? It centers on the real nature and dimensions of the shtetl world created by these great writers. Does this world correspond to the historical shtetl? Are they preserving it for us in all its complexity? The answer to these questions cannot be a simple yes or no. The Jewish classics did, of course, draw upon a historical reality of nineteenth-century shtetl society, although necessarily only partial views of it, in different places and times. Some of their authors may have occasionally entertained the idea that they would "preserve" in the artistic images they created a panoramic portrait of this society as they knew it. This is particularly true of Sholem Aleichem, who told his brother Vevik of his intention to create "a Jewish comedy" as comprehensive as Balzac's *Comédie humaine*.[8] It is not as true of Abramovitsh, who might have thought in these terms only from the late 1880s on, when he promised Sholem Aleichem that his revised and enlarged version of *The Magic Ring* would constitute a veritable "history" of Jewish life in Russia, from the 1840s to the present.[9] Actually, only one of Abramovitsh's major works, the

very late *Shloyme, the Son of Reb Khayim,* was thoroughly devised and composed along the lines of such an ideology of literary "perpetuation." Peretz never intended to preserve or
perpetuate any panoramic view of a given society. To him, the
essence of "reality" consisted of ideas, emotions, and psychic
drives and not of social interactions and institutions. However, even where the intention of perpetuating through art
the rapidly changing historical experience of Jewish life was
present and could influence artistic practices, this intention
represented part of an imaginative aesthetic project and
needs to be understood within the imaginative aesthetic context.

Abramovitsh created an imaginary Jewish space which internalized and fictionalized some of the salient characteristics
of Jewish life in Lithuania and in the Ukraine during the
1840s and 1850s. However, this space was not modeled after
any historical reality, nor was it "true" to any such reality. It
was true only to itself, that is, to the idiosyncratic vision that
was articulated through it. The image of this Jewish space was
complete only in terms of its own aesthetic syntax and grammar. In these terms, it amounted to a full comprehensive
statement. However, in sheer referential terms, that is, in
terms of its correspondence to a complex extrinsic reality, it
was anything but full or complete. Indeed, in those terms,
what it had left out outweighed by far what it included. Its autonomous, intrinsic wholeness might have duped readers
who, driven by various cultural needs, understood it in referential extrinsic terms. Abramovitsh is the first great modern
poet of premodern Eastern European Jewry—as viewed by
modern eyes, of course—not because he replicated its historical reality, which he could not do, but because he projected it
as an aesthetically organized, self-contained image. It is a conceptual image, fleshed out through carefully selected meton-

ymies. The selection of these, however, was determined not
by the "validity" of the metonymies as true representations of
various historical aspects of reality, but rather by their usefulness as illustrations or realizations of a set of abstract cate-
gories around which the author organized his vision.

The best example of this is the structure and organization
of the Jewish geography or space in Abramovitsh's works,
which was said to have encompassed the entire expanse of the
Russian-Jewish pale, at least during the first half of the nineteenth century. Fidelity to an actual geography played a very
minor part in the cultural framing of this space. For instance,
places embedded in what is supposedly the heart of the Volhynian plain, such as the shtetl Kabtsansk, actually reproduced
some of the features of Abramovitsh's own Belorussian-
Lithuanian hometown, Kapulye. Essentially, the Jewish space
of Abramovitsh's works is structured along schematic lines
rather than in reference to "real" space. Thus, instead of
dozens of cities, provincial towns, townlets, hamlets, villages,
estates, and so on, Abramovitsh focuses on fewer than half a
dozen symbolic places, primarily on the three towns Glupsk
(Kesalon in Hebrew), Tuneyadevka (Betalon), and Kabtsansk
(Kabtsiel). The names themselves clearly indicate the satirical
schematization and abstraction we have been describing, for
instead of pointing to any geographic, ethnic, or social speci-
fications of these three towns, they designate them as centers
or enclaves in which a certain attitude or mental disposition
finds its quintessential expression. Glupsk, the home of
Fishke, is an enclave of a certain kind of foolishness; Benjamin
the Third's Tuneyadevka is a place where idleness reigns
supreme; Kabtsansk—Paupersville—immortalized in *The
Magic Ring,* is not just a town of paupers, since poverty is
characteristic of all of Abramovitsh's *shtetlekh,* but a place
where poverty has become a mentality, raised to the "sub-

lime" status of a religion complemented by faith in the miraculous attainment of riches as a result of celestial intervention
without any connection whatsoever to human effort and intelligence.

The space created around these three towns—one (Glupsk)
a larger commercial center and the other two tiny backwater
*shtetlekh*—is unified on the abstract level by the psychosatiri-
cal overall design that manifests itself in the three names, and
on the narrative plot-line level by the mobility of the protagonists, such as Fishke in *Fishke the Lame* and Benjamin and
Sendrel in *The Brief Travels of Benjamin the Third*. Just as important, if not more so, is the mobility of Mendele the Book Peddler, who regularly visits these places and knits them together
into one living space. Thus, embedded within a unified con-
tinuum, which is only marginally envisioned in terms of geo-
graphical contiguity and continuity, the three towns as well as
some less important places are juxtaposed, played one against
the other in a way which allows them to function like pieces
of colored glass in a kaleidoscope. With each motion of the
artist's dextrous hand the pieces settle in a new and exciting
pattern. They relate to each other not in terms of proximity
and distance, but rather in terms of attraction and repulsion,
contraction and expansion.

The towns and villages of Abramovitsh, like the stars on
an astrolabe, rotate around each other to form spheres. The
overall pattern formed by this rotation has a focal point, a pulsating core, which is encircled centrifugally by expanding
spheres, from the center to the outward periphery. The
spaces between the spheres are not completely empty. They
are only empty of "Jewishness" and they are designated as
"Nature"—although Abramovitsh wrote zoology textbooks
and as a writer is justly famous for his sensitive descriptions of
nature, nature in his Jewish space remained a concept, a spiri-

tual condition, rather than a commonplace reality. The protagonists of the stories live in its very midst, and Mendele the
Book Peddler spends more time in the open spaces of the
Ukrainian countryside than in his *shtetlekh,* and yet to them
and to him nature remains an alien entity. It is often projected
in their minds as "she," a seductress. It can be experienced as
sweet, sensual, and beautiful, but also as frightening and even
monstrous. On some occasions it allows itself to become familiar, Judaized, as it is in the sunset episode in *Fishke the Lame*
where the field and the forest form one large roofless synagogue. But more often it is uncannily "empty" as far as the
Jewish sense of space is concerned. It is contrasted with another feminine presence—that of the Jewish habitat, the
town, which can be *ir va'em* (a city and a mother). There Jews
are intimately huddled together like children in the lap of
their mother. Leaving this habitat the Jews encounter a presence with which they are unfamiliar, that of the foreign
woman of the Book of Proverbs. While the mother-town is
Jewish and asexual, this woman is erotic and Gentile. Above
all else, she is "empty" in the sense that one cannot orient one-
self within her expanses, no matter how beautiful and allur-
ing she might be.

   The pulsating center, where space is completely domes-
ticated and Judaized, is the bustling town of Glupsk. The
centrality of Glupsk, a relatively large place, should be em-
phasized because in our sentimentality we tend to identify authentic shtetl civilization exclusively with cozy, tiny places
where "life is with people" and where all the members of
the community know each other personally. Although Abramovitsh did portray such places in his Tuneyadevka and Kabtsansk, he insisted on exploring the shtetl mentality as it
manifested itself in a larger, less intimate, and even decep-
tively semimodern place such as his Glupsk. He was not in-

terested in a sentimental, idealized, ethnographic, or anthro-
pological anatomy of the Jewish "pueblo," as some American
readers might imagine. Rather, he was interested in the historical dynamics of premodern Jewish society, which in the
middle decades of the nineteenth century found its best expression not in pauperized, lethargic villages but in busy commercial towns like Berdichev, which the Jewish sociologist
Yankev Leshtshinsky described as "not typical but very characteristic."[10] By this he meant that the town did not represent
the statistically average Jewish locale in the Ukraine or in the
Pale, but was nevertheless historically "characteristic" because
its growth reflected the dynamic development of the Russian-
Jewish city.

Glupsk is characteristic in this sense because it is dynamic.
This is also why Abramovitsh made it the center, the heart of
his "world." Tuneyadevka and Kabtsansk, genuine *shtetlekh*
though they may be, are characterized by their relationship
with Glupsk; they are either closely related to it (Kabtsansk)
or separated from it (Tuneyadevka). In the final analysis, all of
the *shtetlekh* depend on Glupsk and are drawn to it. The protagonists, born in the *shtetlekh,* are bound in one way or another to leave their hometowns to flock to Glupsk, swelling
its rapidly growing Jewish population. Thus, the "real" *shtetlekh,*
Tuneyadevka, Kabtsansk, Tsviy'achich (town of hypocrites in
*The Little Man*), and Teterevke (named after the river Teterev,
an estuary of the Dnieper), hover around Glupsk, vibrating
and quivering under its magnetic influence. They form the
first sphere which encircles the center of the astrolabe. Their
presence vis-à-vis the center is conveyed by binary opposi-
tions such as passivity versus activity, thinness versus density,
as well as point of origin versus destination.

The second sphere combines widely separated and socially
distinct places such as the cities of Odessa and Warsaw, and

also perhaps the city of Dnieperovits, or Dnieperovna (the name stands for the Ukrainian capital, Kiev, in *The Nag*), large urban centers where relatively modern Jewish communities had formed. This does not apply to "Dnieperovna," which in the 1860s and 1870s still contained only a small Jewish population. The presence of all of these places in the stories is necessary not because Abramovitsh really wanted to integrate them within the Jewish space of his works but because they offer an important perspective—basically, that of the modern reader at whom the stories are targeted—on Glupsk and its *shtetldik* satellites. Even the relatively detailed description of Odessa in *Fishke the Lame* is focused in such a way that the cityscape functions as a mere foil or as a distorting mirror of the image of Glupsk. There is not much that Abramovitsh wants to tell us about the modern world or even the modern Jewish world per se. His target is the premodern world, and modernity is presented only insofar as it relates to it.

Sometimes places even more distant and foreign than Warsaw or Odessa appear on the horizon of the Mendele world, such as the German commercial town of Leipzig, or even Queen Victoria's London and the Rothschilds' Paris. However, these places exist in the stories only to the extent that they excite the imagination of the inhabitants of Glupsk, Tuneyadevka, and Kabtsansk. In the midst of the busy marketplace of Glupsk stands a young man holding a box with a peephole, through which the Jewish passsersby can for a kopek see London—the Pope riding in his red hose—Napoleon battling with the Prussians—a woman riding with the Sultan in a carriage, the Grand Vizier holding the whip and driving the horses.[11] In the synagogues and Turkish baths of Tuneyadevka and Kabtsansk, Rothschild counts his millions and the Queen of England dispatches a fleet of ships to the high seas. All of these are, of course, shtetl fantasies, or rather the reality of Europe in the heyday of colonialism translated into medieval Jewish myth and legend. Thus, the third sphere, a semimythological one, is very close to the fourth, which is completely mythological, or medieval-midrashic. This is the sphere which encircles the Mendele geography with the legendary landscape of India, over which Alexander of Macedon still soars on a huge vulture which he feeds with the pieces of flesh he cuts from his own body; with African and Asian deserts full of dragons; with the frenetic mythological river Sambatyon, beyond which the Ten Lost Tribes of biblical Israel still thrive—but the river, always stormy and throwing big rocks high into the sky, resting only on the Sabbath as God has decreed, renders them inaccessible; with the great oceans of medieval Hebrew travelogues, studded with green fertile islands which are really the backs of dormant but treacherous whales. Obviously to this sphere also belong the Holy Land and the heavenly Jerusalem where the dead, ready for the Last Judgment, do not suffer bodily corruption. This fourth circle represents not the faraway places of which it supposedly consists, but rather the mythological dimensions of the minds of the people of Glupsk and Tuneyadevka. It indicates that the Mendele geography of which it is the outer fringe is essentially a psychic geography; the space it encompasses is metaphorical and mental, psychic and cultural, rather than social and geographic.

## X

We have then to accept the Mendele geography, in spite of its powerful effect of mimetic verisimilitude, as more of a concept than a described object—even in those cases where the correspondence between the spatial image and the historical

fact is abundantly clear. For instance, Glupsk, the epicenter of
this geography, is said to have been modeled after the town of
Berdichev, the Ukrainian "Jerusalem." In a certain way and to
a considerable extent Glupsk may be read as a pertinent commentary on the development of Berdichev, which, starting
around the turn of the nineteenth century as a shtetl of a few
thousand people huddled around the Polish cathedral and the
nearby market square, rapidly grew until it had become in the
1850s, when Abramovitsh first saw it, the commercial center
of the Ukraine, where the agricultural products of Russia's
"breadbasket" were distributed throughout the empire. Berdichev's quick decline, starting in the 1860s, eventually reduced it to relative unimportance by the end of the century.
This is not the place to inquire what triggered these develop-
ments: it is enough to imagine the impression Berdichev must
have made on the mind of young Abramovitsh, who until
1858 had lived only in small backwater places such as Kapulye
or Kamieniec-Podolsk. By the end of the 1850s the Jewish
community of Berdichev, the second largest in Eastern Europe after Warsaw, numbered more than sixty thousand people and was growing daily. The influx of immigrants from
shtetlekh near and far inundated the city. The newcomers faced
a scarcity in housing and an even greater scarcity in jobs. They
thronged the synagogues, shtiblekh (small prayerhouses), inns,
and marketplaces, and lived in shacks and hovels. Many sold
their time and labor as servants for a piece of bread and a roof
over their heads. Others were pushed toward the fringes of
society and the underworld. Quite a few young Jewish
women ended up as prostitutes in Berdichev's own brothels
or those of distant places. Commercial enterprise loomed behind it all, with its promise of affluence on the one hand and
alienation and corruption on the other. Abramovitsh took all
of this in and re-created the hectic atmosphere of the place in

his descriptions of Glupsk, which appear throughout his oeuvre. However, the longer he observed his new surroundings,
the more inclined he was to reify his impressions. What this
place, like every other but more than most, demanded from
his fertile imagination was distillation and abstraction. He had
to identify its literary nature or its essence. He had to develop
in his mind an image which would *essentialize* it into a symbol
of universal human proclivity, an archetypal state of mind.

This was not easy. Superficially, Berdichev-Glupsk stood
for business and commerce: following the line of least resistance, Abramovitsh could have developed its image as that of
a place where only money and profit matter and where the
"average" inhabitant would be the proverbial *Homo economicus.*
In some of his early works, such as *The Tax,* he did this, more
or less. However, even in these works he also expressed a different sense, indicated by the very name Glupsk, which he
adapted from Saltykov-Shchedrin's satire "A History of a
Town," where Russia was projected as Golupov, a town of
fools. Now, foolishness and commercial activity are hardly
synonymous. We tend to equate the latter with cunning and
to associate it not with a lack of brainpower but rather with a
lack of charity, friendliness, and perhaps honesty. But Abramovitsh saw through the cunning of Berdichev, and found a
quality which he identified as foolishness. The "Glupsker," he
thought, acted only *als ob,* as if they were motivated by truly
mercantile motives. In reality, they were only playing a role,
and their activity was aimless, or, rather, had become an aim
unto itself, an exciting way of life rather than a means for
achieving some goal. Thus, fortunes were purportedly made
but also immediately lost. New business ventures were initi-
ated everywhere but bankruptcy was the order of the day.
Credit was easily available but could also be suddenly with-

drawn. The merchants of Glupsk, Abramovitsh mused, were "running like poisoned mice" but getting nowhere.

If in the early works Glupsk was projected as a commercial jungle and its foolishness was identified with the helplessness and naïveté of its exploited artisans and servants, in the more mature compositions the focus of the projected image changed. Glupsk could still be a jungle where the male children of the poor could be impressed into the army and the females sexually exploited; yet now it was essentially a megashtetl where the naïveté of the Kabtsansker and the foolish passivity of the Tuneyadevker were replaced by the clever stupidity of the dumb manipulator. The idleness and helplessness of the *shtetlekh* people were camouflaged beneath the semblance of fierce and aimless activity pursued by people who were too busy to rationalize their efforts. These people were not really examples of *Homo economicus,* since they based their adventurous commercialism on conjecture and make-believe rather than on rational considerations such as the profit motive.

Thus, Glupsk became a satirical symbol of a special kind of stupidity, and its description belongs in the long tradition of satire which, since the days of classical antiquity, had focused on that most multifaceted of all human shortcomings—intellectual insufficiency. Indeed, Abramovitsh was eager to endow his symbol with something of sublime antiquity. He portrayed his ultramundane Glupsk as a town with legendary or even mythological origins. Arriving in its active marketplace, Benjamin—characteristically, Glupsk is often viewed through the eyes of a newcomer—while he sees the ongoing give-and-take of commerce, the crowds of vendors, the grotesque and tragic beggars, the thiefs, the performing gypsies, and the riffraff, also senses the presence of an entity

which transcends the mundane. Glupsk, he reports, is an ancient capital of sorts. Its strange houses point to a connection
with distant ancient cities. It possesses *an alter krepost* (an old
fort) and a watchtower supported by *hinershe fislekh* (chicken
legs) like the legendary hut of the witch Baba-Yaga. The town
as a whole, he says, has an actual body, because it is "a body
politic" in the original sense of the term, that is, a "kingdom."
This is indicated by its topography, which is like that of a body
with bodily orifices (through which it may be entered: Benjamin and Sendrel enter Glupsk through its anus). It is also
confirmed by a pseudobiblical and pseudo-Virgilian myth of
origins which Benjamin repeats in high style and with great
solemnity: the town was founded in biblical times by the Jews
sent by King Solomon to Ophir for its famous gold. They
went to India, where they opened expensive stores and business offices, but then they went backrupt, fled their creditors,
and many perished in the desert. Those who reached the coast
boarded ships and sailed across the ocean. Through the river
Pyatignilevke, a muddy stream in Glupsk, which in those days
flowed directly into the sea, they traveled inland until, shipwrecked by a terrible storm, they were tossed onto an unknown shore. Here they built Glupsk. This mock-epic presents
the town as a locus which originated in bad business deci-
sions, bankruptcy, and shipwreck. At the same time, it pro-
jects the town as a new Jerusalem *manqué,* or as a travesty of
Rome, which was also built by exiles and shipwreck sur-
vivors. Glupsk is the town of ancient Hebrew argonauts, the
capital of precarious commercialism. In *The Magic Ring,* this
"fantastic" view of Glupsk is reasserted through another myth
of origins, according to which the town was from the very
beginning a divine practical joke, played by its founder, the
god Mercury, the god of merchants and thieves. Planting a
reed in the midst of the smelly river Pyatignilevke (in He-

brew, Sirkhon, meaning stench), he allowed it to collect dirt until a precarious shoal was formed around it. Many Jews, looking for a haven under the sun, descended upon the shoal and so quickly and actively treaded its slippery mass that they actually managed to harden it. Then they settled it, multiplied, opened stores, gave and received credit, bought, sold, and went bankrupt. Again the mock-myth indicates the clever silliness of a people who live forever on a floating piece of scum which must eventually founder. Glupsk is, in a way, a version of the eternal ship of fools.

However, it is a Jewish ship of fools, and one can clearly see how it functions within the conceptual context of Abramovitsh's Jewish space. It points to the unifying abstract characteristics of the Jewish fictional "world," to its reified "essence," which is not the brand of foolishness specific to Glupsk, but rather the abstract principle that it incorporates. This principle reveals itself if we compare the foolishness of Glupsk with the miserable poverty of Kabtsansk and the docile idleness of Tuneyadevka.

Kabtsansk is the quintessentially poor, helpless Jewish community. Historically, it underlines the impoverishment of the Jewish shtetl as a result of the modernization of the Russian economy. Economically functional within the feudal system as the tiny local-commercial spot which serviced its immediate agricultural vicinity, the shtetl became increasingly irrelevant and economically untenable as steam transportation and the development of wholesale purchase and distribution of agricultural products enabled the Ukrainian or Belorussian peasants to circumvent the mediation of their Jewish neighbors. Now, the people of Kabtsansk, as Abramovitsh says, had no economic resource but themselves. Kabtsansk took this turning upon itself, the commodification of its own inhabitants, very seriously. The only productive activ-

ity in which the members of the community excelled was re-
productive, or sexual. They could produce children and did
so with both pleasure and pride. The men of Kabtsansk particularly are presented as oversexed and as people whose
pride and authority depends on their virility. However, these
men do not know how to feed, clothe, and take proper care of
the children they sire, so they end up selling them to the merchants of Glupsk. Every year when autumn comes, presaging
the hardships and hunger of the coming winter, a "quarter" of
the inhabitants of Kabtsansk squeezes itself into a few wagons
in order to "emigrate" to Glupsk. Many of the emigrants, particularly the young ones like *The Magic Ring*'s protagonist,
Hershele, never come back.

While all this corresponds, in a symbolic way, to significant historical processes, the actual description of the shtetl
must be regarded as a fantasy attained through the well-
known satirical stratagem of *reductio ad absurdum*. Of course
the projection of Jewish existence in Kabtsansk in sheer
sexual-mercantile terms—the town as a sexual factory which
produces children for export—is as absurd and as fantastic as
Swift's "Modest Proposal," which recommended the rearing
of Irish children as gourmet delicacies for the English. The
absurd quality of this projection is enhanced by the Kabtsansk
myth, which encapsulates its special brand of religious faith.
The myth entails a visit to town by the biblical *ushpizin*
(guests)—the patriarchs King David and King Solomon, the
prophet Elijah, and others. Since the visit takes place during
the holiday of Purim rather than on the more solemn occasion of the Feast of Tabernacles, when the *ushpizin* are nor-
mally expected, the hallowed group this time includes
Mordecai, Queen Esther's uncle, and the biblical drunkard
Lot, a relative of Abraham. However, the guests find Kabtsansk empty. Everybody, with the exception of one Reb

Yudl, who, being the only infertile male in town has no children to worry about, has left for Glupsk to earn some extra money as deliverers of Purim gift packages (mishloakh manot). Yudl invites the guests to the Purim feast and entertains them. They bless him with progeny—the innuendo hinting at an extramarital pregnancy lurks beneath the high hagiographic style—and also put at his disposal a miraculous purse which contains a coin every time it is opened. Thus Reb Yudl's family becomes the only one in town which is not in dire financial straits. The mock-myth of the visit-of-the-god and the birth-of-the-hero type encapsulates the realities of Kabtsansk: fecundity, systematic emigration, and an "economic" messianism, that is, the dream of miraculous riches which through supernatural intervention would put an end to all "Jewish" miseries.

Tuneyadevka is as destitute as Kabtsansk, but unlike the latter, it is docile and even happy. It represents Abramovitsh's sardonic version of the shtetl idyll, a secluded, slow-paced, good-natured, intimate community whose poverty is experienced as being quite bearable. Abramovitsh took care never to describe its plight in the wintertime. Here, frazzled caftans and worn-out socks suggest openness and heymishkeyt rather than penury and slovenliness. There is enough optimism and bitokhn (faith, confidence) to go around for all and sundry. Tuneyadevka does not convey an immediate experience of shtetl life but rather a sentimentalized impression protected from reality by selective memory. It is Egypt—the exodus from which serves as the central myth around which the narrative of Benjamin the Third's departure from the shtetl is structured—as remembered by those who could still savor the pungency of the onions and garlic but had somehow managed to erase the memory of slavery, brutality, and hard labor. Abramovitsh created it for the purpose of attacking a sweetened version of shtetl existence and for analyzing the subtler nuances of shtetl bondage. It was necessary for a major work, *The Brief Travels of Benjamin the Third,* in which he wanted to explore the idea that the situation of Eastern European Jewry called for revolutionary change not because of its self-evident flaws, such as dire poverty, wasted young lives, and ignorance, but because of other, less obvious ones: the hopeless provinciality and immobility of people for whom the outskirts of their hamlets constitute the end of the habitable world, their fantastic-medieval concept of reality, and also—this has not been sufficiently understood—their subverted sexuality. For as much as the men of Kabtsansk are virile, the men of Tuneyadevka, particularly as represented by Sendrel, the best among them, are *yidenes* (housewives). In their passivity and docile acquiescence they allow themselves to be mentally castrated. Their stolen masculinity is then forced upon their women, disfiguring them not only by making them masculine, but also by making them bitter, gruff, domineering, and strident.

Benjamin, who yearns to leave Tuneyadevka—not because of any physical discomfort, but because of his deep need for power and self-aggrandizement—is therefore the only real man in town. But even he, as a Tuneyadevkar, is only half a man. Hence, his "elopement" with "Sendrel, the *yidene*," his mate who is his man-woman. This "marriage" of the two—the matching of two males is a recurrent motif in Abramovitsh's oeuvre—by which the Quixote–Sancho Panza–Dulcinea triad has been shrunk to a pseudohomosexual dyad—represents, perhaps better than any other symbol, the "legacy" of Tuneyadevka. It is a legacy of inadequacy and impotence, which presages the inevitable failure of Benjamin's "exodus." In any case, Tuneyadevka, we realize, is more "unreal" by far than Glupsk and Kabtsansk. It is a psychological projection rather than a historical and social reality, and because of this quality, it plays an important role in the Mendele world, despite the fact that it appears only once, in the first four chapters of *The Brief Travels of Benjamin the Third.*

Now, it is not difficult to put the three towns together and get at their common denominator. Superficially, they represent opposites: the busy and alienated Glupsk versus the intimate, slow-paced *shtetlekh,* the misery of Kabtsansk versus the "happiness" of Tuneyadevka, the virility of the Kabtsansker versus the effeminacy of the Tuneyadevkar and the commercialized, stunted sexuality of the Glupsker, who mate for money and status, and sometimes have to buy illicit sex as a commodity. The list can be extended; however, the opposites are exposed only to be undermined. Abramovitsh knows that they are not genuine. The commercialism of Glupsk is bogus; the cunning of the Glupsk merchants is a form of stupidity. Their fierce activity is dialectically connected to the idleness of the shtetl people. Glupsk parades itself about as a city but it is actually an overgrown shtetl. In Glupsk, the connection between cause and effect, effort and product, gesture and response, has been severed. People run but they do not get anywhere; they buy and sell but they do not prosper; they act but they do nothing.

The same may be said of Kabtsansk. In its own way, the community has severed the connection between cause and effect. The Kabtsansker procreate but they are not real parents. They beget children, but they do not assume responsibility for them. Their sexual activity directly parallels the commercial activity of Glupsk. It is solipsistic, it perpetuates itself without a view toward the results. Thus, in Kabtsansk, fatherhood is as hollow as commercialism is in Glupsk. In Tuneyadevka, the idyllic mood is achieved through mental evasion of reality, or by forcing reality upon one's wife in order to enjoy an endless vacation from responsibility and manhood. Here too, dysfunctional economy parallels dysfunctional sexuality, while excess and deficiency present two sides of the same coin. Too much sex is equated with no sex at all; too much commercial activity is the other side of total idleness. Because of this dialectical similarity, the Mendele world always remains the same, deeply flawed and inherently chaotic. Yet for all that, it makes for an image which is almost mathematical in its precision and neat logical structure. Aesthetically, Mendele's world is perfect. Historically and psychologically, it is a mess. A good reader of Abramovitsh's works is equally sensitive to the perfection and to its dismal opposite. While savoring the first, one remains morally vulnerable to the second. Horrified and intensely pleased at the same time, one goes on reading.

# XI

We must shift our attention from the "geography" to the consciousness through which we become acquainted with it, from the image to the eye in which it glints, from the Mendele world to Mendele himself. As the second major component in the complex artistic entity under investigation he is as important as everything we have encountered so far. We must ask: Who is this Mendele? What role does he play in the work of Abramovitsh? We should be sure that any answer to that question does not shortchange either the character or the reader. The answer, whatever it is, cannot be merely nominal or purely technical, for Mendele transcends nominality and technicalities. Of course he is not just a pen name of Abramovitsh, as readers and critics in more naïve periods have believed, probably because Abramovitsh himself, for his own literary purposes, wanted them to do so.[12] One trusts

that this popular error has been laid to rest now for more than
a quarter of a century. Mendele is a fictional character, as fictional and as "imagined" as any literary protagonist in the
annals of fiction. Moreover, he is a complex character, shifty
and tricky; a character fashioned with skill and subtlety that
clearly belie the allegation that Abramovitsh, as much as he
could describe the material and social world realistically,
could not penetrate individual psychology. He definitely could
do so when it was necessary—as in the case of Mendele, his
chief psychological creation—but he would not allow himself
to indulge in overt psychological analysis because he felt that
it would undermine the authenticity of his narrative as a
"folksy" and "Jewish" discourse. Thus, psychological insight
into his work, as into that of so many other masters, had to
enter the narrative through the back door of an occasional
remark, a slip of the tongue, "faulty" cognitive sequences,
"unnecessary" and "uncontrollable" repetitions, and other little "psychopathologies" of everyday life and everyday use of
language.

True, unlike any other character, Mendele is also a technical "device." At the beginning, he was not even a "dramatized
narrator," to use the rhetorical terminology of Wayne C.
Booth. He was a mere technician, entrusted with the task of
making a "true," bona fide document public. As such, he was
invented in Abramovitsh's first Yiddish story, *The Little Man*
(1864), and he remained tied to similar ancillary services
throughout his fictional existence, which ended only with
Abramovitsh's very late productions, such as *Shloyme Reb
Khayims* (1894–1912) and *Seyfer habeheymes* (The book of cattle, 1902). At the same time, Mendele also grew rapidly,
developing new dimensions and enlarging his presence.
Throughout, he managed to retain a cohesive and unified per-
sonality, a distinct and immediately recognizable voice, tonal-

ity, and manner of speech. For Mendele, although he can by no means be identified with Abramovitsh the author, was conceived from the start as a raconteur, wit, and serious commentator in his own right.

Already in the first version of *The Little Man,* where he was not meant to serve as much more than a cover for Abramovitsh (who, as we remember, did not want to be known as the author of a Yiddish tale), Mendele's unique personality emerges. He is allowed to control only the short introduction preceding the "document," Yitskhok Avrum's confession and will. However, even this minimal introduction sufficiently revealed some of his salient characteristics: his caustic wit, his natural suspiciousness, his need to go beneath the surface to see through any facade no matter how innocent, and to discover the little lie, to expose the self-serving rationalization. Also his specific mannerisms as a talker and raconteur come to the fore, albeit in a very rudimentary form: his garrulousness, his tendency to digress, to tell a story in a meandering fashion, and above all else his penchant for sharp, biting asides. Mendele was an immediate success. The readers of *Kol mevasser* enjoyed his introduction as they enjoyed the juicier episodes of the protagonist's shocking life story. Abramovitsh responded by allowing Mendele to occupy a much larger space in his next Yiddish publication, the first version of *The Magic Ring* (1865), where Mendele's introduction, a long conversational essay, occupies about a third of the slim volume. Abramovitsh's readers now expected every one of his new Yiddish publications to include an extra bonus: a witty, satirical "Omar Mendele" (Thus spake Mendele) introduction. The writer soon learned how to develop such introductions as "a story about the story" which precedes "the story itself." He also made the introduction follow a certain routine, to parody a particular high, somewhat antiquated Yiddish style, studded with Hebraisms—a technique which enabled him to develop the introduction as an autonomous exercise in self-investigation, with Mendele tearing into his own sanctimonious declarations, *qua* book peddler and occasional publisher for "kosher" religious and educational purposes only, exposing the stark truth that he does what he does in expectation of profit, and precipitating every sublime and pathetic gesture into the depth of intentional bathos.

Eventually, Abramovitsh allowed Mendele to assume literary functions which went far beyond his initial ancillary role, such as editing or even rewriting the manuscripts he published. This was explained either as a result of the original manuscript's needing to be shortened (as in *The Brief Travels of Benjamin the Third*) or as a result of the author's unfamiliarity with the tastes and expectations of Jewish readership; hence the need to add Jewish "spice" to his writing (as in *The Magic Ring*). In *Fishke the Lame,* Mendele was supposedly retelling the story told by an ignorant and inarticulate beggar. He therefore had to assume a role very close to that of a full-fledged author. Thus, Mendele's presence became more and more conspicuous in Abramovitsh's work, until in the short stories and novellas of the late 1880s and early 1890s Mendele became a protagonist-narrator recounting his own adventures, rather than publishing written accounts of other people. Only in Abramovitsh's last major novel, *Shloyme Reb Khayims,* did Mendele humbly retreat to his original role as publisher and prologue-author, leaving center stage for the "real" author, who was none other than S. Y. Abramovitsh himself. The border separating Mendele from Abramovitsh was clearly marked for those who wanted to notice it. True, in compensation for this "decline," Mendele was presented with a particularly brilliant and well-developed *Petikhta* (Introduction, 1894) which, even though it belonged within the novel as a whole, also formed an autonomous short story, one of the best Abramovitsh ever wrote.

With all that said, we still have hardly touched upon the crucial significance of Mendele. This has little to do with his usefulness as a literary master of ceremonies. As such, Mendele could have well remained the humble provincial literary entrepreneur he had been when he was originally invented, and one of the many fictional collectors and publishers of stories and documents which fill eighteenth- and nineteenth-century European fiction, particularly when this fiction is presented as "regional." For example, in Gogol's "Evenings on a Farm Near Dikan'ka," colorful Ukrainian tales are supposedly gathered and introduced by a certain Rudyi Pan'ko. Walter Scott's allegedly genuine Scottish novels and tales are collected and introduced by a local schoolteacher and parish clerk, Jedediah Cleishbotham. But Mendele assumed greater importance than any of these publishers, editors, and amateur litterateurs, an importance owing little to his technical tasks and therefore not to be explained as an aspect of narrative technique; or, rather, his importance depends on such techniques only insofar as does everything else in the story—content, ideas, emotions—and insofar as narrative technique cannot be unrelated to whatever is significant in the story.

Nor is Mendele's significance directly connected with the little that we are told about the circumstances of his life. We know he is middle-aged or elderly, but never really old. This is how he appears in 1863, and how he takes his leave at the end of the first decade of the twentieth century. His physical appearance is common, quite indistinct, and his physiognomy characteristically "Jewish." He himself hails from a small shtetl, Tsviy'achich in some stories, Kabtsansk in others. Naturally, he is married and a paterfamilias, a father of grown children (how many we never know) of marriageable age. However, he is hardly a family man, for he sees little of his hometown or of his family, since throughout the better part of the year he plies his trade as an itinerant book peddler doing his "rounds" throughout the *shtetlekh* of western Ukraine. Significantly he never cares to tell us about his short stays at home, during Passover, for instance. We hear nothing in particular about his wife, whom he does not seem to miss, and who is less close to him by far than his horse, his constant companion. He is extremely loyal to his trade, which he took up long ago, after his years of "bed and board" with his in-laws had terminated. Having then lost money in other trades, which were alien to his nature, he finally "found" himself as a book peddler, which is what he is the whole time we know him. Only once, swept along by Zionist enthusiasm, does he dream of getting rid of his books and wagon to become a farmer in the fields and vineyards of Judea (in the short story "Bymey hara'ash" [In days of tumult], 1894). He is easily dissuaded by a wise elderly Zionist leader who makes him realize how unfit he is for such a step and how frivolous his "dream" really is. Mendele is quickly convinced because he is by nature perspicacious, cool-headed, and not given to wishful thinking. Another time, when he is robbed of his horse by the pogromists of 1881–82, he is forced to stay at home for a longer time ("Beseter ra'am" [In the secret place of thunder], 1886–87). He is quite impatient to resume his itinerant regimen, not just because he has to make a living but also because roaming throughout Ukraine with his books has become his real life. His stock is the conventional Jewish one: Talmud tractates, sets of the Mishna, and the *Shulhan arukh,* ethical treatises, Hasidic publications, popular Yiddish chapbooks, women's prayers, as well as ritual articles and even protective magical amulets and cameos. Secretly, he might also carry riskier stuff, that is, books and magazines of the Haskalah—if he thinks they might bring in a profit. Far be it from him to sympathize openly with this "forbidden" literature, but we have the sense that he is acquainted with it, at least superficially.

Of all these rather stereotypical features, only three characteristics are of real importance to us: (1) Mendele completely "belongs," at least outwardly, within the traditional Jewish milieu and can hardly be distinguished from thousands of similar *yidn fun a gants yor* (common Jews). This, on the one hand, gives him access to the innermost recesses of traditional society (while the European-looking Abramovitsh immediately arouses suspicion) and renders him an ideal "spy." On the other hand, it also entails a real intimacy on his part with the cultural codes of that society. Thus, he can serve us not only as one who spies but, more important, as an interpreter, a translator, and a guide in our passage through what is to us an almost foreign cultural territory. (2) Mendele, when all is said and done, is nevertheless an "uprooted" person. He has more or less already wrenched himself out of the cultural and social world he is describing and is now more of an observer than a participant. This has little to do with overt ideological heresy and much more with a sense of individual freedom which he has developed during his life as a lonely itinerant. Mendele *is* a free agent. He *is* a person aware of his individuality. He does not depend on a supportive environment and does not trust collectives. As befits a lonely and free person, he is inquisitive, suspicious, and takes nothing for granted. His itinerant lifestyle frees him from the provincialism and parochialism of his society. As a man who travels as far as Odessa and Warsaw, he can make comparisons, draw conclusions, notice differences, but also detect characteristic infrastructures. He can compare the different towns; he can "Judaize" nature and "naturalize" Judaism, that is, demystify

Jewish codes of behavior and point to their biological origins. In a way he is a genuine intellectual, but his intellectualism is completely different from that of the traditional Talmud scholar or the bookish modern university professor. He is a "natural" and conversational philosopher. He observes, muses, plays with ideas, engages in dialogue, and talks, talks, talks. His thinking and talking are not structured. They are always tentative, digressive, associative, and open-ended. (3) Mendele's attachment to the book trade does not render him bookish. He is relatively erudite on demand. Particularly in Abramovitsh's Hebrew renderings of his works, Mendele must indulge in games of quotation, allusion, and parody, through which he compensates for the racier wit of the Yiddish version. However, he never allows books and sacred texts to control him. At the same time, his "professional" literacy gives him the benefit of familiarity with a disciplined use of language. Mendele knows as well as anyone how to make a point, and also how to conceal a point he does not want to make openly. He is, in fact, a master of the linguistic sleight of hand which allows him to say and unsay something almost in a single phrase. He is precisely the professional stylist, the expert he proclaims himself to be. He is also an ironist, a philosopher who knows how to use language for subversive purposes. Indeed, irony—saying something while meaning its opposite—is his lifeblood, even when he is not trying to be funny or clever. As we have seen, his very existence is double-tiered. He is a shtetl person as well as one who has cut himself loose from the shtetl and its loyalties; he is married and also single; he is gregarious but essentially lonely; he is a "simple" person, who is also an intellectual; he is a traditional Jew, but also the very personification of a Jewish *esprit critique*. How can he function rhetorically if not as an ironist?

# XII

Putting together all that we know about Mendele, we can see Abramovitsh's tremendous literary and cultural breakthrough involved in this invention. We can also see why the inventor became so thoroughly enamored of his creation, to the extent that he almost allowed it to suck him dry of his own identity and virtually strip him of his very name. In Mendele, modern Jewish literature could speak in two voices without lapsing into schizophrenia. With him, the mental chasm separating modernity from tradition, as well as the arrogant rational ego from the less articulate and the less articulated layers of the human personality, could be bridged or at least viewed from both sides. Modern Jews experienced the gap between themselves and those whom they had left behind in the traditional milieu as a gap separating the subject—we, the moderns—from the object—them, the people of the shtetl. If the shtetl civilization was ever to become relevant to the modern experience, even if the relevance was expressed as a serious critique, that mental separation had to be overcome, if only for an illusory moment of suspension of disunity through aesthetic meditation. The "we" had to develop the ability to envision themselves as "them" or, better yet, to discover in "ourselves" the vestiges of "them." A mental enlargement of the modern Jewish identity was absolutely necessary, but not for the purpose of harmonizing the disharmonious or finding the compromise where, perhaps, no compromise was possible. It was necessary for the purpose of buttressing the modern Jewish identity as such. If it was to be not simply "modern" but also Jewish, it had to redefine its attitude to the Jewish "past," and for that some kind of an *interior* dialogue with that past was needed. Mendele supplied the aesthetic literary arena where such a dialogue could take place. His unique voice, as unified and recognizable as it was, created the tonality of dialogue. His meandering narrative followed the convoluted line of the question-answer or charge-countercharge sequence. Mendele's discourse was inherently dialogic, as much as Talmudic discourse is by definition dialogic.

Modern Jewish literature assumed the prophetic role of a "watchman unto the House of Israel." It was meant to replace the rabbis, the Talmudists, the Hasidic leaders, the mystics, and even the biblical prophet himself as a guide of the Jewish people in modern times. That is why it would allow itself to talk through its modern cultural heroes, such as Bialik and Peretz, with the authority of (Godless) Isaiah or Ezekiel. However, without God, from where could this pseudo-prophetic literature draw its authority, its Jewish legitimacy, if not from "the people," from their historical experience? And how could it speak in their name—and thus talk not only *at* them but also *to* them—if it alienated itself from "them"? Thus, without a Mendele of sorts, and his followers (the "Sholem Aleichem" of Sholem Aleichem or the narrator of Agnon's *Bridal Canopy,* for example), the prophetic Bialik and Peretz would be unacceptable and impossible.

The linguistic schism that Abramovitsh transcended by writing in both Hebrew and Yiddish, and also by overcoming the dichotomy between "high" Germanized Yiddish and "low" colloquial Yiddish, as well as that between "high" biblical Hebrew and "low" Talmudic-midrashic-rabbinic Hebrew, was, then, a cultural schism that had to be transcended on many levels. The language issue represented a cleavage at the heart of Jewish cultural identity. Abramovitsh was able to transcend it not only, not even mainly, because he was a super-

latively sensitive and creative stylist, but because he fully
grasped its cultural and psychological supralinguistic significance, and, most important, because he had with him
Mendele, his Janus-faced creation, to show him the way out of
the labyrinth. Simply by following Mendele's *causerie,* paying
attention to his ironic remarks, he would see the way toward
his destination.

In a way, the Janus-faced Mendele became the ultimate
"watchman unto the House of Israel." His critique of traditional Jewish life was bitter, withering, but it did not issue
from beyond the confines of the House of Israel. Mendele's
criticism indirectly reflected Abramovitsh's European humanism, but in his voice it was internalized and Judaized, and
struck roots inherent in Jewish moralism. Mendele did not
try to imitate "their" voice and speech, that is, those of
Abramovitsh's shtetl protagonists. There is very little mim-
icry of this kind in his *causerie,* for Mendele never betrayed
his own tonality and timbre. But Mendele could, at least
occasionally, discover in himself other voices, or the voices
of the "other." He could bring up to the surface the shadows
of the half-forgotten "us" who were still not separated from
"them."

Nowhere does this act of tonal resurrection occur more
openly than in *Fishke the Lame,* which in more than one way is
Abramovitsh's quintessential novel, where Mendele gives his
quintessential "performance." The novel begins with Mendele's triumphantly parading his caustic wit and his fluency as a critic and a rationalist. Metaphorically, he is like the
summer sun, the blazing light of which radiates through the
first episodes of the novel, penetrating cranny and crevice,
shedding light on every dark little indecent secret. Thus,
Mendele blows to pieces all Jewish "spiritual" pretensions.
The Jews pretend to have transcended, or at least sublimated,

all bodily needs—the need for food, sex, shelter, etc.—but actually they have only suppressed and vitiated them. The hairy, heavyset, virile Alter Yaknehoz pretends that he has re-married because he needs a woman to look after his house-hold, but actually he had divorced his first wife, lost track of their children, and remarried because he craved sex with a young and attractive woman. Mendele knows this ugly and potentially disastrous secret of his colleague (Alter is also a book peddler) and he makes it clear to the browbeaten man, as he pushes him against the wall with his bright, scorch-ing, inquisitorial retorts. Mendele is even wise enough to know and point out the historical significance of this terrible insight into the sweaty physicality of Jewish "spiritualism" (for the Jews do not "conquer" the body, they only cripple it), as indicated by the date on which the novel starts, the seven-teenth of the month of Tammuz, the day on which the army of Nebuchadnezzar broke through the walls of besieged Jerusalem. The downfall of the Jewish commonwealth, the Jewish *body politic,* brought about the crippling of the Jewish body.

This bright, almost insufferable omniscience of Mendele, however, attains an altogether new dimension when night comes and Mendele finds himself alone in the forest, without his horse, which, along with Alter's, has been stolen. Alter goes to look for them and, ominously, does not return. Sud-denly, Mendele's *esprit critique* collapses and the wise com-mentator on the national character is revealed—to himself and to us—as a frightened child. Mendele's "wild" imagina-tion, folksy and demonic, overpowers his rational capacity. Mendele experiences a frightening entropy of his entire per-sonality. Everything in him falls apart under the overwhelm-ing impact of the realization of how weak, helpless, and lost he is. Now the weak Jewish body is Mendele's body. The hairy, virile Alters are looked to as possible protectors and saviors. Indeed, it will be Alter who will bravely fight with the thieves to retrieve the lost horses. It will be Alter who will save Fishke from death. Mendele will only lose his way, his earlock, and his dignity. Once he reaches the safe haven of a Jewish inn, he gives vent to his childish emotions of hurt, pain, and loneliness, sheds hot tears, addresses the moon, which he identifies with his dead mother, and pours out his bitter complaints about a wasted life.

We understand that as much as the Glupsker have lost the connective link which could have tied their commercial activity to the desire for profit, and as much as the Kabtsansker have lost the emotional link which should have bound their sexuality to parental responsibility, Mendele has also lost some important connection which might have linked his out-sized critical capacity to a sufficiently developed emotional and instinctive identity; for emotionally Mendele is still a child. The only woman to whom he can relate is his dead mother. In order to survive in an adult world, one in which the legendary "Green Mountain" of Glupsk is only a muddy, dirty heap of rubble infested by thieves and robbers, he has to suppress his emotional being and leave it stunted and weak-ened. Of all the people in the world, it is from Fishke the Lame, the grotesque cripple of whose wedding Mendele speaks with such frightening sarcasm, that he must learn true emotional maturity. Not in vain does he try to tear Fishke's tale of love and loyalty to pieces with his snide remarks, or better, by generalizing and abstracting it into an anatomy of Jewish beggary. The story threatens him directly. It exposes the ugly secrets of his life without love, just as he had exposed the dirty secrets of Alter's life of sex without responsibility. Thus, Mendele's ironic duality is revealed as yet another valence of the national flaw of a disjointed sensibility. Only now, the flaw is experienced from within and not from without. It is an internal bleeding wound, a terrible gash crying for healing and not for sarcastic exposure. Mendele has become one with the Mendele world, and through him we can also integrate ourselves within it or integrate it within ourselves.

Dan Miron
Jerusalem and New York City
May 1995

## NOTES

[1]See "Reshimot letoldotay" (Sketches to my biography, 1889), *Kol kitvey Mendele Mokher Sefarim* (Tel Aviv: 1947), p. 5.

[2]D. Frishman, "Mendele Mokher Sefarim," *Kol Kitvey D. Frishman* (Warsaw and New York: 1931), vol. 7, p. 74.

[3]See Y. H. Brenner, "Ha-arakhat atsmenu bishloshet hakrakhim," *Kol kitvey Y. H. Brenner* (Tel Aviv: 1967), vol. 3, pp. 57–78.

[4]See, for instance, Meyer Viner's Mendele studies in his *Tsu der geshikhte fun der yidisher literatur in 19-tn yorhundert* (New York: 1946), vol. 2, pp. 5–234.

[5]Cf. G. Shaked, *Beyn sekhok ledema* (Ramat Gan: 1965), pp. 22–35, 46–56.

[6]See Yankev Glatshteyn, "Fishke der krumer," *In tokh genumen* (New York: 1947), pp. 453–69.

[7]See Avraham Kariv, "Olam vetilo," "Klalot ufratot," *Atara leyoshna* (Tel Aviv: 1956), pp. 30–115.

[8]See Volf (Vevik) Rabinovitsh, *Mayn bruder Sholem Aleichem— zikhroynes* (Kiev: 1939), pp. 140–44.

[9]See Abramovitsh's letter to Sholem Aleichem of June 10, 1888, in *Shriftn* (1928), vol. 1, p. 251.

[10]Yankev Leshtshinsky, "Di geshikhte fun di Berdichever yidishe kehile fun 1789 biz 1917," *Bleter far yidishe demografye, statistik un ekonomik,* vol. 1, no. 2 (1923), p. 37.

[11]*Geklibene verk fun Mendele Moykher Sforim* (New York: 1946), vol. 2, p. 225.

[12]Abramovitsh often appealed to critics who mentioned him by his real name not to divulge his "secret" and to refer to him as Mendele. He was trying to protect the sense of intimacy that many readers developed with regard to Mendele as a friendly living being.

# A NOTE ON THE TRANSLATIONS

F ISHKE THE LAME WAS INITIALLY PUBLISHED AS A YIDDISH SHORT
story in 1869. When S. Y. Abramovitsh resumed his literary activity in the late 1880s, after a hiatus of several
years, he worked simultaneously in Hebrew and Yiddish.
From 1886 until the end of his life, he wrote Hebrew stories
and worked on Hebrew versions of his prior Yiddish novels.
Since Abramovitsh never merely translated his fiction, the
new editions are actually new books. As he produced his Hebrew narratives, Abramovitsh also revised his Yiddish texts.

Ted Gorelick's translation of *Fishke the Lame* is based on the
second, greatly expanded edition of Abramovitsh's *Fishke der
krumer*, published in Odessa by Varshaver in 1888. This was
the first volume of what was intended to be a complete edition of Abramovitsh's Yiddish works, but only one subsequent

volume—containing *The Nag* (Di klyatshe, 1889)—was printed. The Hebrew version, entitled *Sefer ha-kabtzanim,* was initially translated by H. N. Bialik and printed in *Ha-dor* 1 (1901); Abramovitsh later retranslated his work for the Jubilee edition of his Hebrew writings (1909–12). The subtitle of the present translation, "A Book of Jewish Poorfolk," is drawn from the Hebrew version.

The narration of Fishke's tale is as important as the story itself. Mendele narrates the opening chapters, which describe his chance meeting with Alter; then Alter recalls his match-making fiasco. Mendele picks up the narrative thread, telling what he has heard about Fishke. Finally, Fishke himself takes over and, prompted by Alter and Mendele, continues his story up to the present. This creates a striking multivoiced effect, in which the three different narrators convey distinctive levels of Yiddish speech and Jewish society.

Abramovitsh presents serious problems for the translator because even a century ago his Yiddish had an archaic flavor. Ted Gorelick's rendition of *Fishke the Lame* conveys the intricacies of Abramovitsh's Yiddish diction by echoing the dialects found in English novels of the eighteenth and nineteenth centuries by such authors as Laurence Sterne and Charles Dickens, whose works influenced Abramovitsh. The twists and turns of this translation approximate the leisurely pace of Abramovitsh's Yiddish while highlighting the contrasting voices in the telling of Fishke's tale.

HILLEL HALKIN'S TRANSLATION of *The Brief Travels of Benjamin the Third* strikes a balance between archaic and modern elements of style. This translation is based on the first edition of S. Y. Abramovitsh's *Kitser masoes Binyomin hashlishi,* published in Vilna by the Romm publishing house in 1878. Although the title page indicates that this is only Book One, no continuation was published. The Hebrew edition was printed as a supplement to the Odessa-based journal *Pardes* 3 (1896). The Epilogue has been translated from the Hebrew text.

*The Brief Travels of Benjamin the Third* is the last original work dating from Abramovitsh's first Yiddish phase. He had previously published *The Little Man* (Dos kleyne mentshele, 1864–65), the original versions of *The Magic Ring* (Dos vintshfingerl, 1865), *Fishke the Lame* (Fishke der krumer, 1869), a play called *The Tax* (Di takse, 1869), and *The Nag* (Di klyatshe, 1873). These four novels and one play, together with *The Brief Travels of Benjamin the Third,* represent the crux of Abramovitsh's Yiddish fiction.

*The Brief Travels of Benjamin the Third* employs vigorous satire and parody, satirizing the everyday life of Jews in the shtetl at the same time that it parodies prior works in literary history. The first Benjamin was the twelfth-century Benjamin of Tudela; Benjamin the Second was Israel ben Joseph Benjamin (1818–64), who wrote travel books. Apart from referring back to these previous travelers, Abramovitsh's novel parodies Cervantes's *Don Quixote*—itself a parody of chivalric romances. Moreover, it pokes fun at Hasidic accounts of pilgrimages to the Holy Land.

# FISHKE THE LAME

## A BOOK OF JEWISH POORFOLK

TRANSLATED BY
TED GORELICK

*Epistle Dedicatory*

## TO MY DEAR, CHERISHED FRIEND, THE RENOWNED AND ERUDITE M<sup>R</sup>

# Menashe Margolis,

## THIS BOOK IS OFFERED IN GIFT WITH ALL HIS HEART, BY THE AUTHOR

*My dear friend,*

*I bear only the sad refrain in the chorus of Jewish literature. In my writings you will find revealed a Jew even to the marrow, who, if he falls to singing a lively air, will give the impression, if only from afar, that he is well on the way to tears. His Sabbath hymns are tempered by the quality of sadness; he has only to laugh, and his eyes brim over, and should he allow himself some small measure of gladness, it will instantly snatch from his bosom a sigh of profound sorrow—and so is he ever and always giving out with cries of woe and interjections of grief! . . .*

*Now I would not for the world presume to call myself the nightingale of our Jewish literature. Though I will admit to resembling that melancholy chorister among birds remarkably well in one detail. The nightingale pours out its anguish in, of all seasons, the spring; exactly* at opetide, while the whole world is being radiantly reborn and all's abud, and on every hand pleasant smells invade the air, and every heart rejoices in it.

You and I, my friend, began our work in Jewish literature in the very springtime of Jewish life here in our country. The 1860s marked the beginning of an entirely new life for Jews——a life that abounded copiously in brave promises of later fulfillment. We were both very young then and had taken eagerly to belaboring our pens, each after his own fashion. The public relished your writing, were ravished by your wonderful fluency in discoursing upon the great matters of Jewish life; they thrilled to your eloquent championing of your people's good, and were beguiled by the amiable congeniality with which you taught them to know themselves better and to take their place among the nations as respected equals. Ah, how the pearls tumbled from your mouth then, lustrous, sparkling gems destined ever to remain an ornament in Jewish letters. And I, too, for my part, took occasion to warble in that happy season, scribbling away, making my own music the while. Although I generally set aside one string which bore accompaniment in a minor key and put my hearers into a melancholy humor. Some listened eagerly, albeit with a heavy heart; others fretted and fussed, made disapproving faces, resentful of having had some sore spot of theirs rudely touched, of being too often reminded by me of disagreeable things. In the event, I only persisted in harping on the same string, playing upon it exactly as I was prompted to.

But that joyous spring being over, how dire for Jews its sequel. I was made to withdraw into silence by it, and for a great while unable so much as to put pen to paper.

And if now I take up this poor, withered quill of mine to write, I owe it all to you, and you alone. For it was your healing presence which restored me to myself; your wise counsel, your tireless work on behalf of our people, which had finally roused me to set myself a task that I, also, might put my hand to. A spark of that sacred fire burning *always in your own Jewish heart was carried into my heart, which was rekindled by it and now blazes as ardently as in my youth.*

*Yes, you and I began our literary work at the same time, though our fortunes diverged. You took up lodgings as it were in the upper story, amongst the Quality; dealing there with the most valued treasures of Jewish history, setting out for display only the richest jewels of our people's past, their best, their proudest artifacts. Your business has been with the likes of Rabbi Hillel, Rabbi Meir, and Rabbi Akiva, your custom with our worthiest notables, and only our exalted luminaries bear you company. Whereas my lot has taken me belowstairs, down into the cellars of Jewish life. My stock in trade: RAGS & CAST-OFFS. I have merely to do with paupers and tramps, ragamuffins and rogues, and such other poor human oddments as may come to net, little folk to a man, small fry, and smaller beer. Beggars are the stuff of my dreams; cadging bags the constant subject of my reveries. Whither I turn, where'er I look, that shabby article looms before me; like the string of umbles dangling at the end of the mournful booby's nose in the adage, that lumbering bag of slim pickings and rag-and-bone charity our people have been shouldering since time out of mind is never out of my sight . . .*

*Lordy, lordy, ever and always the cadging bag, that infernal Jewish cadging bag!*

*Yes, my friend, it was through you that I regained my desire to write; and fine thanks you have for it in the person of my Fishke the Lame—cadging bag and all, poor fellow—with whom I now appear before the public after so long an interval. Now, I am only too conscious that this Fishke of mine makes a poor enough gift by way of return for a valued friendship. But knowing your good heart, sir, to say nothing of the affability of your nature, I have every reason to hope that you will receive my poor Fishke kindly when he turns up, and give him warm welcome. And possibly, too, you may invite him to come in, go even so far as to acquaint him with your household and your* guests, among whose company he would then be allowed to set down his bag and bide awhile, and entertain you all for an idle hour with his stories. And so, the happy contemplation of that prospect's having brought a smile to his lips, all that remains to do is to beg you to accept this earnest and heartfelt expression of gratitude, from your most affectionate friend, sir,

The Author

# A PROLOGUE

BY MENDELE THE BOOK PEDDLER

UPON HIS SETTING OUT ON
HIS JOURNEY INTO THE WORLD
WITH THE VERY FIRST PRINTING OF
HIS OWN STORIES

"MA SHMEKHEM"—"So what's your name?" That's the first thing one Jewish gent says to another, and a total stranger to boot, the minute he has slipped him the glad hand and unplugged a how-d'ye-do. And it'd never even enter anybody's head at the time to say: "Now, sir, what makes *you* so all-fired eager on a sudden to know my name? Are we maybe thinking of becoming related by marriage? I go by the name it pleased them as named me to call me, and there's an end!" Why gracious, no! It's a perfectly normal question and quite in the ordinary nature of things, say like giving someone's new caftan an appreciative pat and asking, "How much a yard?"—or like cadging a smoke, just when someone's got his tobacco pouch open; like poking your fingers into someone's snuffbox, and helping yourself to a pinch; like easing your foot into someone else's tub and dipping in a sweaty old handkerchief, and sort of giving yourself one of 'em general allover rubdowns with it; like sidling over to where two people are having a cozy chat, and cupping an ear to listen in; or like suddenly asking somebody, clear out of the blue, about how's business, and then heaping all sorts of advice on him which he has got absolutely no use for and can just as well do without. This sort of thing, and others I could name, happen all the time. They are part of the scheme of things from away back when, and to take exception would be, well, a bit mad, and savage, if not downright unnatural. And not only in this life but in the next, too, we Jewish folks like to think that, no sooner have we got our foot past the door, than the first thing out of the Guardian Angel's mouth is—"Ma Shmekhem, cuz?" And the angel that wrestled Jacob our father, well, even he wouldn't deviate from the custom, and asked his name right off. So, if that's the Angels' way, what's to expect from ordinary mortal folk, like you and me? Now, I'm sure that on my First Venture, so to speak, into Yiddish *Lit'rature,* the first thing folks are bound to ask me is—"Ma Shmekhem, gramps?"

Mendele is the name, sir! It was given to me, your worships, in honor of my great-grandfather, on my mother's side, Reb Mendele Moscower (God rest). Moscower's how they called him back in his day, on account talk was how once he'd been all the way to Moscow, in the way of trade for Russian goods. Now this gave him quite a name in his quiet neck of the woods; for he was looked up to by, oh, just about everybody, as a man of parts, and wise in the ways of the world; so if they got into a scrape, say, and there was maybe a petition needed writing up, they'd always go to him first for advice. But I'm getting off the point.

Though I've still a long ways to go before I'm let off the

hook. Because once that first question's done with, then they really have at you hammer and tongs, with queries of every conceivable description, like: "So where does a fine Jewish gent as yourself, sir, hail from? Married, are you? Children? What line you say you was in? And, where might you be off to now, sir, if you don't mind my asking?" And so on and so forth, with more of the same; the sort of questions thought proper to ask wherever Jews congregate in God's green earth, if you have a mind ever to be regarded by decent folks as someone who's seen something of life, and isn't only a benchwarmer; and which you are also obliged to answer if you've a notion to be civil, the way you do when you say *Why Greetings, sir, an' a Good Year!* if you are wished a good Sabbath or happy holiday. So who am I to pick a quarrel with the rest of the world? Why no, sir. I am quite prepared to answer these questions, too, as briefly and to the point as ever I can.

Now me I'm a native of Tsviyachich myself, a pretty considerable small town, which God prosper, in Teterevka province, celebrated far and wide for its fine cattle, and even more for our own *Tsviyacher Rebbe,* saving the difference, whose name is on people's lips everywhere. But I'm getting off the point. No, but it says right here, in my Passbook, I am fifty-two. Well now I can't rightly say how old I am exactly, and the matter of my years was quite a bone of contention between my mother and my father, God rest. The both of them said I was born at First Candle, during the big Market Street blaze. Only Papa reckoned this was when the Great Frost blew into our parts, the time the Old Rebbe passed on (an' God rest!), but Mama, she'd point out it happened only a year or two after the First Terror of the Pressgangs—*preserve us!* For it only stood to reason, didn't it, she'd say; on account it was exactly the Last of Hanukkah the Red Cow calved and she even made *cream dumplins!* which only set half the town licking its fingers, and the taste of them still hangs in the mouths of some of our old-timers. But I'm getting off the point. Anyhow, the particulars in my Passbook go like this: Medium Height; Hair and Eyebrows Gray; Hazel Eyes; Nose and Mouth Average; Gray Beard; Blemishes None; Distinguishing Marks and Characteristics None. Which is to say a blank, completely ordinary. Just a person, like most people. Mind, even that's something, if only you think about it. I mean, who knows but one might have been born a tomcat, which God forbid—or, say, even beef on the hoof. Now, here's a moot point to split hairs over. The proposition is: Wouldn't a Passbook and no particulars prove exactly the same thing; namely that one was human because since when has livestock taken to carrying Passbooks about their persons? And the argument is: There's no sense at all in raising such questions. Listen, the whole point is that I have just handed you all my particulars on a silver platter, and still you don't know what I am really like . . . No, honestly, though; of what earthly use, for instance, would it be if you knew I have a high forehead with more than its share of wrinkles; or that my nostrils are decidedly oversized and queer-looking; or that I have these slitty eyes, which when I stare at a thing I kind of squinch them up, like I was a mite shortsighted maybe; or that when I crimp the corners of my mouth together, I get this briery kind of a grin on my face which looks like it ought to come with a wry little chuckle. Why it hardly bears thinking about, I dare say—because, believe me, my own wife couldn't've cared less about such trifles, even before the wedding. All they told her was *Congratulations child, we got you a husband!* and that was that. And, besides, whose business is it anyways to know all about other people's noses and faces and things? I mean what difference does it make, and who even cares? So, now the truth's sort of slipped out, you all know. Yes, your

worships, I have a wife. And children, bless 'em, it goes without saying I've got quite a few, because who ever heard of a
married Jewish gent without he has got half a dozen about the
house, at very least. Specially if it happens he is poor. Oh, and
about my living? Well, now, I make that by colportage. That's
to say I deal in sacred books. Which in our business means
Pentateuchs and Prayerbooks, mostly: Festal Prayerbooks
plus your common ordinary variety of Daily Prayerbooks; as
also your Penitential prayers, and your Breviaries for womenfolks, and—well, your other such bookware in kind. Oh, and
storybooks. I carry all sorts of storybooks, and even some of
your modern-type books, now and again. Only I must say I
turned my hand to a lot of different trades in my day. When
I left off boarding with my in-laws, why I set up first as a
money changer, and then as a grocer, a taverner, a corn factor,
a broker, and a schoolmaster. Well I only tried this and that
and t'other thing, just one after the other, don't you know, the
way a Jewish gent will generally do—for how's the saying?
many livings, few thrivings—and remained (an' God only
keep your worships from the same) an unmitigated pauper.
Till finally I took to books. And managing quite nicely by it,
thank you. Though, besides books, I've also took to carrying
Prayershawls, too, and Bershad-wove "Four-corner" weskits;
as also prime Eight-threaded showfringes for the fastidious,
Phylactery straps, Ram's horns, Goodspells, Mezuzahs, Wolfstooth teething-dummies, Amulets, Woolly knitted combination Baby Bootees and Toddlers' Yarmulkes. As a sideline, I
also trade in brass and copper kitchenware, sometimes. Mind
you, even I haven't worked out how the pots and pans got in
with books. But it's the sort of thing that's been pretty much
the rule amongst our kind for, oh, just ages now. No different,
say, from a Jewish writer having to turn his hand now and
then to marriage brokering, or a Polish shammes having to

keep a modest saloon on the premises, in only a small way of
business, or an alderman in a Jewish parish having occasionally to cook fish in the kitchen, and also waiting on table,
when the Quality are holding open house, or one of your
pious shul-service gentry, say the beadle, or the cantor, or the
sexton, who spends most of his time spreading outrageous
slanders, and every so often manages even to make a regular
hash of things—or only your average, ornery kind of a Jewish
Gent of Means, who can't help taking his cut of the kosher
meat tax. But I'm getting off the point. Oh, I been on the
road for years and years now. Been traveling all over Poland,
too, don't you know; yes, and turned up in just about every
city and dinky town they got, whilst at it. Why, I should think
by now they knew me everywhere there (God praise), like a
bad penny. Though, if you happen by, you will generally find
me hanging about my cart, near the shul mostly. And my jade?
Well now that sad little bag a bones is likely been got out of
tackle by then, and turned round arsy-versy like, that's to say
facing the van; and left to make a poor meal—if he's lucky—
of course fodder's been laid out for him on a length of
spread-out bagging, which is tied up on the one end to the
driver's box, and on the other, to both shafts stood upright.
Like as not, there's a gang of little boys creeping up on him,
too, from behind, yanking away bits of his tailpiece. Now,
you'd perhaps of thought *he'd* mind; but no! For that poor
bonehead of mine, why he'll only be standing there, serene as
you please, like he hadn't a care. Sometimes, though, he'll
curl back his lower lip, and show a kind of toothy grin, don't
you know, which looks (only saving your worships' presences)
practically human. But on lean days, when there's nothing to
eat, well he'll kind of only stick up his ears then, and drift off
into a brown study; and take to peering inside the van, you
know at the books, so you'd swear he was making better horse

sense of them than any Jewish schoolmaster's assistant (no offense) in his shoes might do . . . But I'm getting off the point.

Well I'd say I was about done with my end, and have satisfied your curiosity on every point. So I guess I can get on with
a story which I'm put in mind of. Though, I'm only human.
So if I happen to have missed something, you have my word:
the minute I think of it, I shall be sure to put it straightaway
into one of them stories which I have a notion to be putting
out, one after another, an' God willing. And another thing. In
case anybody is too impatient to wait, and will not rest till he
has got absolutely everything down pat, to the last jot and tittle—why, he is welcome to set himself down and write to
me, and is sure to get an exact reply by very next post. So
here is my address: Менделю Юделевичу Мойхерю
Сфорему объ Цвячичу, Book Peddler. Oh, and don't
bother any about tacking on that honorific tag they got at the
end sometimes, "Rᵗ Hon. Hebrew Gent. Esq." They'll know
anyhow.

Tut-tut, Your Worships! Almost forgot. Piece of luck,
catching myself in time like that. See, our Jewish authors are
forever finding ways of dragging their wife's name in right
about now; say, working her initials into one of 'em pert
whatsits, uh, *Monograms,* which you find at the beginning of
their books, and then be praising her into the Seventh
Heaven, rattling on about how she is so Gentle and Kind and
God-fearing and Pious, and, well, Modest, as a rule, too. So I
am sure you will want to know my own missus's name, at very
least. And, why, it is only reasonable and right you should
want to.

Tut! patience— She is called Yenta!

# 1

THE SUN'S SCARCELY begun to shine, and sweet summer's in the land, and folks have got so they are feeling newborn and glad-hearted, for seeing God's good earth looking fair again—well don't you know but that's just when our somber season sets in, and the time comes for Jews to start mourning and shedding tears in earnest. For it's then the whole roster of sad observances must be got through: the drear progression of fastings and self-denials and bewailments, lasting from the Numbering of Days, at winter's end and in the leafy prime of spring, 'twixt the Passover and the Feast-o'-Weeks, till well into the chill, drenching wet and muck of autumn. And it's then that I, mind you, Reb Mendele the Book Peddler, have my work cut out and come into my own, making the circuit of Jewish towns with my cartload of stock, from which I furnish the kindred with all the rueful necessaries of the rites of weeping—to wit: with Fastday lamentations and Penitential prayers, with Ladies' Breviaries and graveside recitals, with ram's horns and Festal Prayerbooks. So, there you are! Because, you see, whilst Jews are sorrowing everywhere and grieve the livelong summer away, wearing the season out with weeping, I do business and ply my living. But I've got off the point.

I remember once of a midsummer morning, on the Fast of Tammuz, I was out on the road betimes, and seated on my perch in the driver's box, wrapped in my prayershawl and phylacteries, and keeping a light hand on the whip, as well, to kind of prod the jade along now and then, and—well, in a word, looking to all the world quite Jewish, as you may say. So, anyway, there I was: deep into my Sunrise devotions, with my eyes closed, and making very certain to keep them shut so

the cheery light of day shouldn't interfere with Fastday obser-
vance, you see. Well, sir, Satan, as we know, is never idle; and
that day he had got Nature all tricked out and frilly, and looking devilish handsome and nice, and pretty as a picture she
was, too; and she had so beguiled me by now, that I'd got this
powerful hankering to have myself a quick look. Oh, only the
tiniest, fleetingest glimpse, to be sure. Well, I can tell you, for
a while there I had me quite a struggle over it. I mean with
myself. Because on the one hand, you see, there was my Good
Side (that's the one on the side of the Angels, you know), saying:—"Oh tush Mendel! No, but 'tain't right! Oh but really,
Mendel, you *mustn't*"; and on the other hand, there's my Bad
Side (my hankering, that is), which is goading me on with:
"Pooh! Get a eyeful, why don'tcha . . . Nah! ninny, it won't
bite. Go on, have a gander—*Enjoy!*" And he kind of prises
open one eye then, just a wee bit. So I look. Well, Glory be! if
I'm not about dazzled by what I see. For, as though for spite,
what greets this one eye of mine is Nature at her primy best:
this gala prospect that is so near perfect, it fair flattens me,
and clean takes my breath away. Yes sir, it was that lovely! Up-
land I saw fields and fields, flecked with pinkish-white buckwheat blossoms, looking like snowdrops fallen between
coarse-matted rows of buff-golden wheat and tall, faded-
green tussocky stalks of Indian corn; and downland a piece,
there's a grassy glen that's verged on either side with stands of
nutwood trees, thickets of pine and walnut; and in the middle, a crystal pool of dancing sunlit water, which is sparkling
and winking with spangles of silver and gold. And from
where I sit, the cattle and sheep grazing in the pasture below
look to be only mere dots, dark bitty points of tawny brown
and red, and—*"Oh, for shame, Mendel!"* . . . Now this was when
my Good Side starts getting preachy on me again; and he puts
me in mind of what the blessed Sages say: if you are studying

on Sacred things whilst wandering about out-of-doors, and you break off meditating, just to say how nice a tree looks, or how pretty a field is, or in fact any other such article in kind is, then it's the same as doing yourself a wickedness. Only just then my Bad Side wafts me a capful of sweet smells that sets my nostrils aquiver with the thrill of it; and I breathe in a fragrant mixed bouquet: the scent of ricks of hay, and of spices and herbs, which courses through me like quickening cordial, making fresh every organ, thew and sinew of my body; and then he lets me hear the artful flutings of all manner of songbirds, whose singing teases and tantalizes my spirit; and he lets me feel a gentle gust of warm wind, which plays across my face and cheeks, and which tosses about my sidecurls and softly whispers into my ears: "Sure, go ahead and look. Oh, come, Mendel! I mean, you can't go on being the pious fool forever. Be a Man for once! Why surely it's there to be enjoyed. So give yourself a proper treat . . ." Well, now, all this time I was still at prayer you understand—that is, if you could call it that. For I didn't rightly know what I was reciting anymore, because by now, you see, my wits had pretty much taken off on their own, as 'twere, and I was just poking along at it, and going through the motions only; kind of grumbling my way through the prayer by rote, without paying it any real attention. And right along that time, I got this pecking sensation back of my mind—something was niggling away at me there, and riling me; and then a parcel of broody notions come crowding in on me, and they begun nattering away furiously inside my head, and scolding and ranting, like some half-crazed fishwife: "Yah! Crowbait! Maggotmeat! . . . Pah! Dead souls!—you've no more life, nor taste, nor smell to you than week-old table scraps! . . . bruised reeds! riven vessels! broken shards! broom fodder! Bah! you're not fit for the wasteyard even . . ." Well I confess it did give me a fright, I

mean thinking these awful things; and I started rocking to and
fro, pretending I was doing an honest job of praying—
though, all I wanted was to keep my mind from running on
so. And that's when I happened to overhear myself muttering
the start of Sunrise blessing—*Blessed art Thou, O Lord, That re-
storest souls to the dead . . .*

—Eh, what's this? thinks I (being suddenly brought up
kind of short by all this, you see). Oh my! what have I said?
Who can I have been railing at so? Well by now I was well-
nigh mortified by the ugly ungodly things I'd been thinking;
so, to smooth things over, I made out it wasn't *them* I meant at
all—O Heavens, no! Why I wasn't meaning but my little rat-
tlebones up front. Why yes, yes, that was it! Only my jade,
that's all! And to only prove this was so, I straightway tetched
him up with the whip, and bellowed at him, as if it was him I'd
been intending all along: *Yah! Crowbait . . . Gee-up! . . . Haw!
Maggotmeat . . .*

Now mind, as dodges go, this one wasn't half bad. Except
it didn't seem to do much good neither. Leastways not this
time. You see, I was more than a bit put out: I mean with myself, for having had such thoughts, and on such a day as this,
when any decent Jew ought to be recollecting and meditating
on the great Calamity and Destruction—picturing in his
mind Jerusalem lying in smoking ruins, laid waste by Nebuchadnezzar and his fell host . . . So, giving over my mind to
this, there and then I pulled a long face, and began tearfully
reciting the Penitential prayer for that day in a keening whimper; which proceeds then to grow weepier, and ever louder,
till I came to the grim and chilling verses of the hymnal:

> *Lo!*
>> *Is not the rav'ning Serpent of the North
>> From out his Fastness issued forth?*

*Aye!*
   *But see how even now he stretcheth out his claws*
   *And snatcheth Man and Beast unto his jaws!*

Well, sir, that about put me back in the pink. Because, well, let's face it—you have yourself a bit of a shout like that, and a pious singsong by way of contrition, and there's not a Jew in God's green earth who won't feel the better for it. Kind of like a child, you know. I mean after you've put it over your knee, and given it a first-class walloping: one good cry, and he's right as rain again, and twice as chipper. So pretty soon I'm back to being my old level self again, kind of lazying back easy in the driver's box, and stroking my whiskers like I hadn't a care, as if to say: "Well, that just about wraps up my end. Yes, sir! the slate's clean now. I've done my duty, as far as it goes, and my conscience is clear. So now sweet Lord, dear Merciful Father, it's your turn, you show *your* stuff: Let Thy gentle Compassion and Loving-kindness shine upon Thy creatures which attend Thee!" —"*So, come on now, forgive . . . ,*" says I, friendly like, talking to the jade this time: because, well, I really felt kind of bad and wanted to make it up to him. I mean about calling him "Crowbait" and "Maggotmeat" and the rest, a while back. And my little chucklehead, why he bends his spindly foreshanks, first the one leg and then the other, and drops to the ground on both his knees; and he brings his head down low, touching the earth with his forehead and— why, yes, I believe I even heard him groan! Well, maybe it wasn't more than only a soft whinny and a snort, kind of like *b'rrrrr!* But spoke low and mournful all the same, as if he had it in mind to be saying: "Beggin' my Master's pardon, and if 'tisn't too much to be askin' of Your Worship, but how about a bit of feed maybe, for a change, huh?" . . . "Whoa now! that *was* sharp," I says, signing to him with my whip hand, so he'd know he had my permission to rise . . . Well, now, did you ever? You know, it's not for nothing that it's written some- where in, uh, yes, in Fast-o'-Ab keenings, I believe: *O Zion, in thee do all beasts of the earth, yea, even the fowl of the air, grow wise!* Which I suppose in plain language means that, when it comes to good ole horse sense, it's your Jewish livestock which'll pretty near always have the beat of just about any ordinary dumb creature in the world, hands down . . . But I'm getting off the point. Though this did set me to thinking some, about Jews and things: you know—about their deep wisdom, and about their customs and practices and such; and about the Quality amongst them which run most everything, fancy high-toned Jews and—well, about how generally bad off and all they are. Well, by now my mind is kind of rambling hither and yon, thinking on this and on that, and whatever. And sud- denly it seems to me Nebuchadnezzar, the Serpent of the North, was on the march, and I hear the roll of drums and the tramp of booted feet; and there's the terrible clamor and smoke of war in the land: the walls are breached, and doors and gates thrown down, and windows smashed; cries of dis- tress and grief from every quarter, and Jews everywhere shouldering their worldly goods and taking to their heels. And, why, I'm there too! And I've sprung to my feet and I have took aholt of my staff, for there was still fight in me left, and —*WHOO-OOSH thwump!* . . . Next thing I knew I was flat on my back, lying slap-dab on the roadside beside my cart.

Well it's kind of shameful to have to admit; but it did seem like, at prayer a while back, I had let myself nod off, kind of willy-nilly. And worse luck: because when I chanced to look round, I saw my cart had run itself right smack into a mud- hole. And mind, none of your bitty puddly things neither, but one of them deep, sloughy sorts, which coachmen call "inky- bottoms," and are no end of trouble getting out of; and look-

ing on down towards the back, I could see where the butt end
of the axle from some other cart had got itself wedged right
in one of my rear wheels. And the horse, why he was looking
in a cruel state as well: what with one leg kind of hitched up
over a cart shaft, and the rest of him trussed up in a mess of
fouled reins and harness; and him a-puffing and a-wheezing
away something fierce, like a pair of leaky worn-out bellows,
so he looked about ready to drop. And from round the far side
of the wagon, I made out the sound of a whole batch of sput-
tering and coughing, and of hawking-up and spitting; mixed
in with about the hottest and flamingest passel of homespun
Jewish cussing as a body was ever likely to wish to hear. Now
that at least was a mercy. I mean its being Jewish swearing
rather than some other kind. Because you see by then I was
hopping mad, and about ready to take on most anybody.
Within reason. "Whew! one of our own!" says I to myself,
kind of relieved. And in a trice I whip over to the other side
so I could give the fool a piece of my mind. Well when I got
there, what do I see but this jackass sprawled on his back, underneath the cart; and he's got himself all tangled up in his
prayershawl, and his whip's somehow become knotted up in
his phylactery straps, and he's throwing himself this way and
that, and generally kicking and flailing about, and trying to get
himself turned over on his belly, to pick himself up off the
ground. "What's this! What's this!" says I, standing over him.
—"*Ya'aaa!* What's this yerself!" says he. Well it went back and
forth like that for a good while, with each giving as good as he
got, and nary a one looking the other in the face. So anyway,
there I am railing away at him: "The nerve, falling asleep at
prayer like that!" And he come back at me with: "*Ya'aaa!*
Nerve yerself! G'wan, lookit what's callin' the kettle black!"
So then I send his pa roasting to blazes, and he does the same
for mine; only he sends my ma in after him as well, just to

keep him company and do me one better. Well I wasn't standing for it. No, sir! And straightway I made for that broken-
down bonerack of a she-nag he calls his mare; and I took my
whip to her, and lay into her good. But just about then he finally manages to untangle himself, so he goes after my own
jade with his whip too. Well by now we are both larruping
each other's beasts; which are up on their hind legs and in a
terrible lather, and screaming and neighing so it's like to split
your ears open. Well, sir, that's when the both of us leave the
horses be, and we make for each other instead; and we're
closing in on one another like a pair of gamecocks, and each is
thinking to get a firm grip on the other's sidecurls, don't you
know. When all at once, we both pull up short, and look each
other up and down. Well, we must have made quite a sight:
two sober Jewish gents done up solemn-like, in prayershawls
and phylacteries, standing toe to toe like that in a raging passion and spoiling to slog it out with one another; as if this
wasn't the wilds at all, but a respectable setting, like say a synagogue maybe, saving the difference. Well, I mean to say,
under the circumstances it did have kind of a novelty about it
which would have merited notice, if anybody happened by,
that is. Anyhow, we're both standing there the while, giving
each other the same hard looks, and any minute now the fur
was about to fly for sure. When all in a moment each of us
kind of staggers back, sudden-like, as though we couldn't
hardly credit our eyes: "*Goodnessgracioussakes!* it's you, Reb
Alter," says I; and him, why he's no less bowled over than me,
saying: "Huh!? *Graciousgoodnesssakes!* it's you, Reb Mend'le . . ."

Now this same Reb Alter was no other than my old crony,
"Wine-'n'-Candles" Alter (this being kind of his trade
moniker don't you know)—who is a very burly, thickset Jewish gent, well-girthed about the middle, with a great heap of
grimy ginger-yellow hair on him, which could have kept half

a dozen Jewish gentlemen, besides himself, in full face-whiskers and sidecurls, easy: that is, if he was ever minded to be generous, and part with any of it. Anyway, this frowzy mess of carroty hair and whiskers is parted in the middle by a broad fleshy promontory, serving old Wine-'n'-Candles for a nose, which article is stopped up for pretty near most of the year. So as a rule Alter doesn't get much wear out of it generally; and it mainly kind of just sets there, more or less at a loose end, without doing much of anything so you'd notice. But at whiles, come season's end—say at floetide for instance, sometime just before Passover time, when the snow melts, and the ice begins to break up everywhere—well, this is when Wine-'n'-Candles' usually peaceable appendage unclogs, too; and then it gets all effluent and willful of a sudden, and the time's come for Alter to take the thing in hand, so to speak. And a mighty handful it can be too, sometimes: for when Wine-'n'-Candles' nose acts up in that way, there's not a trumpet nor even a ram's horn in Creation, let alone in Tuneyadevka, that'll come near it for fancy blowing and sheer loudness. And each time Alter gives it a workout, the eruptions which follow set all the garden poultry in town puck-pucking and a-quacking and a-cackling; so a regular barnyard concert ensues which is so astonishing it about stops everybody dead in their tracks, and leaves 'em stunned with admiration and amazement. And that's when the lids on dozens of snuffboxes will suddenly fly open, and offers of snuff will come at old Wine-'n'-Candles from every side, along with as many dozens of felicitations touching on his good health: *Aah-'CHOOO!* —"Oh, bless you! bless you! bless you, Reb Alter!" . . . Though, now I think of it, you might say that at this time of year most noses are apt to act up that way. Well, in Jewish towns, anyway. And, after all, it's only natural: I mean, seeing as things do tend to get a bit whiffy and high-

smelling around then. You might say it's a matter of estab-
lished custom even. You know, sort of like she-goats, which
are almost always yeaning round about past the midwinter
and in the early spring; and, as like as not, dropping their
litter on Jethro's Portion week, just about in time for Ten
Commandments reading at shul. But let that go. Besides
which, I'm getting off the point . . . Well, anyhow: Wine-'n'-
Candles Alter is from Tuneyadevka, and a book peddler like
myself, and is also an old acquaintance of mine, as I already
told—so we kind of go back quite a ways together, you see.
He's also what some might call a queer fish and has got his
own ways. And another thing: he's a bit slow on the uptake as
well, not being the foxiest of fellows. And not much of a
talker either, is Alter. So mostly he just keeps to himself and
sulks; and is generally cantankerous, as though he's got a chip
on his shoulder about nearly everything and everybody under
the sun. Though, mind, deep down he's not a bad sort at all,
and maybe kind of sweet even, once you get to know him better, that is.

So anyway, after the usual round of hearty nods and bobs
and handshakes, me and Alter commenced to sound each
other out—you know, in the way folks will generally go about
such things, if they're Jewish, that is. A quick peek first into
the other feller's van, just to get the lay of the merchandise;
and then kind of casually working the conversation round to
how he's been keeping lately, and about how is business, and
so on.

"So where's a feller headed?" says I to Alter just to prime
him.

"Where's a feller headed? *T'sk!*" says Alter with a whisk of
his hand, like maybe he was chasing flies. Now ain't that always the way with Jewish folks? I mean quizzing the quizzer
like that, and then fobbing him off with a brush-off "T'sk!"

which got to be studied over to get at what it means. Only your usual dodge in the game of poking your nose into other folks' business by way of minding your own. Anyway so Alter says: "*T'sk!* Danged blazes, that's where to!" and proceeds then to taking his own lick at the pump, asking, "So where's yerself headed, Reb Mend'le?"

"Me? Thataway!" I says to him a bit sharpish. "Where I gen'ly go this time of year . . ."

"Oh thataway? H'm. Well, now, I reckon that's *Glupsk* ways you be meaning, Reb Mend'le. Why I'm of a mind to be going there myself," says Alter, only kind of offhand, like my going there didn't cut into his trade. "But how's it you're traveling there so roundabout, Reb Mend'le? I mean by this bit of back road, 'stead of by the trunk road like you'd expect?"

"Well you might say it sort of worked out so," says I. "Just as well. Why I haven't traveled this way in, oh, must be years now. But how's it yourself's doglegging it from away round back, Reb Alter, instead of along the trunk road like you'd expect? That's to say, where's a feller coming from these days?"

"Where's a feller comin' from? Danged dingdong blazes, that's where from! Been to that fair. Fair over Yarmelinetz ways. Least that's what they calling it back there. Fair? Ha! More ill than fair! Yarmelinetz? Oughter pull the whole place down, y'asks me. Yess'r! Fair, town an' all! Locks, stocks, an' barrels—an', an' plow't under and be done with it, once an' for all!"

Anyhow the whiles Alter's fuming so, and generally working himself up over Yarmelinetz and how disappointing the fair was, a couple of cartloads of heathen yokelry come along the road, traveling from the opposite direction. Well, now, obviously they are sort of riled at seeing a pair of wagons blocking the road; so now they're also shouting at us to clear the way and let 'em pass. But when they pull up close, and see the two of us standing there, cowled in our prayershawls like that, with big scripboxes on both our heads and all the rest, well that's when they get kind of abusive and disrespectful on a sudden; and start into ragging us, don't you know:

—"*Whoa there! B'rrrrr!* . . . Well looky here, boys—*Whoo-oop! yip-yip-yip!* Now ain't that just the most doll'-up swellest-lookin' pair of Jewfellers you have ever lay eyes on? Yeah—*Whoo-oop! yip-yip-yip!* . . . Hey you two! Drat your mammy's paps an' get them rattletraps o' yourn off the road—like about NOW—*whoo-oop! yip-yip-yip* . . ."

Well naturally both me and Alter hastened to comply. And don't you know but a couple towheaded bucks from amongst that rowdy crowd was good enough to climb down from off of their own carts, and bear a hand. Which was kind of nice of them, when you only think of it. Because, mind, it wasn't as if they was of our own kind, or owed it to us. And if the truth be told, it was mostly on account of them that my caravan finally did get hoist out of the mire. Because otherwise me and Alter would've been sweating away over the thing for oh God only knows how long, and probably would've got our prayershawls ripped up something cruel as well into the bargain. But with this pair of "Esau's kin" (as 'twere) giving us a hand, it was a different story altogether, as you might say. Because these lads really did have the knack; for pushing, I mean; whilst me and Alter, well, we were kind of better suited to the grunting and groaning end of the business. You might even say it went a bit like in the Scripture, more or less: you know—about the hands being Esau's but the voice being Jacob's . . . But I'm getting off the point, kind of—so let it drop. Anyway, the moment the road was clear, the whole gang of country clowns went their ways . . . Though they were still laughing uproariously, and ragging us about being all "doll' up" as they called it, and looking like we was priests!

if you please, saving the difference; and about how funny we looked, praying over our carts and horses with our "crosiers" (which is how they called our whips), and so forth and so on. And some of them even bunched up the hem of their blouse, kind of twisting it into a "pig's ear" don't you know; and waving and pointing it our ways, whilst hollering insults at us, along the lines of *"Here piggy, piggy, piggy—Whoo-oop! yip-yip-yip!"*—Now, this didn't seem to trouble Alter very much; and he only shrugged the whole thing off, saying, "Lookit what's doing the name-callin'! Psssh. Ain't only a buncher Esau's jackanapes anyhow . . ." —Oh but it did too bother me; and more than some. Dear sweet Lord! thinks I, but why? And I addressed a prayer to the Almighty in the style much favored of our womenfolk, as it seemed to suit my mood—

### O GOD ALMIGHTY!

*Look Thee down from Thine High Habitation, which is in Heaven, and see but how thy Minions which dread thee are sorely mocked for thy Sweet Namesake; sith they do dread thy Dreadfulness and reverence thy Statutes. Wherefore, O Lord, do thou heap thy Compassion upon them; that they may find Favor in Thine Eyes and be a Delight in the Sight of All Men. Shield thou these thy Seely Sheep, and let thy Tender Mercies roar about 'em like the Whirlwind; forasmuch as they have Understanding and do therefore dread thy Dreadfulness . . . Oh, and Lord—h'rumph!—now I think of it . . . well, maybe if thou couldst sort of see thy way to favorin' the Fortunes of thy Servant Mendele the son of Gnendele, thy Maidservant (tho', forgetting not the Fortunes of All Israel!), and well, kinder prosper his affairs along only a little? I mean, inasmuch as God only knows I could do with a bit of help about now and, uh . . . much obliged . . . AMEN!*

# 2

THERE NOT BEING much point in hanging about anymore, me
and Alter climbed back on our carts; and then it was *heigh-ho!*
and off again—this time in tandem, with me in the lead. Old
Alter's tittuping along behind in this bonejangler of a thing of
his, with a canopy on her that'd been knocked together out of
a bunch of tatty old tore-up rushmats; and with her undercar-
riage riding on top of a job lot of ill-matched wheels, none of
which is of a pair with any of the rest, and each is lashed together by a web of cordage, made taut by togglepegs stuck
through the knots, and twisted tight, so as to keep the spokes
and wheelrims of a piece, instead of coming adrift of each
other. Well, once these got rolling, they gave out with a devil's
chorus of the most awful creakings and gratings, whilst their
grease-clogged hubs jounced and wobbled to and fro on the
axle ends. And the honor of pulling this sorry conveyance was
entirely that of an exceeding lank, mangy-backed, poor excuse for a mare, which was a mess of raw blains and broken
blisters from croup to withers; and which, in addition to
these graces, also had these very long hinny ears sticking up
out of a scruffy, tangled mane, to which there was always
clinging odd bits of hay, and pieces of hemp stuffing from a
bursted horse collar that'd seen better days.

Of morning prayer all there remained to say was the few
bits at the end; which no one makes much of a fuss over anyway, hardly. Though this out of the way, my Bad Side's back to
stirring up trouble again, this time with: "Aw, go on, have
yourself a snort! . . . Oh, tush, only a bitty one—so what you
say, huh?" says he, sassy as you please. "Why, it's just the thing
to put you right. Pick you up in no time. My word on it!"—
*Pugh!* even the thought of it made me wince. Why, this was

the Fast of Tammuz; which is about as solemn a day as ever there was! —"Oh, how you talk, Mendel!" answers my Bad Side. "So what's a Jewish gent nowadays got to do with Nebuchadnezzer of old, anyhow? Why the rascal's been dead for ages! . . . And besides: there's quite as much trouble in the world these days as then—maybe more, even. But do you see folks carrying on about it? No you don't! So stop being such a chucklehead fool . . . I mean—well, a man of your years and uncertain health he can't be too careful, you know. So how's about it, old feller—a toast maybe, huh?" —I swept my hand over my face, sort of like there was maybe a fly there wanted shooing off; and I shot a quick look round back of me, over to where I generally have my wallet with victuals handy. For it's also where I always make sure to keep my supply of spirits within reach: I mean apart from the buckwheat cakes and the gingerbread, which I keep there as well; and also the onions and garlic, of course, and other fruits and greens besides. Well, by now my mouth's gone bone dry, and I'm practically half faint with hunger, and my stomach's making nasty little burbling noises, and—O Lordy! but I could of done with a whet of schnapps then; and maybe even a nibble of something, as well. Oh! it *was* cruel . . . but I only shook off the thought, and I turned my head quickly away and concentrated on the view, and all the bits of scenery about, thinking to put temptation behind me in this way.

The sky was unspotted blue from end to end, without a cloudpuff in it. The sun scorched like a burning-glass. It was windless now. There was not a current of air anywhere. The grain in the fields stood stiff and unswaying; nor twig nor leaf stirred in the treetops in the woods around. Cows lay languishing in the pasture below, stretching their necks before them, twitching their ears at whiles, and chomped wearily on their cud; some raked up the ground beneath them with their horns and pawed the earth, and lowed out loud for the heat. A bull charged about with his tail erect, tossing his head this way and that. Suddenly he'd pull up short, bringing his face hard by the ground; and then he'd snort, flutter and flare his nostrils, and let out a bellow, and blow and puff, and stomp on the ground with his feet. A small troop of horses was gathered beside a part-blighted old willow, its withered trunk bolt-split, riven of yore in a storm. They stood driving flies away with their tails, and draped their heads crisscross, one over the other; each creature offering its fellow the gift of some little shade from the sun. A magpie was swaying lightly on a slender twig, off aways overhead: a glossy black, lustry-tailed little thing; and with its shoulders and breast and its wingfeathers touched with white, and tipped with blue—well, I declare, from afar it did look like it might have a white prayershawl with blue trimming on; and it seemed to be rocking to and fro as if in prayer, reciting the Standing benediction. It bobs and curtseys, bows down its small head as though in supplication, then cuts a short hippety-hop caper, and chirps twice or three times maybe, and grows still again; and then it stretches forward its wee bit of a neck, and cocks a sleepy eye at the world, staring into space, just so—for no apparent reason, except that maybe staring suited it then. There wasn't a sound the whole length of the road; nary a tweet, nor a rustle, nor a twitter. Nor movement of living creature neither—not even if it was only a bird in flight. Only the gnats and 'skeeters danced the devil's jig on the air, darting now and then past your ear, and dropping a secret there on the fly . . . *zi-iiing!*—and then zipping off, out of earshot again. What real sound there was, was amongst the hayricks and the rows of wheat and of maize—where the crickets chirred and grated and clacked incessantly . . .

It was hot and it was still, and—oh! it was wonderful—
*Sh!* . . . Listen! . . . God's creatures are at rest—


I WAS ABOUT gone limp from the heat by now; and I slumped
back, lolling in the driving seat, with my quilted plush cap
tipped all the way back on my head. And what with sitting
coatless by then, too, in only my shirtsleeves and showfringes,
you might say I was practically in undress. For I even had my
Breslau-woven woolly hose (which I wear even in high summer as a point of decency) rolled right down to my heels; so I
was showing a deal more calf below the knee breeches than
modesty might strictly allow—at least in an honest Jew . . .
So, anyway, I was fair dripping with perspiration. Though,
that part of it was really all right. The sweating, I mean. And I
might have even found it agreeable, if the sun wasn't only
shining direct in my eyes. Fact, you might say I was partial to
it. Guess you could even call sweating a specialty of mine: for
given only half a chance, I could spend just hours and hours
steaming myself amongst the vapors in the bathhouse, lying
on the ledge all the way up in the top tier, where it's hottest.
Runs in the family, you know. —Why, yes. Because my father
(God rest) he brung me up to it, from way back to when I was
a little boy and only just weaned . . . Now *there's* a Jew as did
you proud was my dad. In point of sweating, that is. Come
from his exceeding warm nature, you see; hot, passionate,
fiery—"a gentleman of real temperament" is how he was spoken of. And talk of being knowledgeable about steambathing,
let alone about sweating! Why he was absolutely expert in it.
Yes, sir, he was. Because he'd practically made a study of the
subject. And you may be sure that folks just about idolized
him for it too,—because there was something . . . well,
something unspeakably Jewish in the way he went about it. I

mean the burning fervor, the passion, the perfect dedication with which he'd sweat away in the bathhouse from first to last. So people just couldn't help looking up to him, you see. And whenever they'd talk about him, it was always in that reverent sort of a way which folks amongst us use to speak of prodigies of rank or godliness, or other such worthy persons in kind. "Why, that man, sir?"—they'd say—"now, there's a deep gentleman, one as knows what Jewish vaporings is all about. And mark you, sir, why I'll warrant there's not a Jew in a steambath in all Creation what's got a better hang of the finer points of lashing yourself with twigs than that man has. And as for being in a sweat! I mean a real sweat, sir—well now, I lay you, sir, that in that department there's none this side of Heaven, nor down below, which can come even near being half his match at it—no, sir!"

Though, sweating's pretty much of a Jewish thing anyhow. I mean when's there ever a Sabbathday, or even other Feast day amongst us, which is not preceded by everybody getting into a great sweat over it (inside the bathhouse and out); and besides—how many amongst the Seventy Nations, which our Sages reckon to live in the world, gets more into a sweat than Jewish folks do . . . but anyway, I'm getting off the point.

Still, there's nothing puts a man more in mind of drink and refreshments than sweating does. Which is why about now my throat's so parched I'm close to perishing from thirst, let alone hunger. And which is also why my Bad Side's back to badgering me again worse than ever, and has took to reading me out the entire Jewish Bill of Fare: *Beef Sirloin with Buckwheat Mash; Pot Roast; Stuffed Chicken-Neck Surprise in Noodle pudding; Dough crumbs-'n'-Goose-cracklings, DEEP FRIED!* . . . Lord it was dreadful! Practically every organ in me was crying out for Food . . . But the rascal he wouldn't stop, and he just kept rattling on: *Dry-baked Pancakes; Rolled*

*Cabbage leaves with Mullet; Chicken livers-plus-Sippets in Calf's-foot Jelly; Radish-'n'-Onions; Turkey gullet in Parsnip Stew . . . WHOO-OOP! Bottoms-up gaffer, old son! . . . Aw, Mendel, tush! Now don't you be putting it off again, like a fool . . .* —And already my fingertips begun sort of inching themselves along, on over towards the bag of victuals; kind of on their own and behind my back, don't you know. And practically before I knew it, the schnapps bottle's whisked out of its place, and I'm gripping it in my hand. Well, I'm looking about stealthily this way and that, more or less like a sneak thief that's having himself a quick look-see before showing a clean pair of heels. Which is when my gaze meets the jade's, who'd the whiles been rubbing his neck up against one of the shaft ends, and that minute'd happened to turn his head my way to have himself a gander on back, towards the van, you know. Anyway, I see he's watching me; and it seemed to me he was looking, well—more'n a bit miffed, as I thought. Like as if maybe he had it in mind to be chiding me along the lines of: "Now see here! You just lookit this here hinder leg of mine, which the hock's always puffed up and wrapped in tatty old rags; and this eye, which's gone all rheumy and watery; and my throat, which's sore and runny; and my mouth, which . . . well, enough said of that: for I hardly get any wear out of that organ anyhow, lately. Why, I haven't tasted the likes of oats in—oh, I don't recollect how long now. But do you ever hear me complain? No, sir, you do not! Not though I'm hungry and I'm sick and I'm broken-down and I'm scarcely out of harness for a level minute . . ." —I'd quietly let the flask slip back into its place. For I was feeling very ashamed. And I pushed the wallet of food away from me—all the way, as far as it'd go; and I fetched up a great sigh, which came, so it seemed, from somewhere deep inside me. Then I thought: Now here's a pretty pass I come to . . . I mean, only look

who's teaching me my precepts now. Not to speak of Jewish
good sense. And yet: Who teacheth us more than the beasts of
the earth? asks the Scripture. Why, surely, 'tis He that teacheth us through them . . . Well, never mind, Friend Jade: for I
too go through life never out of harness, even as you do. Oh
but no matter, sir! We'll neither of us—nor master nor
horse—be riding to the devil this day. For it's as David's
Psalm tells: *O Lord, thou preservest man and beast.* Which is to say
God looks after his own, I suppose . . . But I'm getting off the
point.

Funny thing, though. I mean about how once a body's got
past this awful hankering for nourishment, he gets so eating
just don't count for all that much anymore. Well, at least
that's so if he's Jewish. Because then, you see, he can get by
without tasting any foodstuffs at all, practically. I mean specially nowadays, when there's so many Jews who have got
scarcely any trace of a innard nor bowel left in 'em to speak
of—except maybe it's that wee nub of a remainder they still
keep tucked away inside. Which is by way of being only a
token of the real thing, don't you know. And there's some,
too, as even entertain great hopes that, given time enough
maybe—that is, if the kosher meat tax and the Patrons of
Charity, and like Benefactions of the Parish Corporation
which we are so fortunate as to enjoy, are allowed to go on
working on our behalf undisturbed—well, anyhow: given
time enough, they say, Jewish folks may eventually get completely shot of their wicked habits in point of eating. So that,
by and by, we'll lose what little gut we've managed to hang on
to up until now—apart from the piles, of course. Why, sir, it
fair boggles the mind to only think what that is like to do for
our reputation amongst the Nations . . .

All of which is really by way of saying that, immediately
I'd worked up the gumption to thrust the wallet of foodstuffs

from me, I was the better for it. Just kind of braced, don't you know. Fact, I'd started in to feeling downright cheerful by now, pretty much. And I let my mind kind of run on business things, and on trade and such; and I even took to humming bits of a tune under my breath—mournful snatches from an anthem for Fast-o'-Ab upcoming, as I recollect, so as to be in keeping with the occasion, you understand. So things were back to seeming about right again . . . Leastways, so I thought: for on a sudden just then, the devil's own luck fetches a young country wench my way, who's none too pretty anyways, and has materialized as 'twere out of nowhere, carrying a bowlful of the plumpest strawberries you ever saw. Which as it happens is about my favorite titbit ever—in the way of food, I mean . . . Well, now, I guess there's some folks, of the better sort (better than me, anyway), that'd just know right off this was no other than my own Bad Side that'd done itself up in female shape, just to lead me on. But it just wasn't so. No; for you see I'd already got a good close look at the creature with my own two eyes (not being above such things, you know); and I saw this wasn't only one of your ordinary, plain homely sorts of heathen misses—who was also in the way of asking me to buy up her entire batch of strawberries, plus the bowl they came in; and, what's more, for just only tenpennies' worth cash! And she'd even raised up the bowl of strawberries closer to my face, so I might see. So that, in the meantime, the whiff of them'd gone straight to my nose: and already my mouth's watering something dreadful, and I'm licking my chops, and my vision's gone all dark and blurry, and my heart's about to give out and . . . well, in a word, I couldn't hardly contain myself no more. So I took terrible fright only thinking about how I may be tempted to give in. And before I knew it I was that scared I'd pitched myself out of the cart in my haste to get away; and it was nothing short of a miracle I hadn't broke my neck into the bargain, tumbling out that way. And in a voice I scarcely recognized for my own I'm next calling out for *"Alter! 'Hoy . . . Reb Alter . . . !"* For I was hoping to make Alter my chaperon, you see—

Alter though in the meantime had laid himself out as 'twere crabways (begging pardon)—that's to say belly down, and was in a deep snooze—his face flushed and head pillowed in his arms, and his shirtfront all undone, so it showed a shag of brambly russet hairs carpeting his naked breast. Well, it made a cruel sight which'd've moved even the hardest heart, seeing how he's blistering all over from the sun and gone all crimson, and is running whole rivers of sweat so he seemed near drowning in it.

*"Huh?"* Alter mooed and then snorted, being finally roused to wakefulness by my calling to him. Though he wasn't showing much in the way of other vital signs. "Huh? Wha-wa's matter?"

Only meanwhiles, that creature with the strawberries? Well, next I looked, she was gone . . . Plain vanished! So I made shift only with:

"Say, um, so what time o' day you make it, Reb Alter?"

"Huh? Timer day? . . . Wha's the timerday?" returned Alter, sounding kind of hollow-voiced, like he was talking into a water butt. "Lor'! how'd I know? Why, I reckon our eyes is like to drop clean out of our heads before either us ever see Fastday through come sundown. I mean with midsummer days bein' so tedious long . . . Well, let it go! . . . *Whew!* Ain't it hot though . . ."

"Uh-huh, I'll say! Marvelous, though, don'tcher think?" I says, ambling alongside so as to keep pace with Alter's cart. "Workin' up a sweat, Reb Alter? Oh, but say now, ain't it about time we let these poor brutes of ours loose to browse for a bit? Look to me about done in. And I make it near of two, maybe three mile yet to the main road on over to Glupsk. Well now I been thinkin' . . . can you make out that clearing up ahead, over to the left there? . . . uh, sorter like at the edge of that big wood, stretching a-way out over towards the highroad yonder . . . Anyway, seem to me the ground do us about fine for grazing, wouldn'tcha say?"

So it wasn't too long before we pulled off the road, at the spot I'd had my eye on. Turned out to be a prime kind of place, too. With all the trees about, and fields and meadows every-where. Anyhow, we'd got the animals out of tackle and set them free to browse at will under the eaves of the wood. Then the both us stretched out under a tree and lay easy the while.

# 3

OLD WINE-'N'-CANDLES was scarcely able to draw breath for the heat; and he appeared as a general thing also to be a con-siderable deal in the dumps, as well. And what with Alter's pitiable suspirations, in the way of sighs and groans, seeming to follow endlessly upon one another, my heart fairly went out to him. And thinking it would maybe cheer Alter up a bit, and might also furnish occasion for some friendly chitchat, to help pass the time, I kind of let myself casually fall into con-versation with him. Which enterprise proceeds in the follow-ing fashion, so:

"Whew! . . . Heat's got to you, I reckon, Reb Alter, huh?"

*"Ba!"* says Alter, a tad shortish, and with more than his usual crotchetiness, I thought. And he kind of wriggled him-self in more 'neath the tree—which anyways wasn't giving all that much shade, on account of the glare being let in from be-tween the branches . . .

"Dead hard, this midsummer's Fastday business—uh, wouldn'tcha say, Reb Alter?" says I, meaning to have another crack at it. For by golly I'd have a civil word of Alter, or bust—

*"Ba!"* Alter says, inching treewards a mite more.

Though, Alter's "Ba!"s were not going to do me for an answer—no, for I wasn't about to be satisfied with no measly bit-off sheepbleats, not this time. Thinks I: Why, of all the mule-headed! Well, you *are* a cross-grained, willful, cantankerous old cuss, Alter. But never mind, Alter. For I shall set you talking, Alter—'deed, sir I will! . . . So, it has got to come down to business, in the end. Only stands to reason, too. For heat or swelter or whatever—there isn't but the one way to get Jewish folks to start jawing; and that is business. Cordial to the dying's what it is. Even if, say, a Jewish gent is mortal sick and on his deathbed, and near breathing his last; why, you only drop a word in earshot about a little trade in prospect, and it's like he's risen from the dead practically. And him so up-and-about spry it's a marvel. Because even Death's Angel's left to cool his heels whilst such a one is at trade. And I wouldn't wish it on my own worst enemy to cross a Jewish gentleman-at-trade's path when his dealings have got completely a-holt on his mind. No, sir; for when such a one's going about his business, there is never another human soul he will take notice of, nor whose sight he'll tolerate if he did—not even it was his bosom pal nor own brother . . . But I've got off the point. So anyhow, I took a new tack with Alter:

"Uh, Reb Alter . . . kind of crossed my mind, that you and me—well, how 'bout we do some tradin', huh? So, whatcher say—yes? . . . Well, now, but ain't this a piecer luck, us meetin' up like this. 'Cause you oughter seed what merchandise I got stowed away on back. And talk about quality! Sweet, mind. I mean *real* sweet . . ."

My tonic'd took, for Alter was a changed man. He'd kind of set up off of the ground and pricked up his ears; and he was watching me intently now. I harped on—

"Though, uh, this time it's to be cash between us, Reb Alter . . . I mean seeing as you are fresh from the fair over Yarmelinetz way; and with a pocketful of brass, as well, as I've no doubt, so I dare say . . ."

"Wha—? a pock . . . O Lor', yes! . . . bellyful o' heart-ache, more like!" Alter was in a fierce temper now: "Oh but I tell you Reb Mend'le . . . Ah, but ne'mind . . . H'm! —Well-a-well! Though, Reb Mend'le, now I tell you a man's better unborn than born without luck. An' more fool I, as been han-kerin' after new pro-spects! Why in my place . . . well in my place, most anybody else'd've—ha! ha! easy—but me? no: 'cause it's always butterside down with me, from the first . . . Oh, woe's me! Why't hurts to even be talkin' of it. Done no better than one as had blowed his nose and snotted up his face! Yess'r . . . Well 'noughsaid, let it go—"

No, all was not well with Alter. I saw that plain enough. Trouble! I reckoned. Though, now I *had* got a word out of the feller, wouldn't only take a little nudge more for my Alter to get downright chattery, nearly. Nor'd I be the one to stand in his way, if it come to it. So that was what I done. Nudged him. Which does, too, set Alter to spinning me the tale of his woes. Only he tells it in his own fashion. More or less so:

"S'ANYWAYS: I COME inter town and drive on over to the fair-ground; and I get my wares unpacked, such's they are, and well—*nothin'!* So that's the short of it, pretty much: 'cept o'course for hanging about and waiting for custom—of which it seems none is coming my way anyhow . . . O Lor'! but I did come down to that fair 'cumbered with a clutter of the worse troubles. For it's a awful bind I'm in, and dead strapped, these days. Why, first off, there's the printer. Well that feller's squawking about his money. So let him squawk, says you. Well, that's fine, an' so I says too. Only he won't give me no merchandise on account now. Well ne'mind that; because that's not the half of it even . . . Huh? Well it's my eldest. The wench, I mean. She's full-growed, don'cher know, and of age now. And a wench of age why *that's* nupt'als—an' nupt'als, why *that's* husbands—an' husbands why *that's* bride's dowers—an' bride's dowers *that's* . . . Well, 'noughsaid. For just you try and find a husband for a maid what's come of age! Mind, it's not like there wasn't plenty in kind around. But what I mean is one as was, well, a *Husband!* Respec'able, if you take my drift. But wait now. 'Cause the capstone's to come yet. For now the wife's gone an' had herself a little boy. And when's she had it? Foretide-t'-Passover's when! Now a boy—well a boy, now, that's one more mouth than I can feed nor keep. So, then, the wench's got to go. Which is now got me to thinkin' on nupt'als again, an' on husbands again, an' on bride's dowers again, an' on . . . huh?"

"Now, you won't take it amiss, my interrupting you this way, Reb Alter," I says. "But why on earth'd you took such a young wife, in place of your last missus? I mean, it only stood to reason you'd be having so many children of one as was so young, now didn't you?"

"O Lor'! how you talk, Reb Mend'le!" Alter says, taken aback some. "For I'd be wanting *Somebody* to look after things to home, wouldn't I now! I mean, what's a Jewish gent want with marriages anyhow. Lessen o' course, it's to have a wife looking after things fair and proper to home . . ."

"Well, now, if that's so," I says to Alter, "well, if that's so, then why'd you divorce your first missus, and left her so wretched, on account of it? I mean but she did keep fair and proper house, now didn't she, by all accounts, and—"

*"Ba!"* A cloud had passed over Alter's face, and he was back to being sullen again . . .

"And besides, she wasn't exactly whatch'd call barren neither, praise Goodness, was she, your first missus?" says I, kind of bearing down on him harder now. "And, since we are on the subject, so what's become of the children, Reb Alter, huh? I mean, well, what *has* become of 'em?"

*"Ba!"* Now there goes Alter again. *Bleat! Bleat!* But he would say nothing more besides—except he'd maybe gave a little tug to his sidecurl, and tossed up his hand, kind of forlorn-like; and a sigh hove his bosom, as will sometimes fetch up out of the deepest part of a person . . .

Now you wouldn't maybe think it, but that whittled-down sheep bleat "Ba!" (plus pause-for-effect) makes for a fair power of a word. Least, as Jewish folks will use it. Why, saying it was even plain noble, wouldn't half do it justice. For it is a positive gem of a word, which can be made to signify most everything you want it to. And there is no construction you cannot put to it, nor situation it won't answer to at need. If you are down on your luck, say, and dead strapped (which God forbid!), a nicely judged "Ba!" will get you out of a tight spot every time. You only ask your out-and-out swindler, or ordinary bankrupt even, and they will tell you outright. No matter how many duns and creditors may come hammering at your door, it don't take but a "Ba!" to sweep the whole pestering clamoring lot off your doorstep. And that'll do about as good as settling up honest ever has done. And, at a pinch, a bleat in kind will do service, as well, for any upright gent as has been—not to put too fine a point on it—caught out on a whopping lie. And it is just the retort to any fool blatherskite who's been rattling away at you for hours about oh God-only-knows-what, so your eardrums fairly ache, never once taking a minute of time to stop and listen, because probably he wouldn't understand anyways if he did. Oh yes, "Ba!" is a tip-top mouth-stopper. And it will lay over any other such, when it comes to getting folks off the hook, no matter how scoundrely or blackguardly. Why, it'll do any old reprobate of a respectable-seeming gent, playing the *Who, me? Never!* innocent, for when you've found out he's doing the dirty on you behind your back; or one of your oh-so-reverent sorts, whose mouth is always so chock-full of God-be-praised pieties you'd think butter wouldn't melt in it, for when he's been caught doing something really low and disgusting; or your type what's always broadcasting himself as being so affable and kind-hearted, and ever ready to do the next fellow a charity, for when he's shown up to be a mean flea-up-the-nose arrogant fraud with a meat-ax disposition. In short, "Ba!" can be taken in all kinds of senses, some of them clean odd and out-of-the-way, too—say like: "Call me nutcracker, 'cause I've just cracked your nut!" or "Go head, sue me! or "Yah, get roasted!" or "I don't value you tantamount to *that!*" and just no end of other such kind of meanings. Though it will take a little Jewish headwork to know where a particular Ba! is aiming. But once you have got the hang of it, why you will know its exact meaning every time, and what it signifies in point of the particular business in hand.

Taken all round, I should say that that last bleat of Alter's bespoke great misery. Mind, it was not just sad. It was downright bitter wormwood sad. And it seemed to have mixed up in it bits of regret, and a deal of dread along with it, and considerable chunks of remorsefulness and guilt, as well. For it would have certainly weighed very heavily upon Alter, how he'd served his first wife so ill, as he did the children he had had of her. And he must have seen, in every misfortune which was now come his way, the awful hand of God chastising him for his sins. There was that, as well, in the unhappy sigh he uttered—as also in the way he'd swatted his hand back then too, and in the bit of a tug he had gave to his sidecurl—which as much as said: "Hush up, Alter! And you bite your lip . . . but oh! 'tis a dog's life—."

Though I was blaming myself, too, for stirring up Alter's old hurts. But that is only the way with us. We go blundering into other people's personal business regardless, and getting under their skins asking questions, when the other person is hurting inside and choking down his griefs, and wanting only to be left alone, and never a sympathetic soul to turn to. But that's only the one side, though. This apart, I was vexed over all the trouble I had taken seeming wasted now. Alter'd been clattering along just bully a while back—like a longcase timepiece. But I *would* go ahead then, and spoil it by sticking my clumsy fingers inside his works; so of course his pendulum'd dead stopped. And now he'd need to be nudged back into it, all over again . . . Still, I'm not one to begrudge an effort, when it was needed. So I started in to harping on this and on that the whiles; and by and by I found the key which fit. And I wound the old boy up—though ever so dainty-like, mind— and then I'd only gave the pendulum a lee-tle nudge. And it was set to swinging just bully again, going *THWUNK-a thwunk! THWUNK-a thwunk!* . . . And Alter, too, why he soon was set to *ticktock-ticktock* telling, sweet as ever.

# 4

"S'ANYWAYS, AS I told, I'm there kind of hanging about, next to the van," says Alter, taking up his tale again, only in his own fashion, so: "And, well, short of it's, I'm standin' there like, looking the fair over, don'cher know . . . Lor'! though it *were* lovely, Reb Mend'le; because you ought've seen it. I mean all that stir! And you talk about your Jewish hullabaloos! Why the place was a-humming with folks. Chock-a-block all o'er the place they was, and never a one of 'em which is not beavering away, doing deals of one kind or t'other. Put me in minder Holy scripture . . . *Huh?* Oh, I mean of the promise what's in Jacob's Blessing. You know, about Jews bein' let to grow into a multitude, and netting fish aplenty in the midst of the earth . . . Nothin' there about fish, says you? My, my! That a fact? Well ne'mind; because anyhow Jews at fairs why that's as fish in water. And 'sides, it is writ someplace, if I recollec' aright, how there's promises of fairs in Heaven for Jewish folks. Well, now, that's as good as to say Kingdom Come's to be a fair. Now that is so, ain't it, Reb Mend'le? Least, it's as I construe it. —*Huh?* 'Tain't writ? My, my! Don't say . . . Well ne'mind; 'cause writ or no's all one, in this case. For anyhow this fair was down here below, and 'twasn't at all to do with fairs in Heaven, or with castles in Spain, nor with pie in the sky nuther. Why 'twere nearer to Par'dise on the earth. And a sockdologer, as well, it was. Yess'r, for you ought've seed the way folks was running hither and yon, doin' business at every turn, and nary a soul keeping to the one place for a level minute. And, mind, some of them was *Quality* too. Why amongs' the big tradesmen which was there, I spotted even the one as once'd went by the name Wee Ber'l Mooncalf. That's him as started off as a schoolmaster's usher, and then weren't only a shopkeeper's assistant; and as is now got that oversize shop, and's addressed as 'Reb Ber,' if you please! and sir'd and kowtowed to by most everyone. —So, this one's there, too, all red o' face and flush o' pocket, going about business hand o'er fist, like a house ablazes. Well 'noughsaid

on that . . . S'anyways, short of it's, I am looking about.
And, well you ought've seed the rumpus. The way folks was
running about every whither, and just tearing that fairground
up with their to-ings and fro-ings. Never seed the like. Why
first the one gent come a-puffing past; and then the other's
a-clutt'ring hard on that one's heels; and the third then come
a-charging along behind them two. Pretty soon there's whole
mobs of 'em just whooshing past. And, why, some is paired
up a'ready, and they're all flush-faced, with their hats tipped
to the back of their heads; and ain't a one what's not awash in
sweat, and trailing wet pools of perspiration after him. And
they all are chaffering away and fingering the other's merchandise, and fanning the air with their hands, and poking the
other in the chest, and throwing up two maybe three fingers
against the other's four or five. And the first'd maybe chaw his
whiskers on that for a bit; and then he'd be throwing up
maybe four fingers—and deal's done! —Well, there was all
sorts there. And the whole lot's in a great twitter, for the excitement. Why there was matchmakers, and there was bro-
kerers; and there was old-clothesmen, and there was
fripperers; and there was gypwives, and there was chicken
thieves; and there was womenfolks with hampers a-hand, and
menfolks with gunnysacks a-shoulder; and there was plain
folks with nothing to hand but their own five fingers; and
there was plump old housewives with walkin' sticks, and there
was householders o' rank with plump bellies. And amongs'
them I don't see a one as weren't beaming for the effort,
nor had a minute's time to spare; for time's money where
money's to be made. —Well, so much was plain. This was
everybody's lucky day but mine. For they was raking it in just
everyways. Whereas me, why I'm standing at a loose end
only, and idle the whiles; with nothing to show for't, but that
old broken-down cover't cart which is strung round outside

with only straggly bunches of showfringes and charms; and
stocked within with only a bunch of rag-'n'-bone goods, and
with tatty old heaps of *Sarah Bas Toyvim Portals-o'-Pieties!* . . .
*Sarah Bas Toyvim*—Humph! . . . Now, I asks you! I mean what
does Ladies' Breviaries fetch these days, anyhow—twopenny,
say maybe three apiece? Well, just you try an' make a living
outer that. Go 'head, play th' bigwig on slim pickings, an' try
and get a maid wed decent! Why, no, it cannot be done . . .
Well I am riled now. And I'm muttering against wenches as is
of age, and muttering against the cart *and* against the bony
nag, as well, what's pulling her. And I'm wishing all the three
was outer my life nor never in it. 'Nough's enough. Take the
thing in hand, Alter, thinks I. Buck up. One has got to try
one's luck some time, an' God send His Mercy. Now,
ain't that so, Reb Mend'le? For Prov'dence apart, what else is
there . . . So to work! Well, nor sooner I'd spit on my hands
than, why, the hat's a'ready pushed back, and my sleeves is
a'ready rolled up; and my legs, why, they had cut a caper on
their own, or so it seemed. For I'm standing there next to this
cart which is not my own; and I'm sucking on a straw as is got
adrift of it, and has slipped somehow into my mouth. And I'm
rumernatin'! Well, I am sucking on that straw and rumernatin' first to the one side . . . H'm! Then I am sucking on
that same straw and rumernatin' to the other side. And
then . . . *WHOO-OOSH!* the heel of my hand come down on
my forehead. *Marriage Brok'rage!* Why, 'twere plainer'n a
pikestaff. No! plainer'n *Two* pikestaffs. For there they was the
both of them, next to the other practically, and in plain sight.
And each is come with a fair store'orth o' stock. As respectable a pair of gentry-at-trade as you'd ever hope to
know. And what is more, which is both got offsprings what's
of age. Well, I expect you do know who I'm a-minder . . .
why, gracious, but who else you suppose? For on the one side,

there was Reb Elyok'm . . . *Huh!?* Who's Reb Elyok—? Why, him what's *the* Reb Elyok'm. Elyok'm the Sharograder! And, on the other side, there's nor lesser a gentleman in the business way as—*Reb Getz'l* of Greiding . . . Uh'huh, the same! So, nothing would do me, you see, but I must throw up tradin' in rubbage. To the dang blazes with cover't carts, I says, and with nags what's broke-winded. And, why, if it come to it, to the blazes, as well, with low miser'y dunning printers what's not brung me aught but grief! . . . Well I set to work, and I am as keen as mustard. Turn out prospects was good, too. For I had a try at whupping the both parties up to it, and they was interested right off. And soon I am doing a reg'lar circuit to and fro, betwixt the Rebs Getz'l and Elyok'm, from the one to the other, and back. And, why, I'm a'ready the equaller of any trading gent, bar none, what's at that fair. I have got my nose hard to the ground, and I am plowing up whole acres between the two of them. Thinks I, why it has *got* to come to it. Now, and at this place. For what better time nor place was there for it, than at this fair? . . . Anyhow, the both my prospective gents-in-laws meets. Though it is done pretty much helter-skelter, and on the fly. But each does look the other over notwithstanding; and by golly the both likes what they seed. D'I say likes? Why *likes* ain't hardly the word. For the both was just hot for t'other! So what could I have wished for more? Fact, by and by, these two'd got altogether so passionate about the thing, that nothing would satisfy but the business must be cons'mated . . . Well I don't mind telling, I was in fine feather. Why it's dead certain the money's as good as to hand; and I'm even thinkin' how much of the fee to set aside for my own maid's dowry. Apart from the trousseau. For I'd already pu'chased striped ticking on account, for the bridal pillows and featherbeddin';

and I was in the way, as well, of dick'ring with the fripperer over a pretty velvet frock, secon'hand; and blouses, why time enough to think on them; for that'd be as God seed fit to provide. And as for the . . . but ne'mind that. For just you wait! Oh, I tell you, Reb Mend'le, a man's better unborn, 'n born without luck. Listen now what happen next. Well, time's ripe for settling the thing, final-like; and celebrations is being even call for, as well. When, on a sudden the whiles, sort of by-the-bye, why the subject of brides 'n' bridegrooms crop up, kinder natur'ly. So whatcher think . . . Oh, it's past bearing to speak of! *Huh?* Why it's all a bubble. Nor ain't even that! For the neither gent's got even one hones' solitary bride between them. Why, no! The both has got sons. *Sons,* mind! Well, I asks you—"

"*WHOO-OO-OOP! Goodnessgracioussakes,* Reb Alter," I says. For I could not help but laugh. "No, but forgive me, Reb Alter. Well, it's not that I'm meanin' to offend, but—well, how'd you ever come to do such a foolishness!? Why it makes no sense at all; trothplighting a pair of boys, as 'twere, without first sexing the happy couple . . ."

"*Course it don't!*" says Alter, looking cross. "Lor'! what you think? I *don't* know it? Got as much sense as the nex' feller. And I certainly don't want none teaching me about it, neither! Why, ain't such a thing as Jewish gents what don't know about how troths is plighted amongs' us . . . Humph! 'Sides, you know nor lesser'n myself, how the custom is with us in the way of betrothals and such. For none ever thinks to consult the couple at issue, let alone looks at 'em. It is only their folks which counts. So what's so astonishin' about this calamity, in particular? It's nor more mistake as anyone may have made! Anyhow, I did know too that Reb Elyok'm had a maid to home. Maid? Say pure spun gold! and be done. And

God only send me her equaller. —Oh but I saw her a'right,
and with my own eyes. And would only I'd seed so much
goodness in this earth as was in that child . . . Well, ne'mind.
For him as wants luck, wit won't ever mend . . . S'anyways,
this same fair creature, why, on a sudden, she up and marry.
Like that! And aforetime, as well. As though for spite. I mean,
wasn't as if the Pressgangs, or the Devil or what, was loose.
But that's what she done. So how was I to know? Why, I hope I
may never know so much of hard times, as ever I knowed of
that! —Now, Reb Mend'le, let me put it to you in a other
way, if you'll permit. For I will have you bear in mind, sir, that
when I broaches that business with the same said Reb
Elyok'm aforementioned, I did it in quite the custom'ry and
altogether Jewishlike manner prescribed, so: 'Um, 'hem! Reb
Elyok'm—h'rumph! . . . ' I says. 'Um, Reb Elyok'm! I am a-
minder proposin' a match, between your own estim'ble self,
sir, and the Reb Getz'l aforesaid!' Now, who else could've I
been intending, if 'tweren't her what's Reb Elyok'm's purty
gel, and that boy of Reb Getz'l's? Why, spelling the thing out
plainer'd be ridic'lous. No need! It'd be as if I was beggin' the
question from the first . . . *Huh?* Well, sorter. 'Cause as any
half-wit'd know enough t'say, 'Why pooh! sir. How you talk!
Why anybody knows, practically, 'tain't gents as pairs with
gents. It's boys with gels as does—as o'course they should
do.' . . . Now, then. I will allow that on my side I done the
thing proper. No; by golly I'll insist on it! For no one
would've done so good. Never spoke but brass tacks, first to
last. And did it clean to the point the whole whiles. You know
the sorter thing—bride's dower . . . groom's board. And you
must consider, as well, sir, that in your business dealings at
fairs—and forget it's to do with such grand trading gents as
these—why, there is never room for chatter on by-matters.

No, sir! For they won't tolerate it. Haven't the time. You have got to be lean, sir; pared down to the business end only. Nub o' the thing, that's what counts with 'em, nothing else! . . . So, there's a answer to you on the my side. —Now, sir, an't please you, let's the both us step over to the Reb Elyok'm; see how that ex'lent gentleman's been faring the whiles. Now, Reb Elyok'm, away over to his side, he's been hearing me talk of a match between him and the Reb Getz'l. So, you see, he has got to be thinking it is his *boy* what's the intended . . . *Huh?* Why, er—why, on *his* side, o'course! Otherwise it cannot be, you see. First off, it cannot be between his own self and Reb Getz'l. Why that's unnatural! An', why, he would never think it was the gel which is to issue. For she's already wed. —Wherefore, er—h'm, lessee . . . Why, yes! Wherefore, turns out the both sides is right . . . Well, 'noughsaid. So I hope none of it were too many for you, Reb Mend'le. And you do understan' now—uh, don'cher?"

"*Ba!* . . . " Now, to tell the truth, it wasn't "Ba!" I'd meant at all then (bit more of *ho-hum*)—but it did too keep me from laughing. Only just. And I had the blazes to do, to keep a straight face. Could've fooled Alter, though—.

"Well Praise be to Goodness that's settled then . . . finally!" And he jerked his thumb forward, stubbing it abrupt-like against a spot midair between us, as if to mark the place where I'd hit bang dead-on with my "Ba!" And then he fetched a long, drawn-out "Ahaaa—!" letting the sound rumble on for a bit. Savoring it, I guess. For plainly it pleased him to hear that "Ba!" from me, which he also took for my assent.

I will own, though, once Alter's explanation had had a chance to sink in, it made considerable good sense. For think only how we're always managing this marriage thing amongst us, so willy-nilly. Tush! why it's a wonder prodigies like this don't happen all the time. Well, whilst my mind was running on in this way, I blurted another "Ba!" at Alter. Genuine article this time, though. For I recollect how I looked fondly at Alter as I said it . . .

"Aha-a-a-a!" Which was Alter being expletory again. And again he jerk-stubbed that digit, same as before. "Well, 'noughsaid o' that," he grumped. Then added: "Only wait, Reb Mend'le! For that's nor more than half a tale. Once I have aholt on a thing, I won't give it up—no; 'tain't my nature. And 'sides: Hope'd sparked up ag'in—."

"Man alive! Reb Alter . . ." No, the man was really quite impossible! "No, no! I shan't let that pass, sir," I remonstrated. "for whatever may you mean—*'Hope'd sparked up ag'in'!?* . . . Oh, pooh, sir!" For that last remark of Alter'd exasperated me so, nearly made me sit bolt upright. Why 'twas all I could do to keep myself prone. Surely the heat had drove poor Alter mad, I thought. Though, to him, I said: "Really, sir. Now what hope was there could remain, Reb Alter, once'd come out, there's only the one pair of bridegrooms between the both gents-in-laws?"

"Oh, now tush! only hear me out, Reb Mend'le! For I promise you I had reason to hope," soothed Alter. "There was life to these old bones, yet. There is never a ill, but God won't send a cure. See it was then that the Mooncalf come into it . . . *Huh?* What's a Moo—? Why, 'tain't *a* Mooncalf; but *the* Mooncalf! Ber'l Mooncalf. —Anyhow, short of it's, I knowed that this same Mooncalf, why, he was chockfuller el'gible gels to home, an' . . . *Huh?* Now tush! How you talk, Reb Mend'le! Course I knowed. Humph! What you think? Fact I was turning all the three of 'em around in my mind at the first: Elyok'm; Getz'l; the Mooncalf—thinking which I'd choose to make the pair. So what did I do but to pick the Reb

Elyok'm, and set Mooncalf aside the whiles. Though, now the
business was spoilt, I had to think what's to be done next. And
that's when I thought to trot the Mooncalf out i'stead. But,
mind, 'tain't the 'Mooncalf' no longer. No, sir. *Sweet, darlin'
Reb Ber'shl* is what he's now; all fatted and pedigreed. —Well,
I managed matters so's to smooth the mistake over with the
both parties previous. I owned some it's my fault; they owned
some it's theirs; and the all three us allowed as, all round,
it weren't only a batch of bad luck. For seemed it were't
meant to be, not in God's books. Know what I mean, Reb
Mend'le? . . . S'anyhow, short of it's, I set to harping that
same tune over again. Only now I am crying up the new gent-
in-law's good points to the other two. Reb Ber'shl!? Oh, my!
Why he's a very di'mont (bless his soul); veritable jewel. Gem
amongs' the Jewish gentry, sirs. Man of Money and Influence.
Yess'r! Stands exceeding high in the Parish Corporation, too.
Trustee an' Officer. Almoner, as well. Why, hand's in about
every charitable till, pra'tically—er, though, mind, that's only
in a manner of speaking, you understan'. Is he book-learned!?
Is he book—? Oh, tush! The Reb Ber'shl!? Lor'! course he is.
Gotter be. Shan't find his equaller in that line, howsomever
afield you may care to go. And wise? Why he's a very Sage!
Only stands to reason, though. For was ever a rich man, as
weren't wise? Sorter come with the station, I should think!
—Well, it went on like that for quite a whiles. And that spark
I told of? Well pretty soon it was nearer a bonfire. Thinks I:
Why it's as well it happened so, casting my bread upon the
waters; and that pair of boys risen atop, like sweet olive oil.
Now there'd be *two* betrothals, not only the one. For at the
end the Reb Ber'shl was sure to put the thing right. Bound to!
(the Lord willing) . . . So I set to work again. And I am back
to rattlin' up and down the fairground, exactly same as be-

fore. Well, that business seem to come quite a considable ways—when . . . O Lor'! whatcher think happen. Reb Mend'le? Fair over! Plumb in the middle, an' the fair's over! For, all in a moment, near everybody's making tracks. Soon they was all gone. The Rebs Elyok'm and Getz'l!? Gone! The Mooncalf!? Gone! My Labors? All that hard, hard work?— Gone, as well. All of it were for naught only; and there weren't only naught to show for it neither . . .

"You do see now, don'cher, Reb Mend'le?" Alter's voice rose and fell in a tearful singsong. He'd stretched out both his hands towards me, his palms cupped, like begging bowls, as though he would implore of me some little comfort I might drop in them. "But you see now what it is, Reb Mend'le, don'cher? Him as wants luck—one such as me, as wants even the smallest crumb of it—why, there's ne'er wit in the whole world will mend him. Oh, but God's poured out his wrath upon me, punishing me for my sins all this while . . . *'Cash'!* says you, *'this time's for Cash'!* And me, what's not got one penny to pocket! Woe's me . . . Oh, woe and woe's me!"

"*Ai,* it's fit for the bathhouse!" I spoke this in bad temper, and quite aloud; and I shifted closer in then, to be more in the shade.

Alter gave me a glare. Then he nodded his head angrily, grumbling the whiles, as if addressing himself only:

"Talk about your Jewish rogues, by golly! For here's a man sits afore him, weighed down so cruel by afflictions, so his guts is near fit to bust for it; and why's even pouring his griefs out to him . . . Though, what's it to him anyhow? Why, ain't naught! For no; he won't turn a hair. Thinks only on his own precious self. *'Aye!'* says he, *'fit for the bathhouse'!* Only fancy! Why tush! sun's got the poor thing all hot 'n' bothered. Bath-houses—Humph! . . . Oh, but don'cher worry, sir! For I do know all about sudden dainty airs, put on by Jewish gents what's backing outer deals, on account t'other feller's got no cash, an' won't turn him no profit!"

"Gracious! No, but Reb Alt . . . ," I'd cried out in protest, and gave Alter's beard a friendly tug—as is only the custom amongst us—saying: "No, but Reb Alter, how can you think such a thing of me? For I'd something very different on my mind. On my honor! Was only the end of your story put me in mind of a yarn what happened on a time. In a bathhouse. Can't seem to get the thing out of my head. And it is a first-rate yarn; why practically the same as the one you told. To the dot, almost. Only this one's shorter, and is got a sockdologer end as well. Worth a listen. Least, so I think. —Whew! . . . Reb Alter! er—um . . . not meanin' to offend really; but that is a whole deal of perspiration you're giving off at present . . . Though, and if it's not putting you to too much trouble . . . well, you might move your estimable self a bit farther off. Only a smidgen, mind. That's right. There now! Think I'll lay me down right over here, so my back's to the sun; and I'll commence telling that tale now—."

Alter mopped the perspiration from his face with the end of his shirtsleeve. He took a small pipe from his breast pocket next. It was a dainty thing, with a bowl of white porcelain had a portrait of a pretty lady painted on it. And, taking a thin wire which hung from a little chain that held it to the pinch-beck lid, he cleaned out the short stem; which was in three parts—the thin, curved mouthpiece and the lowermost piece being of grayish-black bone; and the middle part, the widest of the three, embroidered with glazed, soft plaitwork all round. This done, he lit it, and begun to smoke, whiles cocking a casual eye at the painted beauty. Then he stretched out on the ground beneath the tree. —I hawked, to clear my throat, and settled more comfortable into my place; and I proceeded next with my tale, so . . .

# 5

"AT THE BRICK bathhouse in Glupsk, a young feller I know has been earning his keep for the longest time now, from ever since he was little. Name of Fishke. Fishke the Lame, to be more precise, on account of him being crippled, you see. Ever hear of him? No; thought not . . . So, who's this Fishke feller anyway? you're maybe asking. I mean, where'd the feller come from? how'd he come to be there, in such a place? Well, sir, somehow it just never occurred to anybody, nor to me, to even ask. So that part of it's a blank, pretty much. Though, what else you expect? For here you have this poor article of humanity knocking about the place; and maybe he's even got a name—say, Fishke, or whatever—but, well, after all, he's no different from any of the rest of the wretched cast-offs in our midst which are his equal, and which are forever cropping up amongst us; and seemingly overnight, as well, and fully formed, like so many mushrooms after a rain, with all their distinctive features and parts already pricked out, and in place. Now you'd think maybe *some*body might have taken no-tice of such creatures being born, and growing up, kind of gradual-like; so at least we'd be warned of their coming. But no; ain't nobody ever does . . . See, there are all these poor-folk amongst us have taken to nesting in every sort of odd out-of-the-way hovel and hole-in-the-wall cubby, where they quietly breed away unseen, bringing babies into the world in dark squalor. And, well, whyever shouldn't they? For it's no skin off of anybody's nose if they do; and gracious! why it ought even to be accounted a blessing: I mean, Jewish folks being so fruitful and multiplying like that—as, after all, it's no more than only the Lord's work which they are doing . . . Only think of it. Of a sudden there's this bumper crop of

lively little things which, before you know it, are up and about
and on their own; and, in the wink of an eye, they are already
scampering about in the world on their spindly legs; great
hordes of wee Jewishfolk, called Fishkele and Chaikele and
Yosskele, and any number of other suchlike Jewish children's
names; and they're all of 'em getting underfoot everywhere,
hanging about in the street, and hunkered in the doorways of
prayerhouses, and on the doorsteps of people's homes; and
not a one which isn't barefoot, nor none with any raiment to
hide his nakedness; except for maybe it's a torn weskit-'n'-
showfringes, to cover back and loins with. —Anyhow, getting
back to our Fishke . . . Now Fishke he's not what anybody
would think to call well-favored or prepossessing, exactly. He
has this outsize head, which is flat on top and looks like one of
them shallow, oval-shape basins when it's turned turtle. And
his mouth is a deal on the broad side, as well, with crooked
yellow teeth; and he stammers sort of and lisps quite a lot
whilst talking, and has trouble getting his *r*'s out properly.
And he's also a bit crookbacked, too; and when he walks, he's
got kind of a list to him, favoring the one side like, on account
of this very bad limp he has in his one leg . . . So anyway,
Fishke was way-away past the time of first coming of marriageable age; and certainly he would have wed long ago, and
by now have favored Glupsk with half a dozen or so children
of his own—that is, if the matter was up to himself alone.
Only it weren't, you see. For it was Fishke's particular misfortune that nobody ever gave him a second thought in any regard, never mind in regard to marriage; so he became what in
the book trade we call 'lazy goods'—the sort of merchandise
you can never move and which no one ever looks at, and gets
shelved, and is left to yellow and turn dog-eared and moldy
on its own . . . Anyway, in this matter of marriage, Fishke
was passed over even at the most desperate of times, when

bridegrooms of his like were at a premium, and in very great demand. Like, well, say during the visitations of the cholera; when the arrival of this dread pestilence so terrified the townsfolk, and brought the Parish Corporation into such a great consternation, that the latter gentlemen proceeded in a panic to round up bridegrooms from amongst the most frightful cripples, degraded paupers, and lamentable ne'er-do-wells as were in the district; and would press them into service against the infection by arranging to marry them off to whatever virgin spinsters (so-called) as were their like in misfortune, and happened to come to net—the nuptials being conducted with solemn ceremony in the cemetery of the town, in full and certain trust that, once the union between these 'cholera bridegrooms' and their pauper brides were accomplished, and the knot tied amidst the graves of the parish Dead, the contagion would at last stop. For the remedy had already proved itself countless times, and there could be no question as to its efficaciousness. In such cases, any maiming or blemish, so long as it were sufficiently dreadful, qualified a pauper for entering upon the estate of marriage with a lady equally afflicted. Indeed the worser was the affliction in degree, the better it suited to the purpose; and not even such as were maimed in their private parts—whose 'stones' were crushed, as the Scripture says—were in times like these excepted. But not Fishke—no, sir. For as things transpired, it never was he who was thus honored. In the event, the first time round, Parish's choice fell on the greatly regarded and acclaimed cripple, Yontl No-gams. That's the one as ambles about on his hindquarters, by clutching aholt of these two wooden handgrip things, got like four pegs stuck into the bottom of 'em—look sort of to be midget footstools, don't you know; which he's able to lift himself up off the ground with, and then scuttle along, by working his arms like they was

legs . . . So, anyway, this same Yontl was paired off with a lady
of no less eminence than himself in the pauper line—I mean
the one who is missing a lower lip, and has got a set of teeth
on her which, at a pinch, could as well serve for shoveling
coals with. Well, it seems the sight of this bridal pair gave the
contagion such a terrible fright that instantly it withdrew
from town, so as to be well out of their vicinity. But the retreat of the pestilence notwithstanding, whilst it was so
shamefully taking to its heels, there was a great abundance of
people who took to their beds; and a goodly number of these
even perished, though no one to this day has been able to discover the reason why . . . At the next visitation of the contagion, Fishke was overlooked once more, the favor of the
Parish falling, this time, upon the person known as Li'l
Nahum the Loafer, a conspicuous simpleton and layabout of
the neighborhood. This natural fool performed the ritual of
Bride-Veiling at the cemetery, before a very distinguished
gathering of Parish dignitaries, with a maiden lady that was
getting sufficiently on in years to have long ago left behind her
salad days; and in whose case the solemnity of veiling the
bride's head served also as a charity—she being nearly bald
from her girlhood on, and her scalp covered with sores from
front to back. Mind though, this aside, the whisper in town is
that the bride was not quite the lady she gave herself out to
be, being in truth no female, but a creature of indeterminate
sex, the sort what's sometimes called an Androgyne. Now,
that's as may be; but this seems not to have prevented folks
from having a grand time all the same; and I hear tell that the
wedding guests made very merry this time, consuming prodigious quantities of schnapps, in amongst the tombstones,
whilst drinking the couple's health. For the general sentiment
of all those present was—'Aw, go 'head, be fruitful! Serve
that old rascally cholery right, Jewish folks multiplying like

that, in the face of the affliction. Besides, it's a mercy, really. For ain't even poor misfortunate cripples, such as these, deserving of a bit of fun, as well?' And everyone even took turns in dancing before the bride, and calling out to her *'Behold the beautiful and graceful bride!'* Though this was not—as some wags would pretend—to recommend the poor thing to the cholera's attention (which Heaven forbid!); but rather, I say, to recommend her to the affections of her imbecile husband . . . but I'm getting off the point. So, anyway, the short of it is that the Parish clean forgot all about Fishke. And though there was yet another visitation of the cholera, it availed Fishke no more than those had done which preceded; and he remained still ever the bachelor, and unwived as before. Why even the saintly Granny No-nose, her what dances about in the street like a dervish, collecting alms in a dish, and is accompanied in this by a broken-down gent playing on a beaten-up fiddle and singing tenor; the both them laboring only so poor cripples of neither sex oughtn't to remain unwed God forbid! for want of the means to marry—yes even this dear, kind, sweet, charitable creature had quite forgotten about Fishke, and left him to make his way in the world without a wife. So I suppose there is just no other way of describing Fishke's condition but to say it was unfortunate in the extreme, and that he was greatly to be pitied. Such was apparently Fishke's fate; for there seemed to be no prospect of his ill fortune being ever mended. —Fishke went about barefoot as a general rule, and was coatless always. He had on only a blouse which was botch-patched; and which he wore under an exceeding long, outsize, cover-me-queerly four-corner weskit and showfringes that come down to his knees, and was much soiled, even in the parts that showed through the general grime. A very crumpled pair of trousers of coarse linen completed the outfit. This was all his wardrobe. His public of-

fice consisted in going out upon the street, of a Friday, and
calling out to the townsmen, *'Oyez, oyez, oyez! menfolksh ter the
bathowze!'* and, as well, of a Wednesday, performing the same
service for the townswives, and calling out, *'Oyez, oyez, oyez!
womenfolksh ter the bathowze!'* and in the summer, when the
garden greens began first coming up, Fishke's voice would be
heard in the streets, hailing everyone at large, with—*'Hoy
folksh! thish way fer yer lovely baby onions! Hoy! thish way fer green
garlics . . .'* His duties in the bathhouse were chiefly those of
keeping watch over the clothing, and of carrying in a kettle of
hot water at need. He was also very clever in the way he had
of rolling up a gent's blouse, and stuffing it inside the sleeve,
and then securing it in a bundle by buttoning the cuff. And it
was no less a treat seeing the way he had of carrying a live coal
in from the stove, and tossing it from one hand to the other;
and of holding it steady to the end of a feller's seegar, the
whiles it was being puffed on, to get it lit—such work usually
earning Fishke a tidy tuppenny copper, and even all of the
thruppenny, sometimes. And by virtue of his years of bathhouse duty, discharged in these several capacities, he even
acceded to a dignity very near that of one of the Parish bea-
dledom or Shul-service gentry, thereby enjoying, as well,
some small privileges attendant thereon. Like, well, for instance going door to door, collecting a season's goodwill
gratuities on the feasts of Hanukkah and Purim, in merry
company with the whole gang of bathhouse drudges—which
is to say, with all the twigsmen and rubbers-down and water-
boys and stokers and steam-makers, and the bathboys attending upon the better class of patron in the upper tier; or going
round to householders, to partake of honeycakes-'n'-wine
collation, on any number of solemn or festive occasions, as
after eventide reading of the Shema, and at circumcisions and
weddings and such; or, again, making the circuit of town on

the Passover, with cadging bag in hand, to receive such left-over shards of matzos, as a charitable householder may be willing to part with. ——Now, I knew Fishke pretty good, you see, and always liked talking with him. For he could really surprise a feller, with the clever things he come up with at times. I mean he wasn't at all the fool which his appearance might give you to think he was . . . But this aside, though, the reason I got to know Fishke in the first place is, any time I'm over to Glupsk, I always make dropping in at the bathhouse there my first order of business. Matter of principle, in a way. Why, I won't never even think to touch any other businesses first; no, indeed not, sir! Least, not till I've got all my duds and hose and things steamed out proper (best cure there is for the road vermin, don't you know); and I've clumb up on the top tier, and gave these old bones of mine the prime steaming-out they deserve. Because, well, think what you will, but I'll say it again, if I never said it afore, there's just about never another thing in the whole world will give plea-sure more than having a grand sweat. That's my opinion. Take right now, for instance. Why, I'd be enjoying even this little bit of sweat I worked up this minute, if that sun wasn't only in my face . . . uh, I say, Reb Alter!

——"Say, Reb Alter! Now, you wouldn't maybe mind movin' over some? Oh, my, but that *is* a power of perspiration you've worked up, sir . . . Huh? Uh, why yes—well you might just shift yourself a bit more, maybe, if you're willin'—h'm, well, p'raps only a lee-tle touch fu'ther . . . *There now!* that does it . . . Well, maybe a wee—"

"*Tchah!*" says Alter, his temper having got the better of him again. "Man alive but how far's a feller s'pose to move, Reb Mend'le? . . . An', an', so how long's this yarn o' yourn go on for, anyhow? Why, it'd try the patience of a saint. So I

am beggin' you, sir, do give us the nub of it a'ready, and be
done!"

"No, but bear with me, Reb Alter!" I says to him. "I mean,
it's not as if there wasn't loads of day left yet, till Fast-
end . . ." —And I took up my story again, from where I left
off:

"So, where was I? Um. Lessee . . . Right! —S'anyhow, as I
was tellin': Couple years back, I come into Glupsk, and who
do I see but this same Fishke walking past, with the same hob-
bly crookfoot gait he had. Only now he has got hisself dudded
up like a fashion plate. I mean the feller near floored me, the
way he looked! For this was my poor Fishke, mind, done up to
the nines in a brand-new frock, what's one of 'em dandy Cir-
cassian gaberdine things, and shod in a new pair of shoes plus
hose; and wearing a floppy velveteen bonnet, as well, and the
starchiest calico vest-'n'-showfringes, which looked needle-
fresh, and showed a pattern of red flowers on it that just about
dazzle the eye, even at a distance. Well, I didn't know what to
make of it. First off, I thought maybe this season Parish may
have been brought round to favoring Fishke for graveyard
nuptials. But no, this couldn't be, as there'd been no visitation
of the contagion that year. Though, this wasn't because folks
had maybe got round to cleaning up the old pond, or to rid-
ding the town of the pesky smell keeps hanging over it, or to
even clearing away the dead cats which are let willy-nilly to
lie about the place; nor was it because householders may have
quietly joined against the much revered and time-honored
practice of tossing house slops into the street, right under
people's noses. —Now, really, sir! the last's all but unthink-
able. For it'd be too unspeakably low and mean to even con-
template such a slander against the good folks of what is (if
nothing else) a decent and very respectable community. I

mean, to fly in the face of tradition like that? Never! So I suppose the business must be reckoned Providential. Yes, most assuredly, it *was* a miracle . . . this is not to say, though, that there was not a fair number of people who had complained of a serious distemper of the stomach anyway; and quite a few maybe even died of it. But this was . . . well, kind of a by-the-way thing, so it don't really count. And besides, well, first of all it was only, as 'twere, one of your garden-varieties of epidemics—the sickness being ascribed to an incontinent consumption of unripe cucumbers. And in the second place— well, in the second place, all of it was only the doing of the poorfolk of the neighborhood, who, owing to an access of ill-advised enthusiasm for the fruit, had took untimely to the infant green, whilst it lay still unmature in the ground. Though, thanks be to Merciful Goodness and . . . Oh, let it go! For I've got off the point anyhow. —Well, the whiles I was preoccupied so with Fishke's remarkable appearance, and wondering about what it signified, the feller had gone his way. Now it happened so I had took a very bad fall about then, and the small of my back and flanks was giving me the worst kind of trouble on account of it. So it occurred to me it was quite a time since I let myself be bled—I mean since last I received a proper abstraction of blood, at the hands of the barber-surgeon. For leechings, of which I'd anyways had only a half dozen in as many months, are never quite the same thing, by way of cure; whereas, in all that time, I hadn't allowed myself not so much even as one good cupping, dry nor wet. So I resolved that, first thing on the morrow for sure (an God grant), I should get me over to the stone bathhouse, and avail me of the services of a barber-surgeon in the place. And I would as well spend a couple of hours' time there, at whose end I should pretty well discover everything. Mind, not just about Fishke (though that of course goes without saying), but also about great matters at large, and all manner of other businesses. That's to say about what's called 'Polyticks and Posts' and, oh, near about anything and everything's happening in the world, and in the town . . . Only place, really, for a Jewish gent to get a handle on things is a bathhouse. It's where a feller can always unburthen himself of the things been grumping away inside, and which he's dying to tell about; and he is sure to collect worthy titbits in kind from other folks in return, as well. For it's where all sorts of secrets may come your way, and there is every kind of deal being done. Why, there is always more dealings and give-'n'-take palaver being done in a bathhouse than anytime there ever was or even could be at your market fairs. And Fridays is about the best bathday there is, to get a good eyeful of the goings-on. —Oh! but the place is a bully picture then! For over to one end you may see the pair of barber-surgeons settled down to work amongst the clutter of their tackle and gear and stock in trade. The one of them might be taking his turn at doing the barber's part, razoring the hair off a gent's head, the whiles the second is slashing up backs, and flanks, and sides, and pulling the cupping glasses off of the one gent—*plook!* and applying 'em straightways to a other. Why, it's hard to credit, sometimes, what excesses of innocent Jewish blood may be spilt in the cause of cupping; for there's pools of the stuff fairly sloshing about underfoot then; and getting mixed up with the litter of shorn hair, and of leaves fallen off of whipping twigs. And sometimes, when the wick at the end of the surgeon's candle gets frayed and comes undone, the flame will begin to sputter and to fret, throwing the queerest light on the scene . . . Every variety of wear can be seen hanging from the posts along the walls, and from the roof over the stove; giving the place the appearance of a huge clothing store, draped with an abundance of weskits-'n'-showfringes, and of

stockings and gaiters and breeches, and of every manner and
cut of caftan and gaberdine, and of round felt hat, as well. Of
the noises which fill a bathhouse, the loudest generally comes
from the bathers in the upper tier, where some lie languishing, and groaning pitifully; and others, being furnished with
bundled lengths of twigs, beat away at themselves, crying out
the whole while *'O Lordy!' 'Oh, mercy me!' 'Vapor! More v-a-por, I
say!'* And then suddenly the whole chamber may grow very
cold, and the hubbub is universal. But none ever even thinks
to mend things by pouring hot water on the stones himself—
not till, at the end, some merry rogue come along and warms
the place up so nobody can draw a breath, for the quantity of
steam. —Why, there's just never an end to the diversions of a
bathhouse. There's always the pair of very sodden gents gets
into a tussle over watering rights to the same bucket; and the
each will be tugging at the thing, and cussing the other out in
the shamefulest language. And then a third feller comes by—
say maybe it's the scrawny schoolmaster, as lives in the neighborhood; and it happens he's been looking for just such an
article what's in dispute. Well, he'll just charm the other two
into happy compromise; by which all the three is next cheer-
fully hunkered together, dipping their noserags in, and swab-
bing themselves from the same pail. But it's all the way to the
top you must look, if you want gentry. For that is where the
select clutch of Gentlemen of Consequence in the Parish take
their vapors, and confabulate. Which is to say they talk about
the meat tax, and of folks these days not knowing their place
anymore, and them being so uppity; and about supplying the
new Levy of recruits, and electing the new Aldermen, and
appointing the new Rabbi, and—well, as a general thing, they
talk of Money, as also of the new Police Chief, and what this
gentleman's share in the commodity last named may be. And
one of the better class of hangers-on may sidle over simper-

ingly then, venturing a few opinions, as well—about the running of the Poor School, about the newly published Imperial
Edicts, about several of the recent misconducts perpetrated
by certain Shameful Persons in the community—not forgetting also to drop a whispered confidence in kind, into the
privileged ear of each one of the venerable gentlemen in
turn. And that's when your Young Upstart, eager for public
office lately vacated, makes his play, approaching the most
eminent of these Personages, and craving of His Worship, if
he mightn't be agreeable to joining him on the topmost ledge;
for he'd himself now got the vapors going real crackerjack
there, and my gracious! yes, but there's more than enough to
be enjoyed by two, sir! But Hanger-on he won't be outdone
by Upstart; so he invites another ranking gent, though not
maybe *quite* equal in station to the first, for like ministra-
tions—and then another somewhat less exalted, and yet another, next in order of dignity, and again another . . . till
finally *all* Their Worships are mounted to the topmost ledge,
where the several businesses in hand are amiably concluded to
the agreeable sound of slapping twigs—and what's more,
under so generous a cloud of curling vapors as presently to
overflow, spreading throughout the whole house, and bestow-
ing upon each bather there, some substantial portion of the
general felicity. So that, at last, a great murmur of groans of
contentment and of the happy rustlings of beaten twigs is
heard everywhere in the house. Now, that's when *my* turn
comes to clamber up and to find me a corner all to myself to
lay down in and, . . . REB ALTER! Oh, for pity's sake, Reb
Alter—

"Reb Alter, give us a bit of room, huh? There's a good
feller. Bit more over to the nor'side, though, if you can manage it. Thanks, 'preciate it . . ."

Alter had gave me that beetling leer again . . . He looked

fed up. But then he only hitched his shoulders, and he says: "*Naaa-a-a* . . . ne'mind!"

"Gracious what is it?" I says, beaming at him innocent. "Uh, er, what's that you sayin', Reb Alter?"

"Huh? . . . Wassat *I'm sa* . . . Wassat *I'm say*—? Nothin'! Can't get a word in nohow anyways!" —Alter'd turned away then, grumping to himself: "Listen to the feller. Talk-talk-talk, aller time! An' what about? Bathhouses for pitysakes! An' what's so special 'bout bathhouses? Seen enough of the things to suit me a lifetime . . ." Then he looked at me again, and said, "So what's *s-o-o-o* special 'bout this partic'lar bathhouse, sir? I mean where's th' point, Reb Mend'le? Get to th' nub, sir!"

"Oh, come, Reb Alter!" I soothes. "We'll maybe have us a bit of rest first, and then I'll finish up. No, but I promise—."

# 6

ALTER WAS A tiresome while fiddling with the mouthpiece. Till he gave up trying to unclog it, and unscrewed the thing, swearing irritably. He next got out a goosequill which he stuck the reed of into the shankhole, and got the bowl fired up, puffing short puffs which, for all they was mincing, sent an astonishing quantity of smoke into the air, like from a stovepipe . . . I got the cricks out of my back, and I lay down again and recommenced telling:

"Next day, I was early to the bath, before the place filled up with bathers. Inside the hall I run across Berl the bathhouse 'twigsman' and 'rubber-down.' He was seated between piles of bound twigs, which he'd stacked in columns against the wall, and was in the way of putting together the makings for another besom, and examining the leaves in a twig as earnestly as a housewife picking out peas at market. Itsik the watchman was nearby, warming himself by the stove . . . That's the gent's got the whiskers way down to here, been at the place upwards of thirty year. Though he never does do much of anything there, except it's to maybe laze about, with his hands folded over his belly, keeping an eye on the bathers' things, and saying to anyone as happens to leave—'Yoor v-ery good health, sur! Oh an' bless *Yoo,* sur . . . ,' thereby earning his keep. Right now he was having himself a loud gap and a stretch, raising his arms a-way over his head, and was reckoning up how much his missus expects him to bring home for the Sabbath. The whiles rattling on to Berl, all about how the whole world's come to sich a state, when a feller even cain't make a honester goodness living no more. An' oh! but people *w-uz* close now, v-ery close. For only you lookit what passes for respec'able folks these days!——And he proceeds then to get down to cases; and passes the most outrageous remarks imaginable, slurring the character of this one and of that one, in turn: 'N-o-o, sur! Ain't a one even come upter th' heels of sich gents as once't come round. Not the same sorter place is bath'owzes these days, as wuz once't. I mean, why lookit! Them days you'd not get lesser 'n a solid sixer hard brass from a cust'mer, at very least! even he wuz the biggest skinflint. But nowadays? *P'tui!'* (Itsik says, shooting a gob of spit into the stove). 'Nowadays? God rot'em! ain't even sicher thing as one respec'able gent in the whole mean rotten lot! . . .'

"The both seeing me, they gave me warm welcome. For I'd not been by in a long while, and they had a very good regard of me, so they were pleased to see me. So we got to talking about oh all sorts of things, when the subject of Fishke came up in the middle. So I says: 'Say, what's our Fishke up to these days? I mean, where *is* the feller anyhow?'

"'Fishker!?' exclaims Berl, and he give out with a '*Whoo-oo-oop!!*' and give the new-finished besom a smart swat. 'Fishker? W-ell now!' he says, 'there's one feller which's come up v-ery considable. Got hisself wed! Respec'able householder now. An' happy? Why the word cain't even come near . . .'

"'Fishker!?' says Itsik the watchman, who'd been nodding his head the whiles, and chimes in with: 'Fishker? Reg'lar squire now. An' savin' all harm to the boy—but there's many had traded places with him these days. Why he'd hisself never'd've thought he may come inter sich happy good fortune!'

"Finally, though, Berl the twigsman and rubber-down took matters in hand and told all, so:

" 'OF A EVENIN', Thursday, I finish firing up all the stoves—and half kilt myself doing it, if I may say. So I lay down on a bather's ledge, 'longsides with the rest of the bath'owze drudges, to have a breather. There wuz also some other layabout gentry there besides, as gen'ly beds down here o' nights. So we wuz all laying about easy, and smokin' together and talkin'—and we wuz just fine. But on a sudden then, outside, there's a clatter of coach-'n'-hoss, stops direc'ly out front. Thinks I: H'm! . . . Nah! Coach-'n'-hoss they ain't nothing to be makin' a fuss over. So I don't pay nor mind to it. Well, the thought's scarcely out, when three beefy fellers come in. Big noisy gents, and they wuz belloring out loud, and calling all at once for—"*Fi-i-i-shker!* . . . Where's the Gimper? Give us Fishker!" . . . Well I don't mind telling but I sorter got the wind up. For what way wuz it to behave, shoutin' at folks and talkin' rough, "Where's the Gimper" and "Give us Fishker"? but then I thought better of it. For what's to be scared anyways? Fishker bless him why he ain't no thief;

nor is ever mixed up in business with other folks anyways, never mind shady dealings. Now even jist s'pose these wuz them Gov'mint "snatch-thugs" as been doin' army presswork hereabout. Well, what's Fishker to do with them anyhow? Nor more than may do the butter knife with beefstew. As it is perfec'ly plain, God's mercy is put th' poor boy forever outer the way of bein' the soldier, permanent . . . So this bucks me up some, an' I says to 'em: "Hear you gents is askin' after that Fishker feller. Well happen he's away jist now, so whatcher wan' him for anyhow? State your business, gen'men; for I want to know it!"

" 'Well, that corks 'em up, kinder; so they stood the whiles, exchanging looks together, till the one of them steps for'ards, and he says: "Sure, we'll oblige. For honester goodness, gen'men, this ain't only pious Jewish business, and there is nothin' which is shameful in it. So this is the story:

" ' "Now course, gen'men, you are all acquainted with Blind Orphan-gel . . . Her what's the blind beggarlady . . . The one's got 'er place oh many a year now, nexter th' Deadfolks' shul, over to the Old Cem'tery, and collects alms whiles singing that song ever'body knows, as wuz writ special about her, by one of 'em new whatcher-m'-calls-'ems, er—them 'ere new, uh, *Po-wit* fellers . . . So you know too about her bein' widdered jist recent this year. Only Blind Orphan-gel she won't wait. For nothing will do but she must straighter ways contract by deed-o'-marriage to this porter feller about town. Which deed specifies as follers: Whereas Blind Orphan-gel undertakes she shall, upon sed marriage, decen'ly Clothe, Maintain an' gener'ly Provide for sed Porter feller's needs, plus hand over sich and sich a lump sum to him cash down as agreed, this same feller do promise he shall wed Blind Orphan-gel, the marriage to take place 'pon sich and sicher day. Which event it happen, gen'men, is today . . . An' talkin' about which, you oughter seed the sumpt'ous Banqwert's laid on for it. My word, it is prime! For there's schnapps-likker, and there's whitemeal loafs, and there's pot roas' and there's fish, and there's a 'bridal-broth' with chickens, and all sortser pou'try . . . ever'thing in short what's proper when Jewish folks weds. Mind, it cost dear, though. But never mind; for the feast's set, and anyhow Blind Orphangel as well she's rigged-out jist won'erful-lookin'. Picture of a bride she look, too, in them nupt'al fineries, and raiments all shiny and new, an' cover't all in kerchers and veils. So, time come to fetch her Intended to the Bridal Can'py. We come to Porter feller's door. It's his gran'mar open it. Says we: Where's His Nibs, an't please, ma'am? Says she: Ain't home! So we wait. One hour pass. Feller don't show. Two hour. Still don't show. Porter feller's nowhere to be found. Gone! 'Vaporated, like! . . . So, what happen', you asks? Well, surs, we'll tell you what happen'. Rascally rogue's had a change o' heart, God rot'im! An' why's that, gen'men? Granny's why! . . . Now't appears this lady is dead set agins' the marriage from the start. For she's been in service as cookmaid to *Our Squire* (God bless'm) more years now than even anybody can 'member. And she been raising the most godawfulest stink agin't the whole time, a-scoldin', and a-cryin', and sayin' about how this match was a insult to her dignity. But she do have her point, in a way. She after all bein' with the Squire aller them years, an's a personage of quite consid'able influence, for havin' the ear of some v-ery important tradin' gents what passes through her kitchen all the time, when they come inter the Squire by the back door. For she do make exceptional good puddin' from the recipe which Gra'mar Hanner give her personal, 'fore she passed on (God rest). Nor's her matzo-meal pancakes with almonds got their equaller, in nor outer the district. And her being the cook to rankin' gentry, why that ain't hardly to no account, neither. For her word do carry weight at the Butcher's. And at Feast-o'-Weeks the Beadle why he always come by personal, so she may bless the citronfruit herself. And on Purim the Second Cantor why he's never above dropping inter her kitchen to read from the Booker Esther to her. And why there's never a New Year worship at shul which Rickla the Prayers-promptress don't visit her quite reg'lar, follerin' Torah recitals, to take a cupper two spice chic'ry water with her . . . So wuz on'y to be expected she won't agree to the match. —*NO!* (she says) I ain't havin' it! Never *no*-how! Do whatcher will, I don't care! For I shan't have my *Preciousgoodname* drug down inter the gutter in my old age. I will not have this match. Nor shall my gran'son nuther! You may pull him ter pieces with wild hosses and drag his remainders over burnin' hot coals. He shall not have this bride! . . . And she close the door *bang!*—So there we wuz, lef' out on the doorstep, like a buncher cheeses ripenin' in the dairy larder . . . Well we was in a predic'ment. That were a fact. Though, mind! not so much on accounter losing the Porter feller (to which rubbage good riddance anyhow)—but on account aller that prime pot roas' and fish was goin'ter be wasted . . . Not to speak of nobody which undertook this business in the first place—and what's nigh hand to kilt hisself, in doin' it—will ever see one sol'tary penny outer it. Aller that work! Oh it'd be a terrible thing if at the end we'd have naught to show for it. We couldn't think *what* to do. So the whiles we're chawin' the thing over like, the Gimper feller sudden come to mind. By golly! Fishker's the thing can deliver ever'body outer this quandary. Why, he'll do as crackerjack as any feller. For what difference it make, long as there's a bridegroom. And sure Fishker *he* won't mind. Why ever should he for? 'Cause it'd even be doin' the boy a consid-'able charity, when you come to think on it. So, gen'men, we come express now to only fetch the boy to stand under the weddin' can'py, in place of that 'ere Porter feller which run off.

"'Though, as these fellers is putting the case to us, Fishker hisself come in. Well, you can bet we wuz on him in a instant, and soon herding him out the door, fast as his poor crook-pegs could go . . . *Whoo-oo-oop* Fishker! we says. Now you spare us them questions. Hush up, dear boy, an' listen! For ain't no time to waste. Your days bein' single is over, Fishker! For it's your own turn's come, for standing insider th' weddin' can'py. Oh but it's all been arranged, lad. Come, boy, the Bride attends! . . . And 'fore even the boy's gotter chance to look for his bearings much less find 'em, the thing's over and done. So the whole buncher us is pretty soon guzzlin' up heaps o' food, and drinkin' that couple's health. And a very dandy meal it certainly were, too, inter the bargain . . .

" 'And today? Why these days you may see our Fishker walkin' round the town, and oh! he *do* look the beau o' fash-ion though. With that fancy long coat he got on, and the rester them fine clothes which wuz original bespoke for the Porter feller. And all he got to do in the way of work now is to lead Blind Orphan-gel which is his wife to her beggin' post at the Old Cem'tery of a morning, and then, in the evening, be taking her back home. That apart, he don't scarcely needer worry at all about his meat and drink anymore. An' that mis-sus of his why she's a breadwinning lady which ain't many can boast bein' married to her like. For she got as securer living as most may never hope for. What is more they suits each other

to the dot, and is as satisfy and happy with one 'nother as any
couple may be. Look in the end, like the thing turn out to be a
love match, after all.'


"So THAT, REB Alter, is what Berl the twigsman and rubber-
down told to me at the bathhouse . . . And you do see, sir,
don't you," I says, addressing Alter again, "you do see, Reb
Alter, what sorts of things may happen in the world? How the
lame and the blind may be joined together under the marriage
canopy; how amongst us this business of marriages is conducted, and couples betrothed. And to what end—eh? To
what end, sir? Why, only so the parties to it may eat and
drink. But this isn't only the case of the poor and the humble
in station. It's so, as well, for the rich and great. For even rich
folks are known to arrange some very queer marriages of
their own. Except in their case the meat and drink is, well,
sort of different, if you take my meaning; the enticements,
sir, are of quite another order . . . But no, I'm really getting
off the point now. —No but the point is, Reb Alter—the
point, sir, is that you must put your worries aside. By golly
but you must sir! For even suppose, *just* suppose we do allow
you've maybe not quite managed to pull off that business of
pairing them two boys. Well don't let it get you down! I
wager you'll manage the thing wonderful, next time around;
though maybe with another sort of queer couple, what's
more amenable. For I can see you already have the knack of it,
Reb Alter. Why, you've grasped the principle of the thing just
admirable, sir. Like a scholar his books. No, I'll even go so far
as to declare you have *not* got off on the wrong foot. No, no,
indeed you have not, sir! No, you couldn't have done better if
you was a estates agent. It's only the details which wants

working on. Boys, girls—what's it matter? Pooh, sir! Ba, sir!
With that sure sense of smell of yours, why, soon you'll have
no trouble nosing out the female in any pair. And then, then
my friend, this new enterprise of yours shall (an' God send!)
carry you to heights such as were never dreamed. For the
maid be blind, dumb, lame, or whatever—she shall come
under the bridal canopy for certain! You say the printer's
clamoring for his money? A trifle, sir! Ah but what of the nag
wants feeding (you add), and of my own maid wants dower-
ing, and of my missus, what's been brung to bed of a little boy
God praise! an', an' . . . O Lor'! whatever *am* I to do, sir? Oh
but these, too, are mere bagatelles, Reb Alter! No need to
worry. No; it'll all sort itself out, once you've collected that
first fee. For then your own maid's dowered and paired off,
and room made for the baby boy and . . . Oh, my! —Whew!
Reb Alter!

"Now that *is* a deal of sweating you're about, Reb Alter,
and . . . and why yes! I do admire you for it, really I do. Fact, I
wouldn't dream of having it otherwise, no sir, not a bit—
but . . . but, well, talking of making room—now don'tcher
think maybe, er—well yes! now you mention it . . . maybe
just a little, anyway—."

# 7

"W-ELL, H'M, MAYBE SO," said Alter moodily, as if to himself,
"though, as things stands, can't see 'em mending none
neither . . ." And Alter groaned then, and beads of perspiration beset his brow, for the glooms were on him awful bad.
And when at length he'd raised his eyes, and looked at me, his
features wore such a wistful melting expression, as may be

seen in the faces of babes at breast, hankering for their mama's teat. Only poor Alter he still had his eye on the main chance (as 'twere); and he had got his heart set on us two getting down to business. And that's as well too. For there never was a pair of honester Goodness Jewish gents would tolerate laying easy all day, without nary a thought for trade. Why, if they was marooned on a desert island, plumb in the middle of nowhere, and never another living soul in the whole place but them—ten will get you one, they'd be on to some kind of dealings, before the day was out. I mean the one feller for sure, why he'd already have knocked together a market stall, and be looking out for custom; and the other—well, he'd quick enough have a makepenny scheme in hand; and pretty soon they'd start in to lending and borrowing betwixt them, and swapping this and that, and buying on credit and selling on commission; till at the end, each'd be making a dandy living off the other, easy. Which is how come, on a sudden, Alter up and asks: "Now what may your estim'ble self, sir, have tucked away in that cart o' yourn, I'm wonderin'?" Which was much as to say—*"Mam-m-aaa, titty . . . !"* In other words, *"Reb Mendele, out with the goods!"*

Right! . . . enough idling. To work! —So I haul over my goods and Alter got his. And the pair of us is on our hunkers next, passing wares back and forth, and chaffering and bartering; and generally having a high old time of it all round. Well, I'm thinking to slip a batch of 'em new thingummy books past him—the dinky ones, come out recent, with the short lines, which every other one is got a "Ah!" or a "Lo!" or a "Woe!" or somesuch hoo-ha! gasper tacked on to it. Now I been trying to get shut of these since, well, I can't recollect how long. But Alter he's no such fool, and won't touch 'em with a pair of tongs, even if it was only to look at them.

"Humph! Lazy goods," says Alter, making a po-face. "Why

'tain't only a buncher rubbage, thunk up by bookwormy benchwarmers. An' who for? Well they can go 'head, and call it 'Liter'cher' and 'Po'try' and other such foolishnesses; I don't care! . . . 'cause I calls it double Dutch! For ain't no-body can make head nor tail of it, lessen it's a Mussulman Turk. Been fool enough once, to take such poor fare on board; an' you betcher, I lived to regret it! . . . Pooh, sir! 'Twon't do, sir! So give with the gen'ine article, Reb Mend'le, an' there's an end . . ."

I got out the staple bookware. Which wasn't a one Alter anyways didn't turn up his nose at, or find fault with. Until he lit on this one item he couldn't take his eyes off of. And small blame to him. For it truly was a prize thing, after its kind. Well, first off, the pages come in all different sizes and colors; and the type was all shapes, and sizes, and kinds, jumbled up together—so your Rashi scrip', say, is lumped in willy-nilly with your founts of "Di'monts" and "Pearls" and "Pica ci-cerons" and "Lig'tures," plus your " 'Talics" big and small, kind of thrown in for extras. And, why, it was a dead marvel just the way each page on its own was arranged. I mean how all the dainty writing was made to run down in slender ribands along the sides; and then a swathe of fat letters cut athwart the middle of the page; with maybe a plump oval belly underneath, jam-packed inside with bitty letters, look-ing like poppy seed; and the white frogging which looped in and out through the whole thing, like flagged footpaths laid down amongst the flowerbeds. In short, this particular article offered near every pretty fillip and dainty doodah crocket there ever was, or could be, which Jewish folks hereabout are partial to, in the way of a book . . . Talking of which, natu-rally there was scores of pages out of sequence, as well. Only that's just the beauty of it, you see. It's by way of saying to a feller, "Aw, go on! give old mother-wit a real workout this time . . . I mean, what else's a Jewish gent got a head for any-how?" And that's as it should be. For if everything was cut-and-dried, then any unlettered yahoo'd get to the bottom of things, as well as you or me—and what'd be the point in that, sir? . . . And about misprints, well, it goes without saying there were plenty of those knocking about the place. And whyever not? It's not as if anybody makes a fuss over such tri-fles anyhow. Tush! why there couldn't be much to any book, without them. I mean, given half a chance, there's never a Jewish gent what's not just mustard-keen to cudgel his brains, puzzling over things which other folks will let lie. Which brings me to the matter of Language. I mean about the *way how* a thing's written; that's to say the Art of it, if you take my meaning. Now, this book was just jammed full of art and lan-guage. Had crocks of it, you might say. Why it was so full of it, you couldn't hardly understand a word. Well, of course, nowadays, just about any old Lit'ry gent can manage the thing easy; and I dare say there's many which actually do it quite well. Still, you do have to admit, though, your modern fellers they don't come half near to the old-timers, when it comes to leaving you guessing at what they mean. Take this book, for instance—why you never saw the like in the way of brain-twisters and tongue-teasers . . . that's to say, brain-teasers and tongue-tweezers, uh . . . well, anyways, there was more of them than you could shake a shtick at . . . uh, shtick a stake at . . . Oh, let it go! . . . Anyhow, all in all, there was more than enough to keep a reading feller on his toes—give him something to chew over, and puzzle out . . . Huh? . . . What-ever for, you ask? Why, sir, I say there is no greater pleasure in the world than *not* understanding a thing. Because—and this is strictly from a Jewish point of view, you understand—well, I mean if a thing has absolutely got you stymied and defies comprehension, then of course there has just *got* to be something in it. Only stands to reason, you see. For otherwise, well, I mean otherwise, uh . . . but anyhow I've got off the point—.

Now of course Alter couldn't wait to snap up the said article. And no sooner had he done it than you could see how he'd perked up then and there; so you'd hardly even take him for the same feller. So then the both us get down to swapping off Women's Breviaries for Bubba's Book o' Wives' Tales; Graveside prayers for *The Thousand and One Nights;* Song-o'-degrees Psalters for goodspells; One Hundred Zhitomir Penitences for Bershad Four-corner Weskits-'n'-fringes; Vilnius Fast-o'-Ab Lamentations for Shofars; Hanukkah menorahs for Wolfstooth baby-teethers; and Lathed Brass Sabbath candlesticks for Sabbath-end lighters plus Woolly toddlers'-yarmulkes . . . Mind you, though, for all the quantity of goods had changed hands between us, the neither party had got so much as a plug pennyworth's cash profit out of it. But that didn't signify; because there was satisfaction enough only in transacting the business. You see, it was purely the commerce, the hurly-burly alone of trading, the sheer *doing* of it, and not being idle, which counted. And Alter's cares, as well, they seemed to vanish too, like smoke carried away on a breeze; and you could see from his face, how the memory of that other business at the fair, and the wretched ill luck which seemed to be dogging him everywhere recently, had clean gone out of his thoughts. He'd been adding up sums on the fingers of one hand; and he held his other hand cupped to his ear, and was nodding the whiles, like he'd been listening to a bookkeeper was tucked away inside, doing his double-entry reckoning for him. And Alter did too seem finally to have come out of the red (praise God!)—for I next see a crevice opening up under all that gingery facefuzz; and then—for the space of a bare instant—there's a flash of about the toothiest smile showing through as you'd ever hope to see on a feller.

The time was getting on to evenprayer, and the weather breezed up some and freshened. Bits of ragged cloud overhead made a sight for sore eyes, like dear friends too long gone; and the world quickened to greet them. Trees swayed from side to side, rustling amongst themselves in tree-ish whispers. And the ears of grain in the field sprung up in the wind, and bussed aloud like babes at play. God's creation was come alive everywhere; in the woods and fields, and in the air. Every kind of songbird appeared, one after the other, on branches and twigs, high and low, grooming their feathers with their beaks; and with a shake, then a bob, each gave out with piping clacks, and chirrups, and trills. Butterflies in jeweled satins and silks danced coyly on the air. A couple of white storks too'd stood up in the grass, on reedy red legs and heads stuck a-way up; looking grand and gaudy as any pair of guardsmen turned out in white tunics, and red piping down their britches. One little feller darted from tree to tree, calling *cuckoo-cuckoo-cuckoo!* as were at frolic in hide-and-seek; and another answered, from away off amongst the stalks of wheat and corn, *peekaboo-peep-peep! peakaboo-peep-peep!* as if to say—*Naa-Naa! you cain't ketch me, no you cain't . . . !* And over the way, in a copse, a nightingale'd burst into full-throated chauntings; and every creature, as only could, chimed in then—for now frogs grated out of unseen ponds, and, nearer to, flies and bees were abuzz; and even the scape-grace beetle took to the air, and filled it with the whirrings of its clumsy wings. And the world was full of the making of joyful noises, and pleasant smells drifted in on currents from every side.

—"Oh! but it's grand, Reb Alter. Oh, do say it *is* grand,

Alter . . . Only lookit, how beautiful this old world of God's is, Alter! . . . Oh, Alter, don't it stir you fair to the marrow? . . . Aw, g'wan man, admit it . . . Why, I'll lay, it do set your heart thumpity-thumping . . . Maybe some, huh? —Me, why, makes me want to throw myself into it, right in up to my ears—an', an', well, kind of to let it wash over me forever then, if I could do it . . ."

"Reb Mend'le, how you talk! Oh, you *do* astonish me sometimes, sir!" says Alter, looking very much put out. "I mean talkin' idle like that; 'tain't decent! . . . Best you get on with 'Even-offerins,' Reb Mend'le. For there's more gained—lest you forget, sir!—from recitin' 'Answer-us' suppl'cation than there was ever in mooning an' maundering over aller 'em foolishnesses . . . Humph!"

So I did the decent thing and pulled my hose up, and knotted the coat-sash round my middle. And then proceeded to recite the "Confection-o'-incense" portion for even'-offerings in my best high treble. Nor was old Wine-'n'-Candles (God bless!) behindhand, pumping up his own bellows; and pretty soon Alter too'd set the rafters shaking, with that great barrel-organ he'd for a voice. And the pair of us now joined our evenchants to the rustlings of herbs and grasses of the field, and chirpings of woodland creatures; the which the whiles between had been singing praises to the Almighty on their own account, for only His sweet Namesake.

Though, scarcely had Alter got down to naming the whole 'pothecary's chestful of herbs, spices, and simples went into Temple incense—that's to say, balm, and onycha, and galbanum (which last's called "devil's-turds" by some, on account of its color, plus being high-smelling) and sweet frankincense and myrrh and, uh . . . myrrh, and—H'm! . . . Well, as I told, scarcely he'd began telling all these concoctions-of-scents' names, and only got so far as the myrrh part, than it put him in mind of the old carters' adage, about myrrh's myrrh, only 'tain't worth a shucks (cravin' yer Washup's pardon!), when the wagon wants greasin'. For the very next thing, he'd got his coachman's tar pail whisked from out under where such things is usually slung, which is below the driver's box. And Alter not being in the least a dawdling kind of man, he dashed right on ahead; and, in the space of oh not half a minute, he'd already finished up with praying——leaving me on my own, at only midway. And he commenced then attending to his hubs.

"Gracious' sakes! Oh do try an' make an end, Reb Mend'le! Don't be *l-i-n-gerin'* over the thing so . . . Short's sweet, sir . . ." Alter had begun to fret, and was out of patience. "That's the ticket . . . you go an' see to your wagon, the whiles I hunt up the animals. Time we was under way . . . There's least coupler miles might be cover't till night, if we was t'start now . . ."

Good as his word, too, Alter was. No sooner he'd said it, and he was away like a shot. Me, I got down to daubing up the cart. Done right by her, as well. Took my time about it, for I don't hold with scrimping on lubricants. And, what with taking each hub in turn, and giving it my individual attention, as 'twere (hubs being tetchy things, don't you know, and don't take kindly as a rule to slapdash treatment)——well I was quite a while at it, before I'd done. Alter, though, he still hadn't shown . . . But I allowed then as the horses must have foraged a fair way into the woods—no doubt having a grand feed in between whiles, as well. So that bucked me some. And I took to watching the sun setting over the fields; and stood looking so for a spell. It now dipped behind the horizon, and the last of the sunlight began to fail, inching its way ever-so-slow from down off the trees, which it had lit up and played upon so jolly, not minutes before . . . In a moment it was gone——.

I was uneasy. Something had happened to Alter. I was sure
of it. Takes a awful lot out of a feller, perspiring like that, and
the Fast so long . . . Shouldn't wonder if he'd fainted away.
And wasn't a living soul would take notice of it, if he had. I
mean the place being so out of the way, and off on a by-road.
And there's the forest, too. Who knows what sorts may be
skulking about inside, for a lonely traveler to fall foul of—
No! I shouldn't leave things to stand so. I would go in after
Alter.

I worked myself up to it, and went in. I had gone a fair distance inside; though it didn't do any good. For there was
never a trace of Alter, nor the horses. Till at the end I'd come
to a deep gully which had cut dead across the wood, so I
couldn't get to the other side. And looking down, I made out
where it bottomed-out in scree and a narrow valley, covered
with clumps of sedge and bushes, which were all thorns and
thistles everywhere. And in one direction it ran up to where
the main road was; and towards the other it stretched away off
into the darkness—the deuce knew where to, for I never did.
And the forest lay asleep all round, and nothing stirred in it.
And overhead a heavy curtain hid the sky and not a whisper
was heard for a sound anywhere. Except, at whiles, when
branches on neighboring trees brushed against each other, or
a handful of leaves fluttered here and there on a bough, as
though fretted by dreamers' fancies. It was the forest sleep-
talking—dreaming dreams of oh! such an untold many yes-
terdays, happy and cruel by turns. The brushing of dry twigs?
that was the wood remembering cut-down saplings, felled before their time . . . And the muffled crash, as soft as a bird's
nest fallen to the ground?—a token of a brood of nestling
chicks and their mother hen, brought down by a sparrow
hawk the other day. For it was the same memory had made
the leaves flutter a while back. It seemed to me a cloud of

somber fancies beset the forest on every side, and it bore in
upon my own spirit. And now, Imagination, that father of
falsehoods, did the rest; conjuring out of the still murmurs
and rasps, the wildest and most frightening notions; and setting them in train inside my head. And they were magnified
there, and given grisly substance. For in my mind I had
painted them up into dreadful pictures. I saw my poor Alter
stretched out, pale and lifeless, upon the ground; and his she-
nag and my own little jade lay dead beside him. And their as-
sassin lurked nearby, a huge man with cruel features framed in
a shock of red hair . . . and instantly the man's apparition
faded, and was replaced by a wolf snarling, and baring fell
rows of teeth . . .

I had about resolved anyhow to go down into the valley,
when a thought stopped me. Our wagons were left unattended, and were fair game for anyone, that way. The whole
caboodle of our stock may already be made off with (which
Heaven forbid!); and then where'd the either of us be! So
maybe it wasn't such a bad idea, if I just went to see how our
things fared, before proceeding in this business. Besides, Alter
might be back with our horses, for all I knew, and no doubt
half out of his wits with worry about me. The feeling that this
was so grew stronger; till the hope it nourished in me had all
but driven away the clouds of despair, and my mood light-
ened.

I hurried back as quickly as I could—.

# 8

WITH GOD'S HELP I did get back in one piece, more or less.
For I'd took a couple of spills, smacking up against trees hap-

pened in my way. Though, picking yourself up off of the
ground again isn't half bad in a wood, next to doing it in the
city, where folks is apt only to laugh. I mean that does put you
off a thing, kind of. So this time I managed to get some pleasure out of it. Sort of like a job well done. And I could even
thank God for His Mercies to me in good conscience. For seeing as how He'd been so solicitous of me in matters of falling
down and getting up, I'd reason to think I should find old
Alter waiting for me with the horses at t'other end. This was
greater bounty though than probably I deserved, or His
blessed Name was prepared to give maybe.

For Alter wasn't nowhere to be seen . . .

It'd stopped me cold. I was heartsick. God only knew
what happened to Alter, or where he'd got to. Looked like
Alter's ill luck had really done for him, this time. For wasn't
no accident only. Had to be more of it . . . So what's to do?
That was the question, now. And what of me? I mean, here I'd
all along been counting on selling off my wares in town; and
loading up full instead with Fastday breviaries there, and making the circuit of the parishes hereabout. Which is pretty
much as I always do every year, this season. So it now being
the Three-week, 'twixt the Tammuz-'n'-Ab, there wasn't a
minute to lose. For if I was hung up here all the while,
where'd that leave the folks in this neck of the woods? I mean,
it's no joke; no Fastday Lamentations for Jewish folks at such a
time. Why it's not even thinkable. For you can imagine what
sort of Fast-o'-Ab day would be in store then. Well, picture
it . . . Pre-fast noodles'n'cheese collation's already ate, and
the ash-dipped hardboil' eggs is bolted down. And most
everybody's plumped down on the ground in their stocking
feet now, looking solemn and a bit cross; and maybe the
whiles even took to reckoning up how many toenails there's
poking through their hose. And the fleas are in high feather;

and nearbout every lad in the place's got whole handfuls
ready, of stickseeds and dandelion teasels and beggar's-tick
barbs, only itching to be throwed; and why they're all of 'em
waiting for the good word, to get down to it only. And they
are waiting, and waiting, and waiting, and . . . Oh dear! *Good-*
*nessgracioussakes*—no Lamentations! Now, where's that book
peddler feller got hisself to? Reb, uh, Reb Mendele . . . Tush,
where *is* the feller! —And are they riled, sir? You betcher
they're riled! For dear me, what else might any of us be, if we
was tucked in amongst a press of, oh, maybe a score or so of
like headachy gents, poring over the tats and remainders of
only the one bitty Lamentation book's left over from Fast-o'-
Ab past; which the each is jostling t'other to get a peek at for
himself, so there's such a dingdong confusion of sidecurls and
chinwhiskers, plus the stickseeds and burrs in 'em, as a flea in
midhop couldn't've knowed whose or which gent's facefuzz
he's like to light on. And that ain't the half of it—for the Pre-
fast collation's begun to repeat itself on folks, as well; so the
scent, too, of noodle-and-egg breath's hanging now under
everybody's noses . . . Now about womenfolks, well, in their
case it's different, you see. For they are rather partial to tearfulness as is; so as a general rule, any old printed-up piety, in
the way of prayers, will leave 'em in tears. Why at a pinch
even kosher recipes have been known to set them blubbing
pretty good. Which is only what's wanted Fast-o'-Ab, in the
first place. But menfolks, now what they want is first to be
reading up on a subject, and then—

Oh but things were bad, though—and that's the truth! For
wasn't nowhere to turn to . . .

Still—something had to be done. It wouldn't do to only be
wringing my hands over it so. No; there just wasn't any other
way but going out looking again. From the stars, I could see
Fast-end had already come. So I fished the schnapps-likker

out, and took spirituous consolation out of the bottle, straight: *kloop!* couple of pulls . . . glub-aglub-glub! a-nd down the hatch . . . a-aaah! Had a morsel, too, though more for show only than otherwise, as I wasn't up to eating anything. Then a couple more parting plashes of the schnapps— and I was off again, setting a good pace the whiles into the wood.

In a short while I was over to the gully, and let myself down to the valley below. I should own, though, I wasn't really alone; nor nowise near as spooked and wretched as before. For now there were all of two of me, pegging along through the scrub together; and the pair us was having a very companionable heart-to-heart the whole whiles, about what come to pass, and the proceedings in hand. So, all in all, I was pretty blithe. For it seems a while back, in taking to the schnapps in such haste—I mean, what with all that worry and care which preceded, and doing it on an empty stomach (for I was anyhow too much troubled, to keep any solid nourishment down)—well, let's just say I'd also took a surplus of whet on board. And it was this excess of spirits which certainly stood by me in my hour of need then, as might a father his child. For I had got great courage from it. Though heaven help me but it did make me gabby when walking amidst the brambles. But that is nearly always the way with me. It never takes but the one drop too many, when it's allowed—say Feast-o'-Purim, or on the Simchas Torah—and the gab is sure to come running out at my mouth apace, like meal out the bottom of a tore bushel-sack of feed. And when I have a glow on like that, and happens to be a wall nearby, or other such furnishing, you'll find me talking away at it, and there's the sugariest, treacliest smile on my face. And I go so soft and soppy, you may as well bottle me for a poultice. And my body stretches v-ery thin now, and goes all wobbly as a hill of calf's-foot jelly in a high wind. And oh just dozens of minikin bits of Mendeles will detach themselves from the main body, and take to bobbing about on the air to every side, never quite sure of where's their purchase nor whither their center is. Till all the atoms resolve themselves finally only into two Mendeles; the one looking to go nor'-nor'east, and the other sou'-sou'west, and only the one pair of legs between them going crazy, figuring which to follow after. And the same two are all the whiles making small talk, and the sound of their chatter comes back to my ears, sounding not at all like my own voice, but kind of like it was outside me, as an echo may come back at you from out of a empty cask. Though my wits never quite take leave of me altogether at such times. For I manage always to hold on at least to some token of wit, as were in a dream.

"Ev'nin, frien'!" says I, making a reverence. "So-o, where's coupler fellers headin' middler night?" —"Psssh! Knuck-nuckleheads . . . !" returns my yokefellow, beaming amiably. "Tha's a laugh—haw, haw! L-l-lookin' ter git losht inner w-w-wildernish . . ." —"Hey! watchershelf, ol' man! They's a hole inner groun'!" —"Whoopsh! blankertyblank holes every whichways!" —"Ne'mind, ol' feller . . . Upshy-daishy!" —"Thank'ee frien', mucher-bliged. Besht I use thish 'ere whip fer a cane . . ." —"Oo-o-o look'ee! aller 'em there trees follerin' us!" —"Why, morer merrier, s'what I say! Welcome 'board, treesh!" —"Now you shtop your scratchin, y'hear! Oh, pother! 'nother scratch. Ouch! that'un near took out a eye! Now you shtoppit, y'hear . . . *P'tui!*" —"Atter boy, you show 'em! Sh-shpit on 'em, Reb Men'le! Git ridder 'em thingummy brambles . . ." —"Oo-oo lookit, s'a path! Mus' foller't inter open groun'" —"Here we are—why's a field! . . . Whoo-oop! an', an' lookit that 'ere full moon! Why s'bout as purty an' plump, and as yellery-white as dough in a kneadin'-trough. An', an' there's its eyes and mouth and

nose!"—"Oh, shush-up! . . . sh-sh! Mus' bless the moon! . . .
Hipperty-hop! Hipperty-hop! —Ev'nin, Moon!—'Ev'nin,
Ol' Timer!—Come on, hipperty-hop! hipperty-hop! Lessee
you touch me, Gramps!' —Gracious, 'f only we'd be as outer
reacher 'em what hates us, as that 'ere moon's outer mine!
Oh, why they got it in for us so, I'll n-n-never ever know . . .
For s'no faulter mine, I'm alive and needs meat'n'drink like
t'other folk . . . why on'y look! I'm naught nor skin'n'bone,
and I'm sick and I'm ailin' . . . An', an' I hadder mother
once, too, I did; yessir! which she use to hug me and to kiss
me, and she loved me so much . . . But w-w-woe's me! Ain't
but'er poor moth'less orphan now!" —"Hush-a-bye, Men'le!
Don'cher be takin' on so . . . Oh shame on you, sir! growed-
up man sucher yerse'f, and with'er fam'ly and 'sponserbil'ty,
bawlin' at'er moon like that . . . 'tain't 'spec'able!" —"Huh!
what's that? . . . Why's a fence! Psssh! Give me a turn,
s-shmackin' inter the thing! . . . So, what's ter do?" —"Whatcher mean? Climb over't! Easy, ol' feller, easy! . . . 'At's th'
boy!"—"Thank'ee!" —"Doan' menshunnit . . ." —"Oo-oo!
Looker 'em peas and them beans, an', an' aller them *Cu-cu-
cumbers!* hun'reds of 'em! . . . sh-sh! Gotter say aforemeal
blessins fu'st!" —"Now, tha's the besht cure they is fer hunger,
cucumbers is . . . yessir—mmmmmm! —*THWACK!!*"—
"Huh!? Wassat . . . !"—" 'nother *THWACK!!*" —"Oh fer pitys-
sakes! now where them thwacks come from . . . ?"

Now it so happens the thwacks I'd received came from a
well-set-up heathen buck who got hold of me from behind;
and he now proceeded to let me know, in that same coin as
before, that one didn't go breaking into strangers' gardens
by night; nor eat other folks' cucumbers uninvited, not
ever . . . ! —Well, maybe on account of the pummeling he
was giving me, or only because of the fresh cucumbers I'd ate,
I was stone-cold sober again. Though I did stand about be-

mused for a bit longer, like I'd been asleep and just woken up. Anyhow, as you can imagine, the first words come to my mind, naturally, was: *"H-help! Mu-u-u-rder . . . !"* But then I thought better of it; and, assuming an expression which was innocent and bland together, I addressed the same feller in the sort of rude gibberishy lingo which his kind of folk talk in these parts, saying (more or less): "Say, my good fellow, didjer maybe happen ter see this other Jewfeller—oh, 'bout so tall, and maybe's got this pairer broken-down hosses with him? . . . Well, speak up, speak up! So whatsermatter, cat gotcher tongue . . . ?" But this big yokel only does what he had a mind to do, and won't listen to a word; and sometimes he's dragging me along by the coat sleeve, and sometimes shoving me forward from behind, the whiles talking rough at me, and saying: "Now, gitter long, old feller . . . Gitter long!" But I reckoned it wouldn't do to be uncivil; so I went along anyhow. —Well, after a time, the pair of us arrive at a house somewhere. Ordinary place, really. Except the windows were all lighted up. And outside, too, round the front end, there was a exceptional swell-looking buggy. One of 'em open barouches, don't you know—the kind has got a foldback top on it, and two v-ery cushy facing seats. Fine piece of equipage, by the look of her. Four-in-hand, as well, with as prime-looking a double-tandem team of animals as you are like ever to see in tackle . . .

Once inside, though, the big feller stationed himself next to the door, with his cap off. So off came my own hat too— an' God save! for I couldn't see as how I'd much choice in the matter, anyways. And so I stood there the whiles, scratching my head, and looking pretty hangdog, I suppose.

Over at a table, a notary was noisily scribbling with a pen, of which the nib seemed in need of being dipped into the ink all of the time, after it scooshed out all its contents onto the

foolscap. Well that little scrivener did look to have a cruel
case of the wet runs on account of it; and kept making a wry
face at the thing, and swore at it each time he conveyed it to
the inkstand. It was plain the two were having a pretty bad
time with each other, and neither was happy in the business.
The pen, because of the notary's heavy-handedness and
crossings-out; and the notary, because of the way the pen kept
sicking-up on him. So every time the notary bore down hard,
it got even by squittering and blotching his lines . . . Though,
what held my eye now, was the jowly, big-bellied personage
planted in the middle of the room, had brass buttons down
his front, and was topped up by a red collar. Now that last
item clearly marked him for one of 'em "Red-collar" fellers.
That's to say this gent was a policeman. From which pray God
keep us safe! For Red-collars is a very disagreeable lot, even
ordinarily; and this particular article looked the panjandrum
of the bunch, judging by that nifty carriage'n'four outside,
must have been his. Right now he had a very wild look about
him. It was frightful, the way he darted restless glances all
about him, and was twirling the ends of a very long set of
mustachios. And each time he glared at you, and opened up
'em little slits he had for eyes, the whites around his pupils
shone crimson from being so bloodshot. At the moment he
had set all of his chins a-tremble, bawling at these other two
gents were standing near the door; the both of them hanging
their heads, looking penitent. One was a hefty feller, had a
bull neck which the nape was clean-shaven, and this great
quiff of hair on top, plus a silver earring in one ear. The other
was a deal stringier, with a weedy beard come to a point, had
sort of a dinky seal of office hung on his breast, and was holding a truncheon in both hands; the whiles he cringed and only
ducked and curtseyed the whole time the both were getting
the going-over. Red-collar was in oh a terrible passion with

Quiff-'n'-earring, and was bellowing at him: "Eh? Village
Elder, is it? *Wr—etch!* Oh I shall have you in iwons, suh!
Twanspo'ted, suh! Sibewia, suh . . . !" —And then he turned
on the runty one, and said: "Call y'self Bailiff, eh? Off'cer of
the Lawr, eh? Oh but I'll have the hide off you back pretty
quick, suh! Blame, blankity blankity so'n'so and so'n'so . . .
an' blankity blank y'mother, as well!"

I was numb all over and quaking like a leaf. My head was in
an uproar and my ears buzzed. I was struck deaf and blind,
and couldn't tell what was going on anymore. So I wasn't attending when the big yokel was telling about what I had done
when he caught me. Only when the Red-collar started snap-
ping at me, in his Russky lingo—which I could tell it was, on
account it's drawlier and more high-tone than local gab is—
well you may be sure I came alert and listened. For I saw
Red-collar's fist was weaving up and down before my nose,
and he had commenced howling the most dreadful words at
me: "Thief, eh? —*W'etch!* Bootlegger! Wobber! Swags-
man! . . . C-u-t-purse! . . . Oh I'll have your hide, suh! . . .
Knout, suh! Iwons! Pwi-son . . . *S-I-B-E-WIAH!* . . ." Then he
stopped. It was my sidecurls had his attention now, and he was
giving them the eye, sneering at them in disgust. Then in
anger he swept up the scissors from off the writing table, and
in a trice he had one of the pair shorn clean off. It was only
the work of a moment, and the lock of hair lay already at my
feet. I observed it was gray, and thought how from my
youngest infancy I had had it, and it was grown old even as I
had done; and I wept for the shame which had been done to
me. And in my mind I dwelt upon the years this tuft had dan-
gled at my cheek, and on the joys and no few griefs had passed
in the time between; from when I was a child, and my mother
used to toy with it, twining both of my earlocks round her
fingertips, into two sable ringlets, which ever after hung

down from my temples, and whose comeliness she seemed
never able to have enough of, as much as if the head they
adorned were her dear own. And when I grew into manhood,
and was strong and well, and in my prime, I cherished them
with pride. Though soon enough the black in them faded,
when I turned gray before my time. But there was never
shame in that. For only the excesses of griefs, and of want and
cares, of senseless hatred and persecutions, had made me old
betimes. But Lord!——what offense had my gray hairs given,
that I should be ill used because of it? ——And great sobs
heaved my chest now, so I thought the violence of them must
knock my ribs apart. Though I could not bring myself to utter
any sound; and I remained as still as a lamb at shearing. And
my eyes dropped slow leaden tears—plop! plop! plop! . . .
each as plump as the first drops of the autumn rain. And I felt
my naked cheek flush hot, as it were burning, and the change
wrought in my face must have been awful to see. For instantly
the abuse died on the Red-collar's lips before even he spoke
it, and his manner to me softened. The gray hairs on my head
and my whole appearance had made it plain, I was an upright
man and could never be thief. And he talked kindly to me,
and laid his hands gently upon my shoulders, so I now knew
that a human heart, after all, pulsed beneath the brass-bound
front. And as though seeking to obtain my pardon for doing
me wrong, he began ranting at his yokel that brought me, for
being such "a demmed deuced Fool and most certainly a
W'etch, suh!—yes, I say a *W'etch!* for dragoonin' this poor
grayhead gent, over such twifles as cucumbas, suh . . . !" And
letting out with another string of fearful oaths and assorted
sendings-to-the-devil, he roughly drove his yokel out of the
house. Then he retrieved his hat and took a few idle turns
around the room; and after issuing some last orders he tarried
no more, and saw himself out with no word of leave-taking.

And presently there was the scrape of carriage wheels moving off, and a muffled clop-clop of horses' hooves, and a rattle of harness bells, whose jingling grew ever fainter for a space, till it faded out of earshot in the distance. And he was gone.

Everyone in the place livened up now. The scribbler tossed away his pen, sending it to the black deuce and all o' Satan's cohorts. The village elder and bailiff uncrooked their backs; and, on the instant, each mock-rolled his eyes heavenwards, as were in thanksgiving, and gave an abrupt toss of the hand towards the door, on the streetside, thereby miming the countryman's farewell: "God praise, sur, an' Godspeed, sur! For sooner I'd see yer backside, sur, nor never know yer front . . . !" The village elder tousled his quiff with his hands, giving it a good shaking out. And he said: "*Whoo-oop!* Now whatcher expec' of a *Imper'al Pohlice Commiss'ry . . . !*"

When I got the chance to lay the story of my misfortune before these country gentry, they advised I might go to the village tavern, which, as they assured me, "Why, 'tweren't on'y coupler furlong upter road anyways; an' there was sure ter be a consid'ble crowder folk at the 'boozer,' as happen ter come in from market day; so maybe they knowed something o' y'frien' and them hosses (Godsend!) . . ." —So I picked up my sidecurl from off the floor, and put it away carefully in my pocket. And on the naked side I bound up the cheek with a neckerchief, bidding the company goodnight then. And I went my ways.

# 9

THE TAVERN WAS closely hemmed by a press of country wagons, of which part were empty with only scattered bits of

straw inside, and part were loaded up with all kinds of wares;
some of it unsold goods, and some purchased or traded for at
market, over to the village. Squeezing my way in amongst a
bunch of rigs, I struck a cart had a pig tied up in it in a sack
which the creature had poked a hole through with its snout,
and was going hoarse giving out with wild, crazy squeal-
ings, and piercing shrieks, made you think of nails being
driven into your head. A bit further along, there was a red-
spotted cow missing one horn and tied up behind a big cart
piled high with cheap, country-made bastwork moccasins, and
new earthenware jars and pipkins come in all sorts of shapes
and sizes. The cow kept throwing herself from side to side,
looking with all her might to get free of the rope around her
neck and rejoin the herd. Yoked together, at the front end,
was a pair of sleek, low-slung gray oxen weren't paying no
mind to the commotion going on behind; and only chomping
steadily on their cud, never leaving off their chawing even for
a minute, mulling over some weighty bovine matter no
doubt. The taverner's billy'd meanwhile clambered up onto
the floorboards of another wagon, to the one side, and pushed
his head into a sack from which he had got hold of a mouthful
of whatever, and proceeded now to chew on it, by turns puffing up and hollowing his cheeks, as his tail spun round and
round, and sniffing at the air, and whipping his head abruptly
to this and that side, glancing around fearfully in every direction, so the motion made his goatee quiver each time. A
scrawny pensioned-off old village dog, with a crippled leg,
and a scraggly tangled-up hank of hair at the end of his tail,
had sidled up to near that same wagon, as well; which he
stopped short of, first eyeing it from a respectful distance, and
then approached closer, testing the ground with his nose
along the way; till he'd fished out a piece of used-up dry bone
hadn't a trace of gristle nor marrow left to it, but which he

took and run off by himself with anyways, stretching out on
his belly in the dirt, and gnawed on it, in between his paws,
with his head laid over to one side. Meanwhiles, though, the
nag which was in tackle and grown bored of doing nothing,
only snoozing and working his jaws, and idly twirling his ears
in between times, had got into his head he must drop in on the
two oxen, and help put away their dinner of chaff. Only he
hadn't managed to get very far, before an axlehead on his cart
wedged itself into the spokes of the wagon alongside, nearly
capsizing the thing, and causing the horse there to jump its
shafts, and tread on the fetlock of a neighboring animal;
which immediately was up on its hind legs, and neighing and
laddering the air with its foreshanks; thereby so startling the
goat that it leaped out of the cart, and lit on the tail of the
ratty old dog, which bounded away on the three of its sound
legs, and dangling its gimpy fourth, and was set to yelping and
yip-yip-yipping, so cruelly and loud, that the sound of it
could be heard long after the creature was out of eyeshot.

Somehow I managed to work my way through the whole
clutter of carts and animals, and look all of them over carefully, to see if our horses happened to be among them; till finally I arrived at the boozer.

It took a while, though, getting used to, before I quite
made out everything which went on inside the place. This
being revealed to me only gradually and in sequel, bit by bit,
instead of all at once. It was my nose to which first honors
were done, by way of a welcome. For while standing yet in
the doorway, I was hit by the shock of the mixed reeks of
strong spirits, cheap shag smoking-tobacco, and excesses of
human perspiration, all of which vapors had concocted themselves into one tremendous goaty smell, so noisome it set me
to sneezing with a force that popped my ears. So now these
sense organs, too, were well clear to receive the next impres-

sion. Which was of a sudden violent discord of ear-killing shrill shrieks and coarse throaty roarings, and assorted raucous cacklings and windy bleats that I could scarcely credit were human voices at all, and thought might make me stone deaf, before even I set foot beyond the threshold. Which to do, however, I had need of my sight; for if I wasn't after all struck deaf by the uproar, I was for the moment as good as blind, and could make out nothing solid in the darkness. Though, after I cast my eyes about blankly for a bit, I picked out what looked like a long wooden table, off aways inside; which had a lighted tallow candle on it, set in a pottery sconce, and burning a harsh red flame at the wick, with yellow-green-blue-gray rainbow rings dancing round it that took their radiance from the clouds of hot steam and columns of curling smoke trailing everywhere through the murky interior. Now disembodied human features emerged glistening out of the obscure fogs and hazes within—there was noses first: short noses and long noses, pug noses and bulbous noses, all looking like either gherkins or gourds; this was followed by ruffled beavers and whiskers, and cowlicks and quiffs. Which details presently merged together into entire heads: florid mugs of sodden men and blowzy women. Till, at the end, I distinguished whole groups of countryfolk, some of them tottering on their legs, or already fallen; others keeping their feet, though by now on their fourth or fifth round. A pair of well-sloshed gents had separated themselves from the throng, and were locked in a close embrace, lavishing caresses on each other, and declaring their tenderest mutual regard in the extremest rude and shameful language. One of 'em country misses was standing about near at hand, in her bare feet and a short skirt which reached down from her hips to above the turn of her ankle; and in a skimpy embroidered blouse,

which the top was cut very wide, so her breasts showed. She
was in as hugely good spirits as the fond pair of drunkards,
whom she was clapping upon the shoulders by turns, saying
to them good-humoredly: *"Hoo! Knock off, now, knock off, fellers!*
*time ter go home!"* But the neither tosspot seemed able to get
enough of his fellow; and they only hugged tighter, tumbling
onto the floor, and rolling about on it together. Some folks
were sitting on long benches next to the table, beside part-
full liquor bottles and the remainders of snacks of food; two
very fat topers among them, the both "slosh-happy," as we say,
were drinking each other's health; while a bibulous, pipe-
smoking gent, for whom the boozer was plainly a constant
refuge, kept raising his glass to them, and to anybody else as
happened to catch his eye, giving out with merry salutations
of *"Yer v-ery best health, sur!"* all of the time, notwithstanding
nobody was taking notice of him . . . Looking past the crowd
now, I at last caught sight of the landlady, which personage
was an exceeding brisk, lively Jewish matron with a faceful of
black furry moles, and her head covered with a very nonde-
script cloth which was intended for her kerchief. She was
seated behind the counter at the back, and was surrounded by
casks and flagons and snifters and jigger glasses, and by ropes
of bagels and all sorts of savories besides, in the way of hard-
boiled eggs, small withered kippers, and hardened slabs of
cooked liver. The whole time I observed her, she never once
stopped chattering, nor were her hands idle for a level minute, as she addressed customers about payment in cash or in
kind, and was drawing naughts and dashes on a slate the
whiles, against this or that gent's account, with a stub of broken chalk.

I wandered like an outcast about the place, not knowing a
solitary soul there, and now and again tried talking to the peo-

ple—but, well ne'mind! (as Alter might have remarked) 'noughsaid! For I may as well have been addressing the wall, and that's both the short and the long of it!

After a while the crowd thinned out, and folks began to go their ways. So I walked towards the landlady, affecting a swaggering air as I did so, and keeping my whip in plain sight under my arm, coachman's style, so she would be sure to spot it. Now, mind, this was purposeful flimflamming on my part. For as everybody knows, tavernwives is always partial to coachmen, and they like bribing them with free drinks and titbits, and other favors besides. Though this is only good business and perfectly sensible, and is done to encourage coachmen to stop at their places, next time they're carrying passengers. So my whip was as much a recommendation of my character as any letter of introduction, and was certain to obtain me her favor and good opinion. Anyhow, arriving at her side, I proceeded to engage the lady in conversation; which business went along on more or less these lines, so:

"Good e'en to you, ma'am!" —"Well, now, greeting to y'sef, sir, an' a very good year!" —"And where may the man of the house be, ma'am?" —"Well, now, an' what may you be wantin' of that estim'ble man, if y'please, sir?" —"Oh, just things, ma'am, just things . . ." —"Well, now, let's jus' hear of 'em, for I may do as well. P'raps even better!" —"Well, ma'am, p'raps so, p'raps so . . ." And so it went on; and presently we got to talking away very amicably together, about one thing and another. So I went ahead and told her the whole story of my calamity, and of my present quandary; and she comforted me the while, sighing charitably over my troubles; with her chin cupped in her hand, and two of her fingers pressed up against her cheek, and ever and anon exclaiming "My, my!" and "Tsk, tsk!" and "Oh, dearie, dearie!" each time heaving a great sigh in my behalf. And at her prompting I told her also about myself, and who I was and what was my line of trade. She, for her part, did the very same concerning herself, running on and on, at just an awful streak, about all the little secrets of her household, telling about how her husband was such a stumble-bumble fool muttonhead, and about her children and how business was, and so forth . . . So by now we were getting on just like old friends. Why, even better! For it took only a bit of reckoning on both our parts, for us to discover we was actual relations! Collateral line, if you please . . . Second Cousins! —Now ain't that just grand, says we! Whereat there was sudden great Excitement and Exaltations on both sides. For, you see, as it turned out, she's called Hya-'Tryna, after an old auntie of mine by marriage, on granny's side of the family. Well, now, that just did put the crown to it. Because Hya-'Tryna set in to quizzing me all about my own missus now, and about the children, and how each of them was faring on their own account—and especially about that boy of mine, my only son, was made bar mitzvah (*"La! y'don't say, sir"*), and now was growed-up (*"God send long life, sir!"*). Anyhow, we went on in this vein; till her husband happened in. And she being all of a twitter, told him the news straight out, without no shilly-shallying, scarcely stopping to draw breath: "We've a guest, sir!" says she. "Indeed, a welcome guest, sir! Reb Mendele! Who is a dear, dear relation of mine. Well, now, I'll have you know that's *the* Reb Mendele! the Book Peddler, sir! . . ." And she got so puffed up about her connection with me, she'd now took to hugging her sides with both hands, thinking maybe she might otherwise split her seams for pride. And turning on the poor gent as was her husband, she said:

"Ha! y'see? Weren't no byre nor barn which you got me from, sir—as *you* seems to think! No; 'cause praise to Goodness I've no call to be ashame' afore any person in these parts!

An', an' why it is *my* family, sir, and *my* connections which does *yours* proud—an' not t'other way round, as *you* seems to believe, sir!"

*Whew!* thinks I. Now 'tis as well that's so . . . So if Saul went out looking for only a couple of fool donkeys, and he ended up finding a whole kingdom, whyever shouldn't I come up with dear old Hya-'Tryna, whiles chasing after a pair o' broken-down nags?

Hya-'Tryna's husband's distinguishing feature, apart from his droopy nose, was the near-white yellow coloring, some-times called "flaxen," of that little wisp which passed for his beard, and of his sidecurls and eyebrows and remainder of hair. When he was silent he worked his jaws all the time, so he seemed always to be chewing on his tongue; and when he pre-pared to speak, he wetted his lips first. And looking at him licking his lips only brought home what people meant when they said of someone he was a "driveling fool." For the man himself expressed the very notion of Driveling Foolishness in every inch of his person . . . Giving me greeting, he did it in a soft slushy mumble which I could make nothing of, and hon-estly doubted if he even said anything. His bearing and whole manner of comportment plainly told that Hya-'Tryna's mis-ter was in a condition of being "under his missus's pantofles," as we say; and married life was for him only an endless hagride, to which even the fevers of the nine-years' ague were to be preferred every time. As it turned out (for this I learnt only later on), folks in this neck of the woods referred to him by custom as "Hyam-Hanan what's Hya-'Tryna's mis-sus"; whereas his taskmistress was celebrated throughout the region under the dread title of " 'Tryna the Terrible"—and, more notoriously even, under the moniker of "Hya the Hun."

"So where *you* been hiding, sir, eh?" says Hya-'Tryna, sud-denly turning on her husband. "Where in damnation you

been? Well, speak up now! Ooo-oo, I never see such a fool!
Going off and never no word! Think maybe the business run
itself, sir? . . . Oh, never you mind about dear Reb Mendele
over here; for he's kinfolks, and got the same right as ever'-
body to know what a pesky trial you are! Ooo-oo, jus' look at
the man! Lor' save us, but any piece of deadwood may show
more life—pooh! and him a-chawin' on his tongue all the
whiles . . ."

"Bu-but ch'know . . . ," faltered Hyam-Hanan, wetting his
lips first, "w-was y'self say I mus' go fetcher sacker p'taters,
from that 'ere Gavrilo goyfeller—was y'self say so, 'member?"

"An' what of that dainty rebbe which we keeps in such a
high style, s'posed to teach the boy—now, why couldn't've he
goed for them spuds, eh? 'Bout time he earnt his keep anyhow, that one! Feller eats for ten . . ."

"Bu-but ch'know, the rebbe he 'ready took the brindle cow
to pasture, an', an' that 'ere calf—'member?" whined Hyam-
Hanan by way of exculpation. "Jus' like y'self say he shoulder
done—was y'self say so, 'member?"

"Ooo-oo hush up already, just you hush up, sir! Best chaw
some more on that tongue o' yourn, and leave sensible folks
to look after things!" And when Hya-'Tryna had finally finished looking cross at her poor husband, she commenced de-
tailing all the particulars of her troubles to me, with each of
her household, saying if it wasn't for herself how she reckoned the whole place might have turned topsy-turvy, oh just
ages and ages ago: "But never you mind, dear Reb Mendele!"
she kept saying over and over, "for I may speak to you as I
would to my own father (God rest!), for you are kinfolks,
sir—."

I now took it upon myself to try and patch things up, and
mend Hya-'Tryna's husband's lot with his missus. And for the

sake of securing tranquillity, I thought some small deception might be in order. So I made out it was all men which was to blame—not shrinking from including even myself in the general fault; and I proceeded then to heap every conceivable praise on the female tribe as a whole, and especially upon Hya-'Tryna, as the redoubtable nonesuch of the entire sex; for where'd this whole world be (that's assuming even it *could* be, ma'am), without such dear creatures as yourself in it? . . . Till at last Hya-'Tryna softened and relented.

"Oh, bless you, bless you, Reb Mendele!" she says, her face all aglow with kindness now. And she then addressed herself tenderly even to her husband, saying:

" 'Nough o' your tongue-chawin', Hyam-Hanan! Best you go give them dishes and drinkin' glasses a couple wipes, which 'em Esau's yokels been feeding from. —Well, now, I am bound Reb Mendele mus' be good 'n' hungry by now!" she said then, addressing me once more. And she rose up from off of her perch in the taproom, saying, "And I do believe I'm feelin' not half peckish m'self! For we are always suppin' late, come market day. Ah, dearie me, ain't ne'er a worser time! So, Reb Mendele, whyn't you step over to our house. Oh do come along, for you may always feel y'self to home amongs' us, sir! . . ."

We passed out of the taproom directly into a small dark alcove, with a door opposite leading to another alcove, and another door, this time on the left-hand side—by which we finally entered into a fairish-size room, which nevertheless gave a rather mean and incommodious appearance, for being low-built and bare of any flooring, and having very small windows. None of the last-named appurtenances, though, had a sound sheet of glass in it, all the panes being cracked, or patched and eked out with odd splinters; and there were some that the windowpane had been knocked out of alto-

gether, and only a wedge of it still clung to a corner of the
frame, like the one remaining tooth in an old woman's
mouth, and which every current of air caused to vibrate, so it
gave out with a kind of soft, plaintive whirr 'n' hum—
sounded like *Zi-zi-zi-humm . . . zi-zi-humm-zi-humm . . . !*
which was very melancholy to hear. Against the wall, to the
street side, running the length of it, was a row of unpainted
long narrow benches, with a large table in front; and on the
wall facing these was a bed covered with a hillock of quilts
and bedding, and of bolsters and pillows, and of cushions of
oh just every size and shape, heaped willy-nilly into a confused pile which reached to the ceiling. And over to the stove
side was an alcove with a wide bench, which did double duty
as a bed, to sleep on at night. And around the upper walls of
the room were hung all sorts of pictures, covered in cobwebs
and impressed with the carcasses of dead flies, and with
dried-up cockroach eggs and fly shites. Though, notwithstanding the pictures were so blotched, I made out one of 'em
pious "East-wall" representations amongst them—had these
funny rabbits in it, and a lot of fanciful, even more queer-
looking livestock besides, which were part goat and part hart,
or part lion and part ass, or part leopard and part serpent.
And I saw it showed a figure of Haman hanged from a gallows
in the middle of it, done up like a Cossack ataman—except
he had been drawn uncommon tall, so the gallows scarcely
reached to even his shoulders; and it looked more like the gallows was hung from Haman's neck, instead of t'other way
round. And Mordecai, as well, was there, in sidecurls and a
wide Sabbath-bonnet of shaggy fur, and in a particolored gaberdine tied with a sash and a short cloak thrown over it and a
pair of dainty shoes and long hose—the whole impression
being more that of a strolling player in motley than of a saint.
And he was attended by a troupe of big-beaked scant-

whiskered gents, with heavy ringlets dangling at their ears, who stood about him with bumpers raised, toasting his triumph. And the lady Zeresh, too, Haman's wife, was shown carrying something was very like a chamber pot; which maybe accounts for why the flies took the trouble to settle her hash in so cruel fashion; for all there was left of the creature was only half a face and a bit of frontage, and the pot. Nor even Napoleon had escaped ravagement by droppings. Oh, how was mightiness brought low! Flyblown! —Left to hang between villainous, ebon-faced Zuleika, Potiphar's faithless wife, looking pantingly at pious Joseph, and clutching at his garment; and a very narrow, very dirty, very crooked mirror, with an ancient shriveled-up citronfruit and willow branch stuck behind it, from since only heaven knows how many Feasts of Tabernacles back . . .

There was a remarkably ample, thickset miss making herself busy about the place. Able-bodied thing, you could say. Had these fat, creampuffy cheeks on her, and so small a quantity of hair, as sufficed only for the braiding of two stunted queues at the back of her head. She held her elbows pressed stiffly against her sides, and her forearms level, thrust straight before her, like the shafts on a country cart; between which she ambled along, in a kind of a quick shuffling glide, never once lifting her feet from off the ground, and with her head set somewhat forward of the rest of her. Though she managed to get about withal at a smart pace, carrying a tablecloth with dishes and dinner things, to set the table with. Hya-'Tryna had come up to her, and whispered hurriedly into her ear. Whereupon this ample miss abruptly faced about, describing first a perfect arc with her shafts, her head thrust forward a bit, and the remainder of herself plus her feet following close behind. And immediately she was gone from the room . . . A passel of boys and girls, looked to be four of 'em together, weren't paying us no mind and scuffling with one another to the one side, squabbling noisily over a little pug pup bitch, which gave out with the most frightful puling din was past bearing, never mind the awful mess she'd left on the floor back of her. Hya-'Tryna squelched the business at once, coming down all unexpected on the whole bunch, distributing pinches on the quiet, here, there, pulling at an odd ear as well; and she swept up the bit of scruff was the puggy-dog creature, tossing it out of the house. This action left time enough for the children to put the "fig-finger" (thumb 'twixt fore and middle) in one another's faces; and jerking it round, as though to relieve the other of his nose, before dashing severally away to the far corners of the room. It was Hyam-Hanan come in then with the earthen milk-jar, had sour cream in it; which the missus of the house took away from him, and went off on her own to busy herself with, pouring out the contents into a large china bowl at the center of the table, the whiles calling out to everybody it was time for aforemeal's handwashings.

On a sudden then, another little feller broke in upon us; barefooted lad, bit older maybe than the rest, and dressed only in a fringed four-corner weskit and trousers, with no proper gaberdine on him. He'd arrived breathless and in the extreme of wild transport, announcing to the rest: "Oo-oo it's th' rebbe! th' rebbe he's ketched a li'l *Spaw-wo,* in the stable! Oo-oo, he did too! he did, he did!" —Which news struck all the other children as so astonishing it left them speechless, their faces grown very wide with admiration. And before they regained their composure quite, in came a very brusque young man whose nose was for some reason swollen, and who had strikingly thick lips and still very much a look of the stripling about him. He made straight for the tub of house slops, over which he performed very hasty aforemeal's ablu-

tions—and in the next instant he was at table, and he'd a great
chunk of bread already crammed into his mouth which he
commenced chewing on. All this proceeding had been done
by him in a great rush and uncommon urgency, without once
troubling to bestow a glance in anyone's direction, as if loath
to lose a moment by it, lest the food be gone before even he
began. The same ample miss with creampuffy cheeks had
meantime glided back in, prinked out now in her holiday fin-
ery. Hya-'Tryna turned, pointing to the ample miss, and said
to me: "Now, that there's my *Sweet Belle Maid,* Hassia-Gruna,
sir, my eldest gel, y'know!" —Dinner being got under way,
the company went about it in seemly enough fashion, at first,
everyone daintily putting by his spoon, after the one mouthful, and then picking it up again, for the next. By and by,
though, the meal became more animated, not to say clam-
orous. For presently there began a great bustling whirl of
spoon-borne traffic, half a score of spoons being launched
into dizzying motion together, all plying roughly the same
distance, though bound in as many directions at once, betwixt the one bowl of cream on the table and the half-score of
hungry mouths; from which there issued half a score again
of plashy slurpings and lipsmackings, the general trend of
which, as to sound, was more or less of a continuous hearty
*Ww-wh—oooof! wuff-puff!* Nor indeed was I behindhand in this
by much; for my newfound relations would not rest till I
joined in, and kept urging me to it (in between mouthfuls),
with repeated exhortations of: "Now, don' be shy, Reb
Men'le! Dig in, dig in—an' only welcome to it, sir!" So, very
soon I added my own accompaniments to the gustatory sere-
nade at large—though in more decorous manner than the
rest, as I thought, and after the tuneful fashion of *Ww-wh—
eeeef! wiff-piff . . . !* That brusque young man, though, of the
swollen nose, now I did notice he, as well, was no laggard in

putting it away; and he was easily doing the work of ten good trenchermen such as himself, at very least. So, not surprisingly, he was the first also to scrape bottom; uncovering with his last spoonful the little picture of a bird painted inside the bowl. The meal being thus abruptly terminated, it fetched from him such a sigh of luxuriousness, as only uttermost repletion may bring; and he took time out now to goggle dazedly about him. When, suddenly, he'd fixed a glassy eye on me; and he shot his hand across the table, rising slightly from his seat as he did so, and said: "Hem! Why, how-do, sir! I've a notion I know you, sir! Pray, may one know y'name, sir?" So I told him, as was only proper I should. Though it did appear to rock him some. For, next thing, he'd struck his forehead exclaiming:

"Reb Mendele!! . . . Psssh! Now, that ain't by chance *the* Reb Mendele? The Book Peddler? Gracious, but who ain't heered on you, sir! Was myself once'd the privilege even of pu'chasin' one of 'em gracebooks o' yourn. From y'own estim'ble self, sir! In Glupsk, sir! Paid nor lesser'n halfer goldpiece for it—and wu'th ever penny, too, if I may say!"

"Reb Mendele's kinfolks of mine!" coos Hya-'Tryna positively melting now with happiness over the connection. And pointing at the stripling with the swollen nose, she added: "Now, Reb Mendel, this here's our rebbe! one's been teachin' my li'l Hosea, y'know!—Osee love!" she next coos to the little feller was minus the gaberdine. "Osee you jus' show Reb Mendele here whatcher know—huh? Pl-e-ease? Aw, don' be embarrassed, Oseekins! For Reb Mendele's a nice nunclewuncles, an' he won't bite, I pw-o-mise . . ."

Osee, though, only sat pouting, the while burrowing his finger farther up his nose. And then, jerking his shoulders, he said: "No I cain't! . . . I'm 'bawwwasst! I'm 'bawwwasst! . . . Am too! yes I am!"

"Pray, but how old is the little feller (an' long life), ma'am?" says I to the boy's mother.

"My Osee? Bless him, sir, why he's aw-ll gwo'd up! Ain't you, Osee love! Was bar mitzvah springtide last, he was (an' long life!)—now wasn't you, Oseekins!"

"Well, Osee!" says I, cupping the boy's cheeks in my hand. "Say, I bet you do know what's the Scripture portion for this week—eh, Osee?"

At which point a sudden chorus broke in from all sides, with calls of "You tell 'im, Osee! Atter boy, you tell 'im now—."

Osee remained mute though, showing no response other than to goggle at the rebbe—which gent was then engaged in bubbling chunky lips at the boy, miming a string of silent *b-b-b-'s* . . .

"B-b-b . . . ," says Osee, echoing bubbly lips back at the rebbe—the rounds of bubblings resolving themselves, at last, into a cry of "Oo-oo I know! . . . s' *B-B-Bullox!*" this being followed by wild pealing shrieks of *"Bullox!! B—u—u—l—lox!!!"*

"Why Balak it is!" says I, thinking to give the lad a leg up. "Only tell me this, Osee. Now this feller Balak, what'd he want to do—eh, Osee?"

The boy'd fixed his eyes on the rebbe again, still looking for deliverance from that quarter. Which quarter again obliged, licking his fingertips this time, then popping his lips, as though making to spit . . .

"Oo-oo I know!" says Osee, "s' *lick'ty-spit . . . lick'ty-spit . . . !*" This again followed by deafening screaks, in the way of *"licktyspit!! . . . licktyspit!!!"*

"Hem! Tha's *lickspittle,* Osee!" says the rebbe, who took upon himself now to speed the lad along, saying, "Only lickspittle *who,* Osee? Who'd Balak say to lickspittle? For tha's the whole p'int, Osee!"

"Oo-oo I know! . . . th'*Webbe!! th'Webbe—E—E—E!!!*"

"Psssh—*Muttonhead!*" returns the gentleman last named— modestly declining the honor; though out of all patience with the lad anyway, saying, "But WHO, muttonhead! Lickspittle WHO!"

"Oo-oo I know! . . . s'th'*Juice!! th'J—u—i—c—e!!!*"

"*The Jews?* Hm! Well, child, maybe so!" says I, patting the boy on the cheek. "But 'noughsaid, Osee! For that was smart as paint, that was! Why, it's near word perfect, if I may say! . . . My, my! But ain't that somethin'—."

Hya-'Tryna was beaming, and plainly in very heaven. She had her hands resting amidriffs, in such an attitude that, would it speak, it would say, Oh blest! blest the belly as bare so excellent a fruit! As to the boy's papa, well he chawed at his tongue the while, and was looking uncommon pleased, as well.

After supper, Hya-'Tryna talked over my business with me, settling the matter so: "Well, now, sir, there's my goyfeller—that 'ere Yanko feller, which's over to pasture with the pairer our hosses right now. Now, he's s'pose to be back with the an'mals in, oh, say two maybe three hours. So, I been thinkin', Reb Mendele, how on the morrer, maybe you mount up on the one animal, an' my mister here on t'other, and then, why, the both you ride out to where them carts o' yourn and your frien's is, and hitch the hosses up; an' then why you fetch the whole caboodle back here, plus th' wares. After that, we'll think on what t'do. But meanwhiles, though, whyn't you stay amongs' us for the night; an' ketch up on a lit- tle sleep. For you're most welcome to, sir. Now, that there's the bed, Reb Mendele, which has got all the fixins on it al- ready. So, whatcher say, huh?"

"Now that is kind of you, ma'am, most kind!" says I. "And I do thank you for it—oh, *tut,* but I do, ma'am, I do! And I should so like to oblige as well. But y'do see, ma'am, I mean if ever I drop into all them soft pillows—and oh my! into all that featherbeddin' as well—why I think I shan't never be made to get out of it. No, no, I'm certain of it! For heaven knows how long I may sleep in such a thing! And time presses, ma'am! Oh but it does, ma'am, it does! So, another time p'raps (an' God send), when next I come visitin', with the wife my missus, and also the children, why I might just take my chances then, maybe throw caution to the four winds, take leave of the world and all that's in it (as 'twere), commit my spirit to His tender Mercy; and I may just throw myself down on to this couch of luxury, and then wallow and wallow in the eiderdown, till even Heaven's own Angels come and fetch me away—an', an' . . . well, anyhow, that's my promise to you, ma'am. Word o' honor!"

"An' warm welcome! is what I say. Morer merrier, sir!" returned Hya-'Tryna, very kindly, and with ready hospitality. "And jus' see you bring *all* the children, sir. Oh, an' also the wife your missus, Jochebed-Sossia, as well, y'hear? Only for now, do take this here one small cushion 't least, so you may bed down with it over on the sleeping bench, in the inglenook there, by the stoveside . . ."

And giving me goodnight then, Hya-'Tryna retired, saying to me, as she went: "Now, you be sure and sleep well, Reb Mendele! Nor don't worry y'self none, sir, about over-sleepin'. For time come, my mister's up betimes—early cockcrowing—and he'll just make certain you're woken timely, sir!"

# 10

HYA-'TRYNA'S A DEAR, dear creature, and an exceptional pious Jewish lady, as I've no doubt—though I can't say the bedbugs which she keeps were the better for it. I mean they were the most savage, bad-tempered things after their kind I have ever met. For I had only to put my head on that sleeping bench, and they were all over me and the battle joined, with neither side giving the other any quarter. Why it was tooth and claw between us from the start—that's to say, they bit and I scratched. But for all I scratched and jumped about, they only went on creeping and biting, letting me know with every nip, "Now, now, it won't do, you ack'ing up so—no indeed, sir, it will not! for be it only boards, the bed's ours; so best you ack' civil, as befits a guest, and on'y let yesself be bit!" —Well I groaned and I gritted my teeth, and only redoubled my scratching. Though there seemed to be no end of it. For it was bite 'n' scratch . . . bite 'n' scratch, nor never a letup the whole blessed time. Why, there was hordes of 'em on me— and me, er . . . why I was on the pil . . . on the *pillow* by golly! Damnation it *was* the pillow! —Away with it . . . away, I say! Whereat the rickety bed of boards, which anyway had been rocking the whiles on the three of its legs (there being no fourth), fell over with a terrific *ker-plump!* splintering the jug of "fingerwater" beneath it, so the shock of it caused a general panic amongst the population of black beetles inhabiting the floor—which roachy critters were certainly legion, for they gave out with an astonishing volume of rustlings, as they scrabbled away in retreat before the deluge. The alcove was all spindrift now, with feathers from the pillow, which had split open from the pummelings I'd been giving it; and bits of feathery down had settled on my eyes, and got up my nose. And the bench beneath me meanwhile continued to teeter-totter, giving out with endless scrapings and creakings, as I only tossed about on it. For there was scarcely an inch of me hadn't been set a-twitching, and wasn't in throes. But the biting never did stop, and I was gone near out of my senses for it. And the awful bedbuggy smell, too, had grown strong as to be past bearing. So finally I grew sick of the whole business and I got out of bed, making for an open window, where at least I might draw a breath of clean air. And there I lingered the while, thinking to profit additionally by the occasion, and to look out upon God's world for a bit.

*WHISHT!* —STILLNESS EVERYWHERE . . . And the Moon. A bright wafery circle riding tranquilly in the night sky. Her gilt, shining countenance shadowed by a thoughtful frown. That earnest look cast a sweet melancholy over me, and spoke to my heart; and each glance she returned for mine, drew forth part of my soul; and my thoughts flowed out to her, as of their own accord, one from the other, in a rising tide. Thoughts of wretchedness merely, of a lifetime's afflictions and griefs; of every kind of mortification, some small, some great—some anciently borne, some recent and fresh. And I began to blubber pitifully, as an ailing child might to its mother—*Oh, ma, oh, I'm hurtin', ma*—. Oh the sheer hardscrabble, the cold, bleak misery of it! And as if the troubles and heartaches weren't enough, you're made abject for it, as well, a thing put upon and scorned. And these unending vexations, come by in only an ordinary way, are but a prelude to calamity. For though you may barely be sucking wind, and have only breath enough to keep a feather fluttering at your nostrils, you're grudged even the petty scrap of careworn existence which is left to you, and might pass maybe for a life—

*Oh, ma, I'm hurtin', oh, I'm hurtin', ma*—. And all the while the moon looked down, the same thoughtful frown still shadowing her effulgent face; and I imagined how she tried to comfort me—*Sssh! Oh, hush, child, hush! For it's no more than as things are* . . . But I only sobbed the more for it and lay my head down in the crook of my arm, turning my naked cheek towards her, that she might see—oh! that at least she might see what had been done to me— *Oh, ma, I'm hurtin', ma*—. And my eyes brimmed with tears, and I cried out in the dark for some living soul might come and comfort me. But there was only silence, and no one came. Though now a small dog stationed itself in the street, its tail tucked between its legs. It stood craning its neck, and commenced to bark into the night sky at the moon. But she only went her ways unperturbed, that thoughtful frown ever on her face, and made nothing of the dog's howlings . . .

I was grown easier now, heartened somehow by a feeling which gave me hope and consolation together, without needing to be put into words. It's the pious feeling takes hold of a gent, after he's done unbosoming and bewailing his lot to God, the while having himself a good blub over it. Same feeling as leaves you all doughy inside, and so filled with terrific boundless goodwill, you're ready to burst of it, wanting nothing better than to give away the shirt from your back, and grab hold of Creation, and be hugging it to your bosom, and kissing it, for sheer love of everything which is in it.

Though about bedbugs, now you see they are as much God's creatures as any of us is. Nor is smelling bad to be held against them. For that's more in the way of misfortune than a fault. As for biting other folks, well that's to be put down to force of habit. Or it's in their nature maybe; but they don't do it on account of any ill will or only wickedness. And if they're maybe a bit bloodthirsty, as well, it's no more than by way of making a living. Which isn't all that blameworthy anyway, if you only think awhile on it. Besides which, it wasn't as if this were the first time I had dealings with the pesky things. I mean, there's no such thing as a Jewish gent as hasn't had to do with bedbugs, and which given half the chance won't regale you for hours, with the most hair-raising stories of encounters he's had with them . . .

So this was the turn my thoughts took, when finally I went away from the window and retired for the night—though not before I'd again at least recited "Into thine hand I commit my spirit"; after which—well there's nothing much to tell after that. Because I fell asleep instantly. And if there's one thing I hate telling about, it's dreams. Never did take much stock in dreams, anyhow!


WASN'T EASY GETTING up crack of dawn next morning. I was just a mess of aches and pains all over. Though it was dire need which in the end did rouse me from my bed. Matter of momentum, don't you know. For Jewish folks are always on the go because of it. Live by it, you might say. And it is dire need which winds them up to it, and keeps them running about and in a sweat all the time. Only let a Jewish gent wind down, even for a bit, and directly he'll drop in his tracks and just lay there, with no more motion in him than if he was a dead man. It is only holidays that his aches will catch up with him, for it's then he has got the time to be sick . . .

So it was dire need got me out of bed, and set me on my feet; and it was dire need put me on horseback; and it was dire need whose dead hand finally whacked me across the back, so I was on my way with that same Hyam-Hanan at my side which is Hya-'Tryna's mister. For it's only getting started which is hard. Though once a Jewish gent's spring's sprung,

he's all but unstoppable, and scooting about the place like butter in the pan. Why he'll be shinnying up walls at need, and
getting himself into all sorts of tight spots, as well, where he
oughtn't never to have got himself into in the first place, and
wasn't invited to be in by anybody anyways. In short I was
myself once more, and good as ever.

Well, there's no getting to the bottom of 'em!—Jewish
folks I mean. At least that's according to the adage. And if
everybody keeps saying so, there must be some truth in it, I
suppose. Take Hya-'Tryna now. Well, I was dead certain she'd
made so much of me, on account only of myself alone. I
mean, isn't every day that relations previously unbeknownst
to folks will drop in on them like that. Never mind that said
relations are learned gents, as is on a familiar footing with
pious books, and it is a honor anyhow to be rubbing shoulders
with them. Now, familiar footings and rubbing shoulders,
that's something which is greatly prized amongst us. Why
even a Jewish gent of Quality, if he has got any business at a
Government House, say, well he never is above getting on to a
familiar footing first with the janitor of the place—which latter gent, of course, is all the time rubbing shoulders with the
high-muckety-mucks within—and he'll be talking up a blue
streak with him, and go away altogether pleased with himself
then, thinking: Hm! So far so good. And that there janitor,
he's a right friendly feller, too . . . Well, anyhow, rubbing
shoulders in the right places, and getting onto familiar footings with the right sorts, gets a feller all kinds of rewards.
Like the caretaker in one of them newfangled Government
Schools in a Jewish town (the kind of gent only gets called the
"shammes" if he does the cleaning up in a proper Jewish
heder), well the handle he generally gets hung on him for it is
"His Wu'ship the Principal"; and the feller who comes round
to the house now and then with the mail, well in Jewish

parishes he gets to be "His Wu'ship Officer o' Posts"; and the other one, who scarcely does anything all day long, only sits behind a cage looking sour, he practically ranks as "His Wu'ship the Postmaster General." In a word, there's never a rabbi's housekeeper won't hold court as well . . . Anyway, maybe you remember back then, at supper, the whiles I was staring at that Ample Miss? Well it occurred to me at the time, how she was pretty well of marriageable age now, and ripe to be brought under the wedding canopy. So I kind of surmised then that the extreme happiness which my presence seemed to inspire in Hya-'Tryna was because I might be of use in making a match for her eldest. I even entertained the notion, she maybe had an eye on myself, as the principal in the proceeding. I mean otherwise there didn't seem to be any sense to it, the gel being got prinked up special in fancy dress, on a sudden. The truth, however, was only divulged next morning, during Hyam-Hanan's discourse with me, whilst we were riding along together. He seemed altogether too preoccupied with my boy was just bar mitzvah; and I remember him going on about it for some time, till at the end his conversation took the following turn:

"But ch'know . . . 'bout that there lad o' yourn bein' bar mitzvah. Fine thing, bar mitzvah. Very . . . H'm! But ch'know, to his age, I were 'ready wed. Fine thing, bein' wed. Very . . . H'm! But ch'know, my missus she wun't let me sleep on 'counter it.—'O Gawd! gimme a husbin for the gel,' she say. 'A sonnen-lawr, sir! So when you gonner gimme a sonnen-lawr, Hyam-Hanan? Oh you are a wretch, sir! Whatcher think, sleepin' gonner get our gel wed?' —So, what you think on her, Reb Men'le? My gel, you seed her. Fine gel. Very. Time maybe she wed. So whatcher think? For you are ed'cated, sir. Know aller 'bout such things. An' she do keep fine house. Very . . . H'm! But ch'know, my missus, she think the worl' on you, Reb Men'le.

Wun't let me sleep on 'counter it. Yestiddy abed, bout y'self
she say, *'Why he plain come outer the blue, Hyam-Hanan! Mark my
words. Plain outer the blue! For ain' never no ill which no good come
outer it.'* —'Cause, if wasn't for you losin' them hosses, Reb
Men'le, you wun'ter come outer the blue. An' warm welcome, sir! as the missus say . . . H'm! But ch'know, 'bout that
lad o' yourn, bein' bar mitzvah. Fine thing, bar mitzvah. Very.
But ch'know, to his age I were 'ready wed . . ."

And the while we were chattering so, we arrived finally to
where I had left the wagons the other day. So I made for my
own cart first; and directly I was satisfied nothing was out of
place (God praise!), I proceeded next to where I supposed
Alter's cart to be, and found it too in place and apparently in
good order. Thinking then to lift up the tarpaulin which covered Alter's goods, I had scarcely put my hand to it, when on
the instant I froze. For I received the strong and very sensible
impression that, only that moment, something had stirred beneath my touch. When however the tarpaulin next rose,
seemingly under its own volition, by golly I must have jumped
at least a dozen feet straight into the air, only for the sheer
fright it gave me. But by and by I saw a head emerge from underneath the tarpaulin and—O my Lord! but he were a sweet
sight! For I beheld, as big as life, nor worser for the wear,
apart from his head being bound by a cloth, the cherished features of my dear, good friend, Reb Wine-'n'-Candles Alter.

# 11

THE STORY OF what happened to Alter, of whither he had got
to, and whence he'd sprung from so unexpectedly, and what
the cause was of his head being bound up—concerning all

these circumstances, we received a true and unimpeachable account from Alter's own lips, so:

"S'ANYWAY, I'M OUT huntin' up them hosses. And I am looking all around for 'em don'cher know. Only hard's I look, ain't no hosses . . . Well, weren't to worry about, I told myself. For I only reckon the pair hike off a piece together. Nor I blame 'em for it. What with all that prime grazing might be had in the wood, and cool shady places besides. For gener'ly live-stock's same as your human folks is (saving the difference), which I never know one wasn't only hankerin' after greener pastures. So I kep' on looking, the whiles getting futher and futher in amongst the copses and trees to do it. But for all I chase about the place, it din't do no good. Wasn't a trace of the creatures anywhere. Well this *were* a pretty pass, and I couldn't think what to do next. When on a sudden, I say *Wassat?* . . . For seem I hear kinder a sof' rustly sound, come from over to the yonder side of the gully. So I'm down the one side next, and shinnying up t'other, and I'm cutting in and out amongs' the clumps of trees again; but I done no bet-ter this sider the wood than the other. By now, though, it were gone dusk and growed dark. Well it did look a bad business, and no mistake. But on a sudden, there's that sound ag'in . . . *Wassat?* And I'm zigzagging round the trees once more, this way and that, in one clump, out t'other. But still I don't make head nor tail on the neither animal. Well I begun to feel vexed now. For seem only a fool's errand, to be scooting about in the dark so, chasing after that pairer phantom nags, wasn't even there . . . And the while I'm puzzlin' over the thing—confound! but there it were again. That some sound! This time only, I make out it's a sorter steady crunch-crunch! as were of footfalls moving along the fores' floor. Black Deuce

take them dumb beasts . . . Oh, jus' wait till I ketched up
with 'em! For it were them, I were sure on't! Lay odds if
'tweren't . . . So I'm off again, madder'n a butcher with a
meat cleaver, and oh just swearin' up a blue streak; the whiles
I'm tearing round stands of trees and breaking through the
undergrowth follerin' after that sound. By and by I reach a
thicket, was away off middler nowhere, which I knew they
was back of. So I creep up on the quiet, round t'other side,
and I'm thinkin': Gotcher! y'blame flyblown bag a bones.
Damnation! So whatcher think? Were a cow! Blame or'nary
dumb cow's all it was. Stray from the village herd, prob'ly.
Never knew a cow but didn't do that . . . Well, 'noughsaid of
that. For about now I didn't know if I'm comin' nor goin';
nor where the blazes I even was. Though only standing idle,
that wouldn't do neither. So I put m'self in the hands of
Prov'dence and proceeded my ways, bending my steps just
any whither. And the whiles I'm walking about troubled so, I
make out a crimson glow up ahead, look maybe to be a campfire. Though when I reach it, weren't scarcely anything left of
it, except coupler live embers and some wood bits were still
smoldering. I see though the grass was trod down all round;
and there was bread scraps and eggshells, and scatterings as
well of onion and garlic parings everywhere on the ground,
and just a mess of tore-up old bits of dirty rag and tattered
clouts strewed all about the place. Look like a whole mob of
folks'd camped there. Band of Gypsies, most like. Though
that were a bad sign. On account Gypsies is incline' to bein'
sticky-fingered, and always is pinching what ain't necessary
theirs. Hosses, amongs' other things . . . Anyways, the whiles
I'm looking over the place, on a sudden I started . . . *Wassat?*
For seem I heered a voice callin' from away off somewheres.
And the thought come to me—why maybe's Reb Mend'le
calling to me? Well I wasted no time, and I was on my feet and

chasing about amongs' the copses and trees again. When suddenly the calling stop. Then it start up again, and I recommenced follerin' it. The calling come in fits and starts now;
and me why I'm chasing after it in fits and starts as well,
lookin' to get my bearings. Only the nearer I come to it, the
more dreadfuller it soun'. Like as someone's sore beset, and
in mortal fear of his life. For I swear it got so very dreadful, it
send the cold chills up and down my spine . . . Though
notwithstandin' I got the wind up so, I weren't about to stop,
and only pressed on, the whiles I stayed alert to any trouble
may come my way, and took care to keep my footing in the
darkness. Then, after a while, an abandon' old tavern come
into view; reg'lar sprawling wreck of a place, so ramshackle it
seem like any breeze might knock it down in a heap. Well
somehow I didn't like the looker it; so I go off on a side and
get down behind a bush, back of a screen of branches. And as
happen to be a broken limb to hand there, I also pick it up
from the ground. Just in case, y'understand. Then I set quiet,
figurin' to bide my time, and see first what happen. And the
while I wait so, the worst things run through my mind; cruel
stories, about all 'em cutthroats hereabout and the thieves
they got over Glupsk ways. When I hear a horrific howl which
fair make me jump out of my skin. And it did too seem to
come from that raddled old wreck of a boozer. It was the cry
of pure terror; and it lay a-holt on my heart, and it seem to
draw me to it. For before I knew what I was about, I'm already standing beside the old tavern, without never remembering how I got there. And the whole whiles I kep' thinking
over and over——Why it's one our own, it's one our own!
Why, maybe's even Reb Mend'le! And who's to say it
weren't? Oh, it were fearful to think on . . . But ne'mind. For
I reckon it even cost me my life, I must get to the bottom of
it. Got this stubborn streak, you see. So it come natural . . .

Anyhow, I come up v-ery ginger 'longsides the place, which
the walls of look nigh hand to tumblin' down, they was so
rotted through from old age. And I stood so for a time, the
whiles I kep' my ear cocked. Though weren't long before I
heered a sound, sorter like a muffled-up voice within. Well it
don't take even half a minute but I'm inside, which making
my way through on tiptoe appear a very considerable-size
room, and nary even a whisper for sign of living creatures
about. But it were too dead dark to go poking about blind that
way. So I rummage inside my pockets for a box I rec'lect still
had coupler matches in it; all which but the last I struck, one
after t'other, but couldn't get lit. Well my fingers was shaking
now I struck the last one, which finally did ketch fire though.
And the instant it flare up, why in that same breath there was a
shout come sudden, from t'other end somewhere. Then it
went out and there was only the dead darkness, and silence
again. So there weren't no choice but I must poke along some
more in the dark, over to where that yelling come from. Well
I'm making my way towards the other end of the boozer,
when I trip over something—feel like a body! Well, sir, that
did put the wind up me so, near every hair on my head turn
handsprings. Then happen the moon come up, and it shone in
through a broken window over in a corner; which by its light I
make out I'm standing in a ratty hole of a back room got no
door to it, and there's a gent laid out on the floor, trussed up
hand and foot, like a sheep, and looking the color of death and
ready to expire, the way his breath come so short. —'Oh,
praise be!' the poor feller cries out to me. 'Oh praise be
you're come, sir! Please, mister, oh please untie me. Else I
shall be a goner for sure! For the rope's chafed clean through,
'most near the bone, and I'm burning up for the thirst . . .'
—'But who's done this to you, sir?' I say whilst I cut way his
bonds with my pocketknife. —'The Black Deuce bust him,'

feller says; 'and do double for his pa, and pa's pa!' And he kep' up his swearing, the whiles he get hisself limber again: 'Goniffin' Rogue! Oh, he's a reg'lar apostate bastid, that 'un . . . !' —'Huh?' I exclaims, looking sharp at the feller; 'Goniff!? Rogue!? . . . Why, you don' mean to say the man's a actual thief?' —'Oh yes I do, mister!' he says. 'You name it he take it. Goniff's his moniker, an' thievin's his trade. Ain't nothing in this worl' which the rogue won't pilfer. Why, weren't only today the rascal went and stoled a pair of hosses . . . ' —Well, now, that made me sit right up an' take notice. And I begun now to question the feller more closely, describing our hosses, exac'ly the way they look. Turn out it was them, all right. Oh I knowed it! Why it were plainer 'n crystal. For it appear a whole wagon train of vagabonds was camped down recent, by that fire I found back in the woods. And a dainty gang of gentry they certainly was, I dare say! No question but somebody from amongs' that buncher layabouts come acrost our hosses whilst taking the air, and filched 'em. But now I'd got a fair notion of which road they took, I was determined I should foller them thievin' rapscallions straighterways, and ketch 'em up. But that feller he wouldn't hear of it, and puts all kinds of reasons in my way, why I shouldn't go. For he's scared on my account. Because that bastid Goniff why he'd as soon kill a man as look at him. And the riffraff which tags along after him in cover't carts, they's most as bad as him. But I couldn't afford to let the matter rest. For there was no way which I could live without a hoss. —'No, no, my mind's made up!' I says. 'Come what may, I must go after them. What's more, I'm determined to. For it's a insult, and I won't never stand for it. By golly, ain't nobody ever spit in my porridge which get away with it. So best if I set out direc'ly, for ain't a minute to lose. But y'self, sir, now whyn't you stay hole' up here the whiles and you rest up good. For God send I come back with the hosses, the both us can mount up and ride outer here together . . .' —So that's what I told to the feller, which somehow I took a shine to because . . . well, ne'mind why, for I just liked him. Anyhow, when I done with explaining, I shouldered my pegs and was immediately under way.

"Now, that old tavern happen was tuck into a woody hollow, just below the junction where the main road split up; which the one branch take you direct past Glupsk, and on over to the west country. And the other, it loop down aways an' under; and then it head to the counties south of it. Well, that were where I had them rabble headed to. South! So that were the road I follered. And you betcher I didn't walk that road—no; I chase down it, fast as only I could. An' vexed? Dreadful! Why coulder tore that thievin' scoundrel into more pieces than even a herring on a trencher at a paupers' banquet. For God knows I got trouble enough, without being lef' stranded penniless, back ender nowhere, minus a hoss. Well 'noughsaid. For my legs begun to give out and I couldn't keep up that perishing pace no longer, and presently my stomach commenced kicking up the worst rumpus, and was only clamoring for nourishment. For weren't no joke; keeping that Fast all the midsummer day long, nor breaking it, even the end were away past due. Oh it weren't no good! And then I was thinking, what use were it being run off my feet like that, and them fine gentry having a considable start on me; and being horsedrawn besides, the whiles I'm only ambling along at scarce even a footpace anymore. No, it were hopeless. Oh I'd never ketch 'em up. Though it buck me up, thinking how if a wagon happen come by, maybe he give me a lift. And it's as well the moon were out. For I could see most as good as daylight by it. So I kep' walking. And even it wasn't nowheres as fast as before, least I was movin' and not standin' idle. Kep' my eyes skinned, too, an' half hanging outer my head, looking out for them gentry. Though meanwhile wasn't a soul on the road. But I only stick to it, and press on. See, when I set my mind to a thing, I won't give it up. Ain't my nature to . . . well ne'mind. So anyhow, the time pass. And seem I do hear a rattle of wheel-'n'-harness at last . . . but Confound damnation! Wretched things was coming the wrong ways—*away from,* not towards, where I was headed. Oh talk only about your rotten luck! Well I try and hail 'em anyways. First the one wagon, then the next, and the next one after that . . . but they was too drunk to even notice. Well I was aggervated now. Not jus' vexed, mind, but aggervated! Fact the thing got to me so, even set me to chasing down that road apace again, same as before. Well I'd traveled quite a ways, and time were getting on, so it were pretty late. But I still hope for some country cart may come up from behind, and give me a lift. When I spot another string of wagons up ahead. Only Damnation! they was coming towards me too. By golly this time I weren't giving up. No; I'd turn my pockets out and give ever'thing to the first driver take me where I want to go to. So that give me confidence, and I break into a trot to close up the distance. But Bedam! if them carts don't even look to be moving. Why they was only setting there and not budging at all.

"*Helluverthing!*—So help me I coulder . . . well, ne'mind what I coulder done. For by time I come close enough to give them a hail, I see the whole lot's a buncher cover't carts, one back of t'other, in tandem, strung out like a caravan. Well I stop. For the first notion come to mind was, these must be them traveling gentry I been chasing. So what to do? H'm! I see there was a hedge of trees, though, which run for a bit alongside the road. So I nip down backer it, and make my way for'ards till I come abreast of them; and I get down behind a bush to have a gander, close range. Uh-huh. Were them all

right. Yess'r. Had all the earmarkings. Fact, right now the
whole packer them rabble was lounging round the one big
wagon 'crost the ways, look to be broke down. Thing must've
throwed a wheel, way she heel over . . . And them travelin'
vagrants; why you never seed sucher quantity of beggar'y,
dirty-lookin' scarecrow all at once. For weren't a one wasn't
in tatters; nor even a garment amongs' 'em was clean nor
whole . . . And the all'em being in the one place like that!
Why, there was menfolks and womenfolks mixed up together, and old folks and young folks, and babies in arms and
at breast . . . And such noise? Awesome! Coulder brung
down the roof with it. What with all of them women was
yelling at the topper their lungs, screeching at their infants
and slapping 'em about; so they was set to only bawling the
worser for it. And a clutcher folks was being loud, only jus'
milling about, nexter the throwed wheel plus axle looked
busted. Which itself was the cause of no inconsidable racket,
what with aller them hammerings and bangings-away and
dreadful blasphemings, come from the gents was set to
mendin' it. To say nothin' of the unwanted guff, which these
same working gentry was getting from those were only bone
idle. And for the rest, it weren't but only pandemonical tohu-
bohu all round. Why, that whole place weren't fill' up, but
only with bad-tempered cussings, and punchings-about, and
whingeings and blubberings, mixed in with wild hoots of
laughter . . . But then, of a sudden, I prick up my ears. For
amongs' all the commotion, I pick out what some them folks
was sayin': 'Dang it all! . . . S'all on counter the new hoss!
Stinkin' fool nag! Ain't wuth a lick even!' —'Yeah, see way't
pull ter the one side aller time? Done it fer spite, I expec'!
An' drive t'other an'mal nigh crazy, with them shenanigans.
Dumb bonehead, pullin' off th' road like that! Oughter be put
out of his mis'ry, if you asks me!' —'Yeah, that is sure some

piecer hossflesh, we got landed wiff! And who you s'pose we got to thank for't, gen'men? Fybush, tha's who! . . . Hey, Fybush! Come 'ere! Blame bastid redhead!' Well the whiles they was talkin' so, this other feller come along, so mad, look fit to bust fur it: 'Shuddup!' he say. 'Loudmouffs! . . . Shitebuckets! Buncher lamebrains! Cain't see, cain't even drive! Cain't do nuffin' right! . . . 'Cept maybe it's sleeping and putting away the grub!' —Well, he were a v-ery nasty article, that one. Yess'r. Tough young ruffian. Had these big shou'ders on him, and this mopper flaming hair. And he was a-huffin' and stomping about; poking them hammy fists of his in everybody's faces. Well 'noughsaid. For the meanwhile I been looking the place over. An' that's when I spot him, Reb Mend'le! See, he was standing by hisself alone, back of the las' wagon, so I didn't chanced to see him at fu'st an'—Huh!? . . . Who was standin', y'asks? Who was stan—? Why your own little jade, sir! . . . So then, lessee . . . Yeah, well that jade o' yourn, it appear'd he been took out of harness recent. For all his trappings was in place yet. Which from the shape of the bit, and the way the straps was laid 'crost his back, I judge he been in double harness, as the off-hoss, to foller after the nearside animal's lead. But that little feller, he were too many for 'em, Reb Mend'le! Done you proud! For he'd took that bit between his teeth, and he make *hisself* lead hoss i'stead. On'y imagine . . . *Whoo-oo-oop and hoo-roar!* Oh, yes! for't do look like he led 'em a very pretty dance i'deed! —The whiles, though, I were put in minder my own nag. Now, where might that little rackabone be? But I see then she were standin' backer that wagon, same as yourn. Only tied up to it by a rope. Well now, I din't waste no time on'y in chawing the business over. No. First off I look round for a solid lengther lumber, got a good heft to her. Which happen were to hand, so I pick it up. Then out come the jackknife. And the whiles them vagabon' gentry was so preoccupy' by the busted axle, I commence to inchworming myself along, kinder working my way roundabout, over acrost to where the back wagon were, on the end. Well it don't take only a jiff to cut the mare loose an' hoist myself on her back. So I'm riding away with the both animals now. And it appear all the three us was home free, and weren't even nobody was the wiser. Except happen one of them rogue vagrants ketched sight of us and he kick up the worse squawk. Which set the whole of the rabble by the ears; so the lotter them was all in a uproar now. And I notice too how that redhead feller—that's the hufty young lout I told about—well he was up like a shot then, and come tearing down the road after us, like th' Black Deuce hisself was at his back. Fact by the time I look, I see he were hot at our heels, and within only a ace of ketchin' up. So I took to whupping up the hosses. On'y they scarce don't need no promptin', for once. For they both was fair postin' like the wind this time. So that redhead feller begun to fall considable futher behind; so it look again like we was home free. Well so far so good. But Confound! for just then my mare, she up and founder. Which happen on account she got her feet all tangle up in them straps, which your own little jade, sir, was trailin' from his breechings. See, I was in too much a hurry back there to get all the harnessing off of him. So the upshot was kinder a hitch in the proceeding, as you may say. Though between whiles that redhead feller come pelting up, with murder in his eye. Well he look about as mad as a bull in a heat tantrum, way he come charging head down. So we grapple. Well the both us grip the other round the middle. And we commence to put a pow'ful squeeze lock on the other; the whiles each feller try to throw t'other to the ground. Though the whole time we was only mum, nor neither us exchange one word betwixt us. For we was too furious to talk. Well we was panting and a-heavin' each other about, till we both tumble down in the dirt. Though we never once let go, and only kep' that same grip on t'other, so our ribs near snap in two from it. Well it were a reg'lar dingdong dustup. And at first I'm on top and squeezing him, so he turn crimson and all his cords and veins stand out. Then it's t'other way around, and him doing the squeezing. But there's plenty of fight in me yet. So I chop him where a gent's incline' to be tender. Right below his briskets. Well that jab to his groin, look to have done him. For he went WHOO-OOFF! and he let go. And he appear to fall away in a faint. So I let him be. Which weren't only what he wanted. 'Cause it were all a ruse you see. For that feller was v-ery art- ful. I give him that. And the while my back was turned, he whupped out his own jackknife, from insides his britches pockets. Well I seed it and I say: 'Whoo-oop! my young cock- erel, so that's yer game . . . ,' roaring at him, so it make him start. And I come down hard acrost his knifehand, with my fist. So he let go, and the knife fly out of his hand and into the darkness. But oh he were quick, that one! I give him that. For first he coil up into a ball. Then he flung hisself at me, and pin me down. Well I feel his hands clawing at my throat, lookin' for my windpipes. Be at them soon enough, too, I dare say. So it appear I was done for. On a sudden, though, he cry out: 'Whisht—Dang! . . . *Wazzat!?*'—Now this were only the clink of a hoss-collar bell come from a wagon, which was still a ways up the road yet. But that were enough to put a scare into him. So he let go. Well, what you expec'? Feller was only a thief. Stand to reason the one thing he dread was discov'ry! So he get up and growl at me: 'Boy yous got plaguey good luck, mister! For wasn't fer that 'ere ha'ness bell, I swear yous a goner!' Then he say: 'So here's a present, me to yous—free gratis . . . !' Then he knock me on the head, and clear out . . . Well no sooner he were gone, I'm on my feet and a-hoss and postin' home free ag'in. Was only later I notice the twinge, from the whack on the head I receive. So I put my hand to my forehead. Golly it were a astonishing-size bump! Big as a baby's fist. Well ne'mind. It was wuth it. For I done it. Yess'r. Done what I set out to. I come back with our hosses."

"O THANKS BE it's ended so, Alter!" I'd called this out joyously, and clasped Alter and hugged him, I was that pleased.

"There, there," comforts Alter. " 'Sides! that Redhead cert'nly got considerable more to be thankful for. As I hadn't even a crumb of nourishment aller four-and-twenty hour, to say nothin' o' my being wore to a frazzle besides. For otherwise . . . Nah! it don't signify. For our hosses is safe. That's the main thing!"

"Talking of which . . . well, I mean, where *is* that prize horseflesh of ours anyhow?" I asked. For I'd a good look around, and didn't make hide nor hair of the either one.

"Why, all in good time," says Alter. "Only wants a little patience, Reb Mend'le, and you'll see 'em . . . Now, you rec'lect that gent I come back with? Well so happen that personage is with 'em now. Over by the woody glade, got the running water in it, plus good grass. Went down special, to water the creatures. Dependable feller, though. So there's no need to get into a fret about it . . . I come back myself only now, don'cher know. But Lor' I were wore out! Only flop down in the cart and cover up, and I was out like a light. Though seem I scarcely doze off, when you happen by. And God praise we meet in good health . . . er—say, Reb Mend'le, I notice where you got your jaw tuck up in that bandanna. Sore tooth, huh? Dear, dear . . ."

"Well, I'll tell you, Reb Alter. It's quite simple, really. Now yourself, Alter, you come back with your head wrapped

up in a cloth, *plus* a bump on it. The whiles I come with my
jaw tied up in a bandanna, only *minus* a sidecurl y'see. And,
well, you brung along that Personage; one's gone to water our
hosses. The whiles, y'see, I only brung along *this* Personage;
who's Reb, er . . . Reb, er . . . Well yes, that's to say, who's
Reb Hyam-Hanan what's Hya-'Tryna's mister!"—which latter Personage I now introduced to Alter, for the second time.
Only this time I did it replete; not forgetting to tack on his
distaff-side honorific. Just to kind of nail him down better for
Alter.

Though I observed Alter's features suddenly to widen into
a look of huge astonishment—

"Reb Alter, surely you can't mean?" I says, goggling astonishment back at him. "But you don't mean to say, sir, that you
actually *know* Hya-'Tryna!"

"Hya-'Try—?" returns Alter. "Hya-'Try—? . . . Who in
dingdong blazes . . . well ne'mind! I mean Hya-'Tryna's all
well and good, I s'pose, in her own way—but your *sidecurl,*
Reb Mend'le, your *sidecurl!* Good grief, sir, what she got to do
with bein' short a *sidecurl?*"

"But ch'know, my missus, she kinfolks, er . . . H'm!"

Though the whiles we was setting around so, on the grass,
attending to Reb Hyam-Hanan, about to animadvert on matters of kinship, and sidecurls as well, I suppose—anyhow, the
whiles we three was lounging so, my own little jade and
Alter's skinny she-nag come trotting up (as 'twere), from over
the rise betwixt us and that glade of Alter's, had the water in
it. Now, I am bound to confess I was impressed! I mean not
just with that spirited imitation of a trot they was doing. No,
was more in the way they bore themselves. With their heads
held so away up. Touch of real pride's what it was. Put them
in altogether a different light, so you'd hardly have knowed
'em for the same creatures. It's like they was saying: "Go on!

laugh if you want, feller. We don't care! 'Cause in case you're not satisfy', there's ever so many cust'mers which is only too eager to take us off your hands. And never you mind about us being rheumy-eyed always, and our hocks wrapped up in them dirty rags. For we'll do for off-hosses as good as our betters, anytime. And as to being baulky, that don't signify in the least! Because if it's only busted axles you are interested in, we can do that pretty good, too! Fact, no worser than any your more high-born equines will do it. But you know what our *real* trouble is? It's being Jewish hosses. Now that *is* hard, sir. For a Jewish gent, such as your own estim'ble self, sir, he just won't keep to his obligations, in the way of provender. No sir, he won't! Somehow he seem never to get around quite to feeding us. Whuppings! that's all he ever seem to know to give to his hosses, to make them go . . ." I gave my jade a playful cuff on the jaw, crooning to him affectionately, saying: "Cheeky little rascal, ain'cher, little buddy!"

Then I see Alter's Personage come ambling behind. So I look at him and —Oh my! I clapped my hands together and cried out:

"*Fishke!* . . . Only talk about Messiah. Oh you are a sight for sore eyes! I just can't believe it . . ."

"You don't mean t'say this is your Fishke, the same you was telling about?" asks Alter, marveling greatly.

" 'Tis indeed, sir, 'tis indeed! The very same. One from the bath. —How-do, Fishke!"

"Why, I rec'nize you right off, too, Reb Men'le!" replies Fishke, giving me good day for mine.

"But we both us owe this young feller a considerable debter gratitude!" says Alter. "Why, weren't for your Fishke here, we'd have 'bout as much sight of our hosses now, as we ever had of our own ears!"

"An' if weren't for Reb Alter," says Fishke, "there wouldn't even be no Fishke to have sight of at all. On account he'd be dead . . ."

"Yes, I know!" I says, "heard all about it from Alter over here. Though what I really like to know is where you been keepin' all this time, young feller—eh?"

"W-ell, that's kinder a long story, Reb Men'le," says Fishke, averting his face from me the whiles.

I took the time to look Fishke over. Why the boy may as well have been naked, for all was left of his clothes. Barefoot too. And those poor feet of his, they were a cruel sight. So battered and swoll' up, and covered in sores. And his face blackened by the sun, and him gone as skinny as a stick. Made you sorry only seeing him like that. Must have seen considerably more hard times than is good for anybody, poor feller. I took his hand then, and I said:

"Come, Fishke. We can hear about it later. It'll keep. Meanwhiles, you plump yourself down amongst us, and rest easy awhile . . ."

# 12

BUT YOU KNOW, for a Jewish gent in a *lit'ry* humor, specially one was inclined now and then to put his hand to Hebrew versifying, there'd have been enough material to knock together a very pretty poem with, only seeing the bunch of us there, on that fine early morning. He'd have for a start the picture of four married Jewish gents, carelessly laid out amongst the green grasses of the field, in their several unbuttoned attitudes; and each looking to be enjoying himself enormously on his own account, without exchanging even a word. And round them was a world all sky and dewdrops and sunbeams, and nature and songbirds. And for livestock, there'd be four nags thrown in, which each was more handsomer than the next. And if that wasn't sufficient, he might paint it up a bit, bung in made-up things of his own. And as well maybe toss in a figure or two from the Book, by way of ornament. Say he'd put in a *Pleasant Mead,* and spot it with a *Flock of Placid Sheep that Feedeth Upon Lilies;* or a *Clear Brook,* with *An Hart that Panteth After the Water;* or put *Quaint Flutes of Reed* into our mouths, that each may *Pipe Sweet Rustickal Airs to His Beloved Spouse.* No need, though, to give us bags for sticking all these benefactions into, as we are all of us quite decently equipped on our own, in the way of that article, thank you! Which is by way of saying: Only so far, and no farther. Because I won't tolerate strangers getting inside my skin and poking about in my thoughts, sticking things into my head which aren't there. Unhand me, sir! And next time, keep them footling inventions and idle gimcrack constructions to yourself. Scoot! Go and peddle 'em where they're wanted. For I assure you I am quite able to speak my own mind.

So, in a nutshell, here 'tis. Or, rather, there I was, sprawled out on the grass, one among an amiable layabout fellowship of four, getting the most extraordinary kick out of goggling goofy-eyed at oh anything come within eyeshot. And why's that? No reason. At least none in particular. —Except maybe it is feeling good. Now that is the kind of well-being you don't—no, nor you even cannot put words to. So you don't. You only let yourself tum-de-dumdum along airily under your breath: *Tum-dedumdumm!* . . . *Tum-dedumdumm!* Like that. *Tum-dedumdumm* . . . No words there. Scarcely a tune, if it come to that. I mean you are never doing it intentionally, say to give your voice box a workout or any such thing. *Tum-de-dumdumm* . . . Know what it remind me of? Only thought of it now. It is exactly the sort of thing a gent will do, when the troubles attendant on making a living leave off nagging him awhile. Like on holidays. Or after Sabbathday sweetmeat. That is when you will see whole companies of 'em—oh just regiments of such gentry doing it, parading up and down outside in the street, tumdeduming, bombinating along so, only crooning a half-tuneless air under their noses, each according to his own fancy—whilst, say, idly twirling the tassel of his coat sash; or maybe winding and unwinding a whisker round his forefinger; or only hitching up his coattails and keeping his hands clasped behind his back. *Tum-dedumdum-dummmm* . . .

There, you see? Hyam-Hanan's doing it. And his face aglow like that! On a sudden though he was on his feet and dusting off, saying: "Um, er . . . 'hem!" —Only preceded first by them tongue-chawings and lip-moistenings which he is prone to, by way of preliminary—

" 'Hem!" he says, giving a fussy stroke to his beard. "Reckon time ter go, Reb Men'le . . . Whatcher say, huh?"

"So soon?" I says, risen to my feet now. "Well, I s'pose if you must . . . Well then! Godspeed and safe journey, sir!"

I saw a look of bafflement wash over Hyam-Hanan's face. He said: "But y'self, sir, uh . . . Ain' you comin'? I mean 'twere all agree, Reb Men'le, 'twere all agree! Yestiddy. 'Member? Was y'self say so. Oh dear, oh dear!"

"But how can I?" I says. "Well you can see for y'self, sir . . ." I swept my hand, to indicate my companions.

"Oh warm welcome! Aller you. Morer merrier, as the missus say . . . H'm! But ch'know, she makin' cream dumplins! My missus. Cream Dumplins! Heapser 'em! 'Nough for ever'one. Thinker it! *Cream Dumplins,* sirs . . . !"

"Why thanks! I rejoice to hear it," I says, dropping him a bob, in the way of acknowledgment. "And so we all do, truly! Only no time. Sorry. Business. Won't wait. My best to the missus and . . . Well, you do understand, sir, don'tcher?"

"Bless me whatcher thinkin', sir! My missus she will ki-kill mmm-um——." Hyam-Hanan'd stopped in confusion, then went on agitatedly. "I mean, she wun't never lemme inner house. No, sir, she wun't! Not lessen *you* was with me, Reb Men'le. But ch'know, yestiddy abed, my missus she and me, we 'ready talk it over! 'Bout that 'ere . . . that 'ere *Business,* twix' you and we. For she been countin' on it, sir. Gotter heart set on't. And my sweet belle maid Hassia-Gruna's gotter heart set on't too. Fact the two them gotter heart set on't. You do get my drif', Reb Men'le, don'cher, huh? I mean, sir, you do get my drif' . . ."

"Why, point taken, sir! Only, y'know, this kind of thing wants a little patience. For my missus why she will ki-kill mmm-um . . . I mean she wun't lemme inner house neither. No, sir, she wun't! Not lessen she and me, we talk it over; 'bout that 'ere . . . that 'ere *Business,* 'twixt you and we. For otherwise . . . Well you do get my drift, Reb Hyam-Hanan . . . er, don'tcher?"

Hyam-Hanan's face took on the complexion of one who had only that moment got slapped by his best friend. I mean you could see how on a sudden the color rose in it, and next it flushed out of it. And he begun to plead in earnest now, to beg: "Oh please, please, sir! —You mus' come Reb Men'le! You simply *mus'!* O Gawd! O my Gawd! —What'my to do, sir! What'my to do . . ." —Anyhow, this went on for a time. For it took a bit, before Hyam-Hanan was persuaded that I was adamant, and he left off whining. Though I had still to put up with his wheedling awhiles longer.

"Well, Reb Men'le, if you ree-ly determine. I reckon cain't be help . . . H'm! But ch' know, I been thinkin'. Gotter idee. You write to my missus. Letter maybe, huh? Coupler words. See, my Hya-'Tryna she wun't never take my word on it. No, sir, she wun't. For she only find fault, and say I was nu-

nuthin' butter, butter, dr-drivelin' f-foo . . . well, things like that. Get my drif', Reb Men'le? So whatcher say. Coupler words. That's all what's wanted. Our rebbe to home, why he know to read. He read it to her. Oh you *mus'* do it, you *mus,'* Reb Men'le . . ."

I didn't want to do it. But I did it. Because, well, it was like giving succor to one as went in mortal peril of his life—though, more of limb in this case, perhaps. Why goodness knows what mayhem Hya-'Tryna mayn't visit on him. Mind, though, it wasn't like he didn't deserve it. Husband like that! Condign I call it. But I wouldn't want it done to him on my own account only. So I fished the lead pencil out of my bag, and I pulled a blank endpaper off a cheaper item of bookware, and I set the sheet down on the driving seat, and I composed myself to the task: *Old-Fangled & Flow'ry* would suit fine, I should think. So—

To
**THE WORTHY & ESTIMABLE** *GOODWYFE*
*My most honour'd Kinswoman*
*THE VERTUOUS and PIOUS*
*R$^t$ HON$^{ble}$ M$^{rs}$ Hya-'Tryna*
*Long Life & Good Healthe*
**AMEN AND GREETING!**

*Ma'am,*
  *Know therefore that I am (Praise G$^d$ and Amen) hale & well, and withal in excellente Good Healthe. I pray The ALL-Mercifull Blessed-be-He may keep us Always (even as He hath ever done) in His Good Graces; that soon we may have Joyous News of each other, and such Fair Tidings as bring Great Consolation & Gladnesse & Honour, as also a Cheerful Countenance, Amen selah. Fond Greeting, Ma'am, to your Children (whom G$^d$ prosper and Long Life to!); and, most partic-*

ularly, to y$^r$ Sweet Belle Maid & Chaste Bride, Miss Hassia-Gruna, whom in G$^d$'s Name I beg to be remember'd to most fondly.

Know, too, Ma'am, that our Carts, plus Contents thereof, are found, much as I left 'em. Said Items being all A-one, and (which Praise G$^d$ for) in Apple-Pie Order. And here, Ma'am, is Good News! Our EQUINES (by which read "our Hosses") are Return'd! And we have no other than the Reb Wine-'n'-Candles Alter to thank for it; for he it is who, at Very Great Perill, hath retrieved the both our Beasts from the Hands of the Thieves which stoled them. Surely, Ma'am, our being the Objects of so great Good Fortune must only be put down to Ancestral Merit. For, doubtlesse, these are Wonderfull Prodigies & Miracles which were wrought on our behalf; and we are unworthy, merely in our owne Right, of so much of G$^d$'s Infinite Bounty & Goodnesse. For the rest, Ma'am, your owne R$^t$ HON$^{ble}$ Reb Hyam-Hanan shall disclose to you ALL—to wit, Every-Thing exactly as it come to pass; which by Golly! is One for the Booke, certainly.

Your Pardon, Hya-'Tryna, if now I take upon myself to put in a Good Word with you, anent y$^r$ Husband, the Worthy Reb HH. For, I do assure you, 'twould have fair wrung your Heart (the more, Ma'am, a Heart so Tendre & Fine-tuned as your Owne), only to see into what a State of Extreme Consternation (not to say Alarm!) hath the poor Man fallen, since Receipt from me of the Sad Intelligence—namely, Ma'am, that on no Account can I return To-day with said Reb HH, as per Agreement and My Undertaking of the Evening Previous. —O, pity him, Ma'am! Be charitable, that he may not be brought down betimes to an Early Grave. And chastise him not, for that I Break Faith and come not Home with him To-day, as per Agreement of the Evening Previous. For by golly, Ma'am! if ever were Living Creature which deserveth of Compassion, 'tis this Worthy Gent as is y$^r$ Husband. O, but you ought only to have seed the way that Man did labour; aye, how he would have moved even the Heaven & the Earth, for your Behoof. Why, I swear, he even came near falling down in a dead Swoone, and before my very Feet, so fervently did he pleade your Cause, Ma'am; extolling

not only your owne Vertues into the Seventh Heaven, but (and this
most particularly, Ma'am!) those of y$^r$ Excellente Sweet Belle Maid &
Most Accomplish'd Bride (whom I beg once more to be remember'd to
most fondly). In a word, Ma'am, he, for his part, hath done Every-
Thing that a Faithfull Husband, and a Most Fond & Doting Father,
may be expected to do. ——But you do get my Drift, Ma'am, now don't
you? O, I am bound you do—nay, Ma'am, but you must, you must!
For consider, Ma'am, to what Lengths the Fellow went, only to bring
me round. Why, the Man stuck at Nothing—neither scrupling to
tempt me with Promises of your very owne Creame Dumplins, Ma'am,
and with other such-like Enticements, in the way of Savoury Delicacies. Only think on it, Ma'am—Creame Dumplins! Well I shan't
deny it, Ma'am. For I'll allow I was tempted, most cruelly tempted.
But Businesse, Ma'am, why, Businesse Cometh Always First, as the saying is; and not even the Temptations of your owne Irresistible Creame
Dumplins may be allow'd to stand in the way of earning one's Daily
Breade. And Secondo, Ma'am; that is to say, in the Second Place, I
have "An Helpe-meet"; in other words, I have a Spouse (by which,
Ma'am, read "My Missus"). ——O but you do get my Drift, Ma'am, now
don't you? And who should better know of what I speak than your
Selfe, Ma'am? For, after all, what is a Man—but nay, Ma'am, what
can he even hope to be, without "An Helpe-Meet-for-Him," without
his Spouse; in short, Ma'am, without His Missus? Talking of which, I
pray even now, to Him Who Liveth Always, that soon we shall all of us
come (an' G$^d$ Send)—that is, Me and the Missus My Wife, & Co.——
that soon, I say, we shall all come a-visiting; and, what is more, be
merrily consuming your Creame Dumplins; and, why, who knows, perhaps even y$^r$ Excellente Ginger-Cakes, as well (an' G$^d$ Willing)! ——
Now, you do get my Drift, Ma'am, don't you? Tho', between-whiles, I
pray you, let not that Most Worthy Gent who is y$^r$ Husband, the Reb
HH, to suffer. In any Case, not on my Account, poor Fellow.

    Be so kind, Ma'am, as to receive, from my Hand, these few small
Gifts hereunto appended, which I send by the Agency of the aforesaid

*Reb HH, y<sup>r</sup> Most Worthy Husband. Item: One "Prayer for Prosperous Dealings." Item: One "Blessings-o'-the-Lights" plus "Blessings for the First-o'-the-Moone." Item: One "Prayer to Our Matriarchs, the Ladies Sarah & Rebecca & Rachel & Leah." Item: One "Prayer for Slaughtered-Fowle Offerings for the Yom-Kippur" (N.B. This last being in Mint Condition and, what is more, also Brand-New!); ——and, Finally, Ma'am, a Booke which is an absolute "Must" for Womenfolk, as well as being Indispensable to their Enlightenment & Edification. Namely, Item: "The Fount of Puritie——Which Worke compriseth a Manuall, or a Compleat Guide, for the Practickall Instruction of Women, concerning the Subject of Menses, or Women's Courses (viz. 'Monthlies'), in respect of All Aspects Physickall, Rituall & Theologickall thereunto pertaining; which Matter hath been Faithfully Gathered, Collated, Tabulated & Set Forth, from the Sacred & Learned Sources; as also Translated from the Holy Hebrew & the Ancient Chaldee Tongues, into the Modern Vulgar. Imprinted by ****** & Co., lodging at ******, upon the **th Day of the Month of *****, in the Year MDCC***." You will surely receive considerable Pleasure from it, Ma'am, to say nothing of obtaining great Entertainment from it. ——O but I do assure you, Ma'am, you shall! As most certainly shall y<sup>r</sup> Chaste Belle Maid, the Sweet Miss Hassia-Gruna——for I sincerely doubt she will ever be able to bring her-Selfe to put it down.*

*Hya-'Tryna, I would crave a Boon of you. That's to say, Ma'am, I would ask a small Favour. It concerneth my Breslau-wove Woolly Hose. Which Articles I was constrain'd to throw off Last Night whilst . . . well, not meaning to offend, Ma'am, whilst them Catawampuses of yours (I mean Your Bed-bugs, Ma'am) had set themselves a-nipping away at me, and had generally took to tormenting me in the worst possible Way, so that . . . But enough! for that's all over with now; so there is no Use my going on about it anymore. ——Anyhow, about them Woolly Hose of mine. So as I was telling, Ma'am: In such a Great Haste was I to get away this Morning, that I clean forgot to put the darned Things back on again; so I left them behind on that*

*Sleeping-Bench of yours, the one which is over in the Alcove. So what I
am asking of you, Ma'am, is this: You hunt up them Stockings; and
pray be so good as to give them away to y<sup>r</sup> Husband, the Worthy Reb
HH. They are my Gift to him. And I do wish him the very best
Healthe in the Wearing of 'em. ——Well, I reckon it is Time now I said
Good-bye. So Farewell, Hya-'Tryna. And, once again, Fond Greeting
to y<sup>r</sup> darling Children, Ma'am. And, as well, to y<sup>r</sup> Sweet Belle Maid &
Chaste Bride, the Fair Miss Hassia-Gruna——to whom, by-the-bye, I
beg to be remember'd Most Fondly. ——O, and in G<sup>d</sup>'s Name! try and
remember, Ma'am, what I told you, concerning y<sup>r</sup> Worthy Husband.
For the Man weareth so Doleful a Countenance, it would move any
One to Grief only having to look upon him all of the Time. ——O
dear! Bless me but I near forgot. My Whip! For I left that, too, in the
Alcove where I slept. Well, never mind. For I should anyhow like to
make a Gift of it to the Rebbe. He shall have Good Use of it. Of that I
am certain. And so I say again: Fond Greeting to y<sup>r</sup> dear darling Children, Ma'am——to All of 'em; and most especially to y<sup>r</sup> Sweet Belle
Maid, &c.——As pertaineth to the rest, I remain,*

*Ma'am,*
*As always, ever faithfully,*
*Y<sup>r</sup> humble kinsman,*
*R<sup>b</sup>-Mendele Moykher Sforim*
*The Book Peddler*

I read out the letter, and the effect that it had on Hya-
'Tryna's mister was nothing short of sensational. The whole
time he listened to me read it, his face wore a smile which
radiated only boundless bliss. And what appeared most to
please him about it was its eloquence, the sweetness of expression, as he regarded it. Indeed, so greatly did he marvel at
the language that, practically at every phrase, he would strike

his forehead, doing so repeatedly, whilst crying out to me: "Oh, my! Ain't ne'er heered the like on it, Reb Men'le, not in all my born days . . . Oh, my! Them words o' yourn, why they's on'y pure honey-sweet sugar . . . God's honest truth, sir, pure honey-sweet sugar!" —Till finally we took friendly leave of one another; and Reb Hyam-Hanan went away with a light heart, and in the best of buoyant good spirits.

# 13

SEEING AS HOW me and Alter were pretty much off our feet by now, and were wore out on account of the night before, we thought to grab us a snooze, and rest up for a couple hours. After, we'd start fresh and keep to the road, till away past sunset, and travel well through the night maybe. Fishke said he would look after the horses the while we slept, and rustle up something to eat for lunch later, when we got up. "For," as Fishke explained, "I shan't anyhow be wanting no sleep today. On account when that bad business which I had was over las' night, I slep' ever so sound, like I was after a bath. And Reb Alter here, when he come back, why he couldn't even hardly roust me, that's how good I been sleepin'." —At my bidding, Alter lay his head down on my lap. I got the knife out, which I pressed the flat of the blade up against the bump on his forehead, till I got the thing squeezed level. We next had ourselves a good gape and a stretch; and then the pair of us lay down in the shade beneath a tree.

Now if it wasn't for Old Butterface in the noon sky, roasting the two of us to a pair of crisps, we might have slept for I can't tell how long past the midday. Though it so happened the minute we got our eyes open, first thing we saw was a small cooking fire not a few paces off, which had a potful of taters on it garnished with an onion—and amongst the spuds was oh the longest-looking skinnygut Jewish sorsage sizzling away cozily inside, so it only made your mouth water. We took a quick nip of the spirits first, for eye-openers; and straightway we'd sat down to our dinner, making a hearty meal of it, you may be sure. Well, we couldn't heap enough praises on Fishke's cooking, saying how we never knew anything come near for honester goodness Jewish delicatessen, and it wasn't only just taters we was eating but royal fare, which it wouldn't shame even a king to feast on it. Now, you can just bet it made Fishke so chipper he was fit to bust for it; and he only kept urging us to dig in the more, saying, "Why, sirs, you jus' eat up hearty, an' only welcome to it, I'm sure!"

"So, young feller, out with it!" we says to Fishke. "Now, then, where'd you scare up that kosher sorsage, out in these wilds? Our onion and taters alone, why they wouldn't hardly do for fillet o' spuds, weren't for that m'mmm-m! lu-scious length of sorsage you come up with—"

"Where I get the sorsage from?" says Fishke. "Easy! From my cadgin' bag! Piece of luck, too, keepin' it from that—oh, dang! Black Deuce bust the 'postate bastid—."

"Aw, c'mon, Fishke, whyn't you tell us about it," we pleaded with him. "So, what ree-ly happen to you back there, huh?"

"Tsk!" answers Fishke, heaving a sigh. "Nah, it'd be too much to tell, sirs, long story like that . . ."

"Why, bless you, Fishke, but the day's long yet; and time's one thing we got plenty of, praise Goodness.— So come, sir!" I says to Alter next. "We'll get the hosses hitched up, and we can hear Fishke's story the whiles we're under way—."

———

WHEN THE CARTS stood ready, I invited everybody into my wagon. Only Alter proposed we all pile into his. "On account it's more roomier," he says, "for it ain't quite so clutter' up, as is yourn, with aller them merchandise, Reb Mend'le!" But I come up with a compromise. We'd split the difference, and ride a little in Alter's cart and a little in mine. And that is what we did. So:

## Under Way with Wine-'n'-Candles Alter

"So, young feller, let's just hear it—c'mon, Fishke, give!" says me and Alter, urging him to get on with his story, after we'd finally all took our places and gee-upped the horses. Alter's she-nag had took the lead, and the cart lurched forward, jolting along at a steady pace now, whilst my own little jade, being of a behindhand nature, tardily brought up our rear. Fishke, though, seemed somehow still to be coy about the business, and he would only cast his eyes down, toying nervously with his fingers the whiles.

"W-ell, I dunno. I mean—um—well, s'embarrassin', sirs, tellin' all about it sudden like that, and there bein' no reason for it. Oh but it do give one a queer feelin', sirs, if y'mus' know—."

So I set about to buck Fishke up, jollying him along with words of encouragement. And Alter, too, for his part, though himself never much given to talk ordinarily, commenced sweet-talking the lad, coaxing him round. Which proceeding of Alter's took the following turn:

"La, ninny! Why, ain't but only the start which is hard. For once that first word is out, the rest's only a breeze. Yess'r. Oughter know. 'Cause I got that exac' same trouble. Well 'noughsaid! —So, uh, lessee . . . Now, you an' that, er—that, um, Blind Orphan-gel, the both you get marry. —Y'see? Nothin' to it! Only ne'mind. We 'ready know that . . . Well, c'mon, young feller! Your turn. So, what happen nex'?"

"Nex'?! Dang! Black Deuce bust her nex'! an' bust 'er pa, an' anner p-p-pa's pa!" Fishke shot this out in a paroxysmic fury. Then he said: "Them two! They sure fix me—oh they fix me good!"

"Well? So—so—so, what happen, Fishke? What happen, feller?" says we. For Fishke's awesome fit of temper now subsided, sudden as it come. Though, by and by, he begun speaking again. Only in a more collected manner this time:

"Yeah, wife, some wife, gen'men! . . . Though I mus' say, after the weddin', she and me—well, we done pretty good, considerin'. Exac'ly like a decen' marry' couple suppose to. And I done more'n right by her, seem to me. Honest, gen'men, as God's my witness. Why I hope my mouth may be stopped f'ever, if I'm lyin'. —Mornin' prompt, every day, I use to take her over to the place she got, down by the Ol' Cemetery. Which it were her custom to set on a bit of straw there quite regular, beggin' for alms, in that sad, quavery singsong she put on for it, sound like lamentations prayers for Fast-o'-Ab worship; and which wasn't nobody pass by, without it broke his heart to only hear it. Couple time a day, I brung food to her, so she may eat—say a bowl of grits I cook up; and, after, hot buttercake, or pickle' cucumber, or a crab apple maybe. And I say to her: 'Eat up, dear, 'fresh y'self!' —Which, after all, it were only right I should do. What with her squatted down the whole day like that, in the one place, and never once moving; and all the while so preoccupy' with business. And there was lot of time, too, when I drop by jus' so, for no special reason, except it's only to see how she were getting on, help with the bookkeeping, and with sorting out the coppers she collec' and such: say making change for a threepenny, p'raps, or a sixer. Or reminding her about folks pass by, which t'other day only give alms on credit, 'stead of cash down; and it were time they settle up. And, sometimes, I shoo off stray livestock, sich as cows and goats, as happen by in the street; case any the pesky creatures may wish to make a meal of the straws was tuck under her backside, where she set. Then, come autumntide, month-o'-Elul Penitences, I brung her down to the big fair, for graveside visitations, over to the cemetery outside town. And we certainly done no worser than any of the common ruck of holy-service folks was there, in the way of gravekeepers and sextonesses, and cantors and prayer-promptresses, and bedesmen and psalm-sters, and almonerwives and candlewick-sempstresses, and mourning-'n'-keening wives for hire, and God's-acre wives which measures off the gravesites with cotton thread. —In a word, gen'men, the neither us din't want for nothin'. And our living come as easy as milk from the cow's teat . . . Though, trouble with folks is, good's never good 'nough, and they must always have better. And if there's black bread for the askin', they only craves for white.

" 'Know what, dearie?' my missus say once. 'Folks like you and me . . . I mean, marry' couple, likes of us, they don't scarcely need to go in want. 'Cos when it come to our bread, Fishke, our blessings is in our faults. Seem to me, any other couple was so blest as us, I reckon they know pretty quick to make their fortune by it. Well, what I say is, we been the worse pair of fools, for not doin' right by ourselfs. No, do listen, dearie, an' take the advice of one's a little older p'raps, and more experience'. You take me out into the great world, Fishke, out yonder, amongs' folks which counts, and you shall see—now mark what I say, 'cos it's a promise—how both of us soon be walkin' in gold. Here, in this place, ain't hardly nothing lef' to expect. Sometime, seem you set here forever, before somebody think to take pity, and throw a morsel of charity your ways. Now, I been hearing folks talk some, about the wonnerful good fortune come to that sof'head, li'l Nahum, got hisself hitch' couple year back, to that whatsit, that harumfrodite creetur, Pearl, for cholery nupt'als. Well, no sooner they wed, him and Pearly go off together into the world. And you wun't believe how well they prosper since. Know our Mottie? The psalms almsman? One been travelin' the country, collecting for his gel's bride-dower what's come of age? Well, now, he been away south recent, where he run acrost the pair 'em, over to Kishinev, whiles they been doing the door-to-door cadge, making house calls there. And ever since, Mottie scarcely cain't stop talkin' about how full up their cadging bags was—I mean, they was stuff' to the necks with great chunks of whitemeal loaf, bigger than what folks hereabout gen'ly give even to the Sabbath goyfeller—and with mamaleega cornpuddin', and smoke' mutton, and strings of skinnygut sorsages, and fat tailbone of sheep an' . . . well, I wun't even bother to try and tell what all Mottie say was inside them sacks. And Pearly got sich a glow on her now, from only preening, a body cain't even look at her without it knock his eyes out. Tub of lard's what she become. Why, the creetur got more rolls of fat, and more chins hung on her mug, than anybody may even count. Pass for a duchess, Mottie say. And these days, why she wun't even hear on Glupsk! Wun't have the place, even you offer it on a silver platter. —And 'em folks of ourn, jus' come back from the seaside; now they still cain't get over what a golden streak of luck which t'other cholery groom, Yontl No-gams, come by, down Odessa way. They say they seen him scuttlin' bout on his hunkers there, in and out amongst all them shops, in the high street an' . . . well, what's to say more, 'cept only the Good Lord Hisself looking after him. Make quite a name for hisself, too, Yontl has. Why, them big city folks don't seem able to get enough of him. Wun't let that feller out of their sights even a minute. Now, by all accounts, one'd think Odessa ready got enough broken-down folks to satisfy every taste. Sight too many, some might say. For ain't a cripple born, only he mus' make straightway for Odessa. Thing is, ain't one amongst the whole bunch neither, which hold a candle to our own cripples, even on a bad day. 'Cos such a rare sight of halt, lame, and blime folks as Glupsk give out, you cannot find a equal to, nowhere the world over. Not in England even. And now the word is got about, why, Glupsk's even made its reputation by it. There's people will come from oh miles round, only to admire sich as we, like we was freak prodigy . . . So I dare say God shan't withhold His charity from us, neither. —Come, Fishke! Le's you and me go way this instant, whilst it's summer yet. Why'd be sinful we linger one more day in this dreary place—.'

"And the whiles my wife been talking so, I get fire' up with the notion, as well. —So we lef', halt leadin' the blin', so to say.

"Well, not to complain, gen'men, I shan't say but we done very tolerable on the road. Weren't town or village folks didn't take to us direc'ly; nor didn't stop and take notice when we pass. And weren't nobody ever turn us away. We was always let to lodge the night, at the shambles-house, with the other sick and poorfolk. And there was just no end of houses, which it seem you don't need but only go up to and put out your hand, and folks was only too please' to chuck what-all into it, and *plonk!* down it go into your cadging bag, your shirtfront, your pocket, whichever come the most handy. And Sabbaths, it don't take but the bit of cash we give to the beadle at shul, and he always fix the pair us up with Sat'day charity chits, for free dinner, with folks live by the

same courtyard. My wife, though, she take me in hand, and
set to teachin' me the ways of beggarfolk. For I was quite the
dainty gent yet in that particular line, and didn't know rightly
to observe the proper rules of cadging door to door. Whilst
my missus were well experience' in such things, and knowed
all the ins and outs on it. So she teach me pretty much everything you must know of beggar lore. About how, whilst you
come into a house, you must wheeze and groan; and about
how you must fall into a coughing fit, and must look ever so
sad the whiles you are doing it; and about how you must
whine and plead for a handout, or grab aholt and stand firm
and never let go till you get it; and about how you must bless
folks if they give, and must put a flea in their ear and rant and
scold and blaspheme, in oh just the worse way, if they don't.
Now, p'raps you gen'men been thinking, it don't take much
to be calling on houses, and you need only to go out and do
it. Why, no! That just ain't so. There is considerable art in it.
For being rich and pow'ful amongs' Jewish folks, take only
natural-born luck. And acting uncivil to folks and being high-
handed in your dealings with them, come with time and a
little practice. But when it come to being a proper Jewish
pauper—mind, I mean your gen'ine down-and-out article—
good fortune alone is never enough, and you must know a
great many things which are needful to the business. Oh just
every kind of shift and dodge and trick you may think of. And
you have got to put your whole heart into it, and know to get
under a person's skin, and to latch on so tight he will think he
must drop dead in his tracks, unlest he relent and cough up.

"Me'm my wife, we was foot paupers. —I see you giving
me looks, gen'men, like what I say got you throwed. Only
bear with me, sirs, so I may explain. For now I begun, it's best
I tell you all I know about it. See, poorfolks come in diff'nt
kinds, same as soldiers. So you got your paupers afoot, say,

which is like foot soldiers; and they are call 'infan'ry' and is
different to hoss soldiers, which is call' . . . No, wait! Maybe
that ain't right. Oh! it is such a mix-up. For there is such a
heap of poorfolks about. Hundreds of kinds, which they all
got names I can't scarcely recollect, nor get my tongue round.
Anyhow, poorfolks which walks abroad and ain't hoss-drawn
is called . . . Oh, dang! I forget again. Though they as common as the dirt on the ground. Why every kind of beggar and
down-and-outer is tramping the country afoot, from one end
to the other; and, unless we forget, there's all the beggars
about town, and the almsmen and layabout scholars in shul,
and the whole kit of idle plate-licking toady lickspittles in the
parish . . . Though maybe if you just let me study on it for a
bit, sirs, I shall get it sorted out—."


FISHKE, THOUGH, ONLY got himself lost the more amongst the
tangle of legions which made up the beggar horde; till at last
his speech faltered so, that his account all but lapsed into inco-
herence. Although from all he said, I managed at least to learn
so much. To wit: All beggarfolk after their kind fall into two
great groups: what's called the *Infantry,* or your *Foot-paupers,*
which is the common variety of tramps as go about on foot;
and the *Cavalry,* or your *Horse-drawn paupers,* which travel the
roads in covered carts. But this is not all. For these horse-
drawn paupers are of two kinds. Some of them are really only
*Town-bred paupers,* as happen also to dwell in carts, but are otherwise in the way of being settled down and domestic in their
habits, so they belong with the rest of the decent poorfolk living in the parish; and they mostly live hereabout and up in the
north over by Lithuania, and away also to the west in Poland.
But there is another group yet, as well, which go by the name
of the *Wild-folk,* or *Paupers-of-the-field.* Such as these are born

in covered wagons, somewhere far out on the savage plain, away from any place of settled human habitation. And their fathers, and fathers' fathers were ever on the move. These are your Jewish Gypsies, traveling all the earth hither and yon, and living out their whole lives so. They are born, grow up, marry, have children, and die whilst on the road. They are free folk in every way, neither owing allegiance nor paying tribute to any king or country. For they have cut loose of everything in this world and in Heaven—even of God Himself, whom they neither pray to nor worship in any way. So they hardly even count for Jews anymore. They have no Sovereign. —Now the poorfolk of a parish include every kind of pauper about town. First there are your *Paupers-in-ordinary,* or *Beggars-simple.* They being men and women, and boys and girls, who, prompt upon each First of Moon (or of a weekday as well), routinely take up their cadging bags, and go a-begging door to door, for only petty penny-bits or crusts of bread. And from amongst these, children of either sex will run clamoring at the heels of every passer-by in the street, latching on to a customer at random, and holding on for dear life, till he may be persuaded to part with some token of charity to obtain release. Then there are your *Holy-service paupers,* these comprising the whole class of bedesmen and psalms-almsmen, and the rest of the half-learned layabouts as may be found lucubrating in prayerhouses, and earn their subsistence by saying solemn service over the recent dead, or at the gravesides of the long departed. And we can as well include amongst them your shofar-blowers, as also your gents who, at need, will proofread mezuzah and phylactery scrips, or any other chance scraps of writ as may come to hand. Though a special case of such as make the synagogue their abode and particular resort are your *Torah-and-Devotions paupers.* As, for instance, your schoolmen-cloisterers, men who throw off

wife, home, and children, and bury themselves in a somber
little prayerhouse somewhere in a backwater, there to live out
their days in pious study, with such need of earthly nourishment as they may retain being at the charge of the parish. Or
your yeshiva lads, who scarcely do anything except it is to
only crack lice and mooch around, toasting themselves by the
shul stove betwixt the one day's charitable board and the
next. Though, pious obligations may be gainfully fulfilled as
well by *Mercy's-sake* or *Do-gooder paupers*: folks of oh just any
condition in life who, under the guise of being chariters or al-
moners, go about with a pocket handkerchief daintily laid out
in the palm of their hand, begging alms for this deserving
cause or that—which they give out never to be only themselves. And from among your respectable ranks, too, there
are those who by mere mischance decline into a condition of
being poorfolk in all but name. Such are *Hidden-paupers,*
householders of consequence mostly who have fallen on hard
times, which they relieve by going quietly on the dole, receiving sundry other parish handouts on the sly as well. Likewise
discretion is the part of those but halfway to penury, what you
may call *Beggars-at-need,* who have taken up the profession of
alms only by way of occasional work. Say schoolmasters at
many a parish charity-school, who spend half their time
teaching, and the remainder rattling a collection box door to
door; and much the same may be said of beadles, and cantors,
and rabbis, and other such shul gentry, all of whom are only
half what they profess to be, and half what other gents shouldering cadging bags generally are. Now it is on Feastdays that
your *Pauper-revelers* regularly come into their own; their high
season being the Foretide to Passover, as also the nights of the
Feasts of Hanukkah and of Purim, when all Jews at large take
heart, and some fall in so with the holiday spirit as to band
joyously together and solicit charity door to door—though

only for the sake of other poorfolk, to be sure. But for sheer principled adherence to philanthropy, it's your *Friendly-loans paupers* that really stand apart, giving over the whole of their lives to cadging only so they may persuade others, too, of the virtue of lending money at no interest; and always swearing you up and down whilst doing it, that if you but tide them over with a friendly loan today, why, sir, on the morrow you shall get it back, and be handsomely thanked for it into the bargain!

"Uh, say, Reb Alter!" says I, after I'd done sorting out Fishke's roll of beggarfolk, and more or less set it to rights. "Say, Reb Alter, maybe you can help me out here. For I may have forgot. And gosh I hate to think some poor wretch was left to knock about on his own, and not got on our list of paupers—"

"Oh, what difference'd it make!" grumped Alter, and proceeded to wrinkle up his face into such a scowl, as gents of a certain age will wear any time a boy has got up to no sort of good whatever. "Oh, goshdarn! Feller forgot! Why, a Jewish gent may never get to be a poor miserable pauper, except he is on that fool list! —Oh do ack your age, Reb Mend'le . . ."

"Now that is a fine way to talk, Reb Alter!" says I. For I was determined to carry my point. "Our beggarfolks have got a v-ery dainty notion of their dignity. Quite stuck-up about it even. I mean, you only think to slight any one of them, even it's in a small way, and they will make your life a perfect misery. So I hope you may never cross a proud pauper so. And Heaven help the gent as does . . . Oh but wait! Only hold on for a sec, um, right . . . *Grandchildren!* Now, there's about as artful a bunch of little beggars as you are ever likely to find. See, it's come to me after all, Reb Alter. For praise Goodness there is no end of folks amongst us in the cadging line can be named, if you only trouble to think about it. And some have got stories could wring charity from a miser. You think you got troubles, mister? Well, now, take your *Holy-Land chariters,* for a start. For here you have gents come maybe from all the way out in Jerusalem, only to tell you of hard times will make the hair curl on even the most wretched of our own Parish-bred indigents. Which getting back to—well, what about your *Combustibles* as we call 'em; that's to say folks whom only a chance spark has reduced the homes of, not to mention all their wordly goods, to mere ashes and cinders overnight. Or what of the *Sick-and-ailing folks* keep coming round for handouts? Always turning up at your doorstep with head trouble, with stomach trouble, with backside trouble, adenoidal folks, borborygmal folks, hemorrhoidal folks, each waving sheaves in your face of testimonials plus the handbills of medicine men, of quacksalvers, of alienists, or corpse-cuppers, or feldshers, of tooth-drawers, of sawboneses, and of other such medicos. Then there's the *Widows,* all sorts, young, old, with children, without; and, oh, don't forget your *Grass Widows,* with husbands gone missing or took off. And if the talk's still of paupers, well why not count your *Lit'ry Gents*; and, if it come to that, may as well throw in your newfangled type of author's wife, too, which goes round door to door flogging her husband's books. Nor you needn't worry none about us two, Reb Alter, neither. For not even Old Scratch shall keep *Book Peddlers* off of that list of paupers; because if we aren't richly deserving of being called paupers, then whoever is? And if book peddlers qualify, well why not the rest of the bookmen? That's to say, all of the *Publishers* and *Printers* and *Editors* after their kind; as also their servitors after theirs, in the way of *Journeymen printers* and *'Prentice typesetters,* and *Galley-proof readers* and *Fair copyists,* and *Journalists* and *Correspondents.* —Oh, yes, let 'em each stand up and be counted, for they are all paupers to a man! . . . So, Reb Alter, all which is

left to do now is getting these folks sorted out proper, and put
'em down on that list according to their several precedences
and titles and dignities, and the rest. Well, so what you think,
Reb Alter—all present and accounted for, huh? None missing?"

  *"Oh, foo, Reb Mend'le!"* says Alter, though maybe a shade too
indignantly for the occasion, as I thought. Next he'd stuck his
hand down inside his collar and begun making a tremendous
show of scratching his breast and the nape of his neck, saying,
"By golly, sir, but that's quite enough of them beggars, and
paupers, and scroungers o' yourn! Give me the creeps all over
to be only thinkin' on them, *b'rrrr!* Like I been set on by vermin, or was lousy or somethin'. So give a feller a break.
'Cause short, sir, is sweet, sir. And for my part, sir, you needn't
have said but only *"All Jewry's Paupery!"* and have done. Why,
sir, 'tis all Null! 'Tis Nil, sir! Naught! Nix! In a word, it's all
ONE BIG GOOSE EGG first to last and there's an end! . . .
Only Reb Mend'le, be fair! Let Fishke go on with his story
and don't be interruptin' all the time like you always do. It's
all very well promptin' the lad now and then, when he's bitten off more of a word than he can chew, and the thing's got
stuck in his craw, so he can't get it out and seem ready to
choke on it. And I am sure none of us will mind when you
improve his style in the way of language. But otherwise, well,
just don't you be sticking your shovel in all that much . . ."

AND IF THE truth were told, it was Fishke called the tune from
the very start, and thereafter. For he was the real cantor in
our little consort. Though maybe more of the kind we know
only too well, which don't quite come up to the mark and are
inclined to overreach themselves in the hard parts and go all

red in the face and work their mouths into the godawfulest
contortions trying to mutate to the treble and get past all the
grace notes and flourishes, till in the end they lose their place
altogether, so it is always the first choirboy must come to their
rescue and set them right. So that is what I was: Fishke's little
choirboy, ever ready and at hand to coax the needed words
out of him when the poor boy begun to sputter and gag.
Which happened often enough heaven knows. For it would
otherwise have been nigh hand to impossible to make out anything of what Fishke said. Proof of which I promise you shall
soon enough have. Now as to Alter, well he confined himself
to mostly prodding the lad along in his wonted manner. And
ever and anon he'd be coming up with one 'em strings of
"ne'minds!" and " 'noughsaids!" and "short's sweet sirs!" of
his. Which put me in mind of nothing so much as your congregants at shul near to the end of Sabbath eve worship, with
their minds more on Sabbath dinner and sweetmeat then devotions by now, and mentally urging the cantor to get on with
it and finish up, so they may finally get home and dig in.

# 14

"*MEMA WOIF WE 'uz hinfery po-pes, 'n' jewskin jest pitcheress, shuzh,
owiff ma crewtet pigs, a nabeam blime, d' bofus inchlong, no fasten
paya c-cr-r-rabs, siphon defense.*"——Well that is pretty much how
Fishke resumed his telling, after his fashion. Which, with a bit
of assistance on my part, may be construed: "Me'm my wife
we was infan'ry paupers, and yous kin jus' pitcher us, sirs,
how wit' my crook pegs, an' her bein' blin', the both us inch
along, no faster'n pair o' c-cr-r-rabs, savin' the difference."

Anyway, Fishke picked up the thread of his tale, which is set down in his own words hereinafter, though with such improvements as now and again I may have been constrained to make. So:

*"NO FAS'EN PAYA c-cr-rabs!"* —Tha's what my wife use to say. Well by and by she set to scolding and to nagging me about it. And she even throwed my faults in my face then, calling me by oh jus' the worse names, on account my sick feet and being so gimpy. And she complain how she were plumb deceive through and through over me. For 'twere she which take me out into the world, amongs' respecable folks; and she which raise me up from my low station, of being only a miserable drudge in the bathowze; and she which put me on my feet, and in the way of a handsome living. Whereas, what thanks she git for't? Why, nuffin'! For I weren't keeping to my end of the bargain; and was being unfaithful to her and doing oh she even don' know what all, so as to be vexing her and making all her life a misery to her. —Only this didn't happen but seldom. So I don't let on how it bother me, and I pretend not to pay it no mind. Thinks I: Well that is only the way of marry' women, and it must be how a wife is suppose to carry on. Which is why husbands is got oft times to give the creatures 'what for' and to even be knocking 'em about, when it's wanted. But her tantrums is scarce over, and things get to be quite tolerable betwix' us once more, and her Fishke is even the apple of her eye ag'in. For she would be putting her hand on my shou'der then, and say, 'C'mon, Fishke dearie, gee-up!' And we recommence our traveling, with me up front and her on back, halt leadin' the blin', same as before. And at such times, why, we was jus' *so-o-o* happy together, like—well, I don't know to 'scribe it even—unless it's to say we was as

happy as only happy can be. So that is how we peg along in tandem together the whiles, and drug our selfs from one place to t'other.

"Well I'm bound we was a monstrous long time about it before we finally struck the town of Balta. And we plumb miss that fair which they got over there, too. Know it, gen'men? That's the fair which Jewish folks call the Great Mudhole Fair, and is spoke so well of everywhere, and which is call by that name, on account that's what Balta mean, in the lingo of t'Other Folk which lives there: Mudhole. —Oh but my wife she were beside herself, over only missing that fair; and she work herself up into the most terrible temper about it. Why you might have thought it cost her a whole stack of twenty-dollar gold-pieces—why, maybe even a million in such coin, the way that woman was only carrying on about it. So I try my hand at bucking her up some, by showing her the bright side. 'But my dear!' says I, 'why take on so? Oh it's such a grand town Balta is, an', an', well it ain't as if there wasn't no houses to be calling on; for there is, and lots of 'em too, all over the place, and they are really such fine houses, by the look of them, God praise, an' . . .' But she only come down on me like a hammer: '*O Damnation!*' she say. 'To the dang blazes with 'em y'hear? 'Cos I don't value your Balta tanta-mount to *that!* No, sir, I do not! Nor I won't have it, nuther! Balta, ha! Oh you creetur! Oh you godforsook godawful cree-tur! What use your blankety-blank mudhole, eh? Why I swear I wisht that you and them dang dingdong houses only sunk down in the mud! Down, down, down! Right down to your chinny-chin-chins, y'hear? Yes, I do. An', an', I wisht you only choke to death on them houses, that is what I ree-ly wisht . . . Oh you . . . Oh you . . . *O Damnation!*' "

—"ALTER! I've got it!" says I. Though I confess it come on kind of unexpected. Maybe a bit loud, as well, for it startled even me. "By Gum I've got it, sir! Why I only thought of it just now. No, listen! It's . . . it's, why it's *Pauper-mortgagees*. There! —So, uh, so what you think of 'em, Reb Alter? I mean in the way of being paupers in the begging line, huh?"

"Oh now ain't that a treat!" returned Alter, "Pauper-mortgagees. Hot diggety!" Which remark was followed by a prodigious display of emphatic side-to-side niddle-noddlings of Alter's head, and thrice he clicked his tongue up against his teeth, so: "Tch-tch-tch!" That done, Alter said: "Only I'd sooner forget the whole lot, sir, than venture my opinion of such poor gentry!"

"Why no need, sir, none at all, on account there is one such gent which I know pretty good, over in Glupsk. Reb Simchele *Alive-O!* is the moniker. Maybe you heard of him? Well, never mind, because Simchele *Alive-O!*'s absolutely persuaded he really owns the whole place, lock, stock, and barrel. Why the feller believes—actually *believes!* mind—that he holds the mortgage on all the houses in Glupsk. And d'ye know he keeps a exact record of what each household owes him in back rent? That's right! In a little black book he has got. Keeps the thing up to date, too: 'Why them's *aw-ll* my houses, sir, and you bet I collects the rent on 'em!' That's what the man says. Ever hear the like? And I must say he goes about his business pretty systematical. Got the entire town mapped out into quarters, don't you know; so each day he goes out to a different one. And he'll walk right in on folks, all bluff and breezy like; and with this proprietary little swagger he puts on, and oh just as wreathed in smiles as a brewer's horse. Well if you do give him his handout, that is all well and good. But if you don't, well, that is fine too; because he'll only say, 'Oh, it's all right, sir, not to worry! Half a sec and I shall put you down amongst the debits in this ledger here. You can pay next time!' And out he skips, still all smiles and swag-

ger, making a beeline straightaway for the folks live next door.
And did you ever hear tell, Reb Alter, how these two beggars
in Glupsk married their children off to each other; and how
the one gent-in-law, which is the bride's papa, gave away all
the houses in Glupsk, only by way of dowry? Well, who do
you think that was, but this same *Alive-O!* feller. ——And how
about this one . . . No, but do listen, Alter, because this one'll
just kill you—no, no, really, it's that funny! Anyway, you
know them big paupers' beanfeasts, which rich folks always
give whenever their children marry? Well one of the Quality
in Glupsk threw a shindig in kind once, to honor his daughter's getting hitched, don't you know. Only this squire is most
particular about who he lets in. You know the type. No gate-
crashers tolerated! R.S.V.P. BY INVITATION ONLY! So
while he's keeping a weather eye open for unwanted gentry,
in comes this one pauper which is invited, and he's arm-in-
arm with another which isn't, you see. So when the master of
the house saunters over, and says—'Welcome, friend, but
how come you brung this extra passenger on board?'—the
first pauper says: 'Well, your honor, I'll tell you. This is my
son-in-law, which I made a solemn promise to give "groom's
keep" to. ——Huh? Why, sir, by deed-o'-marriage, it's the custom! Which is to say, he's got free room and board for the
year, gratis. Well, then: *This here's his board!*' ——So that, too,
was good ole Simchele *Alive-O!*, whom no one shall convince
otherwise than that Glupsk is his own private demesne and its
houses are his by right, and they are all there only to await his
pleasure!"

"Well, for my money, you may give this 'good ole' Simchele *Alive-O!* feller the good ole heave-ho. For he only got it
coming . . ." And cutting me short thus, Alter gave the nod to
Fishke, by way of letting the lad know he might proceed,
without suffering further impediment from myself.

Which is what Fishke promptly set out to do, though in his usual faltering way; whilst I yet remained on hand, to only help him get past his stammers, whenever he needed a leg up in that way; so:


WELL, GOOD GENTS, as I told, we'd took to tramping the whole country together. Though we never travel the highway, but only byroads and dirt lanes; ever sidetracking and backtracking, to here, to there, and yonder, oh to just any whither the mood took us. So, in all, things was fine. Only, I will allow we was maybe a lee-tle mite slow about it. But one day we struck a town which I druther the Black Deuce drugged me down to Sheol before we ever come to it. Now, mind, I don't say this on account of the town nor the good folks which live in it. Indeed, no! For they treat me very civil and was exceptional kind when I come calling on houses there. No; weren't any their fault I met up with that atrocious villain which near kilt me and makes my life such a misery—*Oh, dang! Oh, I wisht . . . I wisht he was gutted without a knife! Yeah, that's what I ree-ly wisht!*—Well-a-well . . . Anyhow, sirs, this is what happened:

When we come to town, there was a whole wagon train of hoss-drawn beggarfolk which already stop there. And we was inform', too, that they had been one of them, uh, whatsits, them re-vuh . . . *re-vo-lutions* amongst the townfolks there. For some of 'em new modren-type Jewish folks had took over in the parish, which they don't hold with the old way of charity; so they went and fix things so there wouldn't be no more free handouts to poorfolks. Not except if the folks was old or ailing, or was sorely cripple. But healthy gents and grown boys, and even womenfolks and unmarry' gels, if they was only able-bodied, they surely wasn't feeling too sick to work,

so they oughtn't to be above earning their bread. And they
even said that all the sentimentaring about Jewish charity,
which everyone seem always to be going on about how wonderful it is, none of it weren't only the worse rot, and the
shamefulest and most pernicious humbug which the human
mind ever conceive. For it was because of this folly that there
was such a monstrous many no-account layabouts amongst
us; which was now waxed altogether so great they was like
vermin and only bleeding other folks white, and would eat
your head off if you let them. So the town set up this factory
they call "the Workhouse" which they also welcome visiting
tramps into and put them to work at a trade, sewing sacks
maybe or making string or somesuch thing, in exchange for
board. Well this gradually put traveling paupers off from visiting; so there is only a trickle of such gentry coming now,
while everyone else is staying away in droves. ——Now at the
time we was dossed down in the "shambles house"; which is to
say we was staying at the parish almshouse, together with
them hoss-drawn beggars we come acrost in town. Well they
was kicking up the worse kind of a squawk inside the
almshouse about the business. I mean they ree-ly work themselves into a great stomping passion about it, saying, "Why,
this is a outrage! What they mean, 'No charity'? What's the
world come to if there's no charity in it? It's apostasy! For
these folks ain't Jews. Cain't be! They scarcely got enough
bowels of mercy to count as human beans even; let alone be
taken for sober-minded Jewish folks . . ." ——But the worse
ruckus come from this big pow'ful-looking redhead feller—
*Oh d-d-dang! Only wisht the Black Deuce hisself bust that bastid,
that's what I wisht . . .* ——Well-a-well . . . Anyhow this redhead
feller look to be the ringleader of that whole pack of gentry,
and he kep' stoking the fires, saying, "Brethren and Sistren!
This ain' only them wicked Cities of the Plain which God

pour fire and brimstones on for their sins. It is Sodom and Gomorrah, and surely these townfolks is Sodom and Gomorreans! Now I dessay we know what that mean, don' we, Brethren and Sistren! It mean they is Rich! It mean they is Wicked! It mean they is Mean! —Well why may only rich folks lay idle like they was lord and lady both, whilst others must live by the labor of their hands? For their sweet luxury, ain't it naught but the salt sweat of others? Ain't it naught but the grinding toil of others? Ain't it naught but the cruel travail of others? —Oh but they do think themselves such a genteel lot, and is ever so tender of their own persons, and is only too content that others shall do their work for them. A rich man, the fatter he be, the more healthier he be, the bigger his belly be, the more respec' he got, and folks will think him the finest creature to ever walk the earth. Whereas one of our own kind, let him only be so misfortunate as to enjoy sound health, and he must hide it like a thief! And if he try to earn his bread by good honest beggin', folks will only bridle and point a accusing finger at him, and say, 'Why cain't a big strapping young buck as yerself, sir, get a job!' Well, by jings! I say it is time the tables were turn, and their applecart upset. Let them rich folks try and do a honest day's work for once. What's the matter, they too sick to work?" —Well that piece of speechifying just about brung down the house, for next thing they was all hoist up on their hind legs and a-cheering that dang bastid redhead, and they was saying, "Hooroar for you Fybushie! . . . Atta boy! . . . You said it Fybushie! For ain't we as much God's creatures, and as fine Jews, as any them dainty gentry is or could be? So what make them so high and mighty? The nerve!" Then one by one the whole gang proceed to trickle out into the street, and they go about their separate businesses.

Well it were evenin' of that day, or the next maybe. And it

happen I was out alone, walking along past the shul yard. I remember it was gone dusk by then, and already dark, and even
a bit drizzly, as I recollect. Anyway, the street was just
a-humming with a great abundance of such goodly cheerful
folks (God bless), which the whiles was passing to and fro before the shul. But on a sudden I make out the sound of sobbing, and there was a kind of a prayerful yammer come from
in front of the shul yard, as of a man pleading with the folks
going by, and which I swear to goodness it may have drug pity
from a stone, it were so mournful to only hear it. Well it make
me stop, and I see it come from a pitiful broken-down-
looking gent which is standing nearby. And he were weeping,
with his arms stretch out, and holding a little cushion up for
the passerbys to see; from which a bitty chit of a baby was
wailing and choking and, oh, just crying its poor dear little
heart out so, you may have thought it was like to die of it.
And that unhappy papa he seem to be in the worse way, and
were only pitching hisself to and fro and side to side, cradling
that helpless chil' in his arms, and rocking it; and he clutch it
to his breas' each time, only crooning to it, in a oh-so-tender
voice, to quieten it, saying over and over, "Oh, misery me!
Oh, woe, my chick, oh, woe is you, my poor little orphan
girl! For your dear mama is dead, my dahlin' . . . Ah, ah!
There, there! Hushaby, my ba-by, don' cry . . . Oh, whatever
shall I do with you, my poor little pigeon . . ." —And everybody which pass by, put something into his outstretch hand.
And now and again a lady stop to say a comforting word to
him; though he only go on whimpery-like, saying, "Oh, misery my dove, oh, woe is you, my ba-by!" the whiles shaking
hisself and rocking that tiny infant; so my heart break for pity,
from only seeing that poor grieving gent and his motherless
babe in swaddling clothes, the way the both them was taking
on. So I dug down in my britches pocket and come up with a

threepenny bit. And I go over to him and reach my hand over the pillow to give it to him. On a sudden, though, he shot his own hand out, and he grab holt of my arm and pinch me hard on it, saying in that same whimpery voice, "Woe is *you*, my pigeon!" Only he come down sharp on that "you" like it was *me* he meant by it. Well that pinch of his hurt, and come so unexpected it give me a fright; so I jerk my hand away and jump aside astonish. And then that same unhappy gent turn his head round and nail me with a look. Well, seeing him up close, it about make my jaw drop to my knees, almost. —"Here, bub!" says he. "Whyn't you keep the kid yesself awhile, eh? Reckon I done with it for one day!" and he roughly push that pillow into my hands. And I see the little orphan she was only a doll dress up in rags. And that grieving papa? Why, he weren't no other than that bastid redhead Fybushie—*Black Deuce bust him to Aitch, the misable no-account r-r-rogue!* —Well-a-well . . . But I do own he went about it quite artful. I mean playing the both parts the way he done. First a-yammering and a-whimpering for hisself; and then a-wailing and a-mewling, oh, just fit to die, for that make-believe child! . . . Anyhow. So then he say, "It's the only way, y'know. I mean, dealing with that gumptionless bunch of featherheads pass themselves off for Jewfolks. Why, you have just got to humbug them! By hook or by crook. It's the game. Everybody's doing it. Ain't no other way, y'see. The rabbi, the magistrate, the dang almsman, and the rest 'em ever so holy-service folks, they all does it by putting on saintly airs and graces. Whilst me—*oh, misery me!*—I ain't got but my po' widdle dolly here. Well what's the cow got her tits for, unless it's so she may be milked? . . . Aw, come on, give us the good word from the amen corner, Fishke! G'wan, feller, jus' say it: *A-a-men!*"

Anyhow, whiles we was lodged at the almshouse with them hoss-drawn folks, that bastid redhead come slinking

round to my wife pretty regular, and commence playing up to
her with a passel of sweet talk and dainty twiddle-twaddle
you wouldn't believe. Seem he took a considerable shine to
her. Anything she wanted, she only ask—and he was up like a
shot and fetching it for her straightaway, and was only too glad
to oblige. And presently he work things so he get in real good
with her, and she come to think the world of him on account
of it. Well, he use to sit by her side for hours together, only
jabbering away at her the whole time. And now and again he
would pass the most shameful and rude remarks, so it make
her stop her ears not to hear it—least so it seem to me then.
And when he took to flattering her in the very worse way, saying how she was so buxom and so delectable, and how he was
greatly partial to fat women such as herself which had a bit of
heft to 'em—well she would scold him for it then and wallop
him acrost his back. Though she done it playful, and laugh a
good deal whilst doing it. And I laugh, too, only I confess that
I sometimes gritted my teeth the whiles. But then I thought
better of it: Now why should I waste any bother over that idle
windbag, thinks I. Come tomorrow, or next day maybe, we
shall be rid of this useless baggage anyhow. For it'll be goodbye forever betwixt us then, with each going his own separate ways. And we shan't never see his ugly mug again.
Besides which, when it come to calling on houses, it was only
me which she let to go round with her, praise Goodness. And
when he try and take her hand, to lead her, it make her so mad
she push him away, saying, "Oh pooh, sir! Why, you should be
ashame' of yourself, trifling so with a marry' lady which has
got a husband of her own to be going door-to-door with her.
It ain't decent. So get along with you, sir—go on, scat!"

   The day after I come upon that bastid redhead in front of
the shul—you know, whilst he were 'personating that helpless poor papa—well, that same morning, I was constrain' to

go calling on houses on my own, without my missus come along with me. For prompt she awoke, my wife complain of being poorly, and of feeling heavy and sort of queer all over, so it make her gape and stretch, and set her a-yawning all the time—which she reckon it wasn't the Good Eye but only the other kind (preserve us!) which cause it, so maybe she best stay home today and rest up. Nor was I quite up to snuff myself, really. For I was feeling bilious generally, and my food come up on me every now and again. And I must say it was awful lonesome to be going about solitary without my wife along. Because—well, there seem to be something missing, this time. No I shan't deny it, sirs—for once that bastid come worming his way into my wife's confidences, and got up to his monkey tricks with her, well she somehow become dearer to me for it. Though sometimes it vex me so, I was near to burn up on account of it; but then—oh I dunno—well, it also make me hanker after her too, like I been bewitch maybe. No, 'twere more like . . . more like—well, yeah . . . maybe 'twere more like one of them pleasuring pains which I gen'ly gets whilst scratching on a blister. For it were grief and sweetness both which I feel. —So anyhow the upshot was that the flavor had gone out of the business nor were my heart in it, so I only went through the motions of doing the door-to-door that day—you know, slapdash "knock-knock, in-out, thank'ee ma'am" fashion; and I shut up shop early and hurry on home, before the day were half out. Well, stepping into the almshouse, I observe my missus was there with that bastid, and they was both sitting a-whispering together; and my wife she had her head incline' in his direction, attending to his talk and her face aglow, and there was a kind of a sweet trembly smile which play on her lips the whiles, and which it never leave off even for a minute. Though when I come up to her and ask,

"How are you, dear?" it pull her up short, and she were like struck dumb momentarily, not knowing what to do. But then she roust herself and she touch my hand, the way she use to, and she say, "Know what, Fishke? Turn out I am sick. No, it weren't the Good nor the other Eye (touch wood) which was at fault. It's from all that walking we done. You know, the leechwife which she come round for charity healings; well she say I must try and get me over to the bathhouse (beg pardon), and be worked over with whupping twigs and cupped and bled; and I must have a rubdown all over with vinegar when I retires, so I work up a good sweat overnight. No, Fishke! from now on I cannot walk no more. Now it so happen the good Reb Fybushie here been so awful gracious as to offer to take us on board in his own private cover't wagon, and to do it free at no charge. So, what you think, Fishke? What you say, huh?"

And that dang bastid—which I only wisht he rot fr'ever!—well, he give me this slitty-eye look, with a weasely kind of a smile which it feel like I was being stuck with needles. Well, my heart plumb went out of me. Like I was a little boy at school, been already unbreeched and throwed over a bench, and was only waiting to be walloped by the rebbe. So I only work my jaw for a spell, without making no sound—for I didn't know what to say.

"So, whyn't you say nuffin'? What's the matter, cat's gotcher tongue?" My wife blurt this out fierce, and she commence to scream at me, saying, "Oh I knew it! You never give a dang for my health, do you! 'Cos you druther see me dead, wouldn't you! Well, you stinking li'l no-account—you gonna eat dirt first. For by jings I gonna pull your hair out! I gonna knock you teeth out! I gonna tear your heart out! I gonna . . . O Confound! You jus' wait and see what I gonna do!"

Well every time my wife open up a mouth and let rip like

that, it turn my insides to ice to hear it; and it always leave me all of a muddle and oh jus' about half dead for the anguish it give me. And how it make me feel this particular time, only the Good Lord Hisself can tell about. For what else could I do, except only to knuckle under? So I says, "Hush, dear! Ain't no call to take on so. Sure you can go! Why not! I never say you couldn't, did I?"

"Now that's more like!" says my wife. And her manner soften and she say, "But you might at least answer the next time a body talk to you—'stead of keeping mum like you was a block of wood. For here's ever such a sweet and kindly gent, actually ask us along for free, and you never even say thank'ee to him! Well shame on you, for being such a awful bear . . ."

Well there weren't anything I could do about it. So I done that too. I said thank'ee to the bastid.


—"WHOO-OOP, REB ALTER, another one!" says I, thunking in my shovel again, loud and clear.

"Don't tell me! Got up a new treat for us, huh?" says Alter—though he done it with maybe a smidgen of sarcastical lilt to his voice. "Now I just bet it's another one of them pathetic kinds of beggarfolk, ain't it. My gracious! I should of thought Providence by now put you in the way of a better sort of a bargain. Oh, be done with 'em, sir!"

"Why, no such thing, Reb Alter! All I meant was maybe we got us another Hyam-Hanan here. You know, the one who's Hya-'Tryna's mister? For our Fishke here must of stood quite as much in awe of his own missus, as that other gent done of his . . . er—don't you think, Reb Alter?"

# 15

FISHKE STARTED UP again after his fashion, whereat I set to work helping him out after my fashion, and Alter prodded him along after his fashion—by which several exertions the story was recommenced, so:


NEXT DAY AFTER that talk which I told about, them cava'ry folks pull up stakes and left *Sodom*. For, yes, that is how that town was call by that bunch! And certainly they lit out of there with a bang. For they had made a riproaring departure of it, with near every mouth amongst them was set a-howling and a-blaspheming together, and there being such a great creak and rattle of wheel and wagon got under way. And oh but didn't they just heap the dreadfulest curses on that town, too—saying how they wisht the place got struck by lightning, and all of them folks was burnt out of house and home, and drop dead of famine at least a dozen times every day, and be constrain' to tramp the earth forever a-begging their bread of strangers, like they was only a bunch of poor miserable combustibles whose property been reduce to ashes . . . Anyhow, there was three cover't wagons in that caravan; which each was jam-packed with menfolks and womenfolks of all kind, old and young folks, marry' and unmarry' folks, and little boys and girls. And me and my missus, we was settle' in amongst them as well. For by good fortune we was now come up in the world considerable, being we'd throwed in with them cava'ry folks, you see.

Well, good folks, I will allow it open up a whole new world to me, and at first I had quite a cheerful time of it amongst that bunch. For it certainly give me a chance to see and hear tell of some v-ery exceptional marvels which I never know of before; though there was a-way too many such, for me to describe all of it in every particular. For instance, I use to hear the way they always spoke ill of everything and everybody under the sun, making fun and 'personating them in the most spiteful fashion; and each of them dainty rogues would be telling in that canting lingo they use, about all of the dodges and mean tricks they was always pulling on honest folks. So one feller may come along and tell about the haul he made whilst "stringing beads" (that's to say, he been stealing bread); and another would talk about how he been "hunting beaks and hook hisself a cackler" (in other words he went out looking for poultry and swiped a chicken); and then someone else would tell about how he been "dipping for clangers" (which means he been picking pockets), and also been generally raising Cain and making decent folks' lives a misery for them; and another might boast of how he'd gone and "baldowered a swell" (which is to say he beat up some filthy rich squire's kid and leave him for dead). Now about squires, though—that's to say pow'rful bigwigs—well, there wasn't nobody which they loved to cuss more than squires. Why, they was forever cussing out squires. And they be doing it just about all the time; and at the drop of a hat, too, and for no better reason than only it suited them to do it. For, gen'men, you have my solemn word on it—why, I'll swear to it in prayershawl and vestments, that them folks hated squires a deal worser even than any squire ever hated them. For by their lights, saying someone was a squire was tantamount to calling him a "mean bloodsucking leech"; or a "jellybelly greedygut"; or a "dumb stonyheart bonehead"; or a "sof' mollycoddle' letch"; or a "brazenface lahrdy-dah copperhead" or even—oh, the deuce only know what-all kinds of evil names they thunk up to call them, for they was legion. And what is

more they actually believe it was their bounden duty to be
playing it low-down and mean with squires, and be doing
them wicked turns anytime they was give the chance to do it.
And if ever they was having a bad time themselves, or was in
oh jus' any ole kind of trouble, why they would blame that on
squires too, and be calling bellyaches down on them, and the
dry gripes, and the chilblains, and the ague, and the rheuma-
tism, and near about every painful bodily misery and sickness
which you can only think of. And, why, sometimes they even
use to call *me* "Squire"—though they done it in jest, because
oftentimes I stuck up for squires and took their part when
them folks had went a bit too far in slighting their honor. For I
got to know squires pretty good in my time, on account I was
bred up amongst them, you see. I mean back when I been
earning my keep in the bathhouse, over to Glupsk. And I must
say I did have quite a lot of dealings with them, too—what
with keeping watch over their clothing for all of them years,
and delivering their duds and things when they was finish
bathing, and bringing in a bucket of water whenever it was
wanted and hot coals to light up their seegars with, and oh
just all sorts of other such business in kind besides. —And I
also use to listen to the young fellers and gels, whilst they was
playing and canoodling together, and talking marriage. For
marriages was arrange between the wagons like between families. But what them folks put a particular value on, was the
art of disguise and 'personation. This was their stock-in-trade.
And most any of that fine gentry, male and female both, could
'personate a hunchback or a gimper easy, or being blind, or a
deaf mute, or even being limbless. But genuine articles in this
line was a rare sight amongst them. I mean real cripples, like
me and my wife was. And such folks was therefore accounted
a great asset by them. In fact they was always saying how honester goodness real blemishes, such as ours, was a gift from

Sweet Heaven Itself and a godsend to poorfolks, and was sure to bring great profit. Though it was my wife's blemish which please them best. For blindness was highly prize' by them folks. That apart, she let her mouth rattle on something fierce these days, like it been put on wheels and oiled. Why it make your hair curl, only to hear the way she open up her yap and let rip. Which certainly add considerable to her reputation amongst the crowd.

And that bastid redhead, all he ever seem to do lately was to hang about my wife. Stick to her like glue is what he done, always making up to her and catering to her every whim, and generally spoiling her rotten. Why he'd of even fed her tur-tledove milk straight from the pigeon's own breast, if she only ask for it. But as it was, he only brung her every dainty which was conceivable, in the way of ordinary human provender: like cook' peas, spice' hoarse beans, stew' prunes—and what-all else he manage to get his hooks into. Thinks I: All right, consarn you! Go ahead. Indulge her, pamper her, spoil her. For what you think you gonna gain by it, huh? . . . Why, nix! 'Cause this is one marry' lady which already got a husband. Well, now, that's that, I reckon. Ain't nothing to worry about from *that* quarter. Or ain't there? —Well, now, p'raps it is her blemish which has got him prancing about her so. For anybody know there is money to be made from going about hand-in-hand with blind cripples. Well you can go bust a gut you rapscallionly rogue! 'Cause it is only me which my missus ever go calling on houses with. So what you work so hard buttering her up for, dang fool! For all that skulking about and underhand scheming of yourn will not answer, sir. No, it won't! On ac-count, mister, the point is this—*It is always me she do the door-to-door with.* Me! Always was, always shall be! Got it, mister!?

And that is why, gen'men, seeing as all this been going through my mind at the time, I got the pow'rful notion to make a study of beggarcraft; to learn all about it, even to the las' jot and tittle. For I done it on account of my wife, so she'd like me. And I done tolerable good, too, if I may say. Why, I already got down pat the part about barging in on folks at home. Now, the trick of it is this: You have got to walk in that door looking fierce, like you was in oh the worse temper and fit to bust of it. And you must insist on that handout—not just ask for it, mind—but *demand* it, same as you was collecting a debt. And once you are in, you don't stop at the hall nor in the front parlor even, but you run in and out of every room in that house, comb it front to back, and hunt up the master and mistress, both of which is generally hole' up in the bedroom. So that's one thing. —Anyway, when it come to haggling, I ree-ly got that business pared down to a art. I mean there weren't nobody which I took a back seat to, not in that department. You see, the skill of it is to look always dissatisfy'. No matter how much folks may fork up by way of charity, you don't never let on it is enough. Say they try and fob you off with some lef'over bread. Well, you ask for a proper feed hot off the stove—like a bowl of borsch, for instance; or if they give you money, you tell them it won't do—no, for you must have a shirt or a pair of worn britches maybe. But the main thing is to be always grumbling, to be always turning up your nose and making a face and . . . well, a strong dose of colorful language will go a considerable ways, too.

Between whiles, though, what's that rogue redhead been up to? Scheming, that's what. Yeah, dang him! for that bastid been figuring how to get rid of me. And all along he been thinking: Whoa there, bub! When it come to playing the pauper game, you ain't good enough to even fire up my stove. On account I got you beat a thousand times over in that line. And if I have a mind to pair up in a business way with that blind little lady of yourn, there is sure to be profit in it. So you jus'

wait, buster, for I gonna settle your hash! —Which is what he
done, and in very short order. For he make a patsy of me. And
by the time he get through, I was sunk right down to nothing
in my wife's opinion, and was made to look a complete fool.
In the end all I ever hear from her was: "Oh I wisht you curl
up and die!" or "Whyn't you go feed the maggots!" or "Git
stuffed, you no-account so'n'so and so'n'so!" and near every
other kind of nasty name-calling besides. And that bastid redhead—*(Oh I wisht . . . I only wisht to sweet Goodness he never see
the resurrection, that's what I wisht!)*—Well-a-well . . . Anyhow,
that bastid would not let up on his gibes and persecutions, till
I was sure they would be the death of me. For on account of it
I was made the butt of general scorn and was kicked around
by just about everyone. And soon enough all them wagons
was at it, doing their level best to make my life a constant misery. There wasn't a minute go by, without one of them dainty
gentry playing me for a fool, or thinking up some new insult
by which to call me. Each of them folks done as they please
with me, and I become the whupping boy of that whole gang.
And if I sometimes got riled because of it, they all come
down on me at once, saying: "Why look at our 'Squire' get in a
tantrum! Soon he gonna get all tearful on us, by jings!" And if
I cry in the course of a beating, they only say: "What you so
tickled about, Fishke? Look'ee, folks! Fishke's nigh fit to die
laughing. Why he's been laughing so hard it brung tears to his
eyes!" And then I hear that bastid's voice egging on the rest,
saying: "That's the ticket! Fishke could do with a laugh, poor
feller. Go head, folks, lay into him. More! Harder! Whup him
about the calves, and rub up his hamstrings some; maybe we
get a rise out of him yet. And don't forget to tickle him acrost
the withers too. For that's sure to get a good horselaugh out
of him. And if that don't jolly him up considerable, try
stroking his head and grab aholt of his ear, and then put a flea

up it. See if that improve his humor some. Remember, good folks, it be our bounded duty to try and assist our fellow human beans—specially they happens to be Jewish human beans!" And there was times, too, when they even throwed me out of the wagon; and I was made to hop along crook-footed after it, trying to keep up as best I could, whilst the folks inside was laughing and clapping their hands and a-whooping: "Atta boy, Fishke! Lessee you cut a caper, feller! Dance, Fishke, dance! Whoo-eee! look at that boy go! Why Fishke could dance anybody off their feet, if he'd only a mind to." And one of them took to calling out then (for it were that bastid redhead, dang him!): "Why look'ee here, folks! Fishke ain't no gimp. Why, no! That rascal been pulling our legs all along, letting on as how he weren't but a poor woeful cripple. For shame, Fishke! Now I'll bet a swift boot up his privates would iron out that kink he got in his drumsticks. Haw-haw-haw!" —In short, gents, I was made as miserable and as wretched as a body could only be. And oh how I remembered them early days in the bathhouse, and all the years which I were setting pretty in that place, and living as careless and as easy as any lord might do on his manor. Oh I tell you it were as near as a body could hope to get on this earth to God's own paradise. For I wanted for nothing then . . .

—"WELL, SO WHYN'T you get a divorce?" says Alter, inter-rupting Fishke in his own person this time. "I mean that's what Jewish folks gets divorces for, ain't it!"

WHY, THAT'S TRUE (returns Fishke with a sigh), and I wisht only I done it earlier. For it would of made a world of differ-ence to me and . . . well, maybe also to a certain other person

as well. Only I dunno what come over me. I reckon I was
under a spell. For it truly shames me to confess it, but deep in
my heart I come to hanker after my wife considerable. And
however grievous I was made to suffer for it, the devil had got
into me where that woman was concern'. Now maybe I was
only being stubborn, thinking, Well, you bastid rogue, if you
got a mind to be living in sin with my wife whilst dumping
me, you can forget it! For I shan't never give her up now, and
shall hold on twice as hard, if only for spite . . . Or maybe it
was—well, how shall I put it? Something which come on me
of its own . . . like witchcraft, as I said. For I was bewitch' by
her in a way. You see, I were greatly smitten by her looks too.
For in her way she was quite a handsome women, what with
being so full of figure and well-rounded and plump; and
comely of feature too—not what you call beautiful, but pert
and pretty like. Oh I admit there was plenty of times when
my troubles got so bad, I come nigh to make an end and kill
myself. Today! I says to myself then, I shall tell her today! Divorce! We are finish for good . . . But I scarce work myself up
to approach her about it and she'd be making with the sweet
talk; or she put her hand on my shoulder and say, "Come
along, Fishke, le's you and me make the rounds!" and somehow I lose all power of speech then, and my mood was turn
completely round.

Once, on one of them rare good days, me and my wife was
out together doing our rounds; and don't you know I was in a
high humor on account of it, and feeling right blithe. So I ask
her outright: "Bassia dearest," I says (for that were her name),
"now what earthly good is it our being always on the road like
this? It don't seem right somehow. Least not for our likes.
Back in Glupsk we was people of some consequence and was
well thought of by folks. Now, I be the first to admit that it
was you which took me out of the bathhouse, but . . . well,

after all, a brick bathhouse, such as Glupsk offer, ain't to be dismiss' by a wave of the hand. Only think of all them fine folks and prime gentry which use to pass through its doors. As for yourself, my dear, there wasn't nobody which weren't acquainted with you in that town, let alone fail to treat you with respect. But look at what become of us now, traveling hither and yon in strange places as we do; and in no better company than a lot of mangy tramps and draggletail riffraff. Well, that scarcely adds to our reputation, does it?"—"Don't tell me you actually thinking of going back to Glupsk?" says my wife, looking riled. "Well you go back yerself, if you miss it so much. 'Cos me, I ain't never going back! That fool place got quite enough paupers knocking about it these days, without yours truly being amongs' them. For ain't a day go by, which you don't see some new kind of pauper or fresh almsman mooching around; why, even repectable householders has took up cadging bags and gone a-begging at each other's doors."—"Well, then, forget Glupsk," says I. "Why, gracious! but it don't *need* to be Glupsk, darling. Just *choose* a town— any town your dear heart desire, for us to settle down in. So long as we know it is *our* town, and the houses is *our* houses, and the folks living in it is *our* folks—why it'd be a blessing all round for us. For how's the saying? *Ain't never a dog but don't got its own mess of garbage . . .*"

"Soon, Fishke, soon," says my wife, the whiles clapping me friendly-like on the back. "But first, whyn't we ride about for a bit yet. Maybe see some more of the world, enjoy ourselfs. What you say, huh? For surely I cain't think on nothing which give more pleasure than travelin' about so. All what's wanted is a little patience, and you shall have your town. Soon, Fishke, it'll be soon, I promise!"

Only that "soon" of hern stretch out for such a monstrous spell there seem to be no end to it. And in the course of it we pass through I don't know how many towns. Nor was my troubles grown the less for it. Which last, I only had that bastid rogue to thank for . . .

FISHKE SIGHED DEEPLY. He shut his eyes and had fallen silent, whilst we waited for him to emerge from his reverie. Which he did soon enough without our prompting, and took up his tale again. The sequel of which proceeded so:

# 16

WELL SO AFTER being call the "Squire" for a spell, I got a new title pinned on to me: *Psalms-almsman*. And this new moniker was thunk up especial for me by that same dang redhead rogue as before, deuce bust him! So that is how everyone amongst that bunch took to calling me *Fishke the Almsman*. Now there weren't any more wicked nor fouler utterance which them gentry could ever conceive than "psalms-almsman"; so if they say it, they make sure to spit seven times to cure the evil which come of it. You know the way workingfolks and shop-keepers and commercial gents all hates each other in the worse way? Well, sir, that ain't tantamount to dog flop, next to how hoss-drawn beggars despise the town-bred variety; in particular the whole herd of psalms-almsmen—which I must say was one subject they certainly use to work up quite a head of steam over, grumbling and going on about how them stink-ing vultures wasn't only a shiftless bunch of high-nose mag-goty holier-than-thou psalm-mumblers; and it was intolerable the way they always come down on weddings or circumci-sions, or even a funeral or suchlike festivity like flies buzzing

round a dead horse, stuffing their faces full and pocketing
money; and how they don't never stick at nothing, but make a
easy living off of both the quick and the dead; whilst on the
other hand *we* folks (meaning hoss-drawn gentry) must forever be a-sweating and a-toiling, working our poor heads off
till we drop, only to put short rations on our table. And only
lookit what that rascally namby-pamby lot of mincing rogues
done to King David's Psalter. Only made a game of it! Why if
good King David would of only knowed into whose grubby
little hands them beautiful Songs of his was to fall, and what
sorts of livings them shifty-eye prayermongers was to make
of them, well it's a leadpipe cinch he wouldn't of bothered to
put pen to paper in the first place.

"No Bassia!" the bastid say to my wife once. "It ain't no use.
Nothing ever gonna lick that Fishke of yourn into shape, and
make a proper man of him. He don't have it in him to be one
of us. For he's a almsman, you see. Always was, always will
be. Bred in the bone. Why it's writ all over him. And none of
your traveling about, trying to show him the world, gonna
improve him. I mean look at him! Feller don't know shucks
from sheep dip when it come to beggar lore. For he's just no
good, Bassia, and no good ever come of him. Mark my words,
all you gonna get from him is a busted bladder, poor thing . . .
Oh Bassia, Bassia! If only I had me such a dear precious creature by my side as yerself, why I swear we both be on Easy
Street. Yes, indeed, ma'am, on Easy Street!"

But following all these connivings to make our marry' life
wretched, and the slanders which that bastid dream up about
me, all of which was lies to take away my wife's affections
from me, he now lit on a new thing. Unbeknownst he went
and told on me to the missus, bearing tales to her about how I
been casting sheep's eyes at one of the gels from another
wagon, and was keeping company with her a sight too cozy, if

you ask him . . . Well, you see, amongst them scoundrels there was a hunchback girl, uh, a young lady which, well sure I like talking with her, and a whole lot, but . . .

—"HA? WHAT'S ALL this about girls, uh, young ladies, Fishke?" says me and Alter, breaking in upon Fishke's story. "C'mon, young feller, out with it. 'Fess up now!"

"Well, sirs, she were a complete outsider to the folks on board that wagon; and the poor soul she suffer quite enough afflictions for one as was so young. And I confess I like being with her just to talk. The pair of us would set alone then and be pouring our hearts out to each other. And she'd feel sorry for me, and many a time she use to cry for pity over my trouble. Ah, if you only knew, sirs, what a noble creature that girl is! And oh the trouble she got, poor dear, such terrible trouble . . ." And the tears started up in Fishke's eyes as he said it.

Me and Alter both pressed Fishke to tell us more of this young woman, about who she was and what had happened to her . . .

WELL NOW SINCE you gen'men so insistent (says Fishke after wiping his eyes in his sleeve)—that's to say if you ain't growed tired of me talking, I shall oblige as best I can. Only I hope, gen'men, you won't take it amiss if my telling is maybe a bit rough.

She weren't hardly more than a tot when her mama brung her to Glupsk carrying only a bundle of old featherbeddin' and a couple odd sticks and pieces besides; which along with her little girl the mother drop off at the house of some wrinkle-up old lady which look a right ole witch, she appear

so ugly and mean. Well, it seem like that old woman run a service for housemaids, and she and the little girl's mama use to
go off together and disappear for the whole day, leaving that
poor chil' behind without a morsel to eat all day long. Only
one time the girl begun to cry something cruel, pleading with
her mama to please take her along. Well the old woman got
pretty rile up on account of it, saying, "No, you dassn't! That
chil' must be kep' secret and no one must know; for it be bad
for business!" Though by and by the mama did take her little
girl along, and lucky she snuck it unbeknownst into the
kitchen of some rich folks she been working for. But it don't
take long before she and her mama move on to another
kitchen, and then to another and another, till in very short
order they gone through a considerable sight of kitchens that
way. And each time they come into a new place, well, the way
her mama treat her went from bad to worse. She never really
knowed her father. For back home he weren't hardly around,
him being on the road and traveling all of the time; and now
they was staying in them kitchens, she never seed him at all.
And she'd of maybe forgot all about him, if only her mama
weren't cussing him every minute of the day, whilst she pour
out all the bitterness in her heart against him, going on about
him being some precious father, and how she hope to goodness he only die for the ill he done to her—the way he turn
her out of house on a sudden, her which been a true and faithful wife to him for all of them years; in which time all that
man ever give her anyways was a mess of bellyaches and anguish; and then he hung that troublesome chil' on her neck as
well, which were more like a millstone, when it's hisself
which deserve being hung in the first place—yes, hung by the
neck till his eyes pop and his tongue hang out—for weren't
nobody in the wide world which will have her now, and

nowhere which she can settle down neither—no not with that surplus baggage she been left holding, and which more-over she is constrain' to lug about with her all over; and for-ever hiding it away what's more, on account ain't nobody fool enough to even look at, let alone hire, a cook which is got herself stuck with a little chil' . . . —And it do so happen that more'n once the mistress of the house come a-stomping into the kitchen in high temper, when dinner weren't quite up to her standard. And she raise the roof then, a-screaming and a-hollering about how come God punish her with such a cook; besides which, where do that woman get the raw gumption to be skimmin' the chicken fat from off the top of the soup and feedin' it to that precious li'l daughter of hern?—Though it weren't so; she never done it, and that lit-tle girl only been getting skinnier and skinnier, and was nigh famishing from hunger. For her mama use to stick her well out of sight, like she was ill-gotten goods, a-way up on the mantel ledge over the stove; where she set all day long, scrooch up into a little ball and hunch over, and weren't allow to make a sound, even a whimper. And she used to grow faint from smellin' the savory smoke of that roas' goose and them fry' chicken livers cooking below—but her? . . . *hush!* not one word; for she suffer her hunger in silence. Till at last somebody think to put a dry crust of bread into her little hand, or maybe a bone which already been suck clean of nourishment, or some such played-out oddment from the meal just finish. And there was times too when nobody even thought to bother; and she could not contain herself no more, so she give a little whimper, poor thing. Then *up* come the poker—or a long-handle scoop or a ladle—and down it come again *thwack!* on her head, or on her hand or foot, whichever get in the way first—whilst her mama set to railing again, though in good earnest now, calling down imprecations on her papa's head, and then on *his* papa's head before him, and right on down the line to every papa ever draw breath since ole Papa Abraham was papa to us all. So you see it were on account her being made to scrooch up in the one place for so long and bent double, which make her the hunchback she become.

Now looking down from her perch so, the girl see a gentleman caller which took to dropping by her mama's kitchen quite regular. And Mama go all tender and sof' when he were around. And she fuss over him so, and feed him all kinds of good things, always stuffing savories and sweets down his pockets, and money too sometimes. And quite often this same swell gent come by latish and stay the night. And sometimes, too, her mama went out on a sudden and stay away until all hours. Though she prink up first, and would stare and stare at her reflection in the glass for the longest spell. But off she go finally, and leave her child on its own and unattended. Well seem like the girl's mama had got her mind set on marriage, so all she had any thought for now was the gent which was her betrothed.

Then one day a stranger come round to the kitchen and collect her mama's things. And her mama thank the mistress for her gift of bridal bread and salt, and at last she lift her little girl which ain't only half dressed from off the stove and they both leave. And her mama take the little girl by the hand, and it seem they walk forever before her mama stop in a side street, and she say: "Set and wait here! For kindly folks will surely come by . . ." That's all her mama say. For next thing she were gone.

So that poor abandon' creature done what she been told, and she only set in that one place afraid to stir, just like when

she live over the stove. And all the while a chill autumn driz-
zle come down which soak her to the bone. For she scarcely
had no more cover than that one blouse she wear, and her
teeth was a-clacking and a-chattering from the cold and wet
together. And if a passerby stop and ask, "Who are you,
chil' . . . ?" all she say is, "I'm my mama's . . . Mama says set
quiet, *hush!* mustn't yell, on account the poker come and hit
me . . ." So that is how the foolish thing pass her day until way
past evening. When a woman happen by and sweet-talk her
into coming home with her, which were only a tumbledown
hut "somewheres on the dunes" as we say, in a run-down
neighborhood amongst other shackly concerns same as hers.

Well the girl stay with the woman a long while. But she
never lick no honey there. The woman said she were her auntie, and that was how she must be called. Now Auntie were
one of the barrow ladies which gener'ly stand in the marketplace hawking spuds and hot buttercakes, and what you call
your "All-vows pears" and "Land-o'-Israel apples," and other
cheap truck besides. And first light every morning she use to
go to market, and leave the little hunchback girl behind to
tend the baby daughter which were her own. And the little
girl do the house chores as well. So she pick up wood off the
ground for fuel; and she crawl under the stove amongst
the chickens and collect the eggs which the hens laid there; and
she scrape out the porridge crust in the pot; and she scrub the
night soil out of the baby's frock in the slop pail; and she keep
watch over the wooden dairy-ladle and the baby bedding, all
of which been laid out to dry in the sun, atop the earthen-
work setter outside the house; and—well, she done any number other such household businesses. Come dusk the barrow
lady return. So she send her little maidservant a-begging door
to door, foraging for bread. Some of which charitable crusts

the little girl manage to nourish herself with, giving away all the rest to her Auntie.

One time, summer, it were getting on to dusk, whilst she been out on her rounds, calling on houses. And she were clad skimpy, for all she had on was a mean little blouse of coarse linen and only a skirt beneath. Well she somehow contrive to stray a considerable distance from the house. Till she end up away over in the fields, to the edge of town, and couldn't find her way home again. By now, though, the sun were long set. And by and by a rack of dark angry clouds come a-racing in and blanketed up the sky, and now and again there was even claps of thunder, and white flashes of lightning was seen. But then on a sudden, a couple of teamed-up cover't wagons in tandem come a-larruping pass, which was on their way out of town, and they look to have a monstrous great crush of passengers on board. —"Hey, look'ee!" cries the gentry inside. "There's a poor li'l hunchback girl knocking about on her own out there. Why she's a-crying, poor thing!" And prompt, down jump this redhead stranger—why yes, that is who it were. That same bastid redhead rogue as before—*deuce bust him to Aitch!* Well he ask her who she belong to, and she say, all tearful-like, "Oh please, mister, I want to go home to my Auntie!" —"Hush, my chil'!" returns the bastid. "Don't worry. I'll take you home to Auntie, this minute!" —And he took holt of the girl and toss her into one cart, and then he drive off with her.

And from that time forward the hunchback girl been dragged along from place to place by them hoss-drawn gentry; which for their part make their mite of profit out of her poor broken back. Now, the way they went about it is this. The minute they come into a town, well they just drop her barefoot and in rags in some well-traffic' thoroughfare, where

she suppose to stand about all day, a-snivelin' and a-blubberin',
pleading for a handout from passerbys in a tearful singsong,
and to waylay folks and be clutching at their clothes, or grabbing aholt of them by the hand or by a leg, if need be. And if
it sometime happen she didn't carry off that hokum slapstick
sufficiently lively, and her takings come up short on account
of it—why, them rogues play merry Aitch with her then. For
they beat that girl merciless for it. And in dead of night they
toss her naked and hungry into the street; where she remain
till the morning, a-wailing and a-weeping in good earnest this
time. I remember once she told of how on a bitter winter
night they dump her in street that way. And how the cold had
took aholt of her and lash her body and pinch it so, she were
like to twist into a pretzel and be froze solid by it. Why it
were so perishing cold, she thought her brainpan come adrift
of her head. And her vision blurred so, she was blinded by
light and dark flashes together, till she believed she were
breathing her last. Finally she couldn't bear it; so she took to
yammering pitifully at the door, and was shaking like an aspen
and pleading for mercy. She beg: "Oh please open, Auntie, oh
please open, Uncle!" for that was how she call them folks. She
holler: "Oh Uncle, I swear I'll holler my head off when next I
go a-begging!" She cry: "Oh Auntie dearest, I promise I shall
cry ever so good next time!" But all her begging and all her
hollering and all her crying avail her naught. For no one let
her back in. So she lay quiet, feeling neither pain nor cold.
And a sweet slumber overtook her, and it seem to her she
were being clasp to someone's bosom, and they commence a-
hugging and a-petting her so tender it make her glow and feel
warm all over . . . That was when they were carrying her
back in, more dead than alive. She was sick a long time after
that. Though by and by they took to dropping her off of the
wagon the minute they spy a fine-looking carriage up the road

with prime Quality on board—say maybe one of them swell
heathen country squires, or a rich gent-at-trade or some such
worthy personage. And when they set her down, she was expected to get up to the same monkey tricks as before. Which
is to say, to be stretching out her hands and be hopping madly
about, and be a-jabbering and a-wailing and a-weeping to the
passengers whilst running helter-skelter along the roadside
beside the carriage; and even running ahead of it, to head off
the horses, if it's wanted—in short to do everything she can
do to get that handout, even it cost her life. Sometimes, during such proceedings, she get lashed by the coachman's whip.
But she swallow that without a murmur. For she know it were
nothing beside what she get if she return empty-handed. For
Heaven help her then . . . Oh it can scarce be related what
terrible griefs that girl were made to suffer whilst still only a
chil'. Nor is her life much improve now she grow up. There is
not a tormented soul in Hell which deserve suffering the way
that girl been made to suffer. Oh it make my blood boil only
to think of it. Why, I give my life to save her. For I tell you
flat, gen'men, there was never a finer, nor a gentler, nor a better creature in this world than that girl is!

# 17

FISHKE'S STORY HAD got us all very down, and Alter and me
were put in an exceeding somber mood by it. Alter took to
kneading his brow, rubbing it as if there was an itch there
needed attending to; the while he kept up a mournful cluck-
ing and a-sighing to himself, saying, "Tsk, tsk, tsk . . . Ah,
me . . . tsk, tsk!"

—"Know what, Alter?" says I cheerily breaking in on the

silence. "I think Fishke gone and fall head over heel for that hunchback young lady. I mean only look; for all the signs there by golly—"

WELL, SIRS, I shan't deny it (says Fishke). No. Nor why ought I? For truly I come to love her, on account I was sorry for her. And I were drawn close to her, too. I come alive only setting by her side. Why? No special reason. Sometimes we just talk, and sometimes we only set looking at each other. And oh my how that goodness of hern shone and lighted up her face then! And her glance, why 'twere that which only a loving sister might give to her troubled brother, when she herself was troubled in no small way on her own account. And when she take my grief to heart, so she even come to the point of tears because of it, the feeling it give me was so warm and so tender that I thought . . . well I thought—oh, I don't even know myself what. Only by golly it put fire in my belly, and . . . well, it caress my soul as well. And I says to myself: Fishke, you are not alone in world. No, you are not. Not anymore! And I could feel hot tears of thankfulness rolling down my cheeks then . . .

About my wife though—well, small wonder that it didn't seem to bother me much anymore. I mean about her carryings-on with the bastid. Oh, sure, it burn me up right enough, only . . . well, it weren't quite the same as before. For I thought: Now, Fishke! You ain't ree-ly wishing that your wife up and say to you, "Enough being on the road. Time we settle in town permanent!" So then I contrive ways in my mind to weasel out of it, and be putting her off. For otherwise, who be looking after my poor hunchback girl? . . . Only here's a pretty pass, gen'men! You see, whilst my feelings for my wife been growing colder, so I don't even fret over her shameful flirtations, *she* only begin to show more affection to me. For suddenly she turn butter-soft, and she be clinging to me and hanging about my neck so you wouldn't believe. But just as sudden the whole thing went bust. For she give me the colicks, way she now took to grieving and tormenting me oh just awful, maybe a thousand time worse than before. It got so bad in fact, I begun to wish I was dead all over again. Thinks I: My gracious but that woman do blow hot and cold. Now what got up *her* nose, I wonder? She gone crazy? or she only got a screw loose! I mean the thing had got me completely stumped. Though it weren't long before that boil finally come to a head, and the venom scooshed out all at once. So now I knowed the true cause of her tantrums, and the reason why they come about. Oh I tell you it were a shameful business; and it pains me to be telling of it . . .

FISHKE SAT MEDITATING awhile. Then he roused himself, and commenced scratching vigorously. And seemingly having obtained relief by the exertion, he proceeded with his recital:

NOW ONCE'T, WE struck this small town someplace, and as per usual we make straightways for lodging at the almshouse there. Well, good gents, I seed a sight of almshouses in my lifetime, so I should say I pretty well know what to expect of such places. But this one took the cake, for bad as the rest was, they was gold next to it. Why to be recollecting it even now make my flesh itch so, I must scratch to relieve it. As a general thing, though, it give the appearance of nothing so much as a great big tumbledown old tavern; oh just a most ruinous-looking old spread which well deserve its moniker "shambles house"; for the whole concern weren't only a mess of crumbly rotted timbers, without a upright in it which wasn't at a crazy incline to the rest. And the roof look like granny's ole bonnet been knock'd into a cocked hat, way that huffy-nosed front end point a-way up in the air, whilst the rear look to have give the game up, and plump itself down on the ground. Why 'twere plain enough that that creaky old dump knowed its end was come, and all it want was to be allowed to fall down and expire in peace, and only be let lie in a restful heap of junk. But them townfolks wouldn't let it. No. For whenever it appear a piece of it going to drop, they all only come a-running, yelling timb-e-e-r! and prop it up again with whatever length of board happen to come handy; and then they offer up thanksgiving, wishing it another twice threescore year more of long and happy life. Anyhow we just roll right on in, wagons and all, through what suppose to serve for a gateway, as 'twere. And we come into what look at first to be the insides of a big gloomy house, with a dirt floor. But it were really a kind of a roofed-over yard—like a innyard maybe—which the walls was so broken up from old age, you could see right through to the outside, and bits and bobs of daylight come a-dribbling in everywhere by way of the splits and cracks. For it were a toss-up if the walls or holes had got the upper hand. And the ground round about was a mess of ruts and chuckholes fill' with steaming mucked-up puddles and runnels of ooze. Which they wasn't only the remainders of sluiced-out house slops, and of the rain let in all the time by the thatch; the straw being so old and raddled it only leak like a sieve, and which you could see the rubbed-out fag ends was strewed all over the floor. Although the grounds was just one big wasteyard anyways, what with there being such a whale of a lot of junk and wares kicking about. Like there was torn-up bags and ratty old rushmats, and there was spent shoes gone to bits and pieces, which run to battered uppers,

and wore-out soles, and boot heels with the rusty nails sticking out of them; and there was smashed pots, and busted
hoops, and spokes, and hairballs, and bones, and played-out
broomstubs plus broomsticks which come adrift of them,
and—well, no end of other such garbage. All of which collection of discards just lay a-moldering and a-sweating away,
whiles it give off all sorts of crazy smells that loaned a kind of
a ripe air to the place, don't you know, which only stunk to
high heaven on account of it. Well, now, to get from that yard
into the actual almshouse, you must first push past a mean-
looking rickety little side door, which open with a most
villainous-sounding *scree-k!* into the lodgehouse. This being all
only one room, with very small, very narrow, ill-fitted windows, of which the panes was knocked out of some, and was
pasted over with heavy sugar-loaf wrapping paper, or just
hung with rags. Though there was whole windows, too. Except they was either cover't in filth, with the mold laid on
thick in the corners; or else the glass in them was so old, they
got that 'ere funny-looking sort of a shimmery yallory-green
coloring to 'em, which it hurt your eyes to look at. You know,
same as scraping on a glass will do to your ears. And that
room, well, there was bunks made of boards in it, laid out on
top of a lot of old blocks and stumps and other odd timber;
which they run round the whole length of that grimy beaten-
up wall, and round the big stove set in the middle, and which
they was different sizes of long and short wooden pegs sticking out of the walls above them. Also there was two ropes
with loops at the end dangling from a sooty ceiling, which got
a long pole slung through the loops, so it hung down by its
ends acrost the length of the room. Well that long stick, together with them pegs in the wall, they was draped with
every kind of raggedy attire in the way of tore-up coats and
dresses, and with ratty cadging bags and other beggartruck.

Which property belong to the tramps and hoss-drawn paupers that stops there. All of 'em visiting gentry being made
up of young and old, and male and female both, which they
live mixed up together in that same room. But now that
almshouse wasn't just a stopping place only. It were a hospice,
too, that's to say it was the place for the dirt-poor of the
parish to die in case they was sick. And the town leechman,
well he only done everything he could for them, in the way of
cures: for he would cup 'em, and he would leech 'em, and he
would cut and bleed 'em direct, if that's what was wanted.
For all which charitable bloodlettings the parish foot the bill,
till at last that poor devil give up the ghost and pass on;
whereat the almshouse keeper come in—him doing double
duty as boss of the place and town gravedigger; and straightway he bury the body, proper. Through, mind, this service too
is give away free gratis, and for nothing. Well, now, the
almshouse keeper and his family keep house on the premises
anyways. Where they got themselves a kind of a cubbyhole
which may pass for a room, if you care to stretch a point.
Though, apart from him being Almshouse Keeper, Gravedigger, Sexton in the Burial Society, Superintendent in the Hospice, the Queen Vashti and Mordecai Hisself for Booker
Esther Entertainments on the Purim, the Bear-Mummer who
dress up droll on the Simchas Torah in a coat with the fur lining turned out, and General Funnyman and all-around Jack-
o'-Allwit at Engagements, Weddings, and Circumcisions, on
which several Festal Occasions he also double as the Waiter—
so anyhow what I say is this: Apart from all these livings, he
also got hisself another trade as town Tallows' Chandler. On
account all the households and shuls in the parish order their
tallow candles at home from that same gent, personal—
which, whilst they is being made, certainly are incline' stink
up the almshouse monstrous, as well as throwing off quite a

rank smell for a considerable circonference around and about
that neighborhood.

When our bunch arrive in the almshouse it was book'
solid. The almshouse keeper was even turning visiting gentry
out: "You been settle in for quite long enough!" he say. "So
fare'ee-well and Godspeed, and go park the carcass elsewhere . . ." But you see it was a Thursday, and the morrow
being Eve-o'-Sabbath and all, they got the pretex' to be allow
to stay the weekend out. Well in the night that lodgehouse
look to be under siege. For the grounds was just that thick
with sprawled-out gentry; and there wasn't a inch of floor or
plank, nor of mantel over the stove, which weren't occupy'.
And folks was argying out loud and elbowing one another,
and a-pushing and a-squeezing and a-thumping each other
only over the meanest patch of ground where to lay their
head on. And you can bet that in that general set-to and hubbub, the Cava'ry and Infan'ry both was having themselves a
high ole time, only showing which was the best haters and got
the most muscle of the two. And amidst all that ugly rioting
there was a sick old man lying on the ground a-moaning over
to a corner, which he been brung here for hospice ministra-
tions only yestiddy—as also a little chit of a chil' which, on
account all the shoving been going on, had got its leg
squeezed so cruel that it was only set a-bawling with such a
horrific katzenjammer, 'twere like holes was punch into your
head. Later only, after that shameful melee had tone down—
which God send only the like never be seed again (touch
wood!), I hunted up a remainder of dirt floor betwixt sleepers, which somehow I manage to wedge myself into, and I
curl up and try and catch me some sleep. Though no sooner I
put my head down I were beset by oh just armies of roaches,
bedbugs, fleas—the works. And big? Well they wasn't any
pikers; so bimeby I was set to itching head to foot in the wors'

way; so thinking about them devils has got me scratching all
over again. So when I take notice I wasn't exactly coming out
on top in that bug war——on account you see a roach just gotta
creep, and his buddy the bedbug well he gotta stink and no
two ways about it, an'——well, I figure if them creepers and
stinkers liked that patch of dirt so much they was welcome to
keep it and I say good riddance. So I went out into that covered junkyard in front, where I reckoned I pass the rest of the
night as best I could. Outside it was awful dark, and a cold
wind whupped about howling like famish wolves prowling
the night amongs' the timbers going *a-whoo——eeeee! . . . a-
whoo——eeeee!* whiles it shriek through the cracks in the wall.
And bits of straw flew off the thatch and join up with the
other fluttery junk been set a-whirling round like sperrits
dancing a devil's reel. And now and again big raindrops was
let in by the holes in the roof. So I hunch up chattering in a
corner in a sorrowful mood and I try and fall asleep. ——*"Oh the
Bath'owze, the Bath'owze!"* says I moaning to myself. Oh what
wouldn't I only give to have it back again. For it were Paradise. So comfortable and s-o-o warm. Why I never wanted
for nuffin' there. So what happen but the Black Deuce must
bring me that woman! Which were only on account her in the
first place I got driv out of Paradise, and must now knock
about here, there, yonder. ——*Women!* Ha! They never any
good. Trouble! That's all they is by jings! Nuffin' but
trouble . . . But then I were pull up sharp. For I recollect the
hunchback girl, and I were ashamed. Why she so fine and
good her company alone give pleasure. For you feel so light
and easy then, it is a joy only to set by her side and be talking
with her. No, ain't a thousand bathhouses together worth her
little finger. Why only one glance of hern make you glow all
over, like a healing cordial. "For shame, Fishke!" I says, rating
myself. "Why it is sinful to talk so. Women they a blessing, a

joy! For they is some will make a Paradise of even the worse hell . . ." And whiles I thinking these sweet thoughts I forget my trouble. And I huddle in closer and weren't even cold. For that corner were so comfable snug. And I commence to say bedtime Shema recitals—only heartfelt, mind, the way you suppose to, and bimeby my eyelids flutter and I nodding off . . . and *c-rack!* I were roust awake by the mos' awful belloring come out the lodgehouse door:

*"Now ain't you the dainty one!"* say the voice; and something heavy slam into the dirt, which it been slung out the door. *"Dang high-nose bit of fluff!* My gracious you of thunk that creature was sonabitch Countess Potocki, way it put on airs. Too grand to sleep under the same roof wit our likes, eh? Well you s-ome helluver sonuffabitch Countess Potocki, tha's for sure . . ."

Well I recognize that loudmouff voice for the bastid's right off, which he go on for a bit longer with his abuse, till finally he slam the door to.

Though a sliver of moon broke through the clouds and shone in by the holes in the roof; and it lighted up what appear to be somebody stretch out unconscious which show no more life than may a sack of meal been dump on the ground. So I went over to see who that sonabitch Count S. Poteskey may be which the bastid been abusing so. Well I look and lordy I was thunderstruck! Know how on the top tier, the vapors can hit you first time? That's way it was then. I near black out and my head was set spinning round and round. For it were the hunchback girl—yes, poor thing, it were she was sprawl' lifeless on the ground on account that bastid! Well I just did what-all to bring her round; and praise Goodness she do stir, bimeby. So I snatch her up in my arms and carry her over to my corner. Though heaven know from where I got the strength to do it. For it were superhuman, like f'instance one

'em fires which they incline to come on of a sudden in
Glupsk, and why you just make legs and run like damn-all
blazes to get away? Well that's way it was. For I swear I walk as
straight as other folks and didn't limp even once't. So now I
set her down, and bimeby v-ery slowly she open one eye and
the other, and she let out a sof' sigh. Well I was so happy for
it, I could bust. For the whole world become mine because of
it. Know them stories about the beggarman which *wham
presto!* they a big palace cover't wit' joowels and gold and silver, and him setting pretty on a deevan next to the Princess
which she gen'ly the king's daughter, and having hisself a high
ole time on account it? Well, sir, I pull my coat off quick and
wrap up my Princess in it, for I see she were quaking from the
cold.

—"Ah!" she moan and rub her eyes, and poor thing she
look round like she couldn't tell where she was.

"Why you staring so?" says I. "It's me, Fishke. And praise
God you alive!"

"Ah woe is me," she reply, "for what good is living if I
druther be dead. God is so merciful and good, why must He
make unhappy creatures as me, which only suffer in this life?"

"La, ninny," says I gentle to her, as to a chil', "God knows
what He is about, and surely He must be content to see our
likes walk about in His world. God is a Loving Father and He
sees and hears everything. Silly! Think for a minute God don't
know about our misery? Oh He know all right. You bet! Why
lookit the moon up there. See it? Well that is God's moon
which she look down upon us here, even inside of this house,
from all way up in the sky. Why it is a sin to be talking so,
silly . . ."

Well she give me such a fiery look then, and tears were
come to her eyes which they sparkle like diamonds in the

moonlight. No, I shan't ever forget them eyes of hern, nor that look she give me then, not ever!

Early morning I was up and I saw my hunchback girl lying in the corner huddle' up in my coat sound asleep like a innocent dove. Her face were so pale and in slumber it look as good and sweet as charity . . . Then I see her lips tremble and they appear to move as in a prayer. And it seem to me she were pleading for mercy. Oh don't torment me, she seem to beg. What did I do that I must be made to suffer so on account it? That prayer break my heart so it make the tears flow and I cry then . . .

Come morning, the first of the gentry from inside the lodgehouse which step into the yard was the bastid, deuce bust him to Aitch! Well seeing me and the hunchback girl, he give the both us one 'em knowing leers of his, and then he let out a guffaw and go back inside.

# 18

FISHKE SUDDENLY LAPSED into silence and turned his face away, looking for all the world as though he were ashamed. Nor it seemed would any amount of ole Alter's many pleadings in the matter induce him to change his mind and go on with his tale. "Tsk . . . now, ree-ly" was all Fishke would allow himself to say; and then he blushed and pulled all sorts of self-deprecatory little faces, but not another word was to be got out of him otherwise. Fishke, as it turned out, had at last become embarrassed by his own recital. Before, when the spark was first put to his touchhole as 'twere, he got so fired up by the business of telling he seemed to be talking out of a fever.

He spoke in the extreme heat of passion, pouring out the whole of his heart's burden even to the dregs, and in such words as surely were beyond Fishke's ordinary ken. And the words tumbled out of him seemingly of their own accord, for it was his soul did the talking then, whilst himself he lost touch with everything about him, and he talked, and he talked, scarcely attending at all to what he said; till on a sudden he was pulled up sharp, as if hearing his own words for the first time, and he marveled greatly at the performance, astonished at how such an extraordinary unlooked-for thing might have come to pass, and to himself of all people . . . and he was disconcerted exceedingly by it. Who hath himself not known at least one such resplendent hour, when he need but to open up his mouth, and lo! only the purest, most unadulterate human feelings will come gushing out of it, like the seething vapors tossed from a fiery mountain? Surely such an hour of grace cometh to even the lowliest among us. Why it come to Balaam's ass, when out of the blue that humble beast opened his mouth and out popped an oration which was a sockdologer by all accounts. To say nothing of your circuit preacher, saving the difference, which it happens often enough one of that sort will be rattling away at you at shul worship, giving out with his usual windbaggery which nobody can ever make head or tail of and is so achingly boring it'll give anybody the dry gripes. When, suddenly, the spirit takes a hold on him, and willy-nilly he somehow actually begins to make sense, so the whole congregation and even himself are left agape, marveling at the prodigy. Or take even your worst kind of a make-do cantor, what's called your "punkenhead" songster, who has got about as much of a way with a song as does a bullfrog in high summer, and makes you want to throw up only hearing his quaky trills and outlandish flourishes, never mind the monstrous faces he pulls by way of emoting.

Well sometimes it happens that even such a one will get carried away at Sabbath service, say after "Prophetical readings,"
and he'll suddenly take the bit between his teeth and belt out
about the prettiest *Salvation-be-vouchsafed* you may ever hope
to hear, and is so heartfelt it gives you goose bumps. But that
hour of grace having gone, the ass is back to being just an ass,
and the preacher to being the same old windbag, and the
make-do cantor to being a punkenhead . . . But I've got off
the point. Though there was this pair of Jewish gents I knew
once, worked all of their lives at a Jewish printing house in
the capacity of crankers, which is the name such drudges go
by in the printing trade. That's to say their only employment
consisted in keeping that big sidewheel revolving, which gets
the press rolling and the whole contraption clanking and
moving back and forth. Now, these two would always stand
facing each other in the same place across the great wheel
hooked on to the side of the press, and be endlessly turning
that wheel morning, noon, and night, forever following exactly the same rotary motion, and showing no more sign of
life besides, than if they was only a pair of painted-up clay
dummies. Then one day some inspiriting power must have
gave them the nudge. Because, next thing, their faces were
aglow and their eyes flashing, and they took to turning that
wheel with a will, and with such evident pleasure withal that
they seemed both of them to be lifted up into the Seventh
Heaven by it, as though entire universes were thrown into
motion by each revolution of the wheel, and every hand's
turn were expressive of an idea, of some great passion which
was churning inside of them. In a while, though, when their
ardor subsided as sudden as it come, they stood glaring at
each other dumbfounded and in a daze, and each spat on the
ground and turned his face away, and they were back to being
the same pair of dummies as before.

So seeing as how Fishke had dummied up, I was set to thinking of ways he might be got talking. When the good Rebbe Leyb-Sores's golem come to mind; about how that creature of mere exanimate clay had stood up, after Rebbe Leyb only pushed the Unutterable Name in from behind, and then went and did as he was told. Now there's a notion, thinks I. But different times, different dummies. For what of old had worked for Rebbe Leyb's golem (which God rest!) would by no manner of means do for mine (whom long life). Wherefore I bethought me of a name not quite as awesome, but withal sufficiently so to answer in present circumstances.

Accordingly I began stoking Fishke's fires by prattling away to him about his hunchback young lady. Well, by and by, I got up a considerable head of steam about the subject on my own account, and had indeed myself become so impassioned upon it, that my discourse took the following turn, so:

"How many such innocent young lives have been made wretched in this world because of the sins of parents, who, hankering only after vain trifles, will wrangle on account of it, and divorce, abandoning their own children—yes, the fruit even of their own bodies—and leave them to be buffeted by life's misfortunes, alone like shipwrecked castaways upon the sea. For what do children matter to such folk as they? When it is only their own precious selves which they ever care about—only their precious little selves. And these same nonesuches of devoted parenthood will go then and marry somebody else that's taken their fancy . . ."

The remainder of that speech died on my lips. My poor Alter! He looked in a dreadful turmoil, having been unmanned completely by what I said. And what a grievous wrong had I done to him, speaking out of turn, and in words

which suited his case so exactly they shook him to the core.
And I was so very sorry now, I couldn't forgive myself. And
instantly I took myself to task for it. Ah, Mendel, Mendel,
now see what you've done? Well it is time you came to your
senses and stopped telling the truth right to a person's face
like that, with as little regard of the consequences as only a
schoolboy will have. Why it was shameful of you to have spoken so. And you a gent with a set of manly whiskers at your
chin, stead of peach fuzz; and pretty well on in years, too, if
it come to that. Well it's way past high time to act your age,
sir, and give a little thought to what is fitting and may even
bring some good. Oo-ooo, that loose tongue of yours, Mendel; whatever shall we do about that confarnal clapper o'
yourn, eh?

So then and there I took a silent oath, to hoard my words:
to only listen, observe, and keep my mouth shut. This being,
as we know, the cherished virtue of all fine, clever folk, and
altogether necessary for getting on in life. Henceforth I shall
only praise folks, becoming beloved of everyone thereby. And
in my minds's eye I pictured great mobs of kindly ole gents,
their faces beaming and radiant with good cheer; I mean the
sort generally addressed by one and all as "uncle," and are just
about everybody's pet and favorite. Oh, I can see them all
now—whole regiments of jovial beamish uncles released into
the world, making their rounds here, there, yonder; ever
merry, ever jolly, always the boon companion and friend-in-
need to their fellows; wagging their tails cheerily to whoever
is top dog of the moment; planting wet, loving busses upon
his pate and cheeks, melting with inexpressible pleasure in
the mere contemplation of the other fellow's good fortune,
speaking to him of it with tears in their eyes, with a smile on
their lips, with joy in their hearts; unstintingly retailing his
accomplishments, bending the ear of anyone who will only

listen, distributing plaudits, paeans, and laudations by the plateful, served out in great steaming dollops, hot off the hob; drinking that same fellow's health, and wishing him the best in this world and the next, even to eternity. Why, you'll find that sort everywhere, at every shindig, kermis, and "do"—in fact wherever the fare is good and vinous entertainment plentiful; always there with a twinkle in their eye and roses in their cheeks, their foreheads glistening, their noses ruddy with brandy blossoms and adrip with the sweet essences of black currant and gooseberry. For such gents being wholly content with their own lot are exultant, too, as though by only sheer contagion, in the happiness of others . . . O ye uncles, ye happy, happy uncles! Ah if only I too might share in that same avuncular felicity. Well, sir, I was resolved that from that day forward I should myself become just such an uncle. Why the very sound of that moniker had now grown so pleasing to my ear that I would not rest till I had tried it on for size, troubling even to repeat it to myself several times over: Uncle! . . . Un-cle Mendele! . . . Un-cle Reb Mendele! . . .

And thinking now to make it up to Alter for having wronged him, I tried next gently to soft-soap him out of his ill humor: "Oh, dear me, Reb Alter, but it must be such a trial to be squinched up as you are, sitting at the very edge of the seat, if not half out of it. And for so long, too! Well, now, I'm bound you're sore all over because of it. So how about we change wagons. Why, I can make you up such a comfy seat over in my cart, if you only let me. Besides, I think we could all do with a little pick-me-up in the way spirituous refreshment right about now, don't you? So what you say, huh? Please?" —Well my Alter didn't want much persuading, so pretty soon we'd all climbed down from off of his wagon. And after I had done with coaxing my jade into taking the lead, leaving Alter's skinny mare to bring up the rear this

time, we each had us a bit of a leg-stretch on our own, to back
of the woodpile, so to say. And having severally eased nature
and blessed God, we were all three settled into our places in
my cart, and I broke out the bottle of spirits. By now, though,
my manner had grown so licorice-sweet you wouldn't believe; and I proceeded then to drinking toasts to Alter's good
health and fortune so liberally that it even brought tears to my
own eyes, in perfect imitation of the benevolent gents I was
forever now sworn to imitate. Nor had I forgotten about
Fishke, whose fires I took to fanning once more in that same
avuncular spirit; till at last I succeeded in rousing him to take
up his story from where we'd left off earlier.

## Under Way with Mendele the Book Peddler

FISHKE NOW recommenced his tale after his fashion, with me
improving upon it after mine, and Alter, ever short on patience, spurring the boy along after his, and the sequel of
Fishke's story then followed, so:

NEXT DAY, FRIDAY, the shul in that town was so frightful close-
packed with poorfolks, you couldn't hardly breathe because
of it. And all of them was crowded around the shul beadle,
shoving and jostling each other, just to get first crack at Eve-
o'-Sabbath chits. That's to say they was all busy trying to wangle the choicest meal vouchers for charitable board that night,
with one of the Quality about town, if they could, or perhaps
even with a squire, where the fare was like to be rich and rations plentiful. Now most certainly the best such invite is to
the tax-gatherer's table; on account that gent is usually the
most prosperous and powr'ful personage in the whole parish.

And the worst is gen'ly to the table of such poor holy-service folks and shul gentry as rabbis, cantors, and beadles; or, say, of a alderman or any other such officer of the parish corpora- tion. Because these last-named gents is well enough incline' to stuff their own faces, but they won't share even a crumb of decent nourishment with a fellow mortal on principle, even their own life depended on it. Course, the mos' low-downest of the lot is the trustees of charitable societies; for although they can get quite mournful about poorfolks whilst only talk- ing of 'em, they will so stint any such unfortunate at table that he must rise from the meal even hungrier than when he set down to it. So paupers naturally thinks falling into the hands of such misers as being a great calamity, and will shun them like the plague. And any time it happen someone do re- ceive such a invite, then the rest will make the worse fun of him, and only laugh themselves half silly over it, same as he just been dealt a losing hand, or had drawed the short straw . . . Well, now, the beadle he was in just a awful tem- per, screaming his head off the whiles, and going on about how in all his born days he never seed such a mob of beggars together in one place like that. "Oh for pitysakes!" he says. "What possess you tramps to descend on our poor town on a sudden like a bunch of locust? Why, this ain't to be borne! Surely it must be God's punishment which brung you here. No, I tell you, there ain't place enough for all you!" Only rant and yell as he may, nobody pay him any mind; and they all went on jostling and elbowing as before, with everyone hol- lering together, "Gimme! No, no, me first! No, me, me!"— the whiles each, on his own, try and push a few coppers into the beadle's hand. Which coin being pocketed by him, that poor gent was then oblige to hand out more chits in return for it, even though it make him so mad he seem ready to go through the roof because of it. Me and my hunchback

girl, though, we stationed ourselfs off to a side, kind of apart
from the rest. On account, first of all, we wasn't either us
what you call exactly fit for such muscular doings; and, second, we plain didn't have the gumption to elbow ourselfs in
amongs' the "bruins," so to speak—which is to say, the beggars of quality. For paupers has their squires and Quality, too,
don't you know. Only ours is about a thousand times worser
than the squires and Quality which rich folks has to offer . . .
Like f'instance, the bastid. Now naturly he was amongs' the
first, and he was give two prime-quality meal-tickets: one for
hisself, and t'other for my wife—which she didn't even have
to join in the pushing in order to get. For he only point her
out to the beadle, and he say, "Only look'ee, sir. See that blime
little lady yonder? She be mine, poor thing . . ." When the
shul was finally clear of folks, which they all had got their
chits and lit out by now, each to his own billet, me and the
hunchback girl went over to the beadle to try our luck, maybe
beg a couple chits off of him on our own account. Well, he
only give us a kind of a vinegary little smile, but not a word
by way of a answer. So I says to him, "Oh, please, sir, have pity
on two unfortunate cripples. For neither us has knowed a
square meal these past six days . . ." —"No more chits!"
the beadle say. "Now both you seed the goings-on before. So
you know there's no more places left!" —"Here, sir," I says
then, and I push a sixer into his hand. "Oh, take it, sir, please!
Only do us this one charity, and God bless you for it . . ." —
"See here, young feller," the beadle say next. Though his
manner had growed a mite softer. "I don't want your money.
But it so happens I got this one extry chit on me. So if you
want, you can draw straws for it, flip a coin maybe. What
you say?"

   —"No, no! you'd best give it to her, sir!" I told him, and
pointed to my hunchback girl.

—"No, let him have it, please!" says my sweet hunchback girl, pointing to me. "For I shan't take it!"

Well it went on so betwixt us for a spell, both us argying 'twas the other which must have that chit, and no we shan't never accept it for our own selfs. The beadle, though, he seem to get a kick out of the proceedings, and he grin at us and toy with his beard, looking on quite friendly the whiles. "Know what?" he say on a sudden. "Whyn't you two come by the shul tonight, end of Evenfall worship, and wait in the lobby by the door, till the congregants come out. They's bound to be good folks will take you in then. I'll even put a word in for you my-self."

Good as his word he was, too. For prompt at the end of Friday Evenfall, whilst the shul worshipers was on their way out, the beadle approach two gents, and pointing the both of us out to them, he ask if they might take us on for charitable board. "Ah, sirs," he say to them, "I've hardly the heart to ask it of you. For almost no week go by, which I ain't yet sent you such unfortunates. But if you be willing, here's two deserving poorfolks which perhaps you may choose to favor so."

"Why tush!" they says both. "Where's there a Jew would even think to turn away a guest on the Sabbath? Why, sir, there is only one day in the long week which Jewish folks can rest easy on. So why shouldn't they give pleasure to the needy on this blessed day, and share with them that which the Lord giveth? We only pray, sir, you never forget us in such a matter, not this week nor any other."

So the two gents beckon to us to follow, the while they both walk on ahead, with their young'uns tagging along; lively little tikes and young lads, looking so spic-and-span; and oh my but they was togged out handsome in them fine Sab-bath clothes. And they was all of them aglow and so jolly, chattering merrily amongs' themselves all the ways home.

Why you needn't but only look, to know the Sabbath spirit was come on 'em, and they already receive that extry soul which it's said Jewish folks will get on a Sabbathday. And the whiles, me and my hunchback girl we only walk quietly behind, and we was—well, feeling somehow content, don't you know.

—"Good Sabbath, my dear!" say my gent cheerily to his missus when he come home; which lady was setting in a chair the whiles and were dress up all neat and trim, and she look so radiant she may have pass for a princess, easy. There was a baby playing in her lap, oh jus' a perfect li'l doll of a chil'; and two little girls on either side hopping up and down, as well, which they was got up in the prettiest frocks you ever see. "God hath favored me this day with a Sabbath guest. For else, my dear, you may never have let me into the house, I fear," say my gent humorously with a smile; and he commence then reciting the Sabbath-eve household blessings in a clear, ringing voice, first walking all about the house, hymning *Peace Be on Ye Minist'ring Angels;* and when he come to the *Woman-of-Virtue* part, he approach his wife singing it, and pick up the baby, and hug and kiss it, whilst the rest of the children clung to him lovingly on every side, all of them frolicking and capering joyfully about. And looking on so, you may have thought God's sweet Minist'ring Angels of the prayer was actually come into that house. —Well, anyhow, the reason why I am telling you about this, sirs, is because it was then I really begun to miss my own hunchback girl so much . . .

Well, as it turn out, my gent belong to what is call your middle station. Not quite rich, but comfable off, as was plain to see. The Sabbath lights was burning in a speckless neat pair of glittery candlesticks—which I don't know, though, if they was real sterling, or only your Warsaw silverplate. Whilst the table was set with fine porcelain ware, and the Sabbath white-

loafs was cover't over with one of 'em purty tablecloths got
the dainty embroidery on it. And there was a wine bottle
sparkling brightly on the table, too, which each of us partake
of it, to pronounce bread-'n'-wine benedictions. And the
whiles we was at table, the missus of the house she never once
stint me; but she urge me only to eat up hearty, nor be bashful
about asking for seconds. Well, I own it was a fine enough
meal. Though I weren't really up to enjoying it as I might of
done; on account each time I fork up a piece of fish or a
length of noodle, chaw on some meat or help myself to the
stewed greens, I couldn't keep my mind from *her*. For who
knew if she, poor dear, was feasting so grand as I was. Then,
after dinner, I was ask to sleep over. "Ask him to stay the
night, dear," the woman softly murmer to my gent, "for where
shall he go, poor man? Not that stable we call an almshouse.
No, dear. A decent night's lodging is the least we can do for
him . . ." —Well, after them doings last night (preserve us!),
I could of maybe use a rest even more than a meal, and that's
the truth. So being allow only to lay my head down on a pillow, and to stretch out at full length in a warm bed, were certainly a great temptation, and would no doubt of done me a
world of good. Except I was thinking on her, so I thank them
kindly and decline. And as it happen she was having her Sabbath dinner with folks which lives just down the way, I
straightways went in to fetch her, and we both left that place
together.

It were a clear night. The moon was out, and it did a feller
good to be only walking about so, out in the open. "Come," I
says to her, "let's walk. Ain't all that much waiting for us at the
almshouse anyhow . . ." Though recollecting the almshouse
on a sudden like that, it give me the cold shivers. You remember the sick old man I were telling about? That's that poor
gent was groaning so pitiful the night before, over the

almshouse. Well early next morning the death agonies come on him and he died at dusk, prompt after Sabbath-eve light-blessings. They laid the body out in the lodgehouse, till end of Sabbath, where we was suppose to sleep.

We walk along for a spell so, till we come into a small back street with gardens and trees in it which give off pleasant smells. It was dead still. For as the custom is of Sabbath eve after dinner, the whole town was long gone to bed. Both us set down now in a patch of grass under a fence.

Well we sit so awhile together, just looking on and not talking. Each was wrap up in they own selfs. When my hunch-back girl fetch a deep sigh, and she commence singing under her breath softly. And I recognize it for that song call' the "*Song of a Murdered Chil'*." Which it go,

> *Hoo, hoo,*
> *My father me slew,*
> *My mother me chew,*
> *My sister gathered my bones . . .*

I saw she was in tears and her face was flushed. She look up at me with a mournful smile. Ah, that look of hern, it near drain the strength from me. My heart clenched, and there was a thumping at my temples like hammers beating on them. I scarce knew what come over me. The words come of them-selves, and I blurted them out for the first time: "Oh my love . . ." —"Ah, Fishke!" she say, choking back her sob. "I shan't be able to bear it much longer. You don't know what he's like . . ."

"What *who's* like?" I shot back with heat. "It's the bastid ain't it!"

"Oh, if you only knew, Fishke, if you only knew!"

I took hold of her hand, then her face, and I pleaded with

her to tell me. She buried her face in her hands. Then, bending close, she whisper it to me in a trembling voice (though more by way of hint than otherwise), about what the bastid done to her. Oh, it were monstrous! And that villain deserve to rot in Sheol forever for it . . .

# 19

FISHKE ONCE MORE was grown silent, seeming somehow to have become both greatly agitated and melancholy together. So, to draw him out, that I might only satisfy myself as to every particular of his story, I thought this time to try and tease him back into talkativeness. And so I said:

"You know you haven't once said, Fishke, if your hunchback girl was at all pretty. Now I shouldn't have thought a young woman such as that had much to offer in that way."

"Well, I never!" says Fishke bridling and his dander up. "What's pretty got to do with it? Never mind that we are concern here with a *Jewish* young lady. For if such a one is pretty, it's her own affair and nobody else's! But if you must know, gen'men, why yes she is. Quite pretty, in fact. For she got the sweetest face and lovely hair, and her eyes—well they's daimonts which you never see their like. But what of it? What may a hones' Jewish gent care for such things? An', an', I mean what you take me for anyhow? One of 'em ruffians which got nuffin' better to do, only chase after a purty skirt? Why that's only idleness, and I won't have it. No, sir. On account what I truly was taken by, was only her goodness. Yes, her goodness! Her pitying me, as might a tender loving sister, an', an' the other way around, too—me pitying her, as would

a loving brother when she were in need, for you see, that's
what it really was about, an', an' . . ."

"There, there! Now what difference it make anyhow?" in-
terposed Alter. "For beauty won't buy beef nor make the pot
boil. But ne'mind that. Now, concernin' that girl o' yourn,
Fishke. You say she told you something. Well, what was it?
Well, speak up, lad, speak up!"

And so Alter commenced hurrying Fishke along after his
fashion, and Fishke got on with telling after his, and I with
correcting him after mine—whereby the tale was again got
under way. So:

THE PINCHINGS—WELL, yes, it ready come to my notice for
some time how the bastid sonabi . . . how he . . . Well anyhow I often enough do notice it, how he use to pinch that
poor helpless girl. But I thought he only done it out of spite,
for I knew him for a wicked person, who enjoy hurting others
and giving them pain. Only, as I learn from her now, these was
pinches of a altogether different sort—why, they was . . .
they was, *foo!* they was Satan's pinches, lus'ful pinches! For it
turn out that the rogue couldn't keep his hands off her for
even a minute. Way he always cornering her, pawing her. Like
whenever he ketch her by herself alone—well at first he
commence to try and sweet-talk her round, jabbering away at
her about oh jus' any kind of fool nonsense which come to
mind: saying how he only wisht he may keep her in clover forever, promising her roomfuls of gold, the sun, the moon,
what-all. And when talking smooth don't get him nowhere,
he proceed to the rough and swear he get even, so she regret
it; threatening to give her a bad name, and to make her life
such a misery she'd wisht only she was never born; and the

whiles, why, he din't scruple to even try and force hisself on her. Now, genly she manage to twist free of him; and couple times she even got a good lick in of her own—like she'd biffed him one *wham!* right in the belly with her fist, so it knock the wind out of him and he fair double up from it. Only he pay her back in spades later, working her so hard she drop, and whupping and knocking her about till she were black and blue all over, and half dead of it. Though bimeby he start up again, first fair, then foul. But if she try keeping out of his way, he only kep' after her the more and give her no rest, dogging her everywheres; and when there was people about, he oftentimes give her a knock or a shove on the sly, like bump into her accidental-on-purpose don't you know, or he sneak her a pinch, just to keep his hand in.

There just wasn't a day pass that the most terrible things wasn't done to her which I won't even soil my lips by mentioning. But that awful business the night before, well that was . . . why, it was s-o-o . . . *foo!* the word disgusting don't come near it. After that shameless to-do in the lodgehouse the other evening, everybody went to sleep, and the poor girl had scrooch herself up in a corner by the door and only just doze off. When she was rousted on a sudden by somebody which whisper into her ear, "Psst!" It was the bastid. "You gonna wear y'self out, hunch up in a corner so, poor thing," he say to her gently. "Well, you come wit' me, dear, for I got a place fix up for you which is just dandy, so you may at least rest up some . . ." She thank him most kindly for it, only she say no and please go back to where he been sleeping. So that's when he start the old game again, this way, that way, the whiles dropping hints about how he knowed all about me and was wise to the hanky-panky which the two us been getting up to . . . And he proceed to try and throw a scare into her, saying how she gonna be eating dirt soon enough, and by jings he'd make a proper end of me too. Well bimeby the devil get into him. For that rogue become both beast and pussycat roll' into one—first acting nice, then nasty, till at last he make hisself so obnoxious, it fetch him such a smack acrost the face which it make his head spin. Well that slap of hern send him into oh just the wildest rage; which was when he'd took holt of her so cruelly and slung her into the yard. And the rest, gen'men, you already know.

When the poor girl finish her story the while we was setting so on the grass together—well I tell you it got me down so I couldn't utter a word for a time. But really I was that churn'-up inside, it stab at my vitals like a tangle of vipers was nesting there; for I was furious with the bastid over what he done. Whereas I was only full of pity for her—that and something else, which I can't rightly put a name to it, but it tug at me, and tug, and tug . . . till it grab aholt of my heart and jerk it so hard, my heart seem pulled clean out of my bosom because of it. It was then I took her hand away from her face, and in a voice which I scarcely recognize it for being my own, I say:

"Oh my dearest! I gladly give my life for you . . ."

"Ah, Fishke!" she return with a sigh, and she move closer to me and lean on my shou'der.

And the world appear to me so blithe of a sudden, and my body grow so lightsome and warm. And I commence now consoling her as one might a faithful sister with words of comfort and hope, telling her not to worry, for surely God will provide and won't never forget us. And I swear to her I shall always be a true friend to her and a brother. And she look up at me with that pretty smile of hern, and she drop her head then, and say:

"Oh I can't tell why, but I have somehow got to feeling so glad now. Oh, Fishke, but it feels good only being alive . . ."

We set so for a good while, chattering away merrily together, all lighthearted and hopeful, talking of how one day
God perhaps restore us to the happiness we both dream of.
When we was startle by a sudden knocking noise, which appear it must come from close by. I look round, and commence to edge myself for'ards, the whiles keeping to the
shadow of the fence we been setting under. Well, I scarce
gone a couple paces, when I see somebody was messing about
the shed of the cellar acrost the ways. Now I dunno why exactly, but they was something make me want to get in closer.
So I move two maybe three paces nearer in, to get a better
view, and . . . *Dang!* if 'tain't the bastid fiddling with the lock
on the door. In a minute he'd wrenched it off and vanish
down into the cellar, meaning to haul everything away which
folks gen'ly keeps there over the Sabbath. Then the idea flash
in on me. Thinks I: Fishke! here's your chance to pay him back
for what he done to that helpless girl. For you need only to
shut the cellar door, and that big bruin's as good as netted.
And tomorrow when they find him, by golly that rogue gonna
get the whupping he deserve, and then some! Well, sir, it
were the first time I got my taste of revenge. And, oh, it was
sweet! My blood was up, and I become drunk with it. In no
time I was over to that door and clap it shut. Gotcha, you
bastid! says I to myself, chuckling the whiles. "Now you can
rot in the ground f'ever, like the dog you ree-ly are! And I
proceed now to push the bolt into the hole, but the staple
been bent crooked, so the bar wouldn't slide in. Well I jiggle
the thing, push it, pull it, this way, that way. Still no go! So this
time I commence tugging at it with both hands, and s-lowly,
s-lowly the bar begun inching home, and I were in business
again. But then the door get yanked open from the inside, and
I come tumbling in after it, head over ashtip and ramstam up
against the bastid, which he been standing on the step below.

"Well, if ain't Reb Fishcakes!" says the bastid, after we face off
for a spell, and never a word betwixt us the whiles. "So 'twas
y'own estimable self, sir, which profane the Sabbath, fooling
round wit' doors and locks and sich—and all on account li'l
ole me! Tsk, tsk, tsk. Well I s'rprise at you! Oh but do come
in, sir, make y'self easy. Here kitty, kitty, kitty! There's a nice
kitty . . ." And with that he flung me down the stairs so I were
sent sprawling on the floor and like to have broke my neck.
Then he say: "Well, now, Master Almsman, I got a leetle job
for you which I reckon even you ain't too sick to tackle," and
he punch me in the back saying, "So you stay put whiles I collec' some these savories which I nearly forgot, and I stuff 'em
into this little sack here. Now, lessee . . . Well, h'm, yes,
there's broil' chicken and a plate of fishcakes, and there's
calf's-foot jelly . . . Now see what I almost lef' behind on
your account?" When he hit me again. "Well start counting,
Fishke!" he say. " 'Tain't one THWACK!—'tain't two
THWACK!—'tain't three THWACK!—'tain't four
THWACK!—a-nd 'tain't five THWACK . . . Now them bitty
thwacks was only for li'l ole yours truly . . . But you got a
couple good licks coming yet, for that 'ere hunchback gel! So
go 'head, Fishke, count . . . 'Tain't nine THWACK!—'tain't
ten THWACK! . . . Well, I mus' say, sir, that's a fine way to
behave, gallivantin' about in dark places at night with young
ladies . . . 'Tain't twelve THWACK!—a-nd 'tain't thir-
teen . . . Oh you're artful all right. But you don't fool me
none. No, sir, you do not! For I seed the pairer you skulking
about ever so lovey-dovey in them dark side streets and back
alleys . . . Now, where was we—'tain't sixteen THWACK!—
'tain't seventeen . . ." Only them last insinnations of the
bastid's, they'd made my blood boil. No, by golly, I couldn't
let them pass. —"Bastid!" I scream at him, "You ain't worthy
to speak her name . . ." And in a trice I was on him, and clamp

my teeth in good. It was war! My teeth against his hands. For we was mortal foe, each fixing to do the other in. But he finally manage to tear me off of him, holding me at arm's length and choking me, till I thought I was a goner. Then he just toss me aside, as a chil' might a rubber ball. ——"You best offer up thanksgiving, bub!" says the bastid then, " 'cause it don't suit me a-tall to baldower you today. No, I druther you rest up here, Master Minnow. So when the folks come down to fetch them fishcakes tomorrow, they only find the one live li'l Fishy waiting to have his goose cook. So sleep tight, y'hear? Oh, maybe they's something you want me to tell to the missus? For she is sure to get the word today, that's a promise . . ." And the bastid shut the door then, and he was gone.

First thing when I come to myself, I went up to the cellar door and try opening it. Well I rattle it, tug it, tug it again, but there weren't any point to it. The door been made fast from the outside and bolted. I couldn't think what to do. I was too a-scared of being overheard trying to force that door, so I left off rattling it; but leaving things as they was wouldn't do neither. And I was wobbly besides. For my head was swimming from all the aggervation and fright, let alone I was aching all over from the thrashing I receive. I went back down the steps and throwed myself on the ground, and only lay there all of a dread. For I couldn't think but of that one thing: about what was in store for me tomorrow, and about the warm welcome which be waiting for me then. And how, when the tocsin sound, folks will come running from every side to get sight of the thief which been caught red-handed in the night, and to only give him the licking which he deserve for it, and who knows for what other made-up villainies they thunk up on him for good measure. Why, the hand of every God-fearing person was sure to be raise against me. Nor'd any my pleadings about being innocent save me from the whaling them folks was like to give me. And the thought of it work away inside of me like a gimlet, boring holes in my head so I couldn't lay still for a minute. All at once, though, I feel something scrabbling over me. So I put my hand to it and catch holt of a rat which scuttle away with a squeak from betwixt my fingers. Well that ree-ly give me the willies, and I was up on my feet next and gone all queasy so the cold sweats come over me. But I couldn't hardly keep on my feet; so I feel my way about in the darkness till my hand struck a clammy wall, which I prop myself up against it standing. And I thought drearily: Lord, what kind of life I got? And why you punishing me so? Surely it be better for me and everybody else, if I never was born. Oh what did I ever do to deserve being cast down so and made so wretched for? And I thought my heart may break then, and I burst into tears. And I was crying and thinking: Merciful God, where are you!? And I remained standing downcast the whiles, and made so numb because of it, that I were past all caring if I live or die. When the door give a sharp little screak and were suddenly ajar, and a thin shaft of light broke in on me from the outside; and then I made out the sound of footsteps coming down the cellar steps softly. And on the instant my hair was on end, and I stood hangdog and quaking, waiting to receive a thieve's reckoning . . . Then I heered my name being whispered ever so gentle: "Fishke? . . . Fishke?" And next thing my hunchback girl was at my side and oh! how I jump for joy then and raise a cheer. "Sh!" she say, taking my hand. "Quick, come away quick . . ." —"Oh, dearest, you save my life!" says I, still shouting wildly, for I was quite beside myself with excitement. And being I was all of a twitter then, I—well, yes, gen'men, I own 'twere there, in that same cellar, which . . . well, which I first kiss her. —Well anyhow I ask how she happen to be there. But she only shush me, and remind me where we was: "Sh! come quick!" she plead. "I'll tell all about it, I promise. Only hurry, quick, we must get away!"——And saying this, she led me out by the hand into the street.

And walking along so, she straightway commence telling me about it. How, after I were gone for what must of been, oh, maybe only couple minutes, well she somehow knowed there was trouble, so she follow after. Well she reach to the end of the fence, and had a good look around. When she re-mark somebody acrost the ways which he were hunch up under a low-pitch roof and look to be pottering about there. So thinking it was me, she allow herself to approach quite near. But then she pull up sharp: for she heered that person she seed, saying: "There, that'll keep you, Master Fishcakes! And by jingoes you can wallow in y'own mess down there, like the mis'able runt o' the litter y'are . . ." Well, she about thought her heart give out hearing it. Though, before she chance to quite collect hesself, that bastid were already on to her. And he pinch her, and flash this kind of a funny grin, and he say, "And a pious Sabbath to you too, granny! Well you some modest missy, y'know that? Traipsing round the streets till all hours in the night. Pious my eye! *Foo!*——disgusting is what I calls it . . . Git on home, you shameless hussy!" And he fetch her a rude nudge from behind with his knee, so she force to walk on ahead of him without a word. Now, that feller maintain a v-ery sharp lookout afoot, always casting glances about him from side to side, the whiles each time he'd shift that fat bag of loot he stoled from one shou'der to the other; nor he forget to keep up his gibes, withal playing that same game he always do with her. And that poor girl she only fret away and worry. For she knowed I was in trouble, but she couldn't help me in any wise, on account that bastid held her fast by his side, and he never once took his eyes off of her. But then a party of gents hove into view, which they was coming away from male-chil' celebrations. And they was all carrying on, talking aloud and laughing uproarious—you know, in the way Jewish folks is incline to do gener'ly. Anyhow, these gentry they had all gang up and was twitting this other feller, on account he foolishly forgot hisself, and were still carrying his pocket hankerchief on him on the Sabbath, which the rest seem to think was the funniest thing ever. So just as fast as he could the bastid make for a side alley, and duck into it. Well that were her chance, and she make a break for it and she dashed over acrost the ways in the opposite direction. So that is how she finally give him the slip.

Natur'ly she run fast as her feet take her, so she might get me out of that tight spot. And only think what a terrible state she must of been in, when she chase in and out of them dinky little streets and alleyways, never once hitting that exact street she seed me in earlier. But she knew I was in the worse danger, which I must be got away from quickly, so every minute was precious, you see—the whiles she been only running about distracted, not knowing how she may reach me! Well she do chase about so for quite a considerable time . . . till at last with God's help she struck that place I was in, and she got me out of it.

So now we was walking along quite chipper together and talking away cheerily. Says I: "Dearest, you stood by me when I was in the wors' need today." Says she: "Oh, Fishke, the other night, at the lodgehouse, remember? You helped me like my own brother. Why, last night . . ." Only that almshouse weren't far off then, and our spirits fell and we stop talking. Somehow we just knew the business wasn't over yet, and the night wouldn't end without more ill come of it.

One half of the almshouse gate was shut to, and the other been left open a crack, enough to see the lodgehouse by the

light come in from the street outside. We both stop short of it
though, and we hung back for a bit, with that kind of a sinking
feeling, don't you know. But then I step inside. Well I scarce
put my head in, when I got sight of that bastid—I mean, he
were right there, in the gateway practically, settle' down all
cuddly with my wife, and the pair of 'em plainly been having
a time of it together: way they both was hunch over that one
cadging bag the whiles, stuffing they faces full with what-all
come out of it. On a sudden, though, the bastid whisper
something into her ear, then he up and made hisself scarce.
And next thing she was up on her feet and in a awful rage, and
set her yap going like all hell was broke loose: "Oo-oo,
you . . . how d-ast you, sir!" she say. "How d-ast you—you
blame so'n'so and so'n'so! Whatcha making whoopee till all
hours for, wiff that, that fancy hussy o' yourn . . . wiff that,
that cheap draggletail trollop!? You think I don' know all
about your sinful ways, mister? Well you mistaken. 'Cos I
know, all right! Knowed about it from the start. Only I look
t'other way, see—and dang near bust a bladder on account it.
So that's what poor thanks I gets for taking you into the world
amongs' decent folks! Why you ungrateful flea-bit li'l sonabi . . . Dija ree-ly think you gonna get away with it? 'Cos you
ain't, y'heer? For I see you in hell fust . . . you, and your pa,
and your pa's pa, y'heer? And that trollop o' yourn as
well . . . an', an' *her* pa, and her ma's pa, y'heer? Why, I show
you both who's boss . . . So you take *that!*"—and she next set
to cuffing me—"take *that!* for today . . . and *that!* for
yestiddy . . . and *that!* for all them other dang days . . . Oh I
gonna see you dead, you . . . you . . . *O Damnation!*" —Well I
couldn't scarcely get free of that woman's hands, till I manage
to skedaddle a couple paces into the street, and I finally got
shut of her. Anyhow she remain outside on her legs for a mite
longer, raising the roof like that with her howlings. But at last

she flung round and stomp back inside, screaming the whiles: "So lessee if dossing down in the gutter like the common dog y'are, suit you now, mister!" Then she slam the almshouse gate in my face.

We stood about looking quite somber the whiles, my poor hunchback girl and me. For we was left feeling very oppress by that ugly business which had preceded. And our troubles give us no rest either; so we commence walking any whither our feet may take us. Nor do we exchange a word on the ways, and only trudge along in silence, each keeping to his own thoughts. Though bimeby I come out of myself and look round, and I notice where we was in the yard in front of the shul. And it break my heart then to see how my poor girl looked so wretched. For it were the second night running she been without any rest to speak of. Well, I bethought myself about lodging, where she may perhaps pass the remainder of the night. So that's when the idea come to me. Why, thinks I, the women's gallery in the shul fit the bill just crackerjack!

Though it must of been only with God's help we climb up them shackly steps leading to it, which each one wobble so underfoot it were pretty much of a wonder we ever reach the top in the first place. And then feeling about in the pitch darkness there, my hand struck what appear to be a open door, which when we pass through it we stumble over something soft, and all in a moment of great stomping commotion broke loose, and there was a sudden clatter of jumping about and jostling, which all at once it rush past us, under us, over us. And before we knew it, we was hemmed in on every side and fetching blows, back, front, and sides, so we hardly knowed where they was all coming from. Well by then I were dump flat on my back and rolling round, this way, that way, feet flying, hands flailing about. Anyhow, finally I manage to grab holt of a beard. And whose you think? It were a goat! That's right.

For, unbeknownst, it seem we had broke in upon the slumbers of a whole troop of them skittish creatures, which it customary that the females of such private-owned livestock gets the privilege of spending the night up in the ladies' gallery of the shul with the Corporate billy. —"Where you gone?" I call to my girl. "S'all right, c'mon! They ain't only a bunch of smelly goats here. Boy, the folks hereabout mus' be pr-etty prosperous, to judge by the number of head they keep . . ." And I proceed then to round up them hircky beasts, and shoo them out. 'Cause they gonna have to look for other accommodation, at least for the one night. For the rest, I give my girl good night and departed, closing the door behind me and making certain, too, it stay shut.

Only coming back down the steps, my path cross that of the billy's—which he station hisself at the foot of the stairs, head down and horns at the ready, and looking quite indignant at yours truly, for making so free with his passel of wives. Well I kind of spar with him for a whiles, on account whichever way I turn, he only block my path. But I do manage to sidestep him at last, and make a dash for the shul door downstairs, where I step inside.

There was a mighty sprawl of almsmen and like parish gentry inside; which all of them was laid out, fast asleep, on tables and benches about the premises. And cozy as lords they look, too; and I must say it also make for quite lively listening, what with all the fancy nosework in the way of snorings and whistlings which they gave out with. Though me personal, it give considerable pleasure only to observe how these folks seem to have got the business of nighttime snoozing down so pat. And seeing them so, I got to thinking that almsmen was actually different from other beggarfolks, after all. I mean these gentry ree-ly had the life. They was "quality" beggars, and I confess to envying them a bit for it . . . Anyhow, I went

behind the stove and hunted me up a bench there to sleep on;
which no sooner I laid my head down, I was out like a light.
Though I ain't never been one for much luck in this life. For
I'd hardly shut my eyes, when I was rousted out of sleep by:
"Ahem! G'mornin', young feller . . ." Well, when I rubbed
my eyes out, I made out quite a circle of very sober-seeming
gents looking down at me; which all of them belong to the
Confraternity of Psalmsters in the Parish and come to shul
special, sunrise prompt every Sabbath, for Psalm devotions.
And it appear, too, I was occupying their usual place; so not
having any choice, I rose up from the bench to perform
morning hand-washings and then settle down amongst them.
I couldn't hardly keep my eyes open; but after a gape and a
stretch, I joined them in Psalm recitals anyway.

# 20

WELL, AFTER THAT Sabbath-eve going-over which my wife give
to me, it were made plain to me at last, what all of her recent
crazy carryings-on was really about. For she was burnt-up,
something monstrous, on account of my friendship with the
hunchback girl, which the bastid also told her about. Only he
contrive to twist things so, they was turn into a black lie. For
the rogue was convince that because of it my wife wouldn't
have anything to do with me, and she'd just spit on me and
send me packing, and make an end once and for all. Only he
reckoned wrong. On account instead of her growing cold towards me and leaving me to go my own ways, so he'd be rid of
me—she got hesself all het up and burn with hellfire and
brimstones over it. And she think: Why the very idee! Where'd
any husbin of hern get the raw gumption to do such a thing?

And what is more, with a hunchback! How dast Fishke take a fancy to such a gel more than herself? No! This was a insult, and 'tweren't to be borne . . .

—"*Ah, but the qu-estion i-is,*" Alter chimed in now, in his best scholar's singsong, impatient to set his poser to the company. "The qu-estion i-is, sir, how could she—that's to say, your missus—well, how *d-ast* that, that woman to . . . er, h'm, well, you know, with that, uh, bastid feller, the whole time . . . an', an' then to turn around and . . . well, sir, answer me that!"

"*Well, on the o-ne h-and,*" responds Fishke, chanting back antiphonally at Alter; "On the o-ne h-and, sir, you got a point. Though, on t'other hand, if they's one piece of hoss-sense I pick up over at the bathhouse in Glupsk, it's that this ain't no poser a-tall, and there ain't nothing in it to wonder at. Why, no. Not by a l-ong shot. For where else you see more mud being slung about, and reputations ruined, than in a bathhouse? And who you think do it most? Why, only them as best keep they own traps shut, if they knowed what was good for 'em. Say, like—well, you only take the feller which ain't never spoke a truthful word in his life, why he'll go about saying of someone else how *he's* a liar; or a person which rather give up his own eyes than to part with a penny, will point laughing at another, saying how that one's a cheapskate; or one which is hisself got a heart of stone, calling another wicked and hurtful; or a gent which he's ready to do most anything, only to obtain public honors, will bend folks' ears about how another was too prideful. Now I remember how Berl 'the twigsman'—you know, one at the bathhouse—well I remember whilst talking amongs' ourselfs, how he use to have the worse fits over it; and he'd just grab aholt of his head, and he'd say, 'Ai, ai, I jus' c-ain't unnerstan' it! How *d-ast* folks to slander other folks, when they knows only too well, what a awful gang of thieves, liars, misers, and rogues they all is theyselfs? I mean, they is guilty as sin of nearbout every wickedness in the book, on they own account, and then, on top of that . . .' —'Well, sonny boy, list and larn!' Itsik the watchman use to interrup' then, saying, 'Know what the whole dang trouble ree-ly is? It's nobody ever reconize the fleas up they own noses, so they think it's only the mote in t'other feller's eye which is the eyesore!' —But then that Shmerl feller, which he is one of them layabout gentry come mooching around the bath, well he be stroking his beard the whiles and smiling, and up and say: 'With respec,' Reb Berl, an' you, too, Reb Itsik! You both wrong. For the plain un-vanished truth is—as I been at considable pains to point out—the truth I say is only this: Everybody reckons to hisself: *Well I'm allowed so I can, and you hain't so you cain't!*'"

—"Right you are, Shmerl!"—I shouted this out quite un-expectedly, jumping up clean out of my seat whilst doing so. Though instantly I turned meditative. For that precept of Shmerl's had given a considerable whiff of incense to the Devil, who, as we know, dwelleth in the hearts of all sinful men. And he pounced on me with a sarcastical cackle and commenced playing ducks and drakes with my own heart, thereby throwing me into such a confusion that a congeries of distressful notions was set astir inside my head. And a hotch-potch of half-forgotten old grievances were dredged up now, so presently my mind came to resemble a tumultuous country fair, crowded with a collection of personages that seemingly had all at once materialized out of the thin air; whiles Old Scratch only kept pointing an accusing finger and disdainfully speaking out against them, as though in my own person:

There they are, feller! See them? All them fine upstanding folks out there? Well they are all allowed, and can and do pretty much as they please. And so they do, and do, and do . . .

And these same fine upstanding folks have got their hand in Trade and in Commerce and in Parish Affairs—inclusive of the Charitable Tills—and in Religion and all the rest of the kit which goes with running the World at Large. And there's also womenfolk at this fair. Ladies after every fashion, and suitable to every taste and occasion. Young ones, old ones; and not only your learned modern-leaning kind, but your ignorant old-fashion' sort too. *"Greeting, and God mend your worships!"* says I, though only to myself as yet. For God knows the shameful truth about every one of you. Now then, your worships. If it was up to me, I'd just as soon never look at any your faces again, nor utter your names. Because I'm that sick to death of the lot of you. Only it ain't up to me. For now that the very Deuce has conjured you out of my mind, the matter won't be laid to rest so easily. At least, not till the Devil has had his due. Which in truth he must, if only in token. So I shall have to tell a little something about each of you. So here goes . . .

—"Hold on a minute, Fishke, and your pardon, too, Reb Alter!" says I, making my apologies to both gents. "There's a lee-tle something I just got to tell you about . . . uh, only give me a sec whilst I collect my thoughts. So, lessee now . . ." And I plunged my hand down amongst the crowd, and plucked me out a choice scoundrel at random from that pack of privileged knaves, thinking: Now, now, don' be bashful, li'l man— only come along peaceable and get your comeuppance! Well, he jerked about wildly, and commence flapping and kicking crazily, like a trussed-up scapecock, frantically twisting and begging for mercy, a-going "puck-puck-puck-*Sq-uawk!* . . . puck-puck-puck-*Sq-uawk!*"; whilst the rest of that deceitful

lot stood about pulling grim faces, and giving me disapproving looks, as if to say, "Well, I never! The ruffian! Don't you
do it! Don't you *dare* tell on us, you bully! 'Tain't civil . . ." —
Thinks I: Dang fools! Well, all your silly face-pullings will cut
no ice with me! And I don't give *that!* for your idle chatter,
neither. Because, *your washups,* I'll have you know I am no innocent child to be throwed into a fright by a mere *boo!* of the
Bear-Mummer. So you put off your scruffy ole inside-out
shaggy sheepskins, and them sham headpieces, and show your
true faces. See? You ain't nothing but a bunch of monkeys on a
stick, and there's nothing of the noble bruin in any of you . . .
—But now the Devil had really got into me, and he proceeded to egg me on with: *Whoo-oop!* Atta boy! Take aholt of
'em by the scruff of the neck, scoop 'em up by the handful!
Now give them blankety-blank so'n'so's the what-for they got
coming. That's it! Again! Again! Now, that's more like it,
feller . . . —"Sorry about that, Reb Alter, only listen. Here's
a pretty yarn that's sure to please you. Now, then. There was
this Jewish town somewheres, name of, uh—h'm . . . Well
no matter. Anyhow, you see, the high-muck-a-mucks in it,
they had this kind of a arrangement, only amongst themselves, whereby . . ." —And so I had begun. Though no
sooner was the story got under way than I was suddenly constrained to stop. And try as I might, I seemed unable to carry
on with it. Though it was all on account of the ladies, don't
you know. Because in my mind's eye they were now casting
begging glances in my direction: *Oh, don't you do it, Reb
Mendele, oh pul-ease, pul-ease don't!* they seemed to be saying.
*Oh dearest, kindest, sw-e-e-test Reb Mendele, for pity's sake, don't
tell . . .* —Well, now, those beseeching looks were my undoing. Which is why I relented. For I must confess I have always
found feminine graces irresistible. Never mind having to face
down such a pretty flutter of eyes demurely blinking back

their tears. So needless to say, I was a goner. Besides which I had recalled withal my own recent oath to become worthy of that benevolent fraternity of beloved uncles . . . —*"Tsk!"* I finally remarked, smiling feebly at my companions. Whereat I followed with: *"Oh devil mend your ilk, sirs, and by jings there's an end!"* Though to my two companions I hastened to add, *"A-hem!* Sorry, gents, I meant them high-muck-a-mucks I been telling of and . . . Oh, forget it. And, well, I don't really feel much like telling that story anymore. —*Bah! deuce make off with each of you, and Aitch bedam!* . . . er—only saving both your presences, gentlemen . . ."

—"Oh, not at all, Reb Mend'le, my gracious, don' mind us! Go 'head, be our guest. I mean I'm sure all us druther see that rascally lot well and truly gone, and this very instant. Only I mus' say, sir, what sort of manners is it, always to be interruptin' another feller with all them stories? *Your* stories, mind . . ." —And so observing, Alter give me such a l-ong withering look! And then he shrugged, as much as to say: Why lookit that feller! My goodness I ain't never seed one was so partial to jabbering away all the time. Stories! Humph. That's to say *his* stories . . . I mean who needs 'em? —And turning away from me grumbling then, he gave Fishke a nudge in the flank with his elbow, saying, "Well, le's hear it, young feller. Only the nub, mind. C'mon, c'mon, so what happen then?"

And so Fishke started up again, after his fashion, and I set to work, after mine, and Alter nudged along some, after his, and Fishke's tale was got on with once more, so:


WELL THE TIME pass, and me and my wife we only drif' farther apart. The whiles, though, she come even more into cahoots with the bastid. And bimeby that pair chum up ever so close, and was growed altogether so buddy-buddy, you may have took them for kissin' kin easy—way they use to walk about as bold as brass together, doing the door-to-door so you'd of thunk they was lord and lady both. Only I wasted no bother about it anymore. On account I had no mind but for my poor hunchback girl, which she was never out of my thoughts now. As for them two, well, thinks I, you just run about together all you want—till you run yesselfs into the ground and six foot under it, for all I may care . . . an', an', well you can go choke on them houses of yourn while you at it, too! And when it happen I sometime pass that pair in the street together, the bastid use to give me such a smirk don't you know, as if to say, "Na-na Na-na! I sure has tweeted you good, Master Fishcakes, and boy you been give the bird, bub . . ." —Well gen'ly I only spit on the ground, as one do to ward off an ill thing, and I continue on my ways, thinking, Well what if you *are* going about with my wife? 'Twon't do you any good anyhow, as she is a marry' woman. So ha ha! you been nailed good and sound, bub! And it's me what's tweeted *you,* Master Bastid, so go have yesself conniptions, or bust a bladder, for ain' nothin' gonna change it . . ."

Though now there was this old feller, took to doing the rounds with me, which he was one of the bastid's mob. And boy were *he* the bad'un—and as much the goniffin' rogue as ever the bastid was . . . Anyhow he done pretty good out of me. I mean wasn't nobody dast deny him a handout, least not once he set to working his face into them pitiful looks he put on, and be a-sighing away so, it like to break your heart; the whiles he only point to me, suppose to be his poor cripple boy, don't you know, of which he 'personate the wretched old father. —"C'mon, give us a gimp, Fishke, and mind you make it good, my precious!" That's how he use to talk, whilst he push me through the door of a house. "And you get that mug

o' yourn screwed up nice and pitiful, y'heer . . . and don' you
forget to groan, like you suppose—*groan,* I says, you dawg!
Oh I shall make 'em pay for it all right, through the nose, oh
you bet I shall . . ." And when we walk along together, in the
street, well he larn me how to work that game; the whiles he
only talk ill of respectable folks, making fun of them; and
now and again he give me a pinch, or he poke me on a sudden, and then cuss me out in the worse way, saying, "Death
and the devil both take you, sonny!" And all that time why he
only be doing this as merrily as you please. Once't he punch
me amidriffs—you know, one of them nasty brisket cuffs jus'
under the breast, where it soft—and, well, I swear it near
give me the palsy then and there. Now, as a rule he pocket all
our alms hisself, and try as I may, I hardly couldn't squeeze a
penny of it out of him. "Aw, whatcha need money for,
Fishke?" he use to joke. "When you a walking mint yesself—
money on the hop, in a manner of speaking. And I wisht to
Aitch you may hop along so for the rest of your born days,
and sicken in every limb whiles you at it, till y'own fool head
is laid in the groun', my precious . . ." Well one day I press
him real hard about it. For I was in great want, so I weren't
any too gentle with him. So when he see how things stood, he
open up a mouth, saying, "Shuddup, you gimpy dawg! For
whatcha think, you got a free ride in my wagon maybe? Well
you show me more respec', young feller, else I shall tell your
wife. 'Cause I don't know you, see? No, I don't. It's only your
missus I knows. On account 'twere she which hand you over
to me in the first place, see? And, as it's her which I have to
thank for such ill goods, I s'pose it be hesself which I shall
square accounts with in the end, bub . . ."

Now that was ree-ly bad! For I saw plain that I weren't of
no more value to that bunch, than might be a performing bear
to a band of Gypsies. I was there only to be led about at a

rope's end, and made money of. And now they had took away
my wife, as well. Just coaxed her into a gunnysack and made
off with her. And she were even conspiring with them against
me now. For she had handed me over to that ugly gang like I
was no more than loot for barter . . . Oh, but it were a bitter
pill to swallow! For 'twere a world gone all awry, and no good
ever come of it now . . .

Well, I finally seed it was all over betwix' us, for good and
all. For we should never again live together as man and wife.
So what kept me here still? No, I must run off, and the sooner
I did it the better. On account these was evil folks which have
driv God out of their hearts altogether, and won't do a hand's
turn of honest work. For they have completely throwed the
yoke off, not wanting even to hear of earning their bread
by the labor of their own hands, but only preferring to batten
theyselfs on Jewish folks and bleeding them dry. And withal
they got the brass to be mortally hating them as well. And for
myself, I too had fallen quite low the whiles, considering all
what I done in the time I been with that pack of rogues. Why,
I weren't at all the same person I once was. For I become infected by many of their dishonest ways. So there weren't only
the one way to get shut of this multitude of ills and troubles: I
must free myself of that villainous bunch, and shun them for
the evil they was. But what of her then, what of my poor
hunchback girl? How was I to leave her behind? And in my
mind I imagined myself to be standing in a corrupt place,
which it were a terrible abyss, a very hell. And I could hear in
my one ear a loud voice which it were admonishing me, saying: *Take care, Fishke, lest thy soul shall be forfeit. For as thou cher-
ishest thy God, get thee from this wicked place at once!* The whiles,
in my other ear, my hunchback girl were calling to me: *Fishke,
Fishke . . .* —So, it come down to this only. I should have to
choose one or t'other: Either I shall make my way into the

world of light, which were clean of sin and trouble and wickedness. Or I must stay here, in Hell, together with her. Well I cried most bitterly over it, praying only that God might forgive me. Because in the end I chose to abide with them scoundrels.

Though later on the idea come to me that we might run away together, so the both us may finally be rid of that passel of no-account gentry. Only this could not be unlest I was able to untie the knot with my wife first. For what good come of my going about so with a young unmarry' lady? Why folks was only bound to talk, and who knows what they may make of it . . . So there was only one cure. Divorce! But hold on, thinks I: What of my wife? Shall she ever consent to such a thing? For that woman were a very devil and a scourge, which she be only too glad to torment me. So if ever I was to bring up the subject with her, she only be spiteful and say No! For it were now her greatest pleasure to be always vexing me and spiting me cruelly. But I wouldn't let it put me off. No. For I was resolve' that I should manage the business by any manner of means, fair or foul. And just maybe, Merciful Providence, too, will choose to intervene. In the meantime I would keep my design to myself, so no one may discover it.

But after my run-in with the old feller which I been paired up with—well, now, I was so grieved by it I just refuse to go calling on houses with any that bunch anymore. Well it brung me a considerable sight of trouble to be sure, but I were adamant. For even it cost me my life, I would not go on playing the dancing bear for them gypsies. Now it only stood to reason that the bastid and his gang, they wasn't any too happy about it—which they also didn't spare their fists to make plain to me. Though, once, when they was punching me about, they ask me outright: "Now why should we drag around such useless baggage as yesself, if you won't do a lick of work to earn your keep? So you only take that fool carcass of yourn dang-all-to-Aitch out of here. Well, go head, buster, *scoot!*" But even then I played it cunning and say, "Gimme back my wife . . . I want my wife!" Well, that ree-ly stun them; though it also about broke them up, so they near fell down laughing. Course it were all by way of a ruse, what I said then about wanting my wife back. For to my own self I was think-ing: Well, now, you go keep that nasty piece of goods, and you welcome to her, as long as she give me that divorce. Now, it is very true that all them knockings-about I get on account my stubbornness was pretty painful on the whole. But I got quite a kick, too, thinking: Well, never mind, feller. It'll answer in the end. For when they see I ain't to be moved, nor can I be of any use to them, they'll be too glad to see my back. So it can only help me get that divorce.

# 21

"BASSIA," SAYS I, approaching my wife coaxingly once, mean-ing to sound her out about a divorce. "Bassia, what you got against me?"

"Drop dead!" was all the answer she give.

"There, you see?" says I letting on like I was peeved. "Here I been trying my darndest, only to meet you halfways, and all you do is to act contrary the whiles: *Drop dead!* Now what way is that to talk?"

"Well, so git palsied, if that suit you better," says she pulling a face and moving off.

"Bless you, Bassia," says I sweetly still. "But do put by them foolish notions of yourn just this once, and let us try and live as God intended us to do . . ."

"Drop dead, Fishke dearest! which it only go double for that 'ere hussy of yourn . . ."

Oho, thinks I, and the same to you, dearest—which it only go double for that bastid of yourn, in spades! And I spoke to her plain: "Only hear me out, Bassia: *A woman shan't be compelled!* That is the way amongs' Jewish folks. So if you won't live as man and wife with me, they's always divorce. Live and let live! That is my motto . . ."

"Aha! still lustin' after that hussy o' yourn, I see. So it's *Bye-bye-Bassia an' Hop-o'-my-Knee My Fancy,* is it? Well I see you dead first! For I ain't making you no present of that cheap trollop o' yourn. 'Cos she gonna crawl, she gonna eat dirt! Hear that, Fishke, my pet? For yous nuffin' but couple blankety-blank so'n'so's, which I wisht only all dingdong dangnations on the pair o' yous' papas f'ever, an', an' on their papas, an', an' on . . ."

Well she begun ranting so, I shouldered my legs and got clear; whilst I still might.

I was more sorely pressed than ever, and hemmed in on every side. And my life been made altogether so wretched I certainly lick no honey. Nor in truth did my poor hunchback girl, which she were degraded and made to suffer even more on my account. You see, my wife now took to playing Lady-o'-the-house with her, and order her about like she was only the meanest serving maid. And if even the least thing wasn't to her liking, she made very certain that the girl should pay dear for it. And when my wife was through chastising her, then the bastid come along to have a go as well. Oh 'twere naught but woe and ill for the pair of us then. And our only consolation was, when late in the night, whilst the rest was asleep, we use to steal away and we set outside and tell each other of our troubles.

One night we was together next to the Big Shul. And the

sky was bright with stars, and it were dead quiet and still. And
there wasn't a living creature astir anywhere. And, well, she
set by me, on only a stone, and look to be all crumpled-up-
like, the way she was hunched over so; and her face was awash
in tears, and she been singing so sadly under her breath the
whiles. You know, so sof' you wouldn't hardly of notice it.
Well it were that same song of hern about the murdered
chil':

> My father me slew,
> My mother me chew . . .

Each word cut my heart like a knife. And I try and console
her, chattering away of only happy things, thinking perhaps it
may be of comfort to her. Why (I says to her), 'twon't be any
time a-tall, and we shall be raised up from this affliction. Oh
we shall! And I reckon up for her what our lives may only be,
when God send and we are redeem from our present trouble.
So I paint her up a picture of how that brick bathhouse in
Glupsk look, right down to the last dint and nailhead, making
it lively, so she may see it in her own mind. And I tell her then
about how I shall contrive to wangle my way back in. And of
how, if God see fit and improve my fortunes, I may in time at-
tain even to the station of a watchman. And, why, she might
find employment there hesself: p'raps be a "ducking wife,"
which she attend on womenfolks at immersions rites—or
some other such employment they got. But if not, they is
other livings may be come by. On account, for poorfolks,
Glupsk is the *Promise Land,* which it flow with milk and honey
where they is concern'. I mean, first off it is very big. So
houses is about as common as dirt there, for which praise
Goodness! if you're a mind to go cadging door-to-door. And
folks ain't at all stuck-up, nor they stand on ceremony much.

For everybody does pretty much as they please, and ain't no-body will object. Why, there are quite respectable folks, for instance, which they go about dressed only in rags from head to foot, such as might shame even a tramp, but it won't raise a eyebrow; or others as strut about in the midday, in only a tore-up tatty old dressing-gown, which it been left open all the way down the front, and even that's took in stride, as well. Or, say, the opposite, where a pauper may dress up in satins and silks, and nobody waste any bother over it. So you'd be hard put to distinguish rich from poor there, going only by people's clothes and comportment. Why there's even al-moners of the Parish which they manage charitable societies; well, for all they is gen'ly paupers in their own right, they still draw quite a handsome living out of it anyhow, together with the rich folks. Which is as it should be, for one hand wash the other. So bein' poor ain't anything to be ashame' of there. All you want is luck, and your fortune is made. Why I can't think how many gents I know of, which the one minute they was dirt-poor and humble, say only a shop assistant or other such flunky; and why next thing *wham!* it's rags to riches just like that, and they are transform into great movers and shakers, panjandrums which ain't nothing ever done in the parish, un-lest it's by their leave and say-so. Well, now, who is to say if one day yours truly mayn't hisself become just such a doer; so in the end everything will turn out just fine. And then, God send, we shall both live out our days in happiness and dignity and contentment. For such things happen in only the ordinary way in Glupsk, and aren't to be wondered at. All that's wanted for it, is to trust in God and to never give up hope, and . . . well, in a word, to be Jewish. For that is the main thing. Piety and steadfastness . . . *O Glupsk, Glupsk!* lordy, lordy, how I wisht only we may be shut of this ugly mob, and be back to thee the sooner, Mother—

"Ah, Fishke I haven't the strength to hold out for any longer . . . ," says my hunchback girl then, sighing deeply. And she put her head on my shoulder, and look up at me with a pleading expression. So I caress her, and set myself to comforting her with more talk of good things. And presently her spirits revived and she look straight into my eyes, and she were laughing now. But then she say quietly: "Fishke, you are all I have in the world. You are my father, my brother, my friend—you are my everything! Be faithful to me always, Fishke, never forget me. Oh you must swear it, Fishke, right here in front of this shul, where only the Dead pray at this hour (and amongs' which even my own father, who I scarcely knew, may be praying as well), that these dead may bear witness to it. Oh swear, Fishke, that you shall remain always faithful to me . . ."

So I set to work seriously now, to try and persuade my wife to agree to a divorce, chawing at her ear, only pestering her. Till at last we come to a understanding, which it were this: Whatever money I have put by in the time we was on the road, shall be turn over to my wife immediately and forthwith, without it being deposited with a third party, as is gener'ly done in such cases; besides which, I had also to give my solemn undertaking that, for the term of the whole of that winter (an' God grant we live the whiles), I should allow myself to be led around by the nose by that gang of thugs, without making any complaint or offering the least resistance. In other words, to be a willing party to all their hokum and thievish shenanigans. Moreover all handouts which I receive in the course of such doings, shall be entirely my wife's, as part of her settlement upon divorce, under the terms of our deed-o'-marriage. The agreement being thus concluded, the bastid then flash me a smile, saying *Congrats!* and he proceed to give me a good drubbing as well; which it were by way of telling me the transaction were signed and sealed, so best I run along now, and keep to my end of it. So once again I become a performing bear and a prime commodity amongs' that pack of rogue gentry. And again that same old feller went calling on houses together with me; whilst I, for my part, was constrain' to only hop along, and to make faces, and to gammon folks, and to gener'ly do exactly as the old buzzard bid me to do.

'Twere gone Feast of Passover, and getting well on to spring, when we arrive in this little town in Kherson province somewheres. And whilst there, I at first still stuck by my end of the bargain. But bimeby I thought: Enough! the time come to make a end of it. Though first off my wife only kind of dither about and ask for a couple days to think things over. But finally she give her answer: All right, she say, tomorrow she accept a divorce! Oh it was like a black cloud been lifted off me, I were that overjoy'. And I was feeling a-way too excited, to only be hanging about the one place. For somehow I felt a great need only of getting away, of just being outside in the open for a bit. Well I stroll about so in town for quite a spell, taking in the sights don't you know. When I come upon a run of houses which I get a urge to try my luck with in the cadging line, thinking: Well, why not? Strike while the iron's hot, is what I say. For we was on our own now, and must fend for ourselfs; so it's as well we had a bit of a nest egg laid by for it. So I up and had me a go at it. Well I mus' say I hit pay dirt, gen'men. For I scarce recall when last I had me such a door-to-door as this. Thing like that, why it don't come your ways but only once in a l-ong jubilee. And when God see fit to help a person, he will just go all-out doing it. Why, weren't a house which folks turn me away at. And this one house I struck, which they was having a circumcision in it? Well now that is when I ree-ly luck out. For folks there was quite deep in

their cups and feeling pretty merry, so first off they stood me
a brandy. Though mind this weren't none of your sniffy sips,
but a nogginful straight out of the blessings cup. Which this
were follow by a nice chunk of honey cake and one 'em fancy
holiday breads go by the name "royal loafs" and a kind of a
dainty roll which gen'ly is call a "rosette," plus a tenner in
hard brass, by way of a cash bonus. Only I don't let my appetite get the better of me, no sir. And I touch none of it the
whiles; but only shove that whole lot down the inside my
shirtfront, stashing it away there, reckoning it be a fine rare
treat for my hunchback girl. And, well, you can jus' picture
yesselfs, in what a high humor I went home then. The whole
ways back, all I thunk about was how tonight, when the rest
was gone to bed, I shall surprise her; and how for once that
poor girl at least gonna enjoy hesself, get some real pleasure
out of life. She which been endlessly drug about all over the
place and ill used, and her heart so sorely tried all these long
years. Why, in all her life that poor creature ain't experience
one whole minute of sweetness nor ease. Well it were time
she knowed she had a faithful brother in Fishke, which he
cherish and look after her, like she was the apple of his eye;
and which he druther deny hisself so he may only give away
his last and best to her. And in my own mind I imagine how
the both us was already setting together in front of the Big
Shul, and we was ree-ly enjoying ourselfs don't you know.
And she be treating hesself to that honey cake I brung, and I
be saying then, "Eat up, dearest, and you only welcome to it!"
Whiles to myself I be thinking what a good portent it was; for
we both be eating honey cakes at home together soon enough,
an' God willing . . . And then I let her in on my good news,
about how tomorrow I shall be free and my wife accept the
divorce; which it will set my girl to beaming so, it be a marvel
only to see the way her face light up on account of it. Then we

think about how we make our getaway, and finally give them pack of scoundrels the slip forever. And once we'd laid our plans, they be good reason to hope everything will turn out well for us . . . So this was what I been thinking, and these was the happy thoughts running through my mind, the whiles I was making my way back to the almshouse. And withal, why, I even come acrost a water carrier on the way, which he were carrying full pails of water. Now *there's* a good omen if ever there was one, thinks I . . . Only what you think come of it in the end?

Oh lordy, lordy, lordy—ain't nothin' come of it! For if a body is destin' only for misfortune, ain't no omen in the world will mend it. Not even it was ten goywives crost his path at once, which they was carrying twice ten pailfuls of water. On account when finally I do get back to the almshouse, which it were getting on towards evening then, that whole scoundrely lot was gone. For the whiles I been having me a high time of it in town, they all lit out bag and baggage, every last one, and took my wife along and my poor hunchback girl as well . . . Now this were all the bastid's doing, his trick which he play on me. —Oh how I wisht that feller only knowed as little of the land of the living as I ever knowed where on earth *I* was then—an', an' . . . God in Heaven! I hope his bowels set to churning the way my head span then. Oh the light were gone from my life! For the one little star which brighten my sky, on a sudden it had vanish. Gone! My only consolation, my poor little hunchback girl were gone . . . Woe is me! I had nobody now and were alone in the world and friendless again. And what of her? Where was she now, and what were she doing, poor thing? Who she got now which will listen to her troubles—which she could have hesself a good cry with, whilst telling them to? Oh, good gents, I been made twice miserable now, for thinking on her trouble and on mine as well . . .

And when I drawed that piece of honey cake from my bosom which I had save up special for her, I thought it made a great hole in my breast. And whiles I bit off a piece, I held it tight in my hands, and I cried over it like it may have been . . . oh, I dunno—like it were a sad keepsake, the one little thing left behind by a baby, a only chil', who just die, and which it was all I had to remember it by. Oh my poor girl, my poor unhappy girl! for you ain't been give the chance to enjoy yerself even this once in your life. And I stared and stared at the honey cake—and I kiss it then, and wrap it up carefully, like it was a precious jewel, and I put it away again, next to my breas', patting it and pressing it to my heart. Oh the Lord only knew what may become of me now . . .

# 22

FISHKE HAD PUT both his hands to his face and turned away, and he wept unrestrainedly now. We understood his need, and we let him be. Though truth to say, we ourselves had been put deeply out of humor on our own account, and were fallen silent, each brooding upon his own thoughts the whiles. My Alter only tugged at his sidecurl, toying with it as he ran his hand over his face, starting with his forehead and finishing at his beard, which he took firm hold of now, wrapping all his five fingers about it, the while he said, "Tsk, tsk . . ." Plainly he was upset. No, all was not well with Alter. I, too, was for some reason in no little turmoil of mind, Fishke's story having quite unsettled me. I remember, oh, years back, how I used to wonder about it all the time, asking myself over and over, Godamercy, but what sort of thing is it: "to fall in love"? I mean, to go all soppy with hankering after someone, so you are besotted by 'em. Oh, I had heard talk of such things happening, sometimes; but as to what it rightly is, well I confess it was beyond my comprehension. Back home then, folks used generally to say, it come only of enchantments and spells. And they would tell, too, of a kind of a vial with philters in it, or essences of roots maybe—anyhow, some such article which did it, and come from an old goywife who was well-known in the neighborhood for being a witch. And that such old witches are quite capable of playing a mean prank like that on a body; not to mention, sir, their being able to fly to the ends of the earth on nothing but a broomstick or baker's shovel, only so they may fetch back a runaway husband by such conveyance; who on a sudden had up and done a bolt on his wife, abandoning that good woman to the hapless state of grass widowhood for the rest of her born days, never able to remarry, poor thing—well, sir, what I say is that it is nothing short of an incontrovertible fact, bore witness to by oh countless numbers of folks; nor am I talking here about any your shavelings, but of only your "sure-thing" Jewish gents, in full possession of all their original facefuzz, so their word is their bond and you may bank on it, sir . . . Though, as I told, falling in love was regarded amongst our set as an infirmity which was tantamount, say, to being seized of the Fever, or a Dybbuk, or the Melancholy, or the Falling Sickness—anyhow, to possession by an evil which was so calamitous that only a miracle-worker could be trusted to exorcise it, or (wanting such) perhaps a sorcerer might be induced to do it. And if anybody chanced so much as to mention the subject, even in passing, you can bet they made certain to spit out that evil seven times, covering their eyebrows with their hand whilst doing it; and then they'd give you one of them long-suffering earnest looks, which folks like to save up for just such an occasion, and sigh and say *"God preserve us!"* or *"Heaven keep us from such a thing!"* or some other such piety, by way of averting disaster. And it was thought a very great charity (not to speak of its being a pious duty!) to ply anyone so unfortunate as to fall in love, with generous doses of the "laughing cure"—which is to say, to make fun of them in much the same way as we customarily jeer at fools and madmen. Now, as I recall, if such a thing ever did happen to somebody, it nearly always happened amongst your very rich folks or only your meanest class of paupers. Whereas your ordinary middle-ranking persons, they never had the least notion of what it was, so naturally they were up a stump every time they come across it, you see. Why, surely (so would I often remark to myself), why, surely, this is a mighty mystery! I mean, after all, what was it? Whatever can it be? For, you see, there has just *got* to be a reason for it. Now, all of that silly talk about the old goywife and her dinky bottles of love potions, well of course I knew it was plain foolishness. For I never did take much stock in such tales, anyhow. Even if my attitude in this had given me a reputation, at least in right-thinking quarters, of being something of a maverick in matters of faith generally, and not altogether sound on the subject. "But-but-but," people used to say. "But by *gum,* sir, how can you *not* believe there's enchantments and sorcerers and demons in the world, when most anybody you care to ask knows for sure there is?" Though I persisted in turning the thing over in my mind regardless, never giving up the search till I finally did tumble onto the reason I was looking for. You see, very rich folks have got it a-way too good in this life. For they already have at their beck and call just about everything in the way of luxurious fare which the world has to offer, so they don't have to waste any bother over it or lift a finger to get it. Why, about the only thing which they seem to miss is a little grief. Well, small wonder then that they are given to hanky-panky and making whoopee so much. Now, whether they are only sowing wild oats or good honest grain by such doings, well that of course only they can tell. So we'll let that question ride. But then again your poorest of the poor, on the other hand—that's to say, your beggars and tramps and vagabonds and such—well, now, I should say they had quite an easy time of it, too, though in their own way. For with them it's all only a matter of "nothing ventured, nothing lost"—living shamelessly as they do off of the charity of others and the ready-made. So the world's their oyster, pretty much. Which explains why they are apt to get up to the same mischief as rich folks do. Now though idling about so and mooning and spooning is generally only practiced by only your very highest and lowest stations in life, the remainder of us middling folks never have time to spare for such shenanigans, and are forever preoccupied with the nitty-gritty and homely down-to-earth matters like putting bread on our tables. So with us it's all business and nothing but. Why even marriage is a business, the way we go about it. For one of our sort never merely takes a wife but he *contracts* for one; first haggling separately over every item of dowry and brideprice, right down to the cut of his Sabbath bonnet and holiday vestments, and making very certain, too, that each such article is set down in the deed of marriage exactly as was agreed to, before he will even think to put his mark to it and take the plunge. And when the deal's sewed up at last, and every condition nailed down, as per agreement, then *wh-oosh presto!* it's under the wedding canopy with you, Oh Darlin' Bride o' Mine, along with the marriage broker, the wedding jester, the cantor, the rabbi, and what-all other shul-gentry as ordinarily receive their meed by assisting at such proceedings. —*Whew!*

Now run along, little woman, and show us what you are ree-ly made of. Aw, go ahead, my sweet, be a wife, keep house, bear children, work, slave, wear yourself to a frazzle alongside yours truly, till your portion of threescore years and ten in this world are done—and God only send you are minded to live for so long. As to your being pretty or plain, clever or a fool, pert as primroses or dull as dishwater, all that's your own affair, for I'm sure I don't care about it. *Brains, beauty*— pooh! I mean, who needs any them foofaraws? After all, a wife's a wife, and one's as good as another at keeping house. And besides, no do-nothing gentlemen of leisure *we,* to be putting on airs in that department; but only sober-minded Jewish gents-at-trade, who are far too busy making a living to bother about any such trifles. —Now you'd be surprised how many Jewish gents there are like myself in the world, who scarcely even talk to their wives, or ever sit down to dinner with them. Come to that, they hardly see them at all. But that is all right, really. Because, don't you know, in the end it always works out for the best. Oh, absolutely. For you needn't only to ask either of the principals, and they won't stint telling you about how pleased they have been down through the years by the whole arrangement—and withal be wishing the very same good fortune upon you and yours and all your progeny down the generations, even to the end of time and God willing Amen forever . . . But say even a Jewish gent's wife up and dies on him untimely. Well of course he will do right by her, and he will bury her first thing, and then piously sit out the Seven Days' Mourning which is after all only her due. Though this done, he promptly contracts for another to take her place, even before the full Term of Thirty-Day Be-reavement is out. And if that second missus happens to prede-cease him, why he will just as promptly contract for a third, and then a fourth, and a fifth, and so on, going about the busi-

ness quite systematically . . . Till, being graced by sound
health and a long life, he finally takes up with a little old
granny as much advanced in years as himself, giving it out as
his intention to voyage with her to the Land of Israel, where
in the fullness of time they shall be laid to rest together (an' it
please God) until Heaven's Trumpeters sound the Resurrection. And what do you suppose all this marital to-do gets to
be called? Why, that's right: *Performing the Commandment,* as
God hath ordained it (no less). For Jewish folks won't do anything without the Almighty has told them to do it first. And
what is more has troubled to spell out for them exactly why
and how they must do it. Which is why we are always making
such a solemn production of everything don't you know. Sabbathday dinner, for instance. I mean will anyone amongst us
unceremoniously sit down to it in the ordinary way, only to
tuck in, because mortal flesh is in need of nourishment to
live? Certainly not! Because what we are doing here is (mark)
*performing the rite of Third Feasts.* So much for Saturday afternoon dinner. Or that bit of a tipple we allow ourselves at the
Feast of Passover? Now you just try and catch a Jewish gent
knocking back a glass of wine on such occasion only because
it is a pleasant thing to do, never mind it also helps the diges-
tion along something wonderful. No, he has first got to put a
pious face on the business: *Lo!* (says he) *ready I am and willing
to perform the Commandment of Being-in-My-Cups.* Which is all
by way of saying that when one of our sort eats or drinks or
gets married, he does it in much the same spirit of solemnity
that he undertakes his other pious duties. —Though, this
said, none of it suits the case of Fishke very much anyway. For
in Fishke's wretched circumstances the hunchback girl was
the only real piece of happiness to have come his way. She was
his one consolation, his joy, his very life. They say that a
drowning man will clutch at a straw. Well small wonder that

Fishke should have latched on to that girl, body and soul. And
if the soul's touched, then the heart too cries out in the one
language which is common to us all—both the great and the
small, the learned and the ignorant. So it is hardly surprising
that Fishke's heart should have brimmed over with such sur-
charge of human feeling. Or that he should deliver himself of
his burden of sadness with an eloquence that could exert so
powerful an influence upon myself, moving me as profoundly
and as deeply as will a sad song played on a fiddle. For not all
your circuit preachers and books of sermons taken together
can ever touch my soul in the same degree, and make me feel
so tender and pious and good, as the sigh of a broken heart or
the fiddler's plaintive air . . .

   Hello, hello, what's this? Well, now, it is all very well for
*me* to be moved to meditating on Fishke's tale. But you, little
buddy, what has made *you* so ruminative on a sudden? Come
on, feller, shake a leg . . . Look at the fool creature! Won't
budge an inch. Why that horse couldn't care less about it getting on to Fast-o'-Ab time, and there being so many towns we
have got to visit yet. Really, now! Straying from the straight
and narrow into a wheat field like that, to browse about
amongst the grasses there. And that stringy she-nag of Alter's
isn't any better than my own bag a bones. What with the both
them treating themselves to a feed on other folks' time. Dis-
graceful! Like schoolboys took to woolgathering because the
rebbe's been momentarily distracted by the baby needing to
be rocked or his wife nagging him. But a good dose of the
schoolmaster's cure will generally set things right in such
cases. So I reckoned some of that same medicine wouldn't be
out of place in the present instance, and I give that bonehead
of mine a touch of the whip. Now that did stir him some. For
immediately he quirked up his ears and capered about on his
hinders for a bit. Though these exertions were preliminary to

nothing much, and they petered out in only his flicking his tail
at me a couple of times. Why of all the—! Now if there is
one thing I will not tolerate it is impudence from a horse. So
this time I didn't spare the whip, and there was even some
bite to it now. Well that didn't suit him a-tall. And for a
minute there I thought he looked ready to rear up and ladder
the air with his foreshanks, but then he appeared to change his
mind and want to kick out at me jackasswise with his back
feet—or maybe he only meant to lay down and play dead, just
to show me. But none of it come to anything. Because next
thing he gave the wagon a bit of a jerk so it lurched forward,
and then he plodded on back to the main road as he been bid.
Only by now we had all of us severally snapped out of our
reveries. Well, Alter commenced prodding once more after
his fashion, and Fishke proceeded telling again after his, and I
of course attended to the business of smoothing his way and
prompting him along after mine. Whereat the sequel of
Fishke's story followed, so:

WELL, SIRS, BRIEF is best. So I shan't say any more than that I
next proceeded by the main road to Odessa on my own,
thinking I might run into that gang of rogue gentry along the
ways, or at least hear tell of them. But it were like they all
been swallowed up by the sea, for any trace I ever found of
them. By now, though, I had grown so weary of dragging myself all over, and I was dying to rest up for a while, just settle
down peaceful-like in the one place, don't you know, the way
I use to once. Well thanks to Goodness in the end I finally
drug myself into Odessa.

Now I do own that the first couple days in Odessa near finish me. Mooching about the place day and night, all alone and
friendless, not knowing where to park my carcass even. Well

everything seem so new to me, and plumb odd. Why I couldn't
even find a almshouse which I might doss down in, like you'd
expect to find in any ordinary Jewish town. And would you
believe there wasn't even houses where a begging gent might
do his rounds if he'd a mind to? Not proper ones, anyway. You
know, the kind that Jewish folks is gener'ly got back home?
Comfable tumbledown places which is built low to the
ground, wit' no fancy frills to 'em. And which they is never
any song and dance about getting inside of, on account they
got the front door unbolted and in plain sight, facing the
street, the way front doors is suppose to be. So you needn't
only give it a lee-tle nudge and barge right on in. And once inside, why you just settle in and make yourself to home. No
fuss, no bovver. For everything a body may need in the way of
bed, board, or other domestic convenience is ready to hand in
the one room; which all you got to do is reach out for it. Got
a thirst? Well there's the water, so help yesself. Got the call?
Well no need going a-way back of the woodpile to answer it.
For the cessbucket's right there, over to the corner, where
you welcome to ease nature, wash hands, bless God, and
gardyloo all you want, and ain't nobody be put out by it in the
least. Nor need you look very far for the master and missus of
the house. For the both them plus fambly is all there, too,
right in amongs' the rest of the furnishings. So you only stick
out your hand, say "Thank'ee an' Godbless!" buss the mezuzah
and pocket the proceeds, and take yourself and your business
on over to the next house down. Which there's never a problem knowing whose house it is. On account that hillock of
homey rubbage and played-out houseware dumped down in
the front yard, the drainage ditch running down to the street,
the roof, the windows, the walls, indeed most everything
about the place jumps right out at you and tells you it's Jewish
folks and no other which are domicile there. And if sight fail,

then the smell alone be a dead giveaway . . . Now in this respect it is contrariwise and altogether different down Odessa
way. Because, well, first off, what passes for houses there is
these big sprawling concerns, which is built so monstrous tall,
it give you neck cramps only thinking about them. And they
all got this kind of a archway mostly, which you must pass
under first, just to get into the courtyard. And then they got
you clambering up and down staircases, and in and out all
sorts of passages and corridors, before you ever catch sight of
anything so ordinary as a door. And even you happen to light
on such a article, wouldn't you know it be locked fast from
the inside, and done up with a dinky little bell and a cord plus
tassels, and what-all else in the way of thingummy attachments. Well it kind of brings you up sharp, and that's the
truth. I mean a thing like that, it is only bound to take a feller
down a peg. Make you feel downright poor, and low, and unworthy. But say you try and reach for the cord anyhow, and
you only give it a ever-so-reverent little tug notwithstanding,
not meaning to offend. Well, for all you scarcely laid a finger
on that cord, you never believe what an astonishing crash of
gongs and chimes result from it. Why it make you feel like
you have just passed a rude remark, or blew a raspberry. So all
you can think of is to get away before anyone's the wiser . . .
Though bimeby you hunt up another set of stairs and try your
luck at another door, only to be set upon by the cook this
time, or other such domestic flunky. Or maybe you find the
gent in residence ain't even Jewish. Well, now, that finally do
put the lid on it. Because it set me to wondering mightily
about what kind of city this is, which it got such queer houses
in it. And where in the name of wonder is all of the poorfolks
with their cadging bags got to? For in between whiles I must
say I had me a pretty good look round, thinking maybe to find
a kindred gent of the road shouldering such a article, who I

might quiz about the business of cadging door-to-door in these parts. But it were my ill luck never to run acrost even one such personage. Now the whiles I been hanging about the street so, I make out up ahead what seem to be a young man done up quite elegant, in them modren type of clothes, you know what's call your German fashion, which he was poking about the place, here, there, yonder, looking like he was studying where to turn next. Well, thinks I, now here's a stranger in town, if ever I seen one. So I make up my mind to follow him and watch what he do. And when he duck into a courtyard next, I nip in after him. Well, he look about. Then he whipped up some stairs, and I followed hard behind. But when he turn in at a sort of a vestibule at the top of the stairs, I hung back at the entrance. And sure enough, after a spell, a baldface party come to the door, which I reckon him for being the party in actual residence there, on account he has got on this kind of a lord-o'-the-manor air which it gener'ly go with the station. Anyhow the young gent give him some kind of a book he'd first retrieved out of his coat pocket, which it must of been as deep as a cadging bag easy, judging from the way the feller dug down into it. The baldface party, though, don't give it only a glance and straightway he throwed the book back, saying very riled, "Who needs that rubbage, for I don't!" But that young man won't take no for an answer. And he commence argying then, heaping praises on hisself and allowing as what he done was all too wonderful for words even. Only ole baldface weren't having any. And it near broke my heart to see how downhearted that young man look when he finally go away, poor feller. Howsomever I don't let it stop me, and I jump right in and stick out my hand and receive my couple of coppers, and next thing I'm out of there lickety-split and feeling right proud of myself. Thinks I: Now that's more like! For if, as folks say, God sendeth flax to the spinner and beer to

the taverner, then it only stand to reason he bethink himself
of a poor beggarman, too, and may sometime put him in the
way of a meal ticket. For that is what that feller with the book
turn out to be. And you can bet I weren't about to let him out
of my sights. So I tag along after him, quiet-like, as a cow
might follow after her calf; and wherever he happen to go I
weren't far behind. Well you have never in your life seen such
a feller for bad luck. For he was give the boot just about
everywhere, with folks saying things like, "Oh for pity's sake,
not another one!"; or, "G'wan, shoo, we don't want any!" So
the nub is, each time he got turn away empty-handed and
went off in a huff, I brung up the rear and come away with the
prize: a penny here, a deuce there, a trey yonder, whatever
mite of charity folks might care to give. Which it add up,
don't you know. Well the whole thing got me to thinking. I
mean, what kind of a beggar was this anyway? Now maybe
poorfolks with books is only the custom in these parts. Like
being dressed up natty in them newfangle' clothes. Still it do
seem such a fool thing to do anyhow, to go a-begging with a
book in your hand, and end up with only getting the finger.
When it be a lot less trouble to come right out and ask for a
handout. Now I personal have always favored the old no-
nonsense way of doing the rounds, the way our fathers done
and their fathers afore them. And I will bet you anything I
come out of it better than any half dozen your fancier kinds
of beggars with books. Though that ain't no matter. For fool
or no, I stuck fast to my book-toting gent, and everywhere he
went I followed after. Well I kept out of his sights as best I
could, and for a while things went along pretty good. By and
by, though, he appear to take notice of my trailing after him.
Which I could also see it vex him considerable. For he kept
stopping and glancing about, and seem gener'ly anxious to
shake me off. But I just put on a dumb face, and look this way

and that, letting on like I wasn't paying the feller no mind, nor I couldn't care less even if I was. And I only continue on my ways as before, the whiles in my mind I'm thinking: Oh, no you don't. You ain't never giving me the slip, bub! Cause maybe you are not worth shucks to yourself nor anybody else, sonny, but to me you are as good as money in the bank . . . Anyhow the whole business betwixt us finally finish up this way: It were about noon, and we come to this one place, which the occupant was setting down to his lunch. When my gent drop in on him on a sudden with his books. Well he go through his usual patter, and they both have words, till the master of the house jump up and took holt of my feller and march him out the door. Where he also happen to catch sight of me, so he send the pair us to the devil. Now the both us being give the same boot, as 'twere, it only follow that we was throwed a mite closer together by it. Though on the way down I observe my gent looking very put out with me. Well I couldn't think what to do, so I stood aside to let him pass. And for a couple minutes we both us remain standing so; with the neither gent feeling any too comfable about it, you may be sure. When my partner up and ask:

"Well, what are you after, sir?"

"Me?" says I. "Why nothin', same as y'self!"

"Same as myself?" says he astonish, and he look me up and down: "Are you peradventure an Aw-thor, sir?"

Well he spoke funny, that's the truth. But from the dainty way he had of pursing his lips whilst talking, I reckoned it must be German. So when he asked me about being "an Aw-thor," I judged he was asking if I was "an other," meaning "an-other pauper" like hisself. So in my best German I answered him: "Yeah, sure, you bet, an aw-thor!"

"Indeed?" says he, still marveling. "And pray what have you made in that line, sir?"

"Well quite a bit, all things considered," says I (the whiles thinking: *Oho, and you only wisht you done as well, friend!*). "Well, lessee now, oh I'd say I made upwards of forty-odd today, in loose change."

"No, no, you mistake me, sir!" says he. "I only meant the Fruit of Your Aw-thorship. The title, sir, the name!"

German again, thinks I: *Fruit of Your Aw-thorship!* Dang silly way to ask a body's name. But I give it to him anyway:

"Fishke!" says I short and sweet.

"Fishke?" says he, "H'm! N-o-o, can't say I've had the plea-sure. Though I should deem it an honor, sir, were I allowed to peruse this Fishke. To make his acquaintance, so to speak. May I, sir?" Whereat he put out his hand to me . . .

"Why I be right proud if you would," says I. "So put it there, friend!" And I took his hand and give it a couple of shakes.

"Well, where is it?" says he.

"Where's what?" says I.

"Fishke!" says he.

"Why bless you, sir," says I, "but here you have me, big as life!"

"No, I mean the book!" says he.

"What book?" says I.

"Why of all the—? Oh dang your impertinence, sir!" says he in a rage. And he flung hisself round and rush out of the place in oh just the worse huff.

Presently I left the courtyard, too, and stepped out into the street; and I saw that feller a-way up the road still running like a crazy man. When suddenly he up and jinked round the corner, and disappeared from view. Well I felt like I been slapped in the face, I were that taken aback by it. What sort of creature was this anyway? A real mad 'un, you ask me. Acting one minute like butter wouldn't melt in his mouth, and the

next minute he's raging and gnashing his teeth. And it ain't
even as if I said anything rude or out of the way to him. Why,
I even troubled to talk his own lingo to him. *Aw-thor; Fruit of
Your Aw-thorship*. Tush! In plain language that ain't only fancy
talk for beggarman and handout. Oh, the deuce take him; for
I am sure nobody else will!

# 23

THOUGH IT WEREN'T too long before I got to know Odessa tolerable well. For I got my bearings of it soon enough, and become quite familiar with the ins and outs of the place; that's
to say with all of the marketplaces and alleyways and side
streets they got there, where a feller may expect the doors to
open for him. On account, you see, Odessa's pretty much like
one them nifty snuffboxes which you got to know the secret
of in order to open. You know, the sort which some gents carries, and they got this lee-tle spring hid away which you don't
need only to touch it and the top'll flip open easy, like there
was nothin' to it; and then, why, you only poke your fingers in
and grab holt of a hefty smack of prime 'baccy and stick it up
your nose. So that is pretty much how it were. For bimeby the
lid come open, and I find my way to oh heaps of houses which
they got exactly the same vantages to 'em, as the ones over
our ways has got. Nor I find was beggarfolks wanting. Why I
come acrost mobs of poor gentry now, which they was of
most every kind you care to see, and then some maybe. Well,
to begin with, you not only got your common sort of pauper
with a cadging bag, but you also got paupers without cadging
bags, which amongs' these last there's such as I reckon you
will never find anywhere except maybe it's Odessa. Like say,

for one, they's all them beggarfolks which come from afar.
For, lessee now . . . well, first off, you have got your Jerusalem
chariters; and then, why, there's what's call your "Franks":
which 'nother words they are Jewish folks come all the way
out from Turkey and Persia ways, and which they know to jab-
ber away in God's own Hebrew oh just a treat, like it was only
honester goodness natural-born lingo they was talking. So,
like I told, there's all kinds of poorfolks there. Sick ole paupers on their last legs, paupers which is marry' wit' wives,
and paupers which ain't, even elderly parties such as are on
their way to the Holy Land, so's only to be bury' there when
their time come. Though, you ask me, none amongs' that general ruck of poor gentry seems to be up to doing much of
anything, except maybe it's only hanging about making babies
whilst living off the charitable board of the parish. And then
you got your abandon' wives, too, oh lots of 'em, which they
come looking for their husbands there; oh, and all sorts of
palsied womenfolks, such as falls down and gets the fits, plus
your broken-down sort of sick gent with most every bodily
complaint you may imagine, which they come down special
only to take the waters inside them, er, whatsits, them salty
pools by the harbor; which the mud and stuff suppose to cure
what ails you. Now for all you find quite a few of your comfable old-fashion almsmen, such as is satisfy' to idle about shul
with only ordinary Jewish gents, there's also plenty of your
modren type of more high-tone almsmen, which they all
shaves their faces and prefers rubbing shoulders with other
such baldface Jewish gents as dresses French and sets around
all day jawing in them taverns and coffeehouses with the
tables outside which they got most everywhere there. And
there's your pauper-swells: that's to say gents such as sashays
around dressed up so monstrous handsome, you of thought
they was as flush as lords; though half of them really got noth-

ing, whilst t'other half, which it only appear like they owned
whole houses, is mortgaged up to the eyebrows, so even their
night jars is in hock. —Funny thing, though. For as many
poorfolks from our neck of the woods as I run into, there
wasn't a one which seem able to get his fill of the place, nor
praise Odessa enough. Though I can't think what the big deal
is which make them so happy to be there. But finally this one
feller manage to explain to me the whole difference which is
between our paupers back home and their likes here. It's the
music, don't you know. That's right. For back home a pauper
eats his dry crust feeling just ever so mournful and down in
the mouth, whereas in Odessa he sets down to the same poor
fare whilst a barrel organ plays to him nearby, so he only
chaws the more cheerful for it. Well, you might even say that
barrel organs has gone over mighty big in Odessa as a general
thing. I mean you can't turn a corner anywheres, indoors or
out, without you got a barrel organ or some such wheezebox
grinding away at you there. Barrel organs in the street, barrel
organs at home, barrel organs in taverns, barrel organs at the
circus. Why, saving your presences, sirs, but Gawdelpus they
even got the shameless gumption to be playing them things at
shul! Ever hear of such a thing? Barrel organs at shul. Foo!
Why it make me so mad I could spit. And they is always such a
great hoo-ha uproar going on in Odessa all the time on account of it, what with all them hurdy-gurdy jinglings and pipings, and folks everywhere whistling and singing along as
well. So say you pass a boozer, well there just bound to be
some tearful drunk inside a-sighing and a-singing a sad Rusky
song call' *"My Purty Li'l Miss"* or some other such lovesick nonsense; whilst opposite a Jewish gent which is no less in his
cups may be giving out with Sabbath hymns or blaring *Ashes to
ashes, Dust to dust, Twix one and t'other, Drink we must* to the
merry beat of a tailor's march.

So I was pegging along in the street nearside of the curb one day, when something hit me hard from behind. But I let it pass, thinking nothing of it except maybe that someone in all that bustle only bump into me accidental, not meaning to do it. Though no sooner I had put it out of my mind, there it were again! Felt exactly like I been hit in the back by a block of wood. So I turn round. And you never guess who I saw planted on his haunches behind me in the middle of that street. Yontl No-gams! Remember the cholery groom from, oh, must be nigh two, getting-on-three year back maybe? So there Yontl was, big as life, setting on his hams with his one hand leaning on one of them pocket-size footstools he gets about with, whilst holding up the other footstool and waving it about in the air, with a big sappy-looking grin on his face, so he give the impression of being tickle' half to death just seeing me. And I was pretty happy to meet up with Yontle myself. For the two us got on tolerable friendly together back home in Glupsk; and why I even recollect attending them graveside nupt'als he was give that year when the cholery come, preserve us!

"So, Fishke," says he giving me greeting. "You finally decide to join us over Odessa ways after all! Well what you think on her? I mean this city of ourn. Ain't she sumfin'. Terrific, huh?" But then when I only give him a offhand shrug, as if to say it don't really strike me as any great shakes, his face fell. Like I just put a blot on his escutcheon or trod on a bunion. And he proceed in a hurt tone:

"Why, next you be saying that that fool town of yourn's a city. Call that a city? Psssh! But then what you expec' of a worm which spend all his life in only a mess of horseradish thinking it's just the sweetest place in the world. Now you hold on to your hat, chum, 'cause I gonna show you around.

And after? Well I just bet it'll be a who-o-o-le different tune you be humming . . ."

And Yontl commence telling all about how grand Odessa was. About how the folks there get such a kick from seeing him scooting about so dexterous on only his hunkers. How he hisself is quite the grand personage thereabout and held in such high esteem by the Lord only know how many shop-keepers. How business was so good he dassn't even to com-plain. But when I ask him next how his wife is getting on, he only give a soft chuckle, saying:

"Psssh! Call that a wife? That sure is *s-ome* old lady which that fool town of yourn stuck me wiff! Though what you expec' of a cholery bride? I wisht the cholery had only took her fu'st, before she ever come my way. Why with that lower lip of hern gone missing, you of thunk the woman might manage to button the one lip she got left. For I swear you have never heard the like when it come to cussing and ranting, and plain ole yakkety-yakking. Grinds and clatters away like a mill all the time, so she got your ornery two-lip article beat by a mile."

Well, thinks I, so it seem there's never a cure to a wife which got a big mouth. For if she's the devil, she'll bite off your head no matter if she ain't got no lips, or only the one lip, or got no nose, or is even blind without no eyes . . . So I told Yontl in a couple words the story of my blind wife and all the trouble she give me recent.

"Psssh!" says Yontl. "So whyn't you do the same as I done wiff mine? Spit on her, and there's an end! Give her the bird, feller, the kiss-off . . ."

"Gracious how you talk, Yontl! What you mean, spit on her? Give her the bird, the kiss-off, without a divorce? Well I'm shock' to hear you say so. Truly I am. For ain't I an hones'

Jewish gent which intends to marry again? So how in the dang nation you propose I do that, without I divorce first, huh?"

"Oho, hones' gent intends to marry does he?" says Yontl laughing. "Psssh! So it's true. You really are a genuine bred-in-the-bone Fool Towner, Fishke. For that is what the name Glupsk mean in them Other Folks' lingo: *Fool Town*. In a word, 'Foolsk'! Well you only stick around Odessa for a bit, chum, and we'll see if we can't fix that . . ."

Well from that time on, that's to say since me and Yontl met up that day, we both use often to get together for a leisure stroll about town, with Yontl working them footstools of his, and each time hoiking his backside from up off of the pavement, and setting it down again, the whiles I shambled along beside him on my own bent pair of pegs. Now, Yontl, he wouldn't give up; and he was just so determine' to show off what he kep' calling "his" Odessa, and boasting about the fine streets and houses and what-all other prodigies that city had. Only, from the way Yontl went on about it, you might of thought them streets and houses was his and he was getting something out of it. And every time he'd point out something new, his face lighted up and he'd shoot me this sappy look. And happy? Why, fit to bust! Like, well, like somehow he thought he had growed more estimable in my eyes on account of somebody else's fine house or somebody else's fancy street. And he always poking me in the ribs then, saying, "Psssh! So what you think on Odessa now, Fishke? Terrific, huh? No, let me guess! Next you be telling me that that Fool Town of yourn got sumfin' better, eh? Ha ha. Fat chance!"

"No, you must hear me out this once, Yontl," I says to him at last, after I receive a dose too many of them digs in the ribs he was so partial to. Which he done this time whilst showing me, from a-way off, the Grand Boulevard they got there, which a very considerable crowd of folks was seen promenading up and down on; and from which last, as I notice, Yontl seem only to hang back, not having the gumption to approach any nearer. Anyhow, so I says to Yontl: "What can I say, Yontl, except I own that Odessa is a fine enough place in its way, I suppose. Though more's the pity there are no people in it. Mind, I'm not saying there are no folks actually living in it. Sure they is, quite a few in fact. Only they are not such as I would care to call people; anyway, not such as knows right from wrong. I mean, can you honestly call any of these gentry respectable people? Dast decent folks dress that way, dast they live that way? Go on, Yontl, take a good look at them folks walking on that boulevard. Look at them swells parading about with females on their arm. Why it is plumb shameful! Jewish gents which actually shaves; females which has left their hair to grow, not even bothering to cover it. And, why, only look at them dresses they are wearing, wit' that big crazy kind of a bun which they got stuck to their aftsides, and the rest of it sweeping the floor behind like it was a broom, whilst in front their naked breasts been hung out to dry, for the whole world to look at. Foo! It about make a body sick only seeing it. Now, if we was somehow only to contrive to bring over some real Jewish folks—yes, even such as you were please to call 'Fool Towners' a while back—well maybe then, j-ust maybe, this place might become worthy of being call a city; a proper sort of a place, where folks was modest and be- haved as they was supposed to."

Yontl silently moved on with me, seemingly having no an- swer to give me. And on the way we met up with this very spiffy-looking pair of swells coming towards us. So Yontl stuck out his hand, and one of the gents stop to talk to him; after which he give Yontl a handout, and we all resumed our separate ways.

"Know who them gentry was, Fishke?" says Yontl, now

preening himself considerable and looking monstrous puffed-up again, as I thought. "Well the one which he give me the handout, he's the actual Principal of our Talmud Torah. That's right. And my personal acquaintance, what's more. Satisfy' now, Fishke? Psssh! Respecable enough to suit your taste, huh?"

"Respectable, you calls it? Well I should hope not!" says I spitting thrice and my dander up. "What you mean, Principal of a Talmud Torah!? That Frenchify' dandy? Him? A Jewish schoolmaster? Never in a million years, Yontl. Why from that gent's swell looks alone, I can pretty much guess what sort of a Talmud Torah (ha ha, so-called) you must have here. Only tell me, Yontl, don't you feel the least bit ashame' of saying such a thing is good? No, Yontl, I fear you been corrupted by this place already. You become like the rest here . . . Jewish schoolmaster? Hoo, that's a laugh! I mean really now. You want a Jewish schoolmaster? Well you take our own Reb Hertzele, saving the difference! That's to say 'Murder-'n'-mayhem' Reb Hertzele, which he run the Poor School over to Glupsk. Remember him? Now that's a honester goodness dyed-in-the-wool Talmud Torah rebbe, as does the profession proud. And Jewish? I'll say! To the core. Top to bottom. Inside and out. Why you will find him everywhere in Glupsk doing most everything in the way of Jewishness. And what is more, doing it as it should be done. Looking to get buried? Then Murder-'n'-mayhem's certainly your man. Need a bit of graveside psalmsaying perhaps? Now you just couldn't do better in that line than with Murder-'n'-mayhem. Looking to get hitched? Well it just so happens marriage brokerage, too, is up Murder-'n'-mayhem's street, satisfaction guaranteed. And lest we forget, each time a man of Reb Hertzele's pious kidney sets hisself down to study a portion of the Law—*zap!* for

a bonus there's another soul let past the Pearly Gates. All
which is apart from his more regular duties of giving little
boys instruction. And don't think for a minute that folks ain't
grateful for it too. Why, once every week, regular as clock-
work, when Reb Hertzele makes his rounds collecting cash
donations door-to-door, well I think you will find folks is
gen'ly quite glad to cough up and send him on his ways. Nor it
ain't different when on the Simchas Torah he drops in on the
rich folks about town, along with the whole caboodle of his
Poor School scholars, to recite after-Torah-reading blessings.
For you won't find even a one amongs' all that Quality which
they won't give him the blessings cup to say the festal bread-
'n'-wine benediction. And on such occasion, when Reb
Hertzele only sing out *Sacred Flock, fo'ward ho!* and all them little boys line up by twos, baa-baaing behind—well, now, I
mean you cannot help but be impress by it. But that Frenchy
feller of yourn? Now what sort of graveside psalmsaying you
expect from his likes, huh? And what good will any his after-
Torah-reading blessings do, or his bread-'n'-wine benediction
for that matter, or even his presence at a funeral, if such indeed it may be called, with his likes running it? And, besides, I
mean, well, besides . . ."

"Now that is where you are dead wrong, Fishke!" says
Yontl, interrupting me. "For my gent don't do any them
things, nor choose to what's more. Why, he wouldn't even
know the first thing about it if you asked."

"What you mean, he don't do any them things!?" says I,
much taken aback. "Who ever heard of a Talmud Torah rebbe
which don't do such things, pray tell? Not recite after-Torah-
reading blessings before the Quality, not bury rich folks,
not . . ."

"Whoa, feller, simmer down," says Yontl breaking in on me

again. "Sure he bury them, you bet, only he do it in another way. Which is all right, on account the Quality here seem pretty well satisfy' with how he go about the business . . ."

"Oh, shame, shame!" says I, shouting now, and stop my ears not to hear his sinful talk. But Yontl wouldn't leave off his prattle, and only went on saying:

"And maybe you care to know who the second gent was, that feller was together with my rebbe back there? Well now that one stands pu-retty tall amongs' the high-muckety-mucks here, and has got heaps to say about the way things is run in Odessa. You know, same as your own Reb whatsisface, uh, that there Aaron-Yosl Nipcheese of yourn, which you got back in Glupsk."

"Take care, Yontl No-gams!" says I riled and very loud this time, so the folks walking by was made to turn round by it. "Oh, Yontl, Yontl, how can you even bring yourself to speak of such a dandy in the same breath wit' our own dear Aaron-Yosl? High-muckety-muck indeed! Well you might at least of said 'saving the difference' while you was at it. Show some respect, man! For our Aaron-Yosl is a sure-thing Jewish gent, complete wit' beard and sidecurls and the rest of the fixings which come with the office. Why, Jewishness lieth even upon his face, as we say, never mind all the Jewish money which is left to lie in his hands. Oh just piles and piles of the stuff, which is took from all the charitable tills of the parish, and more of it pouring in every day. And you know why? It's because folks takes Aaron-Yosl at his word, that's why. Trust's the thing, Yontl, folks just trusts him on sight. And, well, after all why shouldn't they? So what if he take their money. It ain't as if he didn't know he took it, nor know what to do with it after. Depend on it, Yontl, he know all right! So you can rest easy on that score. And what about that Frenchy gent of yourn? Now there's one dandy high-muckety-muck, I must say! For what's there to trust in a fancy-looking swell like that anyhow? His word, maybe? Why, next thing you be saying it's his Jewishness which invite trust. No? Well how about them sidecurls which he seem to have lost track of?"

"Take his word? Trust? Psssh!" says Yontl, digging in his heels now. "And by golly as I'm a Jew, sir, what difference it make anyhow if the gent's got sidecurls or don't? It'll all come out in the wash in the end."

"Tsk!" says I. "So what you trying to prove to me, Yontl? Oh, all right, I'll grant you about that 'trust' business. Forget it! But would you let such a gent assist at a circumcision, even be the Godfather to a boy? I mean, would you allow that fop to even hold the chil', let alone perform the 'sucking-rite' in such a proceeding? Well s-ome 'sucking-rite' that's like to be. What a joke! So I guess folks must be right to say that the hell-fires burn for forty leagues round Odessa."

"Though notwithstanding," returned Yontl a mite sarcastical, "I druther live in hell right here, than in that Fool Paradise of yourn back there, chum!"

Well to my mind Yontl had gone over completely and was as good as lost now. Odessa appear to have spoil him considerable, and we use to fight quite a lot on account of it. For whatever Yontl reckon was good, I only reckon was bad. And contrariwise as well. That's to say, if I reckon something was good, he reckon it was bad. We just couldn't seem to agree about anything. Not about the Big Shul they got there, nor about the cantor, nor even about the rabbi. I mean, you only look at what pass for a cantor amongs' that crowd. Why it were a crying shame the way that feller doll hisself up all dainty in that kind of a pinafore which folks gen'ly calls a "arsy-versy" back home, and which anyhow only a priest would allow hisself to be caught dead in. And then to be leading "choir worship" no less, as them gentry is pleased to call it—well now that about put the lid on it, gen'men. Well, I asks you, sirs, what kind of a cantor is it which he won't scarcely open his own maw and must let others do his work for him? For you never catch this gent work up a sweat the same way "Ole Weepy" Katzenjammer do it. That's to say Reb Jerahmeel Katzenjammer, the cantor in shul back home. Either of you gents ever get a load of the way he got of laying his cheek in his hand whilst singing, and then tucking his thumb under his chin and kind of jiggling his Adam's apple around with it? No? Boy you just do not know what you are missing, gen'men. On account you cannot imagine the lovely sounds which Reb Jerahmeel coax out of his windpipes that way. Like first he was screaming his head off and roaring at the top of his lungs, tossing his voice every which ways the whiles; and then, why, he only give the least bit of a thumb-jiggle, and the next thing *whoo-sh!* out come this kind of a thin whimpery yodel, which he commence to stretch it and stretch it, till bimeby it grow so still and small as a chil's voice—but then before you even know it, he is working up a head of steam once more, and has set hisself first to roaring away and then singing small again, up and down the whole while, doing it over and over, wit'out even bothering to catch his breath. And all them different tunes he come up with? My, there seem never to be any end to them, the way he have of tossing them off one after the other. And, why, you wun't hardly scarce credit the way that man will pour heart and soul into *Salvation-be-vouchsafed* prayers. Like, well, first off, he will give you a sweet "Wallachee" air plumb smack in the middle of it don't you know; which he will follow up wit' that dreadful sad song call the "Poor Li'l Beggar-Chil'"—that's to say, the one which come original from Klivan town and is sung by the beggarfolks there, and it go *O-h, Fa-ther, dear Fa-ther, woe's me-e-e* . . . and is like to break your heart; and then he will top it off lively wit' one of them "Merry Ivan" jigs. ——But that other cantor? Psssh, why you can't scarcely get a peep out of that feller. 'Cause no sooner he open up his mouth to get a word out than *bam!* that choir come down on it man and boy, and they commence then tossing it about from one to the other like hot spuds straight off the grate, the whiles each of them seem to be singing whatever come to mind, so you cannot make head or tail of it nor know which end is up. Why amongst all that commotion, I couldn't make out even one tune. Never mind one such as I might know or even recognize. So that is what they got the brass gumption to be calling "choir worship." Well I asks you! And talk about ignorant? Why, you never see the like. I mean they have even got their Sabbathday prayers crossed. For as anybody which got the least bit of sense would know, it is the *Salvation-be-vouchsafed* which is the whole nub of the proceeding. So what they do? Why they only take a little bit of nothin', such as back home we wouldn't account to be shucks even, and we only grumble our way through it—say, the *None-unto-Thee* for instance— and then they go and make such a almighty song and dance out of it you wouldn't believe. What a laugh! And you know the worst of it? They even dast to be sashaying round inside the shul with the Torah Scrolls whilst they was at it. For all the world like it was the Simchas Torah . . . God save us! (you must be saying) but where's the rabbi? For how can that estimable gent allow such wicked shenanigans to go on? Only you see that's just the point. On account, what else you expec' of a gent which all he got in the way of facewhiskers is that trim excuse for a beard, and all he ever do in shul is to prink hisself out in a dainty pinafore same as the cantor's? —— Well I should of thought that was quite enough folly for anyone, so of course I was greatly pained when I see Yontl appear to be enjoying it so much. "For Godssakes, Yontl!" I commence yelling at him. "What has become of you? You gone crazy or something, or you only out of your mind! What can have brung you to such a pass, sir—an', an', well, dash it all, man, how can you of allow yourself to fall so low?" Though, as per usual, Yontl only kept grinning at me with that same sappy look on his face, saying, "Psssh! Fishke, you are a fool which don't even know a good thing when he see it!" Well I mean how was I suppose to reason with someone like that in the first place? For I saw Yontl was a goner and there weren't nothing which anybody could do about it. So I made up my mind that from then on I wouldn't talk of such things with Yontl anymore. Nor was I going to waste any more bother about Odessa, which it could go to the devil ten times over, for all I care.

"Listen, Yontl," I says to him at last. "I don't care to go on fighting with you over what is wrong with Odessa. For you have got a stubborn streak on the subject which is about yea big and twice as wide, and nothing which I say is ever gonna change your mind. So let us just keep to practical things. 'Greed? Well, now, I been meaning to ask your advice about something . . . So what you think I should do in the way of a living, Yontl? I mean I have had it up to here with the business of cadging door-to-door in Odessa. For there is quite enough paupers mooching about the place already, even without me. Why there is hardly a house left which it ain't mobbed by poor gentry, with more of them crawling out of the wood-work every day. Well I am sick to death of having to elbow my way past all them noisy rambunctious beggarfolks which have took to parking their carcasses on every doorstep lately. So it seem to me it is time I found some other employment. So tell me, Yontl, what kind of a occupation you think I might take up? I mean apart from begging . . ."

"Psssh! Now you wasn't perchance thinking on setting up

shop as a moneychanger in a small way of business? Well a
haberdashery maybe. No? Well I should hope not, for that
wouldn't suit you a-tall . . . So what else you got in mind,
chum?"

"Oh do try and be serious for once, Yontl," says I. "Can't
you think of anything besides moneychanging and haberdash-
eries and such? Surely there must be other livings in the world
which might be suitable for a Jewish gent . . ."

"Psssh!" says Yontl. "Course there is, plenty in fact, if only
you care to look. Like, h'm, lessee . . . So how about you
hold a gov'mint patent on collecting the kosher meat tax, or
the candle tax, or—well, you name it, for there's any number
such taxes which Jewish folks is oblige to cough up. And
there's profit to be made out of the charity game as well: say,
be the treasurer of a Benevolent Fund or maybe one of them
Parish whatsits, uh, Eleemosynary Societies. And you could
do considerable worse than having a hand in them 'Meir-baal-
Haness' Holy Land poor boxes which they appear to be making the rounds most everywhere these days. Or try nosing
about amongs' the powers that be—butter up the Quality,
pull strings, hold public office, be a parish-pump panjandrum,
a fixer, the kind of a feller which has got a finger in every pie
and keeps the pot boiling; or even be the sidekick or gofer of
such gentry, or . . . H'm! On second thoughts, Fishke, I think
we may be aiming a bit high here. So whyn't we think on
something which is more modest in the way of Jewish businesses. Say, what about old clothes? Why there's no end of
Jewish gents which makes a pretty good living by trading in
old clothes."

"No," says I explaining to him, "I'm afraid it won't answer,
Yontl. For, you see, old clothes must be bought and fixed up
first; which you have got to have money for. On top of which
you must know something of darning and patching, and other

such seamster's arts. Well, now, that mightn't be half so bad if we was talking here for instance of only your ornery pair of played-out Glupsk britches. I mean what difference it make if they was a little ripped maybe or out at the back. For you needn't only botch-patch the things, and wouldn't nobody find fault with it nor know the difference. But, say, mending one them fancy-pants Odessa trouser seats (beg pardon), now that is a whole different kind of a proposition. Why, even such as may belong only to the most threadbare reach-me-down article in that line will seem so dainty, I dassn't come any-wheres near for fear of giving offense."

"Well naturally, chum, we can't have that," says Yontl. "So if Odessa fancy pants has got your wind up, why not have a go at greengrocer's discards? You know, damaged fruit and veg, in the way of onions and garlics, or maybe lemons and oranges which have gone a mite ripe. Only be forewarned, Fishke. You must get a handcart first. It's the custom don't you know. And you will have to be pulling that thing, and trundling up and down the streets with it, barrow-boy fashion, the whiles you be yelling and crying up your wares in a loud singsong."

"Now I don't mind yelling," says I. "You might even say I got a knack for it. But pulling that cart about like I was a horse, well I just don't know. No, I don't reckon I am equal to it, Yontl. Anyhow not with these legs. And then there is that same problem again. I mean where in the nation am I suppose to get the 'sweeteners' for it, that's to say the mazuma, Yontl, the clangers, the money, the cash, huh?"

"Look'ee here, Fishke!" says Yontl, looking quite solemn now. "There is just no such thing as a living which you don't have to toil over or put money into it. At least none such as I know of, except maybe it is one of them high sorts of livings I told of earlier. So you tell me, chum, because I have clean run out of ideas in that department . . ."

"Well best of all, I reckon," says I, "is bathhouses. On account that brick bathhouse where I use to earn my keep back home, well the folks there was very satisfy' with my work and it suit me just fine. And I should of been a somebody there for sure by now, if it wasn't for that unhappy marriage I made. I mean, who knows how far I might of gone if only I had stayed on? Why the sky's the limit! So if you got any kind of influence in Odessa as you claims, Yontl, be a pal and put in a good word for me. That way I might wangle me a place in a bathhouse here. Aw, c'mon, Yontl, have a heart, only show me your stuff in this one thing, please?"

"For the nonce, Fishke," says Yontl grinning at me again. "For the nonce I shan't answer that request of yourn which you made just now. I only asks you in the meantime to inspect the bathhouses which they got here first, get the lay of the land, so to speak. Then we'll talk . . ."

So I did as Yontl bid and went round first to one bathhouse, and then another. And talk about odd? Well I confess I was took aback monstrous by it. I mean, gen'men, you just wouldn't credit what kind of a place will pass for a Jewish bathhouse in Odessa. Why now first off it look so uncommon spic-and-span inside, you of thunk it was Lady Houseproud's front parlor instead of only a bath. And furnishings? Well you never seed the like. For you only take them lounging benches they got there. Now, mind, we are not talking here of any your ordinary rickety beaten-up chicken-legged variety of article, such as you only expec' to find around bathhouses. No, sir. These was your actual genuine sure-thing luxury wooden bedsteads. And why I even saw big mirrors there, an', an' combs, as well. Imagine. Mirrors and combs! Psssh. I mean what next, for goodness' sake? And another thing. You won't never, ever catch a Odessa gent give his clothes a proper steaming-out in the bathhouse. Oh forfend, perish the thought! Least not as I could make out. For, in all my time there, I never once see so much as a measly shirt or other such item of small wear being hung up to steam over the stove. Though how else the folks in that town contrive to get shut of their lice is anybody's guess. What a laugh! No, thinks I, this won't do. I could never stay in such a bath. Now back home it were different. For that was what you call a proper kind of a bathhouse. The sort of a place which folks might settle down comfable in and earn their keep. Why it give me pleasure even now only thinking about what happy times we use to have lolling about all companionable on them benches inside; and how we be chatting away for hours and hours, yarning, talking about the world and of this and that, and oh just about anything you can think of which may have sprung to mind . . . So I went round to more and more bathhouses, only—well, oh, I don't know: because, well, they wasn't anything at all like what we got back home. I mean somehow they didn't seem to have that same kind of a, h'm—well, lemme see now . . . well, not that same kind of a odorsomeness, as you may say, which our own brick bathhouse back in Glupsk is got. In a word, they just didn't smell right. And come to that, well you ought to get a load on what them Odessa bathhouses has got in way of a immersion-rites pool, so called. Psssh. Some joke! Now you take our own immersions water back home, for instance. Well you only got to step down into it, and immediately you just *know* you are in something special. For it has got flavor, it has got color, it has got body—why, you can actually *feel* you are in it! It is more . . . well, let's just say it is more *Jewish* like, if you take my meaning. Whiles that water they got over in Odessa is . . . well it is just *too* clean somehow. Least to my taste it is. Why it may as well be plain old ordinary drinking water, for all the good it do you. Like . . . well, like nobody ever bovver to use it even.

"So, Fishke," says Yontl later, flashing me that funny kind
of a little grin of his, "got a eyeful of Odessa bathhouses, I
s'pose, huh. So what you think?"

"Tsk!" says I to him. "Well I reckon I seen better. Though
just about everything you got here strike me as plumb odd
when it ain't downright crazy. No, Yontl, it is plain that this
Odessa of yourn isn't for me . . ."

# 24

WELL, I DIDN'T much like Odessa, and that's the truth. Only it
now being winter, I just had to stay put. For how was I suppose to set out on the road alone midwinter, with only these
clothes I got on my back, "barfoot and nekkid," as we say, and
be traveling through strange country to boot? But no sooner
the rains stop, and the sun come out, and it were warm again,
and the smell of summer were in the air, I only begun to fret
for it, and growed so jumpy I couldn't hardly keep to the one
place anymore. Once, as far as I were concern, summer use to
be, well, only summer, as per usual, if you unnerstan' my
drif'. Like, well, nothin'! Oh summer were nice enough. I
mean, with it being so warm and sunshiny then, and the days
being so long, and most everything around being so green—
which it is quite all right, too, really, on account it ain't cold
then. And what with you got all your herd of town livestock
being took to pasture quite regular, there is also milk to be
had, p'raps even a little sour cream too. Plus, now and again,
for a bonus, you maybe got a baby onion to garnish your crust
with, or a green garlic even, or a radish. Well, now, for poorfolks such things is pretty important and certainly ain' to be
sneezed at. So you won't never hear me complain about it,

no, sir, not for a minute. Only this time, though, well, I don't know, this time it were different somehow. The summer, I mean. Like, well, like summer kep' a-whispering and a-murmuring to me, saying things to me which buck me up and give me heart . . . and which cause me to be thinking day and night only on *her*—only on that dear hunchback girl of mine. For each blade of grass, each bloomy shrub, each sweet chirrup of a bird, seem to only bring me greeting from her . . . Why, it got so all I could ever think on was things like—oh, yes, that was how we use to set together so, and that was the look she give me then; and that was how she use to laugh, and that was how she pour out her troubled heart to me. And the thing got my blood all het up and set it a-boiling, and it put me into such a mood, which it were mournful and pleasuring both, and which it seem to be tugging at me, draw-ing me from that place, and pulling me away yonder, far, far away, to where, to where . . . Well let it go. For I can't rightly say what any this got to do with summer anyhow—I mean, whether it was all only its doing, or it was something else, a kind of a ailment maybe, like the fits or the hypos. But I knowed all was not right with me. For I seem to be fading, like a light which was going out.

"Fishke, you sick or something?" says Yontl once't, staring at me kind of narrow-like. "Why, you do look a sight, Fishke, the way your face is fallen in so, and gone pale on a sudden. What's ailing you, chum?"

"Tsk! ain't nothin', Yontl," says I to him; and I pressed both my hands to my breast.

"Well, now, if it ain't only your heart which is acting up," says Yontl, "I got just the cure. Bread dipped in plenty of salt. If took on a empty stomach, why it just bound to put the old ticker right."

"Now what in the world of all mischief would a body be

pouring salt on a heartache for, Yontl, huh?" says I with a sigh. "Ah, me, Yontl, but I got this monstrous tugging feeling, right here, deep inside, which it won't let me be, nor I can't seem to set still in the one place on account of it."

"Oho, I get it now," Yontl says gone all smirky-like. "Why, you only homesick for that Fool Town o' yourn, chum. Psssh. Well I will bet you can't wait to get sight of that reeky crick of ditchwater which it pass for a river back there, huh? What's it call' again? Yeah, I recollec' now. 'Ole Skummy,' ain't it? And now spring's come, why it fair be blooming with that sickly pall of yallory-green slime which gen'ly come over't then. Charmin' prospec', I dessay. Hoo, boy! Or maybe it's that nippy wind you been hankering after, which it got a way of searching a poor man out, and whipping in and out of a body's clothes so it chill him to the marrow; or p'raps it's only the smell of onion and garlic you been yearning to get a whiff of again, which it always hanging in the air out there? Well, ain't no shame in that, boyo. No, not at all! So best you go on back, Fishke. Back to where you most comfable, chum."

So couple days later I said goodbye to Yontl, and I pulled up stakes and went my ways . . .

And tramping the road so, my thoughts flew before me, away ahead yonder, and my heart only yearn for her. And the whiles I only wonder where my darling might be. What she doing now, thinks I, how were she getting on, how she managing without me, all alone, poor dear? And my feet was carrying me on their own like, without even I pay them any mind. Oh, my pegging along so was painful slow, right enough, but it were steady, too, my steps bent ever thither, ever onwards to Glupsk. And I pass through villages and towns, just one after the other, the whiles I only kep' my eyes open, reckoning perhaps any moment I may run acrost her. Well I hiked a great ways, and that's the truth, and I seed a dead load of Jewish towns. Though, the nearer on to Glupsk I come, the more lightsome I come to feel. Nor I could scarcely get enough of the good folks in our parts, now I was back amongs' them. Why, only bein' privileged to observe the way how they talk and comport theyselfs, seeing their old familiar ways, refresh me and make me come alive. For I was amongs' my own kind, and feeling the more to home for it by the minute. Oh, gen'men, you have got no idee how much good it do a body, being round Jewish folks over our ways again. Honester goodness plain-dealing gentry, wit' no frills nor fancy airs about 'em, and which they don't care a straw for what the world think, nor give *that!* for any your modren fool notions. Go 'head, friend, jaw away, shout, yell your head off, if you mus', only act as you will—and be yesself withal, pure and simple, as only the good Lord intended for us to be. Be it handsome or ill, fitting or no—what business is it of other folks, anyhow? For if it happen they don't like it, why they may lump it or do the other thing! . . . So bimeby I come to myself and I growed easy, thinking on Glupsk and on the brick bathhouse they got there, the whiles only putting my trust in His Blessed Name.

Come one fine morning, though, making my way through a field amongs' the wheat and the rye, I struck what appear a considerable stretch of woodland which it were stacked with green timber everywhere. Well I worked my way in some, and unshouldered my bag and took off my coat, and I lay down under a tree amongs' the tall grasses there, which the leaves was sprouted up broad and high, so they keep me hid on every side. Now, it ain't as if nobody ever seed a forest before, so why waste any bother over it, you may be asking. For, after all, a forest's only a forest, and trees is trees, and grasses is grasses, and birds is birds, and me? why, I ain't only yours truly. So weren't nothing really standing between me and forty winks, so to say. Well, sir, I had me a good gape and a stretch, and I close my eyes and—well, here's what I dream about.

Whilst stretched out so, I hear a kind of a crackly sound like somebody treading on dry leaves. I quirked up my ears and listen with my eyes closed. The crackling got louder and the steps come closer. That put the wind up me some; so I forced my eyes open, though I was scarce able to do it. I lay motionless the whiles, like a bump on a log, not being able to move a muscle, I was that tired. But the steps growed fainter and I was easy again; and my thoughts commence to get muddled and I let myself drift off into a sleep which it only become sweeter and sweeter . . . Till, by and by, I seem to hear snatches of a soft, mournful air, which somehow it appear familiar to me. Well that song fairly went through me and touch my heart, so it were like to make a body cry. Though it also brung me ease, as may a healing potion . . . like, well, like the feeling of tearfulness and joy together which come upon a man-and-wife-to-be, at the bridal veiling; or showers falling on a sunshiny day. Then I were startle by a sharp tug at my hair, and I let out a shout. Well I set up bolt upright then and pushed apart the blades of grass, and I take notice of a pot of bright red strawberries been tossed aside willy-nilly on the ground only a couple paces away. A bit farther I make out somebody stirring, look to be female, which she was setting on the ground and casting glances about her, looking very scared. Well I took in the situation straightway. You see, she been out in the wood picking berries, and the whiles she were so preoccupy' in that business she also been singing to herself. Only unbeknownst she tumble onto my head amongs' the grasses there, which it give her such a fright. Well I wasted no time getting to my feet and pick up that pot of berries, meaning to return it to her, the whiles talking gentle to her, saying,

"There, there, not to worry, missy, don't you fear," and such like. Only I scarce manage to come up to her when the pot fall out of my hands and I give a shout, for I hardly knew what I was about, and— Well, next thing, the pair us was standing together holding hands tightly, me and my hunchback girl . . .

I was awake for sure and it wasn't no dream. For I needed only to look about me to see that the trees was as sound as the earth I tread on; and the birds was merrily hopping about in the branches overhead—and oh but wasn't they all of a twitter now, with their happy pipings and chirpings, only too glad to share our joy. And the both us was a-laughing and a-crying at once, each marveling to see the other, and eager to only learn where the other been, and how come he appear so unexpected and out of the blue on a sudden, and each telling the other what had happen to them during the time between.

Well that poor girl told me about all the trouble she had since them rogues lit out a year ago, and left me stranded in that town. And it were all the bastid's doing. On account he didn't want my wife to get a divorce—no, for you see then she were sure to try and make him marry her. Oh, having a blind cripple like her around, serve his purpose well enough—though, mind you, not by way of being his wife. Because as long as he might have both his pleasure and profit of her, she were quite welcome to belong to somebody else. And what he had in mind for me, was to make my life such a misery that I should never be free of my wife. Nor were he at all pleased about my friendship with the hunchback girl. Because it gall him considerable; and for his part he made certain to find a way to end it. And once he manage to get rid of me, he went after my wife, getting his hooks into her bit by bit, and then he ree-ly showed her who was boss. For he knowed only too well that, as she were blind and alone now, she would never get free of his clutches. Later on, though, she latch on to him, and just wouldn't leave him be. So at last he handed her over to the old buzzard, to do the same door-to-door game with her as he done with me once. Well the bastid just squeeze and squeeze the woman till she were dry, and he took to beating her regular something cruel; and then the old man come after her, getting his own licks in as well. So it weren't long before she sicken and grow old before her time; and oh she were a pitiful sight to look upon now. —Anyhow, that gang been dragging about the country for a whole year now, traveling from one town to another. Why they only just manage to make camp here in the wood before sunup. And today somehow she got a yen to gather berries. So that was how come on a sudden (says she flashing me a pretty smile) she lighted on the best "berry" of them all. By which of course she only meant myself . . .

So then I told her about what happened to me, and how I come to be here early this morning on my way to Glupsk. We must never allow ourselves to be parted from each other again (says I); and we must try everything to get my wife to give me a divorce. But if by some ill chance we shan't succeed, we must run off together and get away from these rogues, and then wait for what Providence may have in store. Well the whiles we was setting side by side so, just enjoying each other's company, don't you know, we hear a voice from inside the forest a-calling *Ah-o-o-oeee!*

"That'll be our people," says my hunchback girl. "They come looking for me."

Presently a feller come up which I recognize him, right enough. And seeing the both us together, he only sneer at us at first; but then he put on a smirky expression, like he reckon the joke was only on us. Well we needed no prompting and got up to go, whilst he run on ahead to bring the glad tidings. Though we took our sweet time about it, walking slowly the whiles. Then, after a space, back of a old wreck of a tavern we come upon now, which it were set a considerable distance into the wood, I got sight of a familiar bunch of cover't wagons. And a bit farther on then, there was a clearing, with a campfire going strong in it, which them vagabond gentry was having themselves a high old time setting round it. Well the first to give me "warm" welcome was the bastid; which after he dispense a couple hearty thumps my ways, he follow with a jolly, "Why, look'ee here! If it ain't our dear Brovver Fish-cakes! Well you got no idee how much I been missing you, bub!" And the whole mob get into the act now, all of them a-rioting and a-whooping crazily, calling out to me, "Put 'er there, feller! Make y'self to home, Squire!" and other such foolishnesses. And they all commence then to pummeling me from behind, and punching me about, so finally my hat was knock off my head. Then, as I look round to retrieve it, covering my head for the nonce with the end of my coat, the whiles I was being cuffed and buffeted on every side, I see my wife dash out sudden from amongs' the crowd, crying, "Fishke? Oh, where's my husbin? Oh, show me where's my Fishke!" Well, to my mind, my wife's joy at my coming was worser than the pummelings I receive from all that gang of thugs to-gether. For such happiness wouldn't answer a-tall, not if I was to get my divorce from that woman. Why, ma'am, I druther you despise me any day, thinks I, like all the rest do here! But she only hung on my neck, clinging to me and repeating over and over, "Oh my darlin' husbin, oh Fishke dearest!" And it give me such a turn, too, seeing what a poor blin' shrivel-up bag-a-bones ole woman she become. Oh, where'd all that plump rosy flesh go, and them fat cheeks, to say nothing of that awesome yap of hern? Why, 'twere all I could do to work myself up to only being civil to her, and asking, "Well, how you been, Bassia?"

" 'Member, Fishke, when you says once't how back home in Glupsk we was persons of consequence, and well thought of by folks there? Well, you never spoke truer, Fishke. 'Cos wasn't nobody there which they didn't treat me wiff respect!" So says my wife, speaking aloud that all might hear; and then she drawed herself up, looking very sniffy the whiles. Why, the way she talk, you of thunk she was one of them ex-squires, which been ruined and come upon hard times, and was now rattling on oh just a treat, all about the good old days, and what a grand personage they use to be away back then. Then fetching a deep sigh, she say, "Enough travelin' hither and yon! Oh, take me back home, Fishke. Back to *our* town, to our houses, to our folks . . ."

Oh I thought I was like to die, listening to her talk so, and my heart sunk. For it were the last thing I expected to hear from her. Anyhow I pulled a sour face hearing it. Though I notice, too, where the bastid was put out of countenance considerable as well, thinking no doubt I was fixing to deprive him of his precious meal ticket. Whereas I only been thinking: *Now, now, you keep that article to yesself, bub, and with my blessing. And you welcome to it I'm sure* . . . Only I could see there was murder in that feller's eye, and he were sharpening daggers in his mind. But at last he rose from his place, and only stomp off grumbling.

Womenfolk and young gels was pottering about the fire, raking and feeding it, hanging pots up, and baking spuds. Now and again a couple young bucks would sidle up to them on the sly, and sneak a rude pinch or a slap from behind, the whiles talking saucy to them. Whereat the women was set to rating and scolding them in oh just the worse way, letting on like how they was mad enough to spit, and looking fit to scratch their eyes out—but then they went all giggly on a sudden, and they bust out laughing and a-cackling . . . much as a hen will do whiles the rooster has cast a beady eye her ways, and spread out his wings, don't you know; when all along she was only too glad of the love peck she receive of him, and will let him have his way. Other lads, though, had wandered off into the woods and was now scattered here, there, yonder amongs' the trees. I see one young feller was laid out on his belly fast asleep, snoring steady as a sawmill, and another was mending a coat or some such thing, and a third set around only scratching and looking solemn whilst hunting up more lice to crack. And there was other lads roughhousing in pairs, wrassling one another to the ground and knocking each other about, just for the fun of it. In a word, there weren't naught but funning and merriment all about—whilst my wife snuggle up close to me and had throwed both her arms around me, holding on to me for dear life, and now was rattling endlessly on, and oh just talking up a blue streak, complaining of her poor wretched lot and all the afflictions she were made to bear, and of what a misery her life was become, and wishing for nothing more than that we might live together as man and wife in the sight of God for the rest of our natural days, as only the good Lord intended we should do, even to twice threescore years if not forever, A-men . . . Well she went on talking nineteen to the dozen, the whiles I couldn't hardly mumble a half word now and then by way of a answer, for my heart weren't in it, and all I could think of was how to get loose of her. But when at last she run out of talk—though Lord know for how long we been setting together in the one place so—I contrive to slip away so's to be able to breathe free for a little. First thing then I search out my hunchback girl and we stole away to a quiet corner, out of sight of the crowd. So what it boil down to is this, I says to her. It look to be a bad business. First off, it weren't any use my asking my wife for a divorce, on account she would only stop her ears and never agree. Though abiding

amongs' these dainty rabble was assuredly a bad business, as
well. For it only be tantamount to selling myself to the devil,
and I should once again be a performing bear, dancing about
on my hind paws to any tune that scoundrely mob was please
to call. So the only question remain, what's to be done? Well
we was awhile conferring about it, till finally we conclude as
follows. There was nothing for it. We must do a flit, abscond.
And since these gentry was a mind to camp here till the morrow, there were no better place for it than tonight, here in this
very forest. Though, as we was thinking our plan over, we
catch sight of the bastid, which he was leading a pair of horses
into the camp for some reason. "We musn't wait for him to
come close," says my girl, "for no good can come of his seeing
us together. We best part for a while."

Which we done, she going her ways and I mine.

I notice though where the bastid been confabulating for
the longest while with that old buzzard, which he was his chief
lieutenant amongs' the mob. Only I took care to stay well out
of the bastid's way, keeping gener'ly to myself. Though whilst
everybody were preoccupy' with work or larking about or
whatever, my hunchback girl come over and whisper in my
ear, how the bastid decide they must move on before nightfall. It seem the pair of horses we see him with earlier was
both stolen, which is why he was in such a hurry to get away.
Well that about scotch any our own plans we had about getting away. Oh I couldn't think what to do next. My heart kind
of like jolted in amongs' my lungs, and my head span and my
knees begun to buckle, so my legs seem about to fold under.
And I saw my sweet girl was looking on pityingly, her eyes
burning and cheeks aflame. Though after meditating some,
she presently say to me, her voice gone all trembly-like:

"Fishke, listen! You be inside that ruined house in a little
while; up there in the loft, you understand?"

"Lordy, yes!" says I cutting a joyful caper. "An' why later you come along on the quiet too, an', an' . . ."

"Sh!—yes," say she with a quick little nod. "Only please, please hush now, lest somebody overhear!"

Though I didn't reckon there be much point in taking tender leave of my wife. Now I'm not saying she weren't to be pitied; only whose fault were it anyhow if not her own? For weren't it she made the break first, which it only growed bigger and bigger betwix' us? Well 'twere over, and past my mending it now! Besides which, putting all other considerings aside, I couldn't no more go back to being together with her than, than . . . well, than earth and sky was like to come together. So naturly I only give our "goodbyes" the go-by and slipped quietly away, over to that ruin tavern.

Well, sirs, it be right easy to imagine with what a blithe heart I step into that shackly old house. All the pain and wretchedness which we been made to suffer for so long appear to be well nigh over now; and it seem withal that the Almighty hath ordain that the hunchback girl and myself should be united in a abandon old tavern, wherein our fate shall be determine at last, and whenceforth we shall venture out together upon a new life. Though getting up into the loft were dead easy; on account, to begin with, the house were low built, and the wall round back ways, which I use to enter the house by, had settle 'most to the ground anyhow. Here and there the floor in the loft had big holes in it, through which you might see into the house below. Well I settle into a corner and wait. My heart knocked like a pair of hammers, and each minute drag by as were a hour. I strain to catch the smallest sound. A straw needed but to stir somewhere, and I fancy 'twere the sound of her tread coming near . . . at the blowing of the merest breeze, I thought 'twere she, softly calling my name . . . Suddenly I were sure I heard a sound

very like a voice coming from below. And the thought, hark!
it's her; she's here at last; that's her calling to me; oh, any moment she be at my side; oh, truly, our hour of redemption
were at hand—well it throwed me into such a all-fire great fit
of excitement and feverishness the whiles, I were flashing hot
and cold all over. I wanted only to call out to her; but my
breath hitched and no word would pass my lips then. And
in that very instant I heard my own name being plainly
spoke; and looking through a crack into the room below, I
caught sight of the pair of them—the bastid and that old buzzard! which they both was talking things over amongs' themselves, so:

"Well you make it your business to keep a e-xtry sharp eye
on them goods of yourn, that's all," the bastid were saying.
"Just so long as that blime bitch don't up and go missing unbe-
known, y'heer?"

"Now don' be getting all het up for nuffin'," replies the
buzzard. "The old sow already been took care of. Only thing
worry me, if she peg out on us. Right now she laid out stiffer
than a corpse, nor half so lively. Why, she so sore, she couldn't
move even her life depend on it. Beat her up pretty good, I
did . . ."

"That shiteface gimper, though," the bastid finish off, "he's
aw-ll mine. Cain't even look at his bucktoof mug wiffout I
want to spit in it; that's how much I hates him. Never you
mind. They's a couple old scores which I been meaning to
square with that halfpint sonuffabitch anyhow."

Lordy! I was so a-scared hearing that devil talk, my own
mammy's paps like to of run dry.

"You know, I been thinkin'," the buzzard recommence
again, "about them purloin' equines of yourn? Well, now, I
been suspicioning they was Jewish. I mean, you just cain't
scarcely help but take notice of how awful downtrod and

sorrowful-lookin' them nags is. To say nothing of being sway-back, and stringy-neck, and Adam's-appley—and, well, you ever get a load on the 'rhoids them beauts has got on 'em? Whooee! they *some* sight . . .

"Hold your tongue, ole fool!" says the bastid, "lest some-one yank it out. Anyhow, best make yesself useful, old man. Nose around some, down here, upstairs. This rattrap suppose to of been one 'em ride-in roadhouses once, ain't it? Well, go on. See maybe you get your meathooks on some old coach-men's truck we can use—you know, harnessings an' such, which they still got wear in them."

Oh, I tell you, the frights come over me monstrous now, for them two find me they'd kill me. And my one foot were set to shaking uncontrollable, and it tap out a tattoo a-going *tap-a-tap! tap-a-tap!* on top the ceiling, don't you know? Well, it give them thugs a sudden turn; and, for a level second like, they stare up openmouth. And then they was both a-jabbering at once—

*"Look'ee! —Why, why, it's dust pouring down from the roof! Quick! get up there, see who 'tis . . ."*

My head were swimming and my ears abuzz, and I come near blacking out; and then the ground give way.

. . . Yeah, the ground give way. For I been took aholt of by a pair of iron hands and yanked out of that loft and thrown down in the dirt below. And I hear myself being given greet-ing, "Good cod! what've we here? Why, my widdle Fishy come to net, *miaow!*" and the bastid's face then hove into view—and with such a grin! like a cat cornering his dinner. I notice, too, where the old buzzard was gone, for I see him nowhere; so I were left to the bastid's mercy alone.

"Say your prayers, Master Fishcakes!" says he. "Your time has come! For I gonna do you, bub, the way I should of done you back in that cellar. Fybush don't never forget!"

I fell at his feet, pleading with him to spare my life. But it were no use. He only took out his knife and held it to my face, greatly enjoying seeing me quailing before him and shaking all over with fear. I tried talking him out of it, asking of him to give thought to the Rewards of Heaven, promising him the World to Come and the Earth Entire, tossing in even my own portion in Paradise, and everything else I could think of, if he would but let me live. But he only glared the harder at me for it, and spoke no word besides. So I let Paradise go and set to warning him of the Hellfires and of Eternal Perdition, which they surely be waiting on him in the Next World, on account of God's Judgment, and which the Merciful Lord was going to exact Stern Vengeance by for spilling innocent blood. But he only set his lips, biting down hard on them, and suddenly he had lifted his hand with the knife in it into the air, and in that dreadful instant—whilst there weren't but *that much* between my throat and the fell blow of that villain's knife—the bastid staggered back, and his hand were stayed. Though it weren't his doing. He been pull back by main might, the whiles a wild voice which it was scarcely human were screaming at him, *"No, no, you dast not do it!"* Well that shook him, and it scare him considerable, too, for he were trembling as he turn to look behind him.

It were the hunchback girl which grabbed him!

"Out, bitch!" the bastid let out with a bellow, after he had collect hisself. "Out, you hussy bitch, else . . ."

"No, no, I shan't leave!" she shot back hotly at him. "I ruther be kilt right here with him first!" But next she threw herself on him, hanging on his neck and crying into his bosom, caressing his face, pleading with him, begging him to spare me, promising him a throne in Heaven if only he wouldn't kill me. The bastid roughly cast her aside, and he set to cussing and swearing so, you never hear the like. Till at last the look of murder in his eyes faded some, and then he turned to me, saying:

"Now you have got no idee, my li'l shite, how sorry I am I have not baldowered you personal today. Well you may thank your plaguey luck I ain't crushed you like the filfy little body-louse you are. Howsomever, you ain't getting off dry, not by half you ain't."

So he unwound a rope from around his waist, and he commence binding me hand and foot with it, saying:

"You lay quiet, runt, and not a peep out of you, y'heer? There! now you may lay truss' up like that till you croaked and have growed ripe. One thing though. If by some unforeseed miracle you come away alive, like your saintly ole granny put a good word in for you from the grave, well you just make certain to never stray into my sights, or—y'see this? like *c-r-rick* . . ."

And when he done putting me to rights, he turn on the hunchback girl, which the poor thing lay on the ground and were looking acrost at me wildly, and just a-sobbing and a-wailing and tearing her hair.

"You a proper nice gel, ain' you," the bastid said giving her a prod with his foot. "Well I got you pegged, missy. You cooked all this up with that gimper, din'cher! Wedding in the attic, wiffout no band playing, eh? An' all the whiles letting on like you wasn't only li'l Miss Purity wiff me. Hussy bitch! Well from now on I'll larn you. And how, I'll larn you!"

And he lifted her in his arms and look over my ways, saying, "And you, you dog, be warned! Not a sound!" And then he lit out.

There's no torments in hell which come near to what I suffer then. For weren't me which was in hell—but hell which were in me. A terrible fire was set inside me, burning and consuming me, so I were all aboil. Oh, it were so dreadful it stood my hair on end, which every hair on its own were like a sharp needle that been set a-stabbing and a-stabbing without end. Yet I dassn't utter a whimper, lest it be heard.

By and by the sounds of a ruckus come to my ears from the outside. The scrape of wagon wheels and voices shouting. Folks was astir. Them rabble had broke camp, and was on the move—carrying away with them that sweet blameless creature, my poor unhappy hunchback girl . . .

For a considerable whiles I lay like a dumb beast had all fours trussed up, and my eyes was a-drownding in hot tears. The bonds which held me had rub me raw; and the least motion I made, felt like knives was cutting into my skin. And I were next to perishing of thirst. Well, I thought 'twere all over with me, and my end were nigh. Later, though, when the pain growed so I could no longer bear it, I commenced to cry out, hoping somebody may take notice. I reckoned, too, that them rabble was well out of hearing by now. But cry as I might, it avail me naught; and I may as well have cried out to the walls, for all the good it do. And my throat, too, was become so parched, the yelling come harder and harder; so I wanted resting up for longer each time, before recommencing. And the situation only become worse as time pass. At last my breath fail, and I could scarcely cry out anymore. My soul were fluttering at my nostrils, and I felt the dread presence of the Angel of Death at hand. So there was to be nothing for it, but to die, to depart from this world untimely whilst I were still young. No, I shall gather my strength, thinks I, if only for one last try! And I hove out a great long cry, reckoning to have gasp out the last of my wretched life with it . . .

Only God had brung you instead, Reb Alter! For 'twere y'own estimble self, sir, which come in my hour of need and preserved my life.

# 25

BY THE TIME Fishke finished telling his unhappy story, the night had settled in, and our horses had brought us all the way to the foot of Green Mountain, which lies at the approach to Glupsk.

Now the Green Mountain of Glupsk certainly wants no introduction, for it is celebrated everywhere throughout the world and familiar to all. But there's one song which has been making the rounds amongst folks hereabout since, oh, from way back when, and is known to just about everyone practically, great and small, and which mothers, and wet nurses, and nurserymaids and such, have been rocking babies to sleep with for generations now. Indeed my own dear mother, may she ever be blest with a happy Paradise, used even to sing it to me when I was small:

> *'Pon that Mountain high,*
> *Amongs' them grasses green,*
> *Two* Deutschers *may be seen,*
> *So tall, they nigh-near touch the sky:*
> *They got stout oaken sticks and long black whips*
> *And O! ain't they done up in funny ole clo'se,*
> *Gay galligaskins and candy-stripe hose,*
> *Billycock hats and periwinkle toes,*
> *Tho', chil', Lor' a-mercy nor ne'er forgit*
> The Lord Our God Above . . .

Well I loved that old song better than any of the rest I had heard. For to my infant fancy the Green Mountain appeared a thing both marvelous and unsurpassably fair—not in the least

resembling those pitiful eminences of mere dirt which passed
for mountains in our neck of the woods; but made of a more
noble stuff . . . say of coriander seed and honey, or of Manna
from Heaven, or even of the soil of the Holy Land, as are the
Mount of Olives and the Lebanon. Now as to that pair of outsize German gents—that's to say the Deutschers of the
song—well I painted them up into prodigies most exceeding strange (saving their presences); creatures of a piece
with Shorabor the Wild Bullock of the Field, and the Great
Leviathan of the Ocean—giant sentries cracking their whips
and belaboring with their oaken staffs the shoulders of any er-
rant comer and all such as might dare try and make their way
to Glupsk; much as the mighty Rock-Throwing River Sambatyon is said to keep travelers away from the country of the
Ten Lost Tribes, as live under the guise of the Little Red Folks
there. So you see you couldn't so much as approach Glupsk
without getting walloped first; which was why all of the
townsfolk of that unfortunate city generally went around so
downcast and with a kind of a whupped-dog look about
them . . . Though, later, when I had outgrowed my bootees,
as we say, and been kind of around a deal (even to Glupsk), I
came to know different. For having in the meantime learnt to
accept the evidence of my own eyes, these furnished me with
a more sober picture of the world than that which I entertained in my childish imagination. Well, the upshot finally was
that I found my way to the true meaning of the song. I discovered that Green Mountain was a very ordinary mountain—
more of a hillock, really—and quite, quite indistinguishable
from any other object of its kind in our region; nor was it in
fact green, but more of a muddy complexion, if you take my
meaning; neither was it handsome to look at, being very pitted and scarred along its surface. And the tall Deutschers of

the song? Now, I decided that that stretched-out pair were really intended to stand in for those *long*-handed, very nimble sorts of gents of the road, with the sticky fingers don't you know: the ones who like hanging about the approaches of a town, and will sneak up on a feller unawares, making the long arm to relieve him of his purse and other removables in only the blinking of an eye, and then be making off with the whole lot, without a body even being the wiser or miss it. So customarily your common traveler coming to Glupsk for the first time inclines to arrive minus his purse. Later on, though, being once bitten and made twice shy by it, a kind of a edginess will begin to creep over him when he's yet a mile or two outside of town, and it just won't let him rest. And his eyes will commence to dart about restlessly here and there, on their own, kind of, and without him even thinking about it, and he'll be looking over towards the back of his van, and then to the road behind, and he'll be slapping about his person next, specially round the region of his breast pocket, making sure of his purse, you see, finally ending the proceeding by buttoning his coat up top to bottom. Which is all only by way of saying that, having reached the Green Mountain in one piece, that is, with all our physical appendages severally intact and in working order, inclusive of our noses—that last article, being also downwind of the place then, at last caught a whiff of the distant though unmistakable scent of *Glupsk* in the offing. So it was only after I made inventory of the contents of my cart, you see, that I took notice of Fishke again, looking a study in distress and grief.

So thinking only to comfort the lad, I set to bucking him up with a lot of cheerful patter, also letting on as I myself were in the best of moods; and I then concluded by singing the rest of the ditty I just spoke of.

The Lord Our God Above . . .

*S-o-o let's have a cup and be ever-so-cheery,*
*Eat dumplins, sweetmeats, and strawbeery,*
*Apples, orangers, and figs,*
*Cut merry capers and lively jigs—*
*Tho', chil', Lor' a-mercy nor ne'er forgit*
*Our Ever-Loving God Above.*


"You see, Fishke, you oughtn't really to let your troubles get you down so," I said to him then. "For we must ne'er forget Our Ever-Loving God above, just as the song says. *He* can see you right, you know . . ."

"Well I won't be askin', Reb Men'le (tho', saving your kind presence, sir, if I do anyhow)," says Fishke looking extremely bitter. "But why need God ever of bovver to have brung me and her together again, when nor sooner He done it He parted us all over again? Why, huh, why? So His Light might shine on us for a second and *phut!* everything go back to being black, only worse? Why it's like 'twere done for spite! . . . And sweet Lor' a-mercy! Agin' *who* He done it, huh? Why only a pair of poor misable Gawdelpus cripples, which they druther never seed the light of day, much less only wisht their own mothers hadn't had 'em, as be made to suffer such wretchedess . . ."

I put on one 'em pious faces then, giving a side-to-side noddle of my head, this followed by a string of cluckings, so: *te-te-tai-i-i!* Which was by way merely of signifying, "Now, now, young man! We'll have none of that here . . ." Well, as it happens, I hadn't spoken so because it was a proper reply to that poor boy's poser, but did it off the cuff kind of, only because such is the custom in the world. For whenever a suffering soul, having been tried beyond endurance by his griefs, is heard to ask hard questions of this sort, the other feller will think it his bounden duty to teach him right from wrong, by at least cutting him short with that same monitory *te-te-tai!* if he challenges Heaven's will. So, having done my duty and got it out of the way, I proceeded next to speak plainly to him, as one man ought to another, saying:

"Though tell me, Fishke, what's that young lady's name? I mean till now all you seem to call her is 'the hunchback girl' or 'my hunchback girl.' Well, I should like to know how she's really called."

"Why, what ever for, Reb Men'le?" asks Fishke, greatly marveling at me. "I mean, with respec', Reb Menle, why is it so important you know it? For after all one don't give out a young lady's name like that, without there's a reason for it. It just don't seem right . . ."

"La, silly!" says I, "you needn't fret yourself a-tall on that account. It might come in useful, was all I meant. I do get around some, you know. Maybe if I poked about, asked a few questions. Who's to say? Oh it'll work out, lad. Why it's just possible that what's lost will be redeemed, and I shall be the agent of it."

*"Beyla,"* Fishke called out sharply then. "That's her name . . . She's call Beyla!"

There was a groan followed by a thud, as if something had snapped. I looked quickly round, for the suddenness of it had given me a turn. Alter lay near insensible on the wagon floor, a-moaning. He'd gone deathly pale.

"Goodness! what's wrong, Reb Alter?" I asked. "Here, you have a pull on this schnapps. There now, easy does it! Feeling poorly, Reb Alter?"

*"Ba!"* was all Alter answered coming round, and hoisted himself up and regained his seat.

"So tell me, Fishke," says I, resuming my quizzing of him after I was satisfied as to Alter's welfare. "Now you wouldn't know what her mother's name was or where she come from maybe?"

"Yes, I do," says Fishke. "My hunchback girl told how folks use to call her mother *Elka*. And she recollect, too—though only barely, y'understand—how her mother been divorce from her husband in, in . . . well, now, lessee . . . yes, in *Tuneyadevka*. Why her mother mention it just all of the time; fact whenever she pour her bitterness out on that innocent babe's head—which was often enough, poor thing."

"Divorced from her husband in Tuneyadevka, you say? H'm," says I puzzling. "Now who in the mischief can that husband of hers have been, I wonder? Oh the man's a heartless scoundrel! Imagine abandoning his child and leaving her so wretched . . . Oh but say, Reb Alter! Now you're from Tuneyadevka. So you can give us that villain's name if anybody can."

Alter appeared a dead man, mouth agape and gazing starkly before him. And his eyes! Oh, there was such a wild and distracted expression about them! My own sinews come unstrung, seeing that look then.

"I think he was call," Fishke was kneading his brow trying to dredge up the name. "His name were—uh, now hold on a bit . . . his name were . . ."

*"Alter! That's his name."* And having unburdened himself loudly of this intelligence, Alter threw himself down in the wagon with a great wail.

"Yes, yes, that's so, yes!" affirmed Fishke looking at him, though plainly without a glimmer of a notion as to why Alter had shouted so then. "And there was a moniker tacked on to his name too," Fishke went on. "What was it? Yeah, *Wine-'n'-Candles*. You see her mama use to thrash her something cruel, and be calling her 'Wine-'n'-Candles' ha'penny brat' and 'Wine-'n'-Candles' bundle o' joy,' and other such things besides, when she had troubles on account she been slung out of work someplace."

I had tumbled onto the appalling truth, and could now but look on, aghast.

Alter wept convulsively at my side, beating his fist cruelly upon his breast again and again, saying—*Omnom hotosi*—"Yea, I have sinned! O! I have laid waste her life. O! that poor poor child. O! she were right—

> *Her father her slew . . .*

O 'tis for this dreadful thing alone which I done that God hath brung down his wrath on me, and wheresomever I have bent my steps or turned my face, things have only gone awry for me . . ."

And being moved to pity, I set out to comfort Alter, if only by undertaking to mitigate by a little the gravity of his wrongdoing. He was (I began) but a man, only an ordinary person of flesh and blood, as indeed we all were, and the Evil Impulse hath, after all, ever waxed strong in sinning mortal folk like ourselves. Why, even the unquestionably righteous and saintly were not unknown to give in at one time or another to their desires, doing some grievous wrong thereby . . . ensnared, so to speak, in the toils of this business of marrying one wife and then another, and made helpless by it, unable to get a grip on their passions. O, how many of our forefathers, surely pious, upright men every one, even to a fault—yea, even our Blessed Patriarchs—had in the consequence put themselves under a wife's thumb, become mere putty in the woman's hands, doing her bidding even to the point of driving their own seed, albeit begot of another, out from under their very roof and away from the familial hearth, if their wife had but commanded them to do it . . .

Fishke had sat observing the proceeding, a look of utter incomprehension imprinted on his startled face, and was now staring wildly, first at Alter, and next at myself, knowing neither what to make of the business nor what part he might be expected to play in it.

The meanwhile, evening had turned to night. It had grown pitch dark, and a great concourse of stars had turned out in the firmament, their shining little faces looking down on us, quite as though nothing in the world would suit them better than to be getting in on our conversation. And at the edge of the sky, rising as though out of the earth itself, the great flaming-crimson circle of the moon had emerged, and she too seemed only to have eyes for us. All above appeared to be in attendance, watching impatiently for the turn of events, waiting only to see how it might end . . . When my Alter suddenly sat up determinedly and fixed his gaze upon the heavens, and said with feeling:

"I swear by Him that Liveth Forever that I shan't come home to wife and children, shan't betroth my wench what's come of age, till I have found my unhappy lost child! As Heaven and Earth are my witness! I'm leaving now, this very instant. And woe betide that—that *feller!* if he but dast to dare and try and stop me."

Fishke had thrown himself upon Alter's breast, and hugged and kissed him for a long while without speaking, then lapsed into confusion not knowing what to say or do. Suddenly he was pleading tearfully with Alter, "Oh save her, sir! Oh dear God you must save her . . ."

In a trice my Alter vaulted out of the wagon onto the ground and was climbing into his cart. And taking leave of us at a distance, he'd got his thills turned round and had whipped up his mare, and set out on his way. For a time Fishke and I silently followed his progress from behind. I looked up at the sky again, where moon and stars followed their appointed paths, though the aspect they bore was different from the one they had before—haughty they looked so away up high, and so far, so very far from our paltry, earthbound selves. It saddened. No happy thought that . . .

I gee-upped my "eagle" (so-called in coachman's lingo), tetching him up with my whip by way of inviting him to brisken up his pace some—and at a rather late hour my cart jarred over the pitted, dark streets of Glupsk, the clop of hooves and rattle of wheel, and the chinking of collar bell, all seemingly drumming up the clamoring call of the town crier by night: *Oyez! O-yez! a-Here b-eee a fresh pair of Jewish gents made their way to Glupsk!*

# THE BRIEF
# TRAVELS OF
# BENJAMIN
# THE THIRD

TRANSLATED BY
HILLEL HALKIN

# The Brief Travels of Benjamin the Third

BEING A DESCRIPTION OF HIS EXPEDITIONS,
IN WHICH HE REACHED THE FAR MOUNTAINS
OF DARKNESS AND SAW AND HEARD
MANY A FINE AND WONDROUS MARVEL,
HITHERTO RELATED IN ALL SEVENTY OF
THE WORLD'S TONGUES AND NOW MADE
AVAILABLE IN OUR VERY OWN YIDDISH

## A Prologue by Mendele the Book Peddler

A WORD FROM MENDELE THE BOOK PEDDLER:
Praise be to the Creator, Who guides His heavenly orbs in their paths and His earthly creatures in their ways! Surely, if our holy books relate that not even the tiniest blade of grass can stick its head above ground unless an angel taps it and says, "Grow, little grass, get thee up and about," surely, I say, a man must have his angel too, tapping and crying: "Up and about with thee!" And even more so must this be the case with our fine Jews, each of whom most cer-

tainly has one hundred legions of angels at least tapping and rapping and telling him: "Heikele, dear soul, go borrow whatsoever money thou canst, and get thee west of the border to the German, and buy there all the goods that thou art able to. Sprout, Heikele, wax, Heikele, up from thy bog, thou villain! Filch the selfsame goods from thine own store and flinch not when thou claimest the insurance! . . ." Or else they say, these angels: "Go, Itzikl, thou rascal, get thee to thy Polish manor lord and flim him such flammery and skull him such duggery that the tale of it be music to all ears! . . ." Or perhaps they exclaim: "Grow, ye beggars, sprout like grass, like nettles, in the streets. Go, Jewish children, hie ye from door to door and knock on each for your living! . . ." Or it may be: "Go, ye wealthy Jews who lack for nothing, cease twiddling your thumbs and get ye to the bathhouse and start to sweat! . . ."

But I fear that this is all beside the point. The point, ladies and gentlemen, is that one of our own brethren has gone far, far into the uttermost regions of the earth and has been crowned with universal renown.

For the past year all the English and German newspapers have been full of dispatches about a most wonderful journey to the East undertaken by one Benjamin, for thus they spell our Hebrew name Binyomin, and thus we shall spell it here too. Just think of it, they have marveled: a Jew, an unarmed Polish Jew on foot, with but a knapsack on his back and a prayershawl bag beneath his arm, has ventured into climes beyond the ken of the most famous British explorers! Only a Superman, they say, could have done it; that is, our Binyomin may have been human, but just having been human never made a Binyomin . . . Be that as it may, however, the world is indebted to him for his many prodigious discoveries, in consequence of which no atlas will ever be the same. Never has a medal been more rightfully merited than the one presented

to him by the Royal Geographic Society of London. His acceptance speech was rushed into print by all the Jewish
gazettes, which talked of nothing else the whole of last summer, as everyone who reads them knows. Lists were drawn up
by them of the great Jews in history from Adam to the present day, and of the Jewish travelers, starting with Benjamin
the First of Tudela seven hundred years ago and down to Benjamin the Second of Poltczeny, who died a while back in London while looking for the Ten Lost Tribes—not to mention all
our innumerable compatriots currently roaming the globe
and typically compared by our Jewish correspondents, for the
greater glory of our Benjamin, to a pack of poor stumblers, a
hapless herd of footloose tramps, the roads taken by whom,
set beside those of our intrepid adventurer, are so many blun-
derings from here to there, like beggars' rounds or the scam-
perings of monkeys. Of Benjamin's exploits and the books
written about them they have said, quoting Scripture on the
gifts of the Queen of Sheba: "Never were such precious spices
brought from afar." Blessed be the translator, they have declared, and well worth his weight in gold, who will extract
the pure nectar of this treasure from its beehive of foreign
tongues and serve it to us in our native buzz for our eyes to
light up with enchantment.

Thus it was that I, Mendele, having no other purpose than
the advancement of my fellow Jews insofar as I am capable of
it, could no longer refrain from vowing: If our Hebrew authors, whose knowledge is to mine as a man's waist is to his little finger, do not cast off their slumber and render the books
of Benjamin's travels into our holy tongue, let me at least
abridge them in plain Yiddish. And old and feeble though I am,
dear reader, I girded my loins and laboriously set about select-
ing from this bounty all the items that might be of interest to
our Jewish public and transcribing them freely as is my cus-

tom. I felt, if truth be told, as if I were being tapped from above and told: "Arise, O Mendele! Get thee from thy cozy corner by the hearth, and take thou a pinch of Benjamin's spices, and whip up a dish for thy Jewish brothers such as they relish!" And this, with God's help, did I do, and now the tasty meal is set before you. Eat up, ladies and gentlemen, eat hearty and may it please you! Let us all set out in the wake of Benjamin's travels howsoever and wheresoever we see fit, each keeping to his own pace and inclinations—and if any of you, God forbid, should meet with a mishap on the way, you need only thrust it from you as if it were a plate upon a table and remain well and firm in your faith, as I, your humble servant, Mendele the Book Peddler, most devoutly wish you to be.

# 1

## IN WHICH WE ARE TOLD WHO BENJAMIN IS, WHERE HE HAILS FROM, AND HOW HE CONCEIVED OF HIS JOURNEY

"ALL MY DAYS," Benjamin has said, "I was raised in Tuneyadevka—that is, until my grand voyage. I was born there, I was schooled there, and I was married there to my faithful wife, Zelda, may she have a long life."

The small town of Tuneyadevka is a God-forsaken place, far off the beaten track—so removed from the world indeed that, should a visitor appear in it, every door and window is opened at once and all stare at him in amazement. Leaning into the street, the neighbors ask each other the Four Questions. Who is this fellow? Where out of the blue has he dropped from? What is he doing here? Can he have come for no reason at all? Tuneyadevka is not the sort of place that a person just happens to turn up in. And since there must be more to him than meets the eye, it is imperative to eye him well.

Whereupon each and every Tuneyadevkan feels obliged to prove his sagacity and the speculations fly like dust. The old folk spin yarns about similar visits made fifty years ago; the wits crack jokes, not always very nice ones; the menfolk stroke their beards while smiling into them; the old women scold the wits with one baleful and one gleeful eye; the young ones steal a glance from lowered visages, hands hiding their giggles. Rumors grow like snowballs, getting bigger and bigger until they roll right into the synagogue and stop before the cast-iron stove, where all things reach their final destination: family secrets, business deals, Turkish and Austrian politics, the wealth of Rothschild, the latest mail delivery with news of recent pogroms or the discovery of a tribe of lost Jews, and so on and so forth. All this is duly examined by a panel of distinguished citizens, which sometimes sits late into the night, leaving wives and children waiting anxiously at home while it selflessly examines the intricacies of each case without receiving a farthing in recompense, after which its conclusions are presented for approval to a plenary assembly of Tuneyadevkans convened on the upper benches of the bathhouse. Such are the by-laws of Tuneyadevka, and it would not avail to change a single one of them if all the monarchs of the East and West were to descend on the town and stand on their heads with their feet up. More than once at such sessions the Turkish Porte has nearly come to grief, and if not for the efforts of certain prominent tribunes the Sultan might long ago have been thrown to the dogs. Rothschild himself, on one occasion, lost nearly fifteen million rubles in an hour, which he did not recoup until several weeks later, when, the topmost benches being in a mellow mood and several sheets to the wind, he made a good one hundred and fifty million.

Although the inhabitants of Tuneyadevka are almost all famous beggars, they are also most merry ones, with a faith that might be described as reckless. Ask one of them where and how he makes a living, and you will get a bewildered stare. Soon, however, he will come to his senses and answer frankly:

"You want to know what I live from, is that it? Well, let me tell you, there's a God above and He doesn't forget us down below. He's provided until now and He won't stop now, that's what my answer is."

"But what is it that you do? Do you have some kind of trade or occupation?"

"God be praised! I happen to have, believe me, a fine gift that He gave me, a voice that makes music like an instrument. On the High Holidays I work as a cantor; I'm also a circumciser and a matzo roller, the best you ever saw; I dabble a little in matchmaking too, that's a fact; I keep on the side—this is just between the two of us—a little tavern that doesn't bring in much; but my goat, knock wood, is a good milker; and I have a rich cousin not far from here who can be milked in a pinch too. The main thing, I tell you, is that God is our father and no one is more merciful than a Jew, don't ever say I said otherwise . . ."

It must also be pointed out that the inhabitants of Tuneyadevka are content with what they have and not choosy about their garments or their food. Let their Sabbath caftans be ripped or torn, or less than immaculate, or down at the seams, none of this matters as long as the satin still has a bit of shine. In fact, it can be as full of holes as a sieve, through which the wearer's skin shows; since no one looks at such private parts anyway, why worry about them? They're no different from the bottom of a man's foot, which belongs to him too. What Tuneyadevkan would go around with his nose to the ground just to see whose shoes have soles on them? . . . While as for victuals, a bit of soup and bread, if it's available, is a meal; and if there's some challah and a soup bone on Friday night, why, a king could eat no better. Try mentioning anything fancier, unless it happens to be a piece of stuffed fish, a plain pot roast, or a sweet carrot stew, and your Tuneyadevkan will give you as strange and mirthful a look as if you had told him that your cow flew over the roof and laid an egg. A dry carob pod on Tu b'Shevat is his idea of a luscious fruit; just looking at it makes him roll his eyes and sigh, thinking of the Land of Israel from which it comes. "Merciful Father," he prays, breaking his teeth on it, "bring us back to Thy promised land, where even the goats eat such treats . . ."

Once, it so happened, someone arrived in Tuneyadevka with a date. You should have seen the town come running to look at it. A Bible was brought to prove that the very same little fruit grew in the Holy Land. The harder the Tuneyadevkans stared at it, the more clearly they saw before their eyes the River Jordan, the Cave of the Patriarchs, the tomb of Mother Rachel, the Wailing Wall. They bathed in the hot springs of Tiberias, climbed the Mount of Olives, ate dates and carobs, and stuffed their pockets with holy soil to bring back to Tuneyadevka. There was many a heartfelt exclamation and damp eye on that day.

"For a moment," Benjamin has recalled of that occasion, "the whole of Tuneyadevka was in the Land of Israel. The coming of the Messiah was all anyone talked about. If from the Creation to the millennium is but a week in God's eyes, the Lord's Sabbath seemed just around the corner. There was at that time a new constable in town who had introduced a reign of terror. He had snatched skullcaps from men's heads, snipped off someone's earlock, raided a back street late at night for Jews without their papers, and even arrested a Jewish goat for eating the straw roof of a local peasant. Since, though a Christian, he was possessed by the spirit of Ishmael, of whom Scripture says that his hand is against every man, the panel by the stove debated the future of Mohammedanism. Then it turned its attention to the latest communications concerning the whereabouts of the lost tribes beyond the River Sambatyon and I first conceived of my expedition."

Until that day Benjamin had lived like a chick in its egg or a worm in a jar of horseradish. Beyond Tuneyadevka, he had thought, the world came to an end, nor was there a better or sweeter place anywhere. "I believed," he has been quoted as saying, "that the richest man on earth was our tax collector, and the finest mansion, his house. It had in it four solid brass lamps, a six-branched candelabrum topped by an eagle, two copper pots and five copper frying pans, a shelf full of pewter plates and no less than a dozen fool's-gold spoons, two silver kiddush cups, a spice box, a Hanukkah menorah, a grandfather clock in a silver case that hung from a chain of glass beads, two cows and a pregnant heifer, two Sabbath caftans, and no end of other good things. I thought there was no wiser person anywhere than our rabbi, Aron-Yosel-and-Soreh-Zlote's-Eizik-Dovid, who was said to have so excelled at algebra as a youth that he could have been an adviser to the Czar; no one more impressive-looking than Heikel the Stammerer with his winning smile; no one more knowledgeable than our doctor—who, it was well known, could bring the dead back to life and had studied medicine with a gypsy possessing a degree that was written in Egyptian hieroglyphics."

In a word, Benjamin's life in Tuneyadevka lacked for nothing. True, he lived in penury while his wife and children went about in tatters—but before eating of the apple, did it occur to Adam and Eve to be ashamed of going naked and barefoot in Paradise? Now, however, the fabulous tales of distant places worked their way into his heart, which went out to them and drew him after them like the arms of children reaching for the moon. On the face of things, one might not expect much to result from a date, a constable, some skullcaps, an earlock, a Jew or two caught in an alley late at night, a goat with a taste for straw roofs; yet taken together these wrought a great change in Benjamin, nor would he otherwise have enriched the world with his voyage.

Indeed, one frequently observes in life how great and even monumental consequences are the product of minute causes. A peasant sows wheat; a miller mills some of it into flour; the rest finds its way to a distillery where it is made into vodka; a portion of both is delivered to Gittel the tavernkeeper; she adds a bit of yeast and water to the flour, kneads it, and rolls it into knishes; in her pantry, thanks to the Phoenicians, who invented the art of glassmaking thousands of years ago, are some glasses; and when the vodka is poured into them, and the hot knishes are put on platters, and these are set before a band of hungry and thirsty Jews, there is no telling what may happen . . . It may well be, in short, that Benjamin's soul always housed a traveler's spark; but this same spark might have died long ago had not circumstances breathed it into a flame; and even had it not gone out entirely, it might have flickered too feebly to produce anything more than a coachman or the owner of a water wagon. I have known many a hack driver in my time who, had things gone differently, might today be circumnavigating the antipodes . . . But this too, I fear, is beside the point.

From that day on, Benjamin began avidly immersing himself in the Talmudic stories of Rabba bar Bar Hanah, the great traveler who once was carried so close to a star by a wave that he was nearly burned to a crisp. Next he turned to the adventures of Eldad the Danite, to the travel book of Benjamin of Tudela, to Ya'akov ben Moshe Hayyim Baruch's *Praises of Jerusalem,* and to Matityahu Delacrut's *Shadow of Eternity,* which explained the Seven Arts in as many brief pages and listed the greatest wonders and strangest beasts in the universe. Such books opened Benjamin's eyes and transformed him. "I was tremendously excited," he has written, "by all their wonderful stories, sometimes to the point of crying out loud: 'Ai ai ai, if only God would enable me to see a hundredth of this with my own eyes!' My thoughts were carried far, far away."

Tuneyadevka was now too small a place for Benjamin. He was determined to venture forth from it, just like the chick that pecks at its egg before emerging into the light of day.

## 2

IN WHICH BENJAMIN BECOMES A HOLY MAN
AND ZELDA AN UNMARRIAGEABLE WIDOW

BY NATURE BENJAMIN was a great coward. At night he was afraid to step out by himself and all the money in the world could not have induced him to sleep alone in his own house. Little dogs made him quake with fear and straying beyond the confines of Tuneyadevka struck him as risking his life. "Once," he relates, "on a sweltering summer day—I remember it as if it were now—our rabbi set out with one of his fellows to take a dip in the stream outside of town. A few young friends and myself walked at a respectful distance behind him, confident that no harm could befall us in his presence. He was not just a rabbi, after all; he was a man universally esteemed and most venerable. Why, his rabbinical titles alone filled a whole sheet of paper! He reached the stream well ahead of us, having walked at a brisk pace, and had begun to undress when a peasant boy appeared out of nowhere and sicced his dog on him. Holding, to put it plainly, the open fly of his pants with one hand and his round fur hat with the other, our Shield and Protector turned and ran for dear life. This made us youngsters lose our heads also; when the whale is hooked with a fishing rod, what are the small fry to think? We galloped off like wild horses, hollering all the way home and arriving helter-skelter on the heels of our hero. You would have thought from the uproar that the town was on fire. Help! Murder! Police! No one could hear his own voice."

Prior to setting out on his expedition, therefore, Benjamin had to vanquish his fears. To this end he forced himself to go out alone late at night, to sleep by himself, and to venture beyond the town limits, all of which gave him an extreme pallor and cost him no little health. His changed behavior, wanly preoccupied look, and new habit of disappearing at all hours were a puzzle to everyone and soon made him the talk of the town. According to one theory, he was quite simply mad. In the first place, it was said, he had been born a bit soft in the head; secondly, there hadn't been a madman in Tuneyadevka for years and it was common knowledge that every town had its idiot; and thirdly, even if Benjamin hadn't been crazy to begin with, the summer heat was clearly making him so . . . To this, though, an opposing school of thought, led by Rabbi Aron Yosel and Soreh Zlote's Eizik-Dovid, said: "Feh!" Granted, Benjamin had always had a screw loose—indeed, he had several; but this in itself explained nothing, since it failed to answer the question of why these had fallen out now and not the previous summer, when the heat was even worse; while as for town idiots—how, if they were so necessary, had Tuneyadevka gotten along without one until now? . . . This latter objection, however, was easily refuted by the first school, which pointed to the stream outside of town. It was, that is, no secret that its waters took a life every year; yet in the past several years they had not taken any, as a result of which they were now so low that they could be crossed in some places without even getting one's feet wet; from which it followed as night follows day that even an absolute law had its exceptions . . .

In short, Benjamin remained a conundrum. Nonetheless, the majority opinion, which also happened to be that of all the womenfolk, was that the matter had something to do with . . . that is, that Benjamin had taken up with . . . well, quite simply with the Devil. Why else would he go out on midnight rambles? Where else could he be vanishing every time you turned your back on him? What else could make him sleep in the pantry? His wife, Zelda, even said that she heard the floorboards creak at night, as if someone were walking on them!

Like everything else, these rumors reached as far as the synagogue stove and from there to the top benches of the bathhouse. Although the plenum was not of one mind, it unanimously resolved to draw up a list of Tuneyadevka's houses and deputize its leading citizens to accompany the local Torah scribe on an inspection of their mezuzahs, a flaw in any one of which could easily have let the Evil One into town; and since the expenses of this delegation were a public responsibility, it was also decided to raise the tax on meat. In Tuneyadevka indeed there was a saying, "No matter what gossip starts with, it will end with someone's death, and no matter what is debated, the price of meat will go up," thus accounting for the presence of death and taxes in the world, two things that only a heretic would question, although why everybody died while only Jews paid taxes remained an unanswered riddle.

Subsequently, Benjamin had an adventure that greatly enhanced his reputation. One hot midsummer day at exactly twelve noon, when the sun was at its fiercest, he set forth from town and wandered into the forest a distance of some three permissible Sabbath walks, that is, about six thousand ells. In his pockets he had several of his books, without which he never went anywhere, and after a while he sat down beneath a tree and lapsed into thought. Before long his imaginings flew far away to the ends of the inhabited earth. He crossed mountains, valleys, and deserts, following in the footsteps of Alexander the Great, Eldad the Danite, and others; he saw the hideous basilisk, the fire-breathing cockatrice, the Minotaur, and the roc; he reached the lands of the Ten Lost Tribes and spoke there with the descendants of Moses; until at last, arriving safely home again, he roused himself from his reveries and wondered when he would set out on his great journey.

By now night had begun to fall and Benjamin rose, stretched himself, and set out for Tuneyadevka. But though he walked and walked, he did not emerge from the forest. He tramped for an hour, for two, for three, for four, deeper and deeper into darkness too thick for the eye to penetrate. Suddenly a storm blew up and it began to rain. Thunder and lightning crashed all around and the trees shook with frightful sounds. Cold, wet, and frightened, his teeth chattering from the downpour, Benjamin came to a halt. It occurred to him that he might be attacked by a bear or torn to shreds by a lion or a leopard, or perhaps even by a wyvern, which was a kind of dragon with a barbed tail that could lift and fling an elephant. Worse yet, he was terribly hungry, having had nothing to eat all day but a single buckwheat cake.

Beset by worry, Benjamin stopped to say his nighttime prayers, reciting them with all his heart. And indeed they were answered, for it soon grew light out and he resumed walking as though at God's behest. He hiked on and on and came at last to a narrow path, which he followed for an hour or two until he heard a voice in the distance. And yet, confound it all, this only made him shudder even more. Suppose it was a highwayman? The thought frightened him so that he turned around and started to run the other way as fast—may it never, dear readers, happen to you—as he had fled the rabbi's floggings as a child. Before long, though, he told himself: For shame, Benjamin! You dream of voyaging to far deserts and oceans teeming with griffins, hydrae, and anthropophagi yet tremble at the thought of encountering a robber in the forest? I swear, I thought better of you! Did Alexander the Great turn and run at the first sign of danger? Did he cower like you when astride his trusty eagle that he spurred skyward with a piece of meat held before it on his spear point? No, he did not. He hacked off and speared a fresh piece and rose higher. Courage, Benjamin! This is God's test. Pass it and you will be worthy of finding the lost tribes and telling our Jews all about them, even in this little neck of the woods. Now is your chance to put your fears behind you. Just think of the glory—of the honor to your people—of the fame to your native town—when Tuneyadevka and Macedonia, the birthplace of Alexander, are mentioned in one breath . . .

Whereupon Benjamin about-faced again and strode bravely forward to face the highwayman, a peasant in a wagon loaded with sacks and pulled by a team of oxen. "Good morning!" he called out in a passing strange voice, which had in it all possible shades of exclamation and entreaty, as if to say: "Well, you can see for yourself that I'm at your mercy, and mercy is what I demand—for me, my wife, and my poor children . . ."

After uttering this combination of a shout, scream, and supplication, Benjamin stood still, unable to get out another word. Then his head began to spin, his eyes went blank, his legs buckled beneath him, and he toppled to the ground.

When he came to, he was lying in the wagon on a large sack of potatoes, covered with a rough cloth coat. By his head was a trussed rooster, which gave him a one-eyed stare and clawed at him with a toenail; at his feet were crates of fresh garlic, onions, and other greens. There must have been some eggs around too, for their packing straw kept getting in his eyes. The peasant was calmly smoking a pipe and calling "Gee-up!" to the oxen, who plodded along so slowly that each wheel had its own distinct sound, all four adding up to a single creaky quartet. The rooster, it seemed, did not like this concert one bit, because each time a wheel reached its groaning crescendo he raked Benjamin with a talon and emitted an angry cock-a-doodle-doo that went on gurgling for a long while in his throat.

Benjamin, who was having trouble telling his limbs apart, lay there feeling stunned. In his imagination a Saracen had taken him captive in the desert and was on his way to sell him into slavery. He fervently hoped it would be to a Jew, who might set him free again; if bought by a Christian prince, or worse yet, a Moslem princess, he could bid the world farewell. Thinking of Joseph languishing in the dungeon because of Potiphar's wife, he let out an anxious sigh. The peasant heard it, turned around, and asked:

"Nu, zhidka, a shtsho, troshki lipshi?"

Indeed, Benjamin really did feel a bit better and had sufficiently recovered to remember what had happened. Still, knowing only a few words of Ukrainian, his situation was far from promising. How could he answer a goy who spoke no Yiddish, much less inquire where he was being taken? Worse yet, when he tried sitting up, his legs refused to obey him.

"*Troshki tebi lipshi?*" asked the peasant again between one "Gee-up" and the next.

"*Lipshi,*" replied Benjamin. "But my legs," he added, pointing to them as best he could, "*ribi moi,* ouch!"

"*Izvidko ti, zhidka?*"

"*Izvidko ti, zhidka?*" Benjamin repeated, chanting the words as though he had found them in a Torah scroll. "*Ya* Binyomin. Binyomin *ub* Tuneyadevka."

"*Ti iz Tuneyadevki? Kazhi-zhe shtsho ti vitarashtshil na meni otshi i glyanish yak shilani. Alye mozshe ti take i shilani. Trastse tvoi materi.*"

And having delivered himself of this speech, in which he asked why Benjamin was blinking like a madman while declaring that he must have the very Devil in him, the peasant turned back to his oxen and cried: "Gee-up!"

"That's so," agreed Benjamin, who had understood only the first three words. "I already told you, *ya ub Tuneyadevka.*" Making a beseeching face and raising a hand to his mouth as if emptying a glass, he went on: "*Ya* have wife in Tuneyadevka, give you *tsharka vodka* and *zhidki hallah.*"

The peasant must have guessed Benjamin's meaning, for he replied "*Ti iz dobri zhidka,*" to wit, "Thou art a good Jew," and geed his oxen up again.

A few hours later the wagon drove into the marketplace of Tuneyadevka. Men and women came running. "*Tshoyesh skilke khotshes za pivan? Za tsibuli?*" called a prospective buyer of the rooster and the onions. "*Mozshe mayesh kartofli, yaytsi?*" shouted a customer for potatoes and eggs. It was a while before someone thought of asking about Benjamin, who had disappeared

as if swallowed by the stream. Before the peasant could answer, the women, who were going through his wagon like lo-
custs, pulled back the coat and let out a scream. "Benjamin!
It's him! Tsippe Kroyne! Basheve Breindl! Go, run tell Zelda
that she's not a widow after all!"

Bedlam broke out. There was not a dry eye in town. Young
and old ran to see Benjamin. He was besieged by congratulations, by questions; all day and all night, he was told, he had
been searched for everywhere. In fact, he had been given up
for dead, assumed martyred by man or the elements. Soon
Zelda arrived, sobbing at the sight of her husband, who was
pale as a ghost, and wringing her hands so hard that she nearly
broke a finger. She did not know whether to relieve her vexed
spirits by cursing him roundly, or to dance with joy at having
been spared a long widowhood, forbidden to remarry until
his body was found and he was declared officially dead.

Before long Benjamin was carried home, still lying on his
sack of potatoes, in a grand parade that wound through the
marketplace. Every last soul in Tuneyadevka was there. No
one waited to be invited and the hallelujahs in his honor were
like the cries of *Holy, Holy, Holy* during the kedushah prayer in
the synagogue.

Indeed, Benjamin was beatified that same day. Henceforth
he was known as Holy Benjamin and his wife as The Widow
Zelda.

The gypsy-trained doctor was called for and prescribed
every remedy he could think of. He treated Benjamin with
cups and leeches, shaved all the hair from his body, and
promised before departing that his patient would, with God's
help, feel well enough to go to synagogue the next morning
and give thanks for his miraculous deliverance.

# 3

## IN WHICH BENJAMIN FALLS
## IN WITH DAME SENDREL

IT STOOD TO reason that this adventure of Benjamin's, which caused his wife much grief and led to no end of debate by the stove and upper benches, would have rid him once and for all of the thought of his grand expedition. In fact, it only made him more determined. He now regarded himself with new respect as an experienced man of the world and held in highest esteem the courage and strength exhibited during his recent ordeal, in which he had displayed such self-mastery. And having become something of a hero and an adventurer in his own eyes, a man versed in the Seven Arts of *The Shadow of Eternity* and replete with scientific knowledge, he felt distressed that a person so well-informed should have to languish, a veritable lily among the brambles, in a backwater town like Tuneyadevka, the simple inhabitants of which had no notion of anything. Their homely sayings and platitudes grew onerous to him and heightened his desire to escape. If only, he thought, my voyage were accomplished and I were already home again, world-honored and acclaimed, with rare tidings for my fellow Jews! Everyone in Tuneyadevka would then know who I am—yes, they would know what it means to be Benjamin . . .

Nothing but a few last details now stood between him and his departure. Where, to begin with, was he going to get the money for his trip? He didn't have a farthing to his name, having spent all his days in the study house while his wife struggled to make a living from a little store she had opened after her parents ceased supporting them as newlyweds, the entire stock of which consisted of the socks that she knit, the down feathers that she stayed up plucking on winter nights, the chicken fat that she fried and rendered before Passover, and the bit of produce that she haggled for with the peasants on market days and resold at a scant profit. Should he pawn some household item? But apart from two brass candlesticks, an heirloom from Zelda's family that she polished faithfully and lit the Sabbath candles in, there was nothing pledgeable in the house; its sole jewelry was a silver headband with a pearl inherited by Zelda from her mother and used for fastening her kerchief on special occasions. Should he sell off something of his own? All he had was his Sabbath caftan, which, though new when he was married in it, had become so bedraggled that its yellow lining was falling out. True, he owned a sheepskin coat too; but the lower half of its wool nap was worn away and its fur collar had not a filament of fur. This coat had been a wedding gift from Benjamin's father, who had told the tailor not to skimp on the collar and to line it temporarily with the leftover cloth from an old gaberdine until the dowry was paid off and he could afford a bit of gray squirrel; the dowry, however, was never paid off and the squirrel remained in the trees.

Secondly, Benjamin had no idea how to part from his wife. Should he take her into his confidence and reveal his plan? This could only lead to wild tears and the conviction that he had taken leave of his senses. How much, after all, could a Jewess from Tuneyadevka understand? She might be a brave breadwinner, but she was still a woman, and there was less in the head of the canniest female than in the little finger of the most doltish man. Should he slip away without saying goodbye? This struck him as disagreeable, the kind of thing that only a cold-blooded Lithuanian Talmudist might do. But what other choice was there? To sit at home for the rest of his life? The prospect was intolerable. He might as well lie down and die, since he and his journey were one; as other Jews turned toward Jerusalem in their prayers each day, so it was constantly before him. He even thought of it when he slept, for it was all he dreamed of at night, and his waking eyes and ears saw and heard not the world around them but the exotic places that he yearned for. Often, in the course of an ordinary conversation, he found himself uttering words that only he understood: the Indies, Cathay, Timbuktu, the Northwest Passage, the source of the Nile . . . No, there was no going back. He just didn't know how to proceed. He felt that he needed someone to talk to, a kindred soul.

NOW IT CAME to pass, dear reader, that there was, in those days, in Tuneyadevka, a man named Sendrel, thus named after his great-grandfather; and he was, this same Sendrel, a simple soul, that is, a man without guile. In the synagogue he had his place behind the dais, which is sufficient to tell you that he did not belong to Tuneyadevka's upper crust. In discussions he generally kept silent, as if he were a mere bystander, and any words he spoke were greeted with hoots of laughter though uttered with no intention to amuse, not because they were witty but because they were his. And yet this laughter, which made him look round with wide eyes for the cause of it, was never minded by him, for being as meek as a brindled cow, he was not one to take offense. Someone had laughed? Well, then, let them laugh; if they did, it must give them pleasure. Sometimes Sendrel spoke truer than he knew.

People liked to play pranks on him. When the children threw burrs at each other on Tisha b'Av, most landed in his beard, and he received more than his share of blows in the traditional pillow fight on the long night of Hoshanna Rabbah, though not of the cookies and vodka consumed on the same occasion. He was, in a word, the butt of every joke, which was why people called him Sendrel the Kickpuppy. He never insisted on his opinion if there was a different one, let others have their way when they wanted it, and did what he was bidden. "What's it to me?" and "Why should I care?" were his mottoes.

With the children Sendrel was a child. He liked to talk and play with them and suffered them with bovine good nature to ride his back and pull his beard. "You young rascals!" folk scolded them. "Where's your respect for your elders? A Jew's beard is not a bellpull!" "Eh, it's all right," Sendrel would say reassuringly. "What's it to me if they stroke my beard? Why should I care?"

At home he did not lick honey either. His wife wore the pants and let him know it, and his fate at her hands was a bitter one despite his loving efforts to put up with it. Worst of all were holiday eves when, tying a kerchief around his beard, she ordered him to whitewash the house, peel potatoes, roll and cut noodle dough, stuff fish, and kindle the oven, all women's jobs that earned him the additional name of Dame Sendrel.

And it was to Dame Sendrel that Benjamin now attached himself and opened his heart, asking for advice. Why Sendrel? The fact was that Benjamin had always liked the fellow. Something about Sendrel appealed to him. Since the two of them generally saw eye to eye, conversing with him was a pleasure, nor did it escape Benjamin's attention that, with his yielding nature, Sendrel was likely to go along with most any plan laid before him. Even if he had a qualm or two, there was nothing, with God's help and Benjamin's quick tongue, that could not be overcome.

AND SO IT was one day that our Benjamin went to see our Sendrel; and he found him, our Sendrel, seated on a milking stool, and he was peeling potatoes. One of his cheeks was flame-red and beneath his eye was a bluish mark that could very well have been made by a fingernail. He was in mournful spirits, like a bride whose husband has abandoned her for some adventure or returned from it to give her a beating. Sendrel's wife was not at home.

"Good morning, Sendrel," said Benjamin. "What are you moping about, old fellow?" He pointed with a finger at Sendrel's cheek. "Again, eh? Where is she now, your beloved?"

"In the marketplace."

"Most excellent!" Benjamin exclaimed, nearly crowing with delight. "Put down your potatoes, my dear boy, and come with me to the back room. Are you sure no one's there? I need to bare my breast to you. I can't keep it to myself any longer. My blood's on fire! Quick, my dear, quick! She mustn't come and take us by surprise before we're ready."

"What's it to me?" said Sendrel, heading for the back room. "If it's quick you want, I'll be quick. Why should I care?"

"Sendrel!" said Benjamin. "Do you have any idea what's beyond Tuneyadevka?"

"Of course I do. A tavern with first-rate vodka."

"You *are* a booby. I mean beyond that."

"Beyond the tavern?" Sendrel shook his head wonderingly. "No, I don't. Do you?"

"Do I? What a question! Why, the whole world!" said Benjamin as grandly as if he were Columbus presenting the king of Spain with America.

"But what's out there?"

"What's out there?" Benjamin could not control himself. "Sea monsters, that's what! Basilisks . . ."

"You mean the little creatures that cut the stones for King Solomon's Temple just by looking at them?"

"The very same, dear boy! And the Land of Israel is out there too, with all its holy places. Wouldn't you like to go there?"

"Would you?"

"What a question! I not only would, I soon will!"

"I envy you, Benjamin. Just don't get a stomachache from all those dates and carobs."

"They can be yours, too, for the asking, Sendrel. The Land of Israel belongs to you as much as to me."

"So it does. But right now it belongs to the Turk."

"The Turk can be dealt with, Sendrel. Tell me, my dear, have you ever heard of the Ten Lost Tribes?"

"A lot, by the stove in the synagogue. Not that I know who they are or where to find them. If I did, I'm sure I'd tell you. Why shouldn't I? What's it to me?"

"Well, I do!" said Benjamin excitedly, pulling *The Praises of Jerusalem* from his pocket. "Here, listen to this. 'Reaching Baruti,' he commenced to read, 'I encountered four Babylonian Jews and was able to converse with one of them, who spoke the Holy Tongue and was named Moshe. He told me indubitable truths about the River Sambatyon that he had heard from some Ishmaelites and about the Sons of Moses who live beyond it.' And look at what it says here: 'The governor of the province revealed to me that thirty years previously he had entertained in his home a man from the Tribe of Simeon, who told him that four tribes of Israelites reside in his district, including that of Issachar, which devotes itself to the study of Torah and sires the royal house.' And there's also this passage in *The Travels of Benjamin of Tudela:* 'A march of twenty days brings one from there to Mount Nisbon, on the bank of the River Gozan. Four tribes live there in many towns and cities: the Tribe of Dan, the Tribe of Zebulun, the Tribe of Asher, and the Tribe of Naphtali. The river runs around them on one side, and they are subject not to the yoke of the Gentiles but only to their own king, whose name is Yosef Amarcala Halevi. And they are the allies of the heretical el-Torek.' Besides which, I can show you numerous references to the descendants of Yonadav ben-Rechav in the Land of Tema, who have a Jewish king and pray and fast constantly for the end of the Exile. Just suppose, my dear fellow, that I should suddenly turn up there, their brother Benjamin from Tuneyadevka, as their guest! What do you think, Sendrel? Tell me."

"They'd be honored to have you, Benjamin. A guest like you is nothing to sneeze at. I'm sure they'll all invite you for dinner, King Amarcala too. Please give him my best regards. I wish I could be there."

"Eh!" A new idea took hold of Benjamin. "Maybe, Sendrel, my dear, you'd like to come along. I swear, this is your chance, you silly goose! I'm going anyway, and I'll be glad to take you with me. Two is jollier than one. Who knows? Perhaps they'll crown me their king and you can be my grand vizier. Here, let's shake hands on it. Why go on living under the thumb of that shrew of yours? Just look at what she's done to your cheek! It's a wretched life you lead with her. Come, Sendrel. You won't regret it, I promise."

"All right," Sendrel said. "Have it your way. Why should I care about her? I'd be a fool to even tell her where I'm going."

"Dearest, I could kiss you!" said Benjamin blissfully, taking Dame Sendrel in his arms. "You've just answered a question for me, a fool's question, you're quite right. Why should I care about my wife? But that still leaves one problem. Where do we get the money for expenses?"

"What expenses? You don't plan to outfit yourself especially for your trip or have your coat turned in its honor, do you? There's nothing you need for it. On the contrary: when you're on the road, the older your clothes, the better. We're sure to be given new coats when we get there."

"That's true. What happens when we get there doesn't worry me. But we still have to eat along the way, don't we?"

"Eat? A person might think you planned to bring a chef along! We'll pass plenty of houses, you can be sure of it."

"Sendrel," said Benjamin in bewilderment, "I don't know what you're talking about."

"I'm talking about the fact that if there are houses, they have doors to knock on. Isn't that the Jewish way? Today I knock on your door, tomorrow you knock on mine. How else would we all get to give charity?"

"I'll be hanged if you're not right!" exclaimed Benjamin. "And now that I know that I'm ready to leave, I feel like a new man. We can start out early tomorrow morning when the town is still asleep. It's a sin to lose a single minute, isn't it?"

"If you say tomorrow morning, let it be tomorrow morning. What's it to me?"

"But early, Sendrel, do you hear? I'll slip out of the house and wait for you by the deserted windmill. Don't forget!" Benjamin turned to go. "Don't forget!" he repeated.

"Wait a minute, Benjamin!" Sendrel reached into his jacket pocket and took out a blackened bit of old leather tied with a string and knotted in twenty places. "In here is all the money that I've managed to put away in the years I've been married. It will come in handy, don't you think?"

"I swear, one kiss isn't enough for you!" cried Benjamin, embracing Dame Sendrel again. "Here's more!"

"The plague take you both!" they suddenly heard someone cry. "The goat's in the house eating the potatoes and these two lovers couldn't care less!"

It was Sendrel's wife, furiously holding the goat with one

hand while beckoning to Sendrel with the other. Like a naughty child resigned to a paddling, he hung his head and walked as slowly as he could across the room to her.

"Courage, dear boy!" whispered Benjamin in his ear. "This is the last time. Just don't forget: tomorrow morning!" And quick as a cat, he was off.

## 4

### IN WHICH BENJAMIN AND SENDREL SET OUT FROM TUNEYADEVKA

EARLY THE NEXT morning, before the town shepherd took the cattle out to pasture, Benjamin was waiting by the windmill with a bundle under his arm. In it were all the necessary items for his journey: his prayershawl, his phylacteries, a prayerbook, a Psalter, and several other volumes that he could no more do without than a worker could manage without his tools. His Sabbath caftan was packed away too for occasions on which he would have to look respectable. In his pocket were fifteen and a half farthings, taken from beneath his wife's pillow. He was prepared for all eventualities.

A fine sun had risen and was beaming down on the world, its every glance a wholesome tonic. As an infant will go from tears to laughter at the sight of a shiny bauble, so the grasses and trees smiled through the night's dewdrops that had yet to dry on their leaves. Frolicking birds took to the air with a song as if to say: "Come, let us chant our matins for that fine-looking fellow by the mill! Why, 'tis Benjamin—Benjamin of Tuneyadevka, the latter-day Alexander—the stalwart soul who has set out from his native land, leaving behind his wife and children, to follow God's path where it leads him! 'Tis Benjamin the Great, come forth from his tent like the sun in the Psalm, like the strong man that runneth his course with joy, yea, with a bundle under his arm! Sing, ye winged creatures, frolic, ye feathered ones, trill ye, tra-la-la ye, for his pleasure!"

Indeed, Benjamin felt most pleased with himself. I am without a doubt, he thought with no offense meant to the Evil Eye, the happiest man alive! What do I lack? I have left my wife, God be praised, well provided for, with a living she knows how to earn, and I am now as free as these birds. The world lies before me. With my experiences, my courage, and my knowledge of the Seven Arts, how poorly can I fare? And besides, I'm a Jew, which means that I have faith. Even when things seem less than bright, we Jews know there is a God who looks after us.

Benjamin was in such fine fettle that his lips parted by themselves and out came a High Holiday tune that sounded like a royal march. Accompanied by the song of the birds, the buzz of the flies, and the shrilling of the crickets, it was an oratorio fit for God's throne in His highest heaven.

After a while, however, there being no sign of Sendrel, Benjamin began to fret and his spirits flagged. In vain he looked everywhere, straining to catch a glimpse of him: Sendrel was not to be seen. Could his old battle-ax have given him some last-minute chore? But it was too early for that; Tuneyadevka was still fast asleep. It was not yet time for peeling potatoes, which no housewife put her mind to before having her morning spat with her husband, soundly beating all her children, and putting the bedding out to air. Benjamin was in a quandary. Should he retrace his steps and go home? The very idea was repugnant. Why, Alexander the Great had burned every bridge on his way to India to make sure there was no turning back! Should he set out by himself? This appealed to him even less. Sendrel was indispensable. It had been a great boon when he decided to join the expedition, which now seemed no more conceivable without him than a ship without its rudder or a kingdom without its lord chancellor.

Just then Benjamin spied a figure in the distance. Could it be Sendrel? But no, it was wearing a calico dress and had a kerchief on its head. Benjamin's heart skipped a beat and he turned white as a sheet. For sure, it was his wife!

The figure approached—or rather, came toward him on the run as if to seize him by the collar and drag him yammering home. "God alone knows," Benjamin has told his biographers, "how, at that moment, I would have more gladly faced a hundred fire-breathing dragons than my wife; for an angry dragon devours only the body, while an irate wife consumes body and soul. But God in His great mercy gave me courage, and I quickly hid behind the windmill and lurked there like a lion in the bush."

A minute later Benjamin sprang from his hiding place with a frightful cry that sounded like a madman's:

"Sendrel!"

It was indeed Sendrel in a calico smock and a greasy kerchief clinging to his cheeks. He had a gash beneath each eye, a stick in one hand, and a large pack on his back—but to Benjamin he was as beautiful as a bride. "As a hart longing for a spring, or a thirsty man in the desert, when water gushes from a rock," he has said, "so I leaped for joy to see my trusty companion!"

"What took you so long?" asked Benjamin. "Where have you been?"

"To tell you the truth," answered Sendrel candidly, "I

started out from home quite some time ago and even woke your Zelda."

"You woke my Zelda?" gasped Benjamin. "Sendrel, you lunatic, what did you do that for?"

"What do you mean, what did I do it for?" asked the surprised Sendrel. "What should I have done after knocking on the pantry door and not finding you? I went around to the front door and knocked again. Pretty soon Zelda came and opened it, looking like a warmed-up corpse, and I asked her where you were."

"Sendrel, we're in for it now! You've gotten us into a pickle, you have. Zelda will be here any minute and she'll—"

"Never fear, Benjamin. She sent me to the Devil so fast that you'd have thought I'd stepped on a new dress of hers. 'You can go with my husband straight to Hell!' she said and slammed the door in my face. I stood there for a while not knowing what to do until I remembered that we had agreed to meet at the windmill and reckoned you must be there. But if that's where your wife told me to go with you, I suppose she must know that you've gone."

"What? Do you think she saw me leave? Do you think she'll come after us?"

"Not a chance, Benjamin. I heard her put the chain back on the door. She didn't even say a word when I asked her, 'Zelda, is there any message you'd like me to give your husband? Anything I can bring him?' She must have been still half asleep. And so I told her, 'Go back to bed, Zelda, and take your time getting up,' that's exactly what I said."

These last words braced Benjamin like a spoonful of valerian drops. A load off his mind, he sighed with relief and brightened up. "Well, then, Sendrel," he said with a whoop, "we're off!"

From the nearby pond came a croak of frogs, as if in a fanfare of farewell. Your Tuneyadevka frog may live in muck and mire, but it has a voice like a brass trumpet. It's as famous in its way as the bedbugs of the Dnieper.

# 5

## IN WHICH OUR HEROES HAVE
## THEIR FIRST ADVENTURE

OUR TWO HEROES set out at a breakneck pace, as furiously as if tugged by a leash or driven by a whip, their broad coattails flapping in the wind like a schooner's sails. To tell the truth, more than one drayman in our parts would have been delighted to see his nags run half as fast. Alarmed by such swift bipeds, the crows and magpies hopped deferentially out of their path, squawking and flying off in all directions. Words cannot describe our couple's contentment with themselves and with the world. Sendrel was overjoyed to have cast off his wife and the bitter existence he had led with her; his last day in Tuneyadevka had been his worst and had left a trail of bruises all over his body, a missing clump of hairs in his beard, and a conspicuous black-and-blue mark on each cheek. Lucky is the male of the species who need not suffer such mayhem from his consort.

For a long while the two men raced along in breathless silence, exchanging not a word. Large drops of sweat ran down their flushed faces. Little by little Sendrel began to lag and huff like a goose. "Faster, Sendrel, faster!" Benjamin spurred him on, flying forward like a warrior into battle.

"Have a heart, Benjamin," Sendrel pleaded. "I can't keep

up with you. You're running, God bless you, like a mountain goat."

"Faster, Sendrel!" Benjamin urged again, much taken with his own mettle. "I'm telling you, I could go on running like this to the end of the world!"

"But what for, Benjamin? Good Lord, it's not as if we're late for anything. If it takes us a day more or a day less to get there, what difference does it make? The world won't come to an end. God made it, so I've heard, to last seven millennia, and there are still a few hundred years to go."

"Faster, Sendrel! It's a crime to lose a single minute. The sooner the town is behind us, the better. Try to push yourself a little harder. You'll make up for it when we arrive and you can live like a king without lifting a finger."

"I don't doubt that you're right, Benjamin. If it's faster you want, why should I care? But it isn't me you have to convince, it's my legs. What do you suggest I do about them?"

Benjamin had no choice but to slow down. Meanwhile, the sun rose like a great ball of butter from its churn and shone down on our two travelers, who soon dropped by the roadside in the shade of a little woods, panting and sweating. The perspiration dripping on his cuts and bruises stung Sendrel like sharp needles. After resting a bit, the two men took out their prayershawls and phylacteries and said the morning prayer, which Benjamin recited with much ardor and strenuous rocking back and forth. A bit of grog, such as was set out after Sabbath services in the synagogue, would have been his just reward, but where was he to find it? Worse yet, he had not brought with him a single piece of bread, not even a thumbkin's worth, and the appetite worked up along the way now made him faint with hunger. He glanced about, cracked his knuckles, yawned, scratched himself fiercely, let out a few grunts, smoothed his beard and earlocks, scratched himself again, grunted once more, and finally extracted a quarto volume from his bundle and perused it while humming a tune. After a while he stopped and asked:

"Sendrel! Do you know what I'm humming?"

"What I know," came the frank reply, "is that you're hungry."

"Thunderation!" exclaimed Benjamin. "How did you guess?"

"With the help," answered Sendrel, "of the Ukrainian proverb that says that the hungrier the Jew, the louder he sings. Go ahead and sing, Benjamin, while I attend to some business."

Whereupon Sendrel reached into his pack and pulled out a small bag.

"Tsk, Sendrel, you ninny," chided Benjamin, "I can see that my purpose escapes you."

But Sendrel was occupied with slowly undoing the bag, which made Benjamin glow all over with pleasure as soon as he caught sight of its contents. In it was all a body could desire: a piece of leftover Sabbath challah, some pickles, radishes, onions, and even a bit of garlic. Good housewife that he was, Sendrel had thought of everything, which made Benjamin prize him more than ever and thank the Lord for providing him with a fellow explorer every bit as precious as the manna with which He sustained the Children of Israel in the desert.

After they had eaten to their hearts' content, Sendrel repacked what was left and said:

"This food will be good for another meal and this bag for another thousand. We need only go with it from house to house and let God worry about filling it."

What, indeed, compared to a Jew's bag, are the magic tablecloths of fairy tales on which one knocks while declaring, "Tablecloth, tablecloth, give me all I crave to eat"? The tablecloth grants every wish, but so, with wondrous ease, does the bag, which can be handed down to one's children and grandchildren. Moreover, it changes its shape quite magically too; for while among most Jews it is a simple haversack, among others it may resemble a satchel, a suitcase, a brief-case, a carpetbag, a saddlebag, a billfold, a basket, a casket, a hamper, a hopper, a rucksack, a reticule, a pottle, a punnet, or a pannier. And yet each and every one of these still serves as a bag, the authentic Jewish almsbox.

"Sendrel," said Benjamin, heartened by his friend's words, "the two of us are a pair made in heaven. We go together like a body and its soul. You'll be in charge of the physical half of our expedition, eating and drinking and all that, and I'll be in charge of the mental half. And by the way, do you know what I was humming? It was the Akdomus for *Shavuos,* and don't think I didn't have my reasons. You see, once we arrive, God willing, in the land of the ten tribes, we're going to have a great deal to talk about, and the language spoken there is the very same Chaldean that the Akdomus is written in. In fact, it was composed by Eldad the Danite and I'm brushing up on it right now. *Shorayes shusa,* Sendrel, how's that? That means, 'Attend and lend an ear.' You see, I'm pretty handy at it al-ready! If we were bound for Europe we could get along in German, which is what they call Yiddish there, but I'm quite certain that none of the ten tribes knows a word of it."

"I'm sure they don't," said Sendrel humbly. "You're an edu-cated man and can look things up in your books. There's no doubt that you know what you're doing. That's why I haven't even asked you if we're heading in the right direction. If you say we are, why should I care? You go ahead, Benjamin, and I'll follow you like a cow behind its calf."

Sendrel's faith in his wisdom was greatly to Benjamin's liking. He pictured himself as the captain of a ship, steering his vessel over the boundless main. And yet it did not fail to occur to him that he had no idea where they were. Could they have strayed so soon from their route and gotten lost? He was still mulling the matter over when a peasant appeared, driving a wagon piled high with hay.

"I declare, Sendrel!" said Benjamin. "Just to be on the safe side, why don't you ask this fellow where we are? You're better at speaking these foreigners' tongue than I am. After all, your wife dragged you to the market all the time."

Sendrel rose, walked over to the peasant, and said as politely as he could:

"*Dobry dyen! Kozhi no tshelovitshe kudi dorogi Eretz-Yisro'eyl?*"

"*Shtsho?*" asked the peasant, eyeing him bewilderedly. "*Yaki Yisro'eyl? Nye batshil ya Yisro'eyl.*"

"*Nye, nye,*" interrupted Benjamin impatiently from where he sat. "He thinks you're asking about a person named Israel, not about the land. What a pumpkinhead of a peasant! Tell him it's the land we're looking for. Come, Sendrel, be sharp!"

"*Kudi dorogi Errrretz-Yisro'eyl?*" asked Sendrel again.

The peasant spat, told them both to go to the Devil, and drove away muttering: "Eres-Srul, Eres-Srul!"

Our heroes set out again. By now Benjamin's calves were aching and his feet felt like two stumps. Nevertheless, he sought to take heart and ignore them; and since walking like an ordinary Jew was not possible, he advanced with a hop-step-and-jump, an awkward gait that he struggled to keep up. What other choice, hang it all, did he have? To lie down in the middle of the road? But this was not something that a Jew did and would only have distressed Sendrel and impeded their progress even more.

In short, they walked all day until God brought them safely at nightfall to the town of Pievke.

Once arrived, Benjamin went straight to the local tavern, where he threw himself down in a corner to rest his legs and catch his breath while Sendrel went to see about supper. The tavernkeeper looked Sendrel up and down, concluded that he was no ordinary wayfarer, bade him a hearty hello, and inquired where a Jew like him might hail from and what his name might be; to which Sendrel replied forthrightly that it was Sendrel, that for all practical purposes he was already a Jew from the Land of Israel, and that he had the honor of being the valet of the illustrious Reb Benjamin who was now relaxing in the corner. Adopting a thoughtful and pious mien, the tavernkeeper told Sendrel to take a seat.

But let us leave the princess of our tale with the tavernkeeper and return to the prince, who lay like a stone in his corner, barely conscious of his surroundings. The blood in the swollen veins of his legs roiled and rankled like a swarm of biting gnats; his temples throbbed as if struck by hammers; and when his ears were not blasting like a shofar at the end of Yom Kippur, they were crackling like fireworks, each rocket exploding before his eyes in bright colors—yellow, green, blue, red, orange, and still more and more. All at once, though, the fireworks ended; he could now see nothing but darkness; and the sound in his ears resembled the rumble of millstones.

For a long while Benjamin lay in a daze, from which he was roused by a distant chime of bells. These drew nearer, becoming clearer and louder, and suddenly there was a creak by the gate like a wagon coming to a stop. All kinds of shrill, hoarse, gurgling, drowsy, piping, throaty voices tumbled out of it, as if a momentous town meeting were being held and everyone was trying to be heard. When the cats yowled on the rooftops of Tuneyadevka, Benjamin may not have understood them, but at least he knew he was listening to caterwauls; now, however, it was impossible to say whether he was hearing screams, cries, laughter, groans, whispers, shrieks, or grumbles, brash razzing or obsequious cajolery, the hawking of throats or the blowing of noses, the rattle of rales or the clatter of handclaps. Who could begin to figure it out?

Just then the door opened and a gang of men poured pell-mell into the room. Benjamin huddled in his corner, trying to make himself small. The room was now full of light, which came from many brass candlesticks. Some of these were stuffed with old tallow that fused with the candles in strange shapes; others had sockets that were too wide and shallow, so that the tapers stood at mad angles, propped up by lumps of coal. Around a long oak table in the far corner sat a group of musicians tuning their instruments, the fiddler tickling the strings of his fiddle, which chuckled that they were ready and that all that was needed was a bow. This he proceeded to produce, poising it for the first stroke; the flutist spoke quietly to his flute, which answered with a soft note; the cymbalist ran a pair of little hammers slowly over his cymbal; and only the blind drummer slumped over his drum went on snoozing beneath his fur hat while making no move to begin.

Near the musicians stood a man on a small stool, who reduced the room to peals of laughter each time he attempted to speak; even the children crowded outside the windows giggled and made funny faces. Finally, he opened his mouth one more time, let out a loud "Hear! Hear!" and proclaimed: "In honor of the bride, and of the groom, and of their parents, and of our host, and of all of you gathered here tonight, I say: Strike up the band!"

Men and women leaped up and began to dance in a circle. In no time the room was so lively that even the cockroaches crawled from their holes and hopped upon the walls. Suddenly a dancer tripped over Benjamin in his corner, took a good look at him, and exclaimed:

"Benjamin! By God, I've found him! It's him, all right, the lost sheep in person!"

At these words, people came running. Benjamin recognized some of Tuneyadevka's finest Jews, Rabbi Eizik-Dovid too. All called in one voice:

"On your feet, Benjamin! Dance, Benjamin! Benjamin, get up and dance!"

"I'm afraid I can't," Benjamin pleaded. "There's no way I can move."

"But there's nothing to it!" he was assured. "Anyone can dance. It's as easy as duck soup. Shake a leg, you lummox! We'll go spread the news that you've been found."

"Zelda!" Benjamin let out a croak. "Please, don't tell Zelda!"

"Shake a leg!" the voices repeated. "On your feet!"

"Have pity on a Jew," begged Benjamin. "I swear, I can't move. There's a reason why I can't, but it's a secret. I can only tell it to the rabbi." He grabbed Eizik-Dovid with both hands and began whispering into his ear, but just then he felt a blow in his ribs that was as sharp as a mouthful of horseradish. Starting with pain, he opened his eyes and saw that the room was dark. The moon was shining in the window, and by its light he saw that he was holding on hard to a calf.

You may wonder what the calf was doing there. Had Benjamin given birth to it? And if so, how could that be? Even assuming that he was an ox, the biggest and lummiest ever, since when do oxen bear calves? And while calves were abundant in the houses of Pievke and Tuneyadevka, these were mooncalves with human faces, like as not pretty ones with dimples, whereas the creature that Benjamin was gripping so tenaciously most definitely had a brute's physiognomy.

Where had it appeared from? Did I hear you say straight from the sky?

Wrong you are, gentle readers! Put no stock in heavenly calves, not a single one of which is to be found among all the yearlings of our region. Let us keep our explanations sweet and simple. What actually happened was this:

When Benjamin collapsed in his corner more dead than alive, he was too exhausted to notice that next to him was a calf. As he lay there with aching legs he dozed off, and in his sleep he dreamed the whole wedding with its musicians and its guests. Tossing and turning, he rolled onto the tavernkeeper's calf, and mistaking it for the rabbi of Tuneyadevka, began to confide in it. The calf, however, seeing no reason to suffer such unwanted intimacies, gave Benjamin a good kick.

Groggy at first, Benjamin hung on to the calf with all his might. It took him a while to push it away, jump frantically to his feet, and beat a hasty retreat. The calf, for its part, sought to get away too, which it did by charging straight into Benjamin and knocking them both with a loud crash into a water bucket.

Sendrel and the tavernkeeper were alarmed by the noise and rushed from the next room with a candle to see what the matter was. It was not a laughing one. Benjamin and the calf lay sprawled on the ground in a pool of liquid. Had an inspired poet been present, he might have vied with David's elegy for Saul and Jonathan by saying, "Lovely and pleasant in their corner, in their puddle they were not divided." But the tavernkeeper and Sendrel were distinctly prosaic souls and the two lovelies were quickly pulled apart. The calf was sent back to its mother with a scolding and Benjamin was led off to be washed, after which he was taken to an alcove and laid down on a straw mat with a pillow underneath his head.

# 6

BENJAMIN'S LIMBS FELT better after a tub of cold water was poured over them. Indeed, he awoke in the morning feeling so chipper that the calf now struck him as having been sent by the healing hand of Providence. How often men rail at some misfortune, he told Sendrel, without perceiving that it is for the best, nothing being too tiny to serve as an agent of God's will. Why, God could even make a physician of a calf or drive a man mad with a bug, like the gnat that crawled into the ear of the emperor Titus and grew to the size of a bird that pecked his brains out. The incident of the water bucket was an auspicious sign that their expedition had the Lord's blessing and would, with His help, achieve its goal.

"I suppose," replied Sendrel, loath to disagree, "that if breaking a glass at a wedding brings good luck, kicking over a water bucket must bring even better."

Nonetheless, still feeling a bit achy and happy to have a soft mattress beneath him, Benjamin spent the entire day in Pievke like a beached ship waiting for a wind. The next morning he rose early and resumed his journey with Sendrel.

For a long while he walked in melancholy silence, sunk in thought. Suddenly he struck his hand to his forehead and came to a troubled halt. After a few more minutes he sighed:

"Ah, Sendrel, I totally forgot!"

"What? Where?" exclaimed Sendrel, running his hand over his bag.

"At home, Sendrel. That's where I left it."

"Benjamin, what can you be thinking of?" Sendrel asked.

"Everything is right here in our bag. We have our prayershawls and prayerbooks; we have our Sabbath caftans; and I'll be blamed if we need anything else. What can you possibly have forgotten?"

"The most important thing of all, Sendrel, and I only hope that God looks after us, because we'll wish we had it if He doesn't. It's a spell from an old manuscript, which I left behind in my hurry to set out. It's to be said at the beginning of a journey, as you pass the first tollgate, and it's a sure protection against all accidents and dangers. And now I've gone and forgotten it!"

"Maybe," said Sendrel straightforwardly, "you'd like to turn back."

"Are you out of your mind?" cried Benjamin, the blood rushing to his cheeks. "After all that we've been through, how could you even think of it? And the world, what will the world say, tell me that!"

"But what does the world have to do with it?" asked Sendrel. "Did the world ask you to take this trip of yours? Has it given you a signed contract to walk to the other end of it with all expenses paid?"

"What logic!" jeered Benjamin. "I suppose the world asked Alexander the Great to go fight his wars in India! Do you think all the Jews roaming the world right now are being paid to do it?"

"How should I know?" shrugged Sendrel good-naturedly. "For my part, they needn't roam at all. I'm sure they'd be better off if they didn't. Your Alexander must have been a great fool not to have stayed in his palace, eating and drinking and having himself a fine time. What did he need India for? They say there's no place like home, and a saying's as good as an old manuscript. I swear, Benjamin, why ruin your health and your boots just to get to the far side of nowhere? If I ever see your Alexander that's what I'll tell him, manuscript or not."

Our two worthies had it out at length, Sendrel thrusting away and Benjamin riposting each time that his friend was a dunderhead to think he had any notion of such matters. Like a horse that always has done its master's bidding, following him to the ends of the earth until one fine dudgeony day it rears and balks, Sendrel dug in his heels. But resorting to the whip, Benjamin gave him such a tongue-lashing that in the end he pricked up his ears like an old dobbin and whinnied:

"All right, have it your way. What's it to me?"

And so the two set out again, and after following many a high road and byroad they arrived dead on their feet in Teterevke.

Teterevke was the first large town that our wanderers had ever seen. No wonder that they gawked at its broad boulevards and tall buildings and all but tiptoed along its sidewalks, treading queerly, as if afraid to damage the cobblestones, on small-town feet that never had been pampered by so much as a floor beneath them; that had floundered in mire all their days like the trotters of swine; that had hurried humbly to and fro on their bumpkinish business; and that now wavered as though drunk in the big-city streets, uncertain where to put themselves down. Timid and tense, our Tuneyadevkans stepped aside for everyone, Sendrel seizing Benjamin by the coattails and yanking him out of the way.

And then Sendrel began to dance. It happened when he encountered someone coming straight toward him. The man stepped to his right just as Sendrel stepped to his left and the two remained facing each other; then Sendrel stepped to his right just as the man stepped to his left and they were facing each other again. In the end they do-si-do'd around each other, but another time, when his opposite number was in no dancing mood, Sendrel found himself hurled so violently sideways that his teeth nearly tumbled from his mouth.

Everything being new to them, our two heroes kept pointing with their fingers. Droshkies clattered by; phaetons rattled along; the tall buildings looked haughtily down from their glass windows; the passersby threw them strange looks. "Stand back, you yokels!" these seemed to say. "Yield and make way!"

"I tell you, Benjamin," said Sendrel, craning his neck to look timorously up at the buildings, "we must be in Stambul!"

"What a nit you are! How could this be Stambul?" asked Benjamin as assuredly as if he had been born there. "Why, Stambul has tens of thousands of main streets, and each street has thousands of buildings, and each building has hundreds of people and ten or twenty floors. And that's not even counting the side streets, and the back streets, and the alleyways, and the lanes, and the walks, and the squares, and the courts, and the yards, and the passages."

"Ai, ai, ai!" exclaimed Sendrel in amazement. "It must give a body a great fright to live in such a place, I swear! But I ask you, Benjamin, where do all these big cities come from? You might think there was no room left anywhere else, the way people are piled on top of each other here! There must be something that makes them want to live so high, up in those tall windows. Do you think it's because our souls come from heaven and are always being drawn back, so that if only we had wings we'd fly right up there? What do your books say, Benjamin? I'm sure you've run across some explanation."

"The most reliable sources," Benjamin replied with a frown of concentration, "have a lot to say about the matter. Once, by the stove in the synagogue, there was a discussion of a passage in the Talmud concerning the verse in Genesis, 'And the earth was filled with violence.' I'll try to explain it—after all, Sendrel, even you have studied some Bible.

"Well, then, according to the Bible, our ancestors long ago lived in tents. Just before Noah's Flood, though, they all got together in a place called Babel and began to make bricks and build a city with tall houses until they started to bicker and fight. The trouble was, you see, that they couldn't understand each other's language and bollixed everything up. Luckily, God chased them out of there and they went back to living as men should. But the sin of Babel is still with us. In every age the old craving returns to get together. That's why Abraham said to Lot, 'Is not all the land before you? Separate yourself from me.' What he meant was, stop being such a leech. You've got the whole world to live in, so shove over . . ."

Benjamin was only halfway through his dissertation when he was interrupted by the cry of a coachman who nearly ran them both over. "Looksmartyoutwo!" he shouted in one breath, cracking his whip, which scuttled devilishly in front of them like a crab and blocked their path. "Heads up, you hayseeds!"

Our two heroes took to their feet and dodged in circles like poisoned mice. Sendrel tripped over a stoop and went flying headfirst, while Benjamin crashed into a basket of eggs borne by a woman shopper. The eggs broke, but this was nothing compared to his own fate: the oaths, the screams, the mouth on the woman! Every egg was paid for with curses and blows, some merely promised and others delivered in advance, plus a power of hair-pulling. In a word, he barely escaped with his life, taking refuge in a back alley, where he was soon joined by Sendrel.

"How do you like your big city now?" asked Sendrel, wiping the sweat from his face with a corner of his coat. "No walking allowed, no stopping allowed, no looking allowed. The Devil take it!"

"It all goes back to Babel," panted Benjamin. "Everything you see here, Noah saw too. A thieving bunch of murderers!"

"Well, I say to hell with them!" said Sendrel with a wave of his hand. "Come on, Benjamin, let's find a place to rest. You look awful and one of your cheeks is all red. A pox on the old crone's father! And you'd better wash your face, because it's got egg yolk all over it."

# 7

## IN WHICH BENJAMIN CAUSES
## A POLITICAL UPHEAVAL

IN ONE OF the little synagogues of Teterevke the Crimean War was being hotly debated. The parliament by the stove was divided into factions, each with its party whip and politics. Heikel the Engineer and his band were ranged solidly on Queen Vicky's side, which they upheld with a plethora of proofs. Actually, Heikel was something of a watchmaker, but he was no mean matzo roller either, to say nothing of a master sukkah builder: when it came to constructing a holiday booth from a noodle board, an old shovel, a milking bench, a stove lid, a broken chicken coop, and other such things, no one could hold a candle to him. As a result he was deferred to on all mechanical questions, to which "That's something for Heikel," or "Heikel will know," was the standard response. When he delivered a lecture on the latest English machine he could make your hair stand on end with its marvels, and if interrupted in the middle by a skeptical question about it, his smiling explanation of the thingamabob that made it work left his questioner feeling benighted. There were, his listeners knew, thingamabobs in watches, in telegraphs, in windup toys, and in all manner of other inventions. Only Itzik Show-Me, who scoffed that if Heikel was to be believed, the Lord God must have created the world with the help of a thingamabob too, dared deny their existence.

Needless to say, all of Itzik's objections stemmed from ignorance and envy, but since Heikel the Engineer was enamored of Queen Vicky, Itzik Show-Me, as loyal leader of the Opposition, took the side of Mother Russia with all the means at his disposal. Both vied for the votes of the other parties, and just as Heikel was about to strike a deal with Shmuel Bokser, the head of the pro-Turk faction, and was far advanced in negotiations with French Berl, the chief supporter of Napoleon III, Itzik Show-Me staged a parliamentary coup by coming to terms with Tuvya Mock, an ally of the Austrian Kaiser. The floor buzzed with rumors; tempers flew; the Crimean War seemed about to take a new turn; the whole synagogue was in an uproar. And it was at this exact moment that our two worthies, in search of lodgings, walked in.

As in all other things, Sendrel was only too happy to yield in politics too. "If that's your opinion," he told everyone right off, "why should I care?" This greatly pleased the members of parliament, who deemed him a likable chap and not the least stubborn or devious. Benjamin, on the other hand, though choosier about his associates, took instantly to Shmuel Bokser, with whom he hit it off so well that the two of them were soon fast friends; hearing of Benjamin's expedition, Shmuel went to tell Heikel, who ruled that it merited serious consideration, problematic though it was. He therefore conferred with French Berl and Tuvya Mock, both of whom were equally impressed. From the very first, they said, they had realized that Benjamin was not your run-of-the-mill individual. There was a remoteness about him; often he seemed lost in thought; when he spoke it was hard to grasp his meaning; when he smiled his eyes were far away; his gestures and demeanor were uncommon. In a word, all things pointed to the fact that, far from being a simple Jew, he was a person of rare degree. Who was to say? Perhaps our Benjamin was more than just a mere man . . .

By now there was a frightful commotion in the synagogue, for Itzik Show-Me, beset by his opponents, had cleared his throat and was tapping a book with one finger while shouting:

"Here! See for yourselves! It's written in Yosifon's history, and I quote: 'When Alexander the Great desired to visit the descendants of Yonadav ben-Rechav, he and his warriors set out for the Mountains of Darkness. They were unable, however, to proceed, for their legs sank into mud up to their knees, the region being a swampy one on which the sun never shone.' And I ask you: if the great Alexander, who flew his eagle to the very gates of Paradise, could not cross the Mountains of Darkness, how, no matter who he is, is this Benjamin going to do it? Not even all of Heikel's thingamabobs could help!"

"You numskull!" thundered Heikel, poking Itzik with his thumb while snatching away the book. "Where are your eyes? It says on the same page, and I quote: 'Then Alexander heard birds speaking to him in the tongue of the Greeks, one of which said: All of thy efforts must come to naught, for thou mayst not enter God's house and the house of His servants, the sons of Abraham, Isaac, and Jacob.' Is it clear to you now, you dunce, why Alexander the Great couldn't get across the mountains?"

"That's all very well, my ingenious engineer, but the best authorities believe that the lost tribes live far beyond the

Mountains of Darkness, in the land of Prester John, and I'd like to see this fine fellow of yours find *that*. We'll all be eating cold porridge before he does."

"Good Lord, Itzik, you're talking balderdash!"

"You just wait, my genius. He's got to cross the Sambatyon too. How is he going to do it when its waters are full of hurtling rocks? Even if he crosses the mountains and finds Prester John, he's still got the Sambatyon, blast it all! He'll never get his foot into it, not even if Queen Vicky does cartwheels with her arse up."

"Leave Vicky out of this! This time you've gone too far."

"Really, Itzik," French Berl intervened angrily, "there's no need to make fun of royalty. We're talking about Benjamin. You can mock him if you want, but not kings and queens."

"Why mock Benjamin?" cried Tuvya Mock. "Benjamin is setting out on an expedition that will be a great thing for the Jews."

"Ah, Mock, Mock, it's you who mock, Mock!" cried Itzik, shaking an aggravated head. "I never would have thought that you would be taken in by all this talk about Benjamin. What do you see in him?"

"Will you listen to that! *What do you see in him?*" repeated Shmuel Bokser sarcastically. "Have you gone totally mad today, Itzik? Why, his bearing, his breeding, the way he talks, the brains he has—they're all the mirror of the man. If that's not enough to convince you, I don't know what is. Why don't you take another look at him and tell me which one of us is crazy. Look at how his cheeks glow! Look at the three lines under his eye that form a perfect Shin, the first letter of Shaddai, the name of God! Well, what do you say now, Itzik?"

Itzik stepped up to Benjamin, surveyed him from head to toe, barely missed hitting him with a gob of spit, and walked irately away. Benjamin had caused a political upheaval.

Shmuel Bokser and French Berl now joined forces with Heikel; Queen Vicky sent thousands of warships from England, bristling with fearful guns; the Turk retreated across the Prut; Napoleon ordered a bombardment of Sebastopol; Tuvya Mock stood saying now one thing and now another, not knowing with whom to cast his lot; and Itzik Show-Me, having resorted to every possible device and all but leaped out of his skin, was left high and dry. Such a setback was no joke. From then on he had it in for Benjamin.

"God is my witness," Benjamin has written, "that I never intended to become involved politically. In the first place, what good could it have done me? And in the second place, what business was it of a Jew's? As far as I was concerned, the Crimean War could have ended however it wanted. My Sendrel, of course, kept strictly aloof from such matters, and subsequently, Itzik did his best to make my days and nights difficult. Once he stuck tarred feathers to my back; another time he threw a cushion at me; yet another, he hid my shoes while I racked my brain looking for them. He tickled my heels with a straw when I was asleep, making me jump out of bed, and blew smoke in my face, so that I awoke coughing like a consumptive, all because of his political debacle."

# 8

IN WHICH OUR HEROES MAKE THE
ROUNDS OF TETEREVKE

OUR HEROES SPENT the better part of their days providing for their needs. They made the rounds of Teterevke's homes and before long became so well-known that people pointed them

out in the street and even stopped to laugh and grin at them.
Others might have put on airs upon seeing the delight they
were glimpsed with, the pleasure brought by a word from
them, and the smiles that ushered them in and out of houses,
but our two Tuneyadevkans were unspoiled souls who took
such honors in stride. Benjamin was preoccupied with the
next stages of his expedition, while Sendrel's main concern
was keeping his bag full of food and his purse with a few farthings in it. As long as Jews gave, he did not particularly care
if they looked happy or sad. In the words of the old Purim
ditty:

> A penny is all I'm asking for:
> Fork it up and I'm out the door!

Often indeed as he made his rounds Sendrel would hum
these lines, which so well expressed his and Benjamin's simple
modesty. "A good morning to you and God bless!" he would
say as he entered a house with Benjamin in tow. Giving Benjamin an encouraging push and reminding him in a whisper
that there was no need for embarrassment, he would let him
do the talking while standing respectfully to one side.

On one of these visits our heroes encountered a young
man who had preceded them and was talking intensely to the
owner of the house. He was, it appeared, seeking to persuade
the latter of the importance of a certain undertaking that the
whole world was agog over while taking care to promote his
own self with the help of some documents he displayed. His
host, who was frowning and fidgeting as if to evade the young
man's clutches, grasped at Sendrel and Benjamin like a
drowning man at a straw, obviously hoping that they had arrived on some urgent business that would allow him to show

his petitioner the door. Upon hearing what they had come for he stood there dumbfounded, like a man overwhelmed by adversity.

"More travelers!" he exclaimed to the young man as soon as he recovered his speech. "These two Jews are travelers too! You can see for yourself, there's nothing but travelers!"

The young man and our Tuneyadevkans exchanged glances.

"Did you hear that?" whispered Sendrel to Benjamin, pulling him aside. "Maybe this young fellow is headed where we are. Suppose he gets there first and leaves us in the rear?"

"You wouldn't happen to belong to the same party, would you?" inquired the owner of the house.

"Not a chance!" cried Benjamin and Sendrel in one voice. "We're on our own, entirely on our own."

"Well, have a good trip then," said their host, reaching into his pocket for a coin. "You still look like one party to me, though."

"Here, sir, let me, sir, I'll be glad to relieve you of that, sir," cried Sendrel, holding out his hand. "We'll see to it that this young fellow gets his share. Come, young man, we'll settle with you outside. I have some change."

Just then the kitchen door swung open and a horrid voice shrieked:

"It's him, it's him! The one standing next to the small, thin Jew! They were hanging around together then too. I'd know him anywhere, the innocent angel, by that face and that yellow beard. Oh, I'd give it a good trimming, I would! God in heaven, the plague take him and his scheming heart! May his brains melt and ooze out of every bone in his body!"

"We'd better get out of here," said Sendrel, tugging at Benjamin's coat. "A pox on the old crone's father! She still hasn't gotten over her broken eggs."

# 9

## IN WHICH OUR HEROES ARE SAVED
## BY A MIRACLE

ONE CANNOT BUT heave a commiserating sigh upon reading the histories of the many renowned men of intellect who suffered so greatly at the hands of a world for which they sacrificed the best years of their lives, while making it the gift of their invaluable discoveries. The world is like an infant that likes to cuddle in its mother's lap, from which it fears to take the slightest step, and its favorite stories are the credulous tales that it hears a hundred times a day from its nannies and grandmothers, the moral of which is that nothing exceeds its childhood games, so that, although beyond its doors are wisdom and science, it kicks and screams as if kidnapped by a murderer when the time comes to be taken off to school. Its greatest desire is to remain as it is; nothing provokes it more than what is new; and then it fights back with tantrums and mud-throwing. And for the same reason, once the new has taken root, and the world has grown accustomed to it and its benefits, it embraces these with such pleasure that it forgets the sweat and tears of the poor genius who first thought of them even as it honors him with a mass or a monument.

Do not millions of men today live happily and breathe free in America? And yet when Columbus first conceived of setting out for that continent, he was called a lunatic and made to suffer for his views. Such, dear reader, was the case with Benjamin. Those who saw him considered him mad; hearing of his journey, they clutched their sides with laughter; they played pranks on him, abused him like an alley cat. It was a great stroke of luck that he failed to notice any of this, for otherwise he might easily have grown disheartened, or worse yet, physically ill, and abandoned his expedition. Indeed, if we have chosen to omit here the greater part of the world's tomfoolery toward him, we have done so only to prevent the eternal shame of it from being transmitted to future generations. Keeping our knowledge of these indignities locked forever in our breast, we shall resume our tale.

Teterevke, Benjamin relates, is inhabited by a large number of Jews, may they continue to be fruitful and multiply. Just who they are, whereof they are composed, and whence they hail are weighty questions to which they themselves have no answers; yet there is an age-old tradition among them that they derive from Jewish stock, and a goodly portion of their apparel, language, business practices, and other habits clearly points to such an origin, albeit one traceable to diverse uprooted tribes that chanced to settle in one place, as is evidenced by the fact that they have to this day so little to do with each other that, if one of them falls in the street, the others, strange to say, will refuse to help him up even should his life depend on it. Not a few of them understand and talk thieves' Latin or *jargonus iudeorum,* and they are highly versed in the art of palmistry or palm-crossing and often expert cutters, pressers, and turners, for they will cut each other on a whim, press on when told to desist, and turn their backs on those in need of them. Notable among their customs is a prohibition on uttering God's name in vain, which they obey by pronouncing it in all other fashions, such as whispering, shouting, crying, and sobbing it until they bring tears to your eyes. According to one school of thought, they are all that is left of the ancient race of Caphtorites mentioned in the Bible, for Caphtor is Crete and there are not a few cretins among them, but in any case, concludes Benjamin, "They were good and honorable souls who always greeted me with a special smile that expressed their contentment with me. My profoundest wish is that man and God be no less content with them."

One of the marvels of the region, Benjamin has said, is that one frequently encounters in it two-legged creatures with the faces of swine. One theory holds them to be a separate species, while another maintains that they are local variants of men. Benjamin himself has no firm opinion on the matter, being of the view that it is best left to further scientific investigation. In either case, he observes, the phenomenon was noted long ago by Matityahu Delacrut, who wrote that "In the land of the Britons there dwells a people that has tails on its behinds like animals. Moreover, there are women there, large as giants, who have bristles like pigs . . . And in the land of the Franks a people has been sighted that grows horns, and in the mountains of that country are women with crooked limbs, and the crookeder they are, the fairer they are deemed." To which Benjamin adds: "Such women, indeed, wanting in symmetry, can be found among us Jews today too, for often, if I may express myself indelicately, we see them with drooping rears that dangle to the ground like tails. How true is the verse that says that there is nothing new under the sun, and that what is, is what will be!"

Teterevke, reports Benjamin, is a sizable town with fine buildings and long streets, but despite one's first impression of a place teeming with vitality, it turns out on closer acquaintance to be little more than a magnified Tuneyadevka. Its inhabitants rise every morning just like the Tuneyadevkans, and they too divide their days into waiting for breakfast, waiting for lunch, and waiting for supper, the three oases for which they long like a cow in barren fields for green pasture. It is commonly said that the very air of Teterevke makes a man sluggish and slothful, and that whoever arrives there with a bit of pluck or drive soon loses both and wishes only to eat, sleep, and rise to eat some more.

During his stay Benjamin met a number of provincial accountants and lawyers who had come to Teterevke from elsewhere. "A man has to get out into the world," they had told the folk back home. "He has to roll up his sleeves and apply himself and get ahead and do some good." In point of fact, being an accountant or a lawyer in Teterevke was like being a fifth wheel on a wagon, since the taxes remained just as high even without anyone's help, but so great was the ambition of these Teterevke-bound souls that they borrowed money to pay their bills and travel expenses and set out for there full of hope. And yet fiendishly enough, no sooner did they set foot in the town than their initiative declined. Declined? Disappeared totally! Sluggish and slothful, they so quickly fell to eating, drinking, and sleeping like a native Teterevkan that one might have thought them the victims of a spell. The days and years went by; the folk back home sent them money on request, and one request followed another; and their lives passed like Sleeping Beauty's in the fairy tale, no medicine man or wonder worker being ever again able to conjure them forth from Teterevke.

Benjamin was all afire to make the acquaintance of the town's renowned scholars and authors. He was, after all, something of a scholar himself, having read many a Jewish book; furthermore, he knew the titles of many more, in both rabbinics and the Seven Arts; what, then, could be more natural than to introduce himself to his fellows? Moreover, he sorely desired to talk to them about his expedition. These were the people who could best understand and appreciate him, and who might give him letters of recommendation that would open doors for him. Missives of this sort were routinely issued for all sorts of trifles; in a truly important case like his, he had no doubt, they would be written so avidly that the pen would gallop across the paper like a horse.

There was just one problem, which was that whenever he came to the house of one of these learned gentlemen, the latter was either eating or sleeping. Once, however, he found one of them, a quite splendidly famous writer, reclining on a wooden bench in his study. "Good morning," said Benjamin. "And to you," replied the man. "What can I do for you?" "Oh," said Benjamin, "I just dropped by for a chat." But the chat went none too well. The writer looked comatose; his lips barely moved when he spoke; his eyelids kept drooping; and he seemed in all respects about to give up the ghost. Although Benjamin did his energetic best to keep the conversation going, he might have had better luck with a block of ice. In the end the man roused himself, let out a mighty yawn, and called for his wife. "Tell me," he asked, stretching himself so hard that Benjamin heard his bones crack, "when are we going to eat? I hope it's soon, because I'd like to take a little snooze . . ."

In a word, Teterevke was one big bedroom in which everyone and everything slept well: the scholars, the merchants, the banks, the courtrooms, and the shops. There was no waking them from their slumbers, and even when the Teterevkans spent time in company, they sat staring at each other like so many mannikins until, one by one, they dozed off. The only thing that could breathe a spark of life into them was the dinner bell, which they responded to with great gusto before turning in for the night.

It was not long before Benjamin began to feel the influence of the town. He did little more than eat and sleep himself, and his enthusiasm for his expedition waned. He was like a ship becalmed at sea, in danger of being stranded in Teterevke. And there indeed he might have remained for the rest of his life were it not, luckily for him and the world, for a stormy incident that drove him out of his lull.

Itzik Show-Me's hatred of Benjamin had grown from day to day and he plagued him with arguments against his expedition, one more discouraging than the next. Benjamin, said Itzik, would see hair sprout on his palm before he reached the Sambatyon, and his chances of finding the Ten Lost Tribes were like those of glimpsing his own ears. Benjamin did not take this lying down. There was, he retorted, a God above who did not forsake those who put their trust in Him, and with God's help he would reach his destination whether his enemies liked it or not. The more heated he became, the more fiery was the stream of words that issued from his mouth: basilisks, sea monsters, Minotaurs, juggernauts, jackasses! In a word, he was saying: "You can go on barking up that tree forever, but I myself will soon be far away, trekking across the wilderness, on and on . . ."

Itzik's response to all this was to spit three times against the Evil Eye and declare that Benjamin was out of his mind and in need of an exorcist. It reached the point that, as soon as Benjamin stepped into the street, he was followed by ragging idlers who cried: "Sea monsters! Basilisks!" Once, as he and Sendrel were out walking at night, they were set upon by such a swarm of ruffians that they had to escape through a back alley. In the course of their flight they found themselves speeding downhill toward a long, narrow footbridge, coming across which was a man who could not be avoided without breaking their skulls, or at the very least their legs, in a last-minute leap. Since both these parts of their anatomy were crucial for their expedition, they had no choice but to run into him nose first.

"Well, well, well, if it isn't Benjamin!" exclaimed this personage with a humph of a laugh. "Of all places to meet up with you, my word! I couldn't have wished for a better."

"Well, well, it's Rabbi Eizik-Dovid," answered Benjamin in a voice not quite his own.

It was indeed Rabbi Aron-Yosel-and-Sorah-Zlote's-Eizik-Dovid, the sage of Tuneyadevka.

"A fine pair you are!" scolded Rabbi Eizik-Dovid. "Since when does a man get up and walk out on his own home like a thief in the night, eh? Who goes and makes a widow out of two wives without dying? It's beyond me, it is. There's a way to do everything and some things aren't done! And of course—because it isn't as though—since even without that—although on the other hand—but the fact is—well, of course, of course! And not that I'm asking, but what are you doing here? I mean you too, Sendrel. Don't think I don't see you standing in back of Benjamin. Your wife, Sendrel, is going to give it to you good, she'll wipe the floor with you like a herring. Something told her, it did—I mean your wife—she had, your wife, a notion that—she even said to me—and now she will!"

"There he is!" cried a voice belonging to a woman looming behind Rabbi Eizik-Dovid.

Sendrel recognized it as his wife's and turned white as chalk. Catching his breath, he clutched at Benjamin's coat with both hands to keep from falling off the bridge. Not that it mattered, he thought, because he was about to be split in two like a log.

"Just look at the lovely couple!" shrieked Sendrel's wife, pushing Rabbi Eizik-Dovid aside. "They can both go to the Devil! Wait until I get my hands on that worthless tramp. I'll teach him that there's a God, I will!"

"Come, calm down," urged Rabbi Eizik-Dovid. "What's

the rush? If you've waited this long, you can wait a little longer. A widow, thank God, you'll no longer be. And as for the rest, well, what is there to say, eh? A woman can't help being a woman. Just when you think she has a bit of brains, that's what she turns out to be. Because if we begin with the end of the story, why fret? Of course, he shouldn't have done it. Some things aren't done and there's a way to do everything! But since he did it, it's done, and since it's done, what are you doing? Forgive me if I talk to you like a mother, but you're acting just like a woman."

Rabbi Eizik-Dovid was just getting going, which usually happened in his case only after turning everything over backwards and forwards several times with pepper and onion, but by now there was a line of angry people at either end of the bridge, grumbling about the Jews who were blocking traffic in order to have themselves a chat. The bridge was so narrow that it could only be crossed in one direction at a time, and as the pedestrians at Sendrel and Benjamin's end began to surge past them, Rabbi Eizik-Dovid and Sendrel's wife were forced to retreat to the other side. Benjamin was the first to rally himself and say:

"Sendrel, what are we waiting for? We're standing here like the boy in the story who was tied to a table leg with a rope the other end of which was put in his mouth. This is the time to drop it and clear out!"

"As I'm a Jew, you're right!" answered Sendrel as gladly as a man released from irons. "Hurry, Benjamin, hurry, if you don't want to fall into her hands! This is no ordinary bridge. God's put it here just for us . . ."

Our two heroes made a quick getaway and were soon at the far end of town. Without further ado they took their packs and said farewell to Teterevke.

# 10

## HURRAH! THE LOST TRIBES!

"HEY, HEY, OUT of my way!" shouted a driver from the seat of his coach as he nearly ran into two women standing in the middle of the busiest street in Glupsk, both carrying baskets of foodstuffs—meat, radishes, onions, and garlic—under their arms. The two were exchanging confidences in voices that could be heard a mile away, each hastening along on opposite sides of the street, so that by the time they finished their conversation they were shouting operatically above the din of coaches, cabs, wagons, and carts piled high with firewood, which formed a long, impassable column of traffic.

"Hasya-Beile! Will I see you at the gypsy fortuneteller's tonight? I'll be there with my boyfriend, and he told me that yours will be there too. We'll have a grand time. Come on, you goose, you'll enjoy it! Won't you come, Hasya-Beile?"

"My missus, drat her, has given me the honor of making farfel and sourdough bread tonight, but I'll try to slip away. Please, though, Dobrish, not a word of it to anyone!"

"Listen here, Hasya-Beile! Your missus won't croak if she has to wait another hour for her dinner. If she gets hungry, tell her to eat worms. And Hasya-Beile, don't sift your flour so well, because all you'll have left is the bran. How much did you manage to pocket from your market money today?"

"The rascal! The rascal! Somebody grab that sneak! What the Devil does he think he's doing? He should be strung up from a lamppost!"

"Why, what happened, Hasya-Beile? What are you screaming for?"

"A thief, Dobrish! He very nearly made off with my basket. It's a lucky thing I had my eyes open."

"Then look up ahead, Hasya-Beile! What's that crowd doing there? There must be a fire. That's the second one today, and I'll bet it's not the last!"

"But there are no fire bells, Dobrish. We'd be hearing them if there was a fire."

"Wait, here comes Sima-Dvosse the market-woman, I'll ask her. Sima-Dvosse! Sima-Dvosse! What's all that commotion?"

"I don't know and I'm not sure I care to. Maybe Nehame-Nisa does. Nehame-Nisa, sweetheart! What are all those people standing in a circle for? Tell your ducks to pipe down, because I can't hear you. I'll bet Hodl will buy them all for the feast. Didn't you hear she gave birth this morning? Ooh, my, what fat ducks! There wasn't an egg to be had in the market today. What's going on there?"

"How should I know? I suppose it's the lost tribes. I heard someone shout something about them."

"What, lost tribes in Glupsk? Ai ai ai! We'd better go take a look!"

With a cry the women ran to join the circle. In it a large gang of drifters was hooting:

"Hurrah, sea monsters! Hurrah, basilisks! Hurrah, the lost tribes!"

The lost tribes were none other than our two heroes, Benjamin and Sendrel, who, shortly after the incident of the bridge, arrived in Glupsk and within a few weeks were quite famous. The town's leading Jews were as excited about them as they were about the local shoemaker who was discovered in those days to be a hidden miracle worker. First to come across the two was a pair of proper old ladies, Toltze and Treine, whose well-known habit it was to don their best Sabbath jackets and kerchiefs every evening and sally forth from town to greet the Messiah. One day as the sun went down, it fell to their happy lot to encounter our worthies, freshly arrived from Teterevke, on the hither side of the tollgate and to escort them into Glupsk. It did not take long for the old women to find out everything about the two strangers entrusted by fate to their care. Toltze and Treine exchanged wondering glances and poked each other smilingly in the ribs. "Well, Toltze?" "Well, Treine?" they whispered, yielding quickly to their premonition that the travelers were no ordinary mortals. So overcome with joy were they that, hearing of the two men's journey, they seemed to grow younger on the spot. "Well, Toltze?" "Well, Treine?" they whispered again, staring at the heaven-sent figures and nudging each other once more.

In the days that followed, Toltze darned the newcomers' socks while Treine patched their shirts and made new laces for their shoes, and both were as blissful as a pair of young brides. Nor were our heroes well received just by them. Where else but in Glupsk, indeed, could they have been so appreciated? Yea, get ye Glupskward, Jewish children! Why languish in loafery by the stoves of small-town synagogues when you can be in Glupsk, blast it all! There you will meet your true equals, your Toltzes, your Treines, and your thousands of other Jews, fine, reputable folk every one; there you will prosper and be made whole again; there you will find favor, there you will gain merit, there you will begin at last to live . . .

Glupskward ho and the Devil take the hindmost!

Here is Benjamin's description of the place:

"Arriving by the Teterevke Road, you must indulgently cross a large bog, then a second, and then the third and largest, into which, to put it baldly, empty the sewers and chamberpots of Glupsk, bringing with them all the town has to offer. Each day has its own items, colors, and smells and can easily be guessed by what comes along. If, for instance, you encounter an effluvium yellowed by scrubbing sand and mixed with fish scales, the heads and toes of chickens, animal hairs, and charred bits of hoof, you may, confident that it is a Friday, reach for your bucket and birch rod and run straight to the bathhouse. On the other hand, if floating your way is a solution of eggshells, onion peels, radish stems, herring tails, the gristle of calves' livers, and empty marrow bones, it is time to wish your fellow Jews a good Sabbath and hasten home to eat your weekly noodle pudding. Sundays, the tide slows to a bare trickle; now it carries bits of burned kasha, dried lumps of dough, torn dishrags, and an occasional scouring pad; the water carrier has not begun his weekly rounds and there is barely enough in the bilges of the barrels to wash out the Sabbath stew pots. And so it goes throughout the week, no two days of which bear the same sludge or stench.

"Once you have safely passed the slop-bogs, you will come, gentle reader, to a small mountain of debris that is the remains of a burned house. On top of it, looking like an itinerant preacher on his soapbox, generally stands a cow, serenely chewing her cud while staring bemusedly at the throng of Jews below running back and forth like drugged ants with their walking sticks, canes, and umbrellas. Now and then she lets out a bovine sigh or exhalation, as if in pity for the world, and also, alas, for her own wretched fate at having fallen into the clutches of such a people . . .

"Putting the burned house behind you, you may now proceed straight ahead, and if, as I most sincerely hope, you do not slip and break a leg on any of the treacherous cobblestones that lie somewhat oddly distributed, but rather regain your footing each time, you will reach a kind of square, in which you will find the true life of Glupsk. Indeed, if there is reason to call the Teterevke Road Glupsk's guts, this square can rightly be considered its heart, which beats without stopping day and night. Here are the shops with their shelves of goods, and especially, with their odds and ends of cloth, lace, ribbons, satins, and furs that are Glupsk's famous discount fabrics, so called because its tailors disdain to count them as the customer's when they are left over from what he has paid for. Around them noisily swarms a solid mass of Jews, pushing, pushed, and poked by carts and wagons; but although it is claimed by Glupsk's doctors that the average autopsy of your local Jew turns up at least one wagon shaft in his body, little credence can be put in their statistics, most of the town's medicine being practiced by its barber-surgeons.

"Among the familiar voices in the town square of Glupsk are those of its little ragamuffins, who go about shouting in a peculiar singsong: 'Hot kasha cakes! Hot pudding! Come and get it! Get your onions! Get your Jewish garlic!' Vying with them are the sounds of outdoor prayer, a group for which can always be found before sunset, while loudest of all are the cries on nights of the Sanctification of the Moon, when passersby are accosted with the call of 'Yes sir, come and bless 'er!' Porters, their bodies coiled in thick rope, wait for work; retired veterans stand about in their puttees and tattered greatcoats; rag ladies hawk old underclothes, caftans, jackets, and other wear; and in the midst of all this stands the town watchman, a Gentile munching on a piece of Jewish challah given him for snuffing out the Sabbath lights in houses and guarding its crumbs as zealously as if it were the Passover afikoman. Pickpockets are hard at work; out of nowhere springs a grimy, wild-haired beggar girl and shrieks in a practiced voice while grabbing your lapel, bawling as if she meant to kill you for your money; scamps run jeering after a madman in a crumpled cap who is crooning a sad ballad; and a young man stands by a chest with a peephole, into which Jews peer while he mimes and chants:

"'That's London that you're looking at . . . There goes the Pope in red breeches—see how people doff their hats . . . Here are Napoleon and his Frenchies fighting the Prussians. The Prussians are running like roaches! . . . And now see the Sultan with a fine lady in his carriage. The man holding the whip and reins is his grand vizier. No, the horses are rearing! The carriage has turned over! The Sultan has taken a spill! They're trying to free themselves . . . All right now, that's enough! How much do you expect for a copper farthing?'

"In the town square of Glupsk you may also see long rows of Jewesses sitting with baskets of garlic, cucumbers, cherries, gooseberries, currants, crab apples, Kol Nidre pears, and all sorts of other wares. Slightly beyond them is a tumble-down, windowless, doorless old shack, which the graybeards remember as once having been the barracks of Glupsk's single hussar; the whole town, they recall, turned out to see his wondrous spit-and-polish. Next to this shack, which is spoken of with the reverence due an ancient fortress, beneath a roof of moldy boards covered with rotting straw and rushes and supported by four crooked corner posts, sits Dvosye the greengroceress, surrounded by more baskets of her own. Before her is a heated pot, which she roosts on in winter like a hen on its eggs, rising only to blow new life into the coals or to retrieve a roasted potato.

"There is a very old legend about the Jews of Glupsk, which relates that they are descendants of the Israelites sent in ships by King Solomon to the Hindoo port of Ophir, where they traded for gold and other exotic things. For sundry reasons they remained there and opened shops and counting-houses, buying from the local Teutons, as the natives were called, at great discounts and selling to them at high profits, so that they prospered for long years. But in the end the wheel of fortune spun round and our merchants lost all and were forced to wander on. Some perished in the wilderness; others safely crossed the border and set out in ships, ultimately reaching the Fetidnelevka River, which in those days debouched into the sea. Up it they sailed until assaulted by a terrible storm; waves high as the sky battered the ships and swept their passengers ashore. Here they built a town and called it Glupsk.

"Our modern historians, whose erudition can build monuments from mustard seeds, have written volumes about this legend, demonstrating with a thousand clever arguments, in each case leading to different conclusions, that it contains a grain of truth. Among the proofs advanced by them are, first, the structure of Glupsk's houses, which, though oddly built, are in an ancient style going back thousands of years to the times when men lived in tents and caves. And yet while many a home in Glupsk resembles a burrow or the yurt of a Mongol, none looks quite like any other. If one leans this way, the next leans that way to spite it; if the first stands broadside to the street, the second stands lengthwise; if this one has steps, that one has a ladder designed for acrobats; if your patchwork roof slants crazily up, mine slopes wildly down. If you don't like it, you don't have to look.

"Architecturally, in a word, there is plentiful evidence of antiquity. Secondly, many of the customs of Glupsk that continue to be observed to this day bear clear traces of the heathens among whom the town's inhabitants lived long ago. Reading, writing, and arithmetic are practically unknown, in consequence of which all communal business is conducted without books and no accounts are given or expected.

"Thirdly, like the Hindoos, the inhabitants of Glupsk are divided into castes. First and foremost are the Muck-a-mucks, who hold sway over the rest; next come the Harum-Scarums, who fight their masters' battles in return for divers favors and the choicest cuts of meat; and after them are the Slipslops, who are the cause of many a downfall but always land on their feet. They consist of the Banca Ruptas, or merchant class, and the Januses, or priests, and are followed by the Untouchables, or common folk, who serve all the others, for which they are rewarded with the rheum, the ague, the catarrh, and the pox.

"Fourthly, there is the old coin that was found in Glupsk in the course of digging a ditch. On its badly effaced obverse side it is barely possible to make out what appears to be part of an apron attached to a stick, below which is an object resembling a mixing bowl full of human skull bones; the reverse side is practically blank, yet careful scrutiny reveals the letters YESHELG VEANAF in ancient Hebrew characters. This inscription has taxed the ingenuity of the scholars, each of whom has sought to decipher it in keeping with his views. Some are of the opinion that the Y and G of YESHELG are not letters at all, but rather remnants of illustrations, thus leaving the words ESHEL, 'a tamarisk tree,' and VEANAF, 'and a branch,' which explain the apron and stick. Others have disputed this, occasioning a fierce debate, the latest contribution to which is the striking theory that YESHELG is an acronym of *YEhudim SHE-ba'u Le-Glupsk,* 'Jews who came to Glupsk,' and VEANAF of *VEnityashvu Al NAhar Fetidnelevka,* 'and settled on the Fetidnelevka River.' The apron, stick, mixing bowl, and skull bones, it is claimed, are actually a ship with its mast, sail, and passengers. The author of this theory has written a lengthy book defending it, in which he proposes that the Fetidnelevka be drained in the hope of finding further evidence bearing on the origins of Glupsk's Jews. The Jews of Glupsk themselves, however, reject the idea, insisting that the waters muddied by their ancestors be left unclarified.

"Close to two score more slops-bogs are to be found in the

town itself, some large enough to contain meadows, and all linked by a series of underground passages to the source of the Fetidnelevka. At certain times of the year, especially before Passover, these erupt and flood the streets with such a deep current of filth that not even the tallest pedestrian can keep his hat clean.

"At night Glupsk is lit by a small streetlamp and patrolled by two watchmen. Those walking where the houses block the light often fall and break their necks, and there are frequent thefts while the watchmen watch each other. The conclusion reached by the Glupskians is that such protective measures are in vain and that what is fated will happen regardless of men's attempts to circumvent it."

And so, Benjamin concludes too, the best way to tour Glupsk is with one's eyes closed, trusting in the Lord and His angels to guide one safely through its streets. There's never a slip unforetold from God's lip, as the saying goes. Besides, Benjamin relates, "The only possession I had to guard was my prayershawl bag, which I left on a shelf in the synagogue, surely the safest place imaginable. If it was nevertheless stolen like everything else in Glupsk, this could only be because the Divine Will did not decree otherwise."

# 11

IN WHICH WE HEAR OF THE WONDERS
OF THE FETIDNELEVKA

THE FIRST TIME our heroes caught sight of the Fetidnelevka they were startled and amazed, for they had never seen such a river. Sendrel reckoned that it must be the largest in the world. He had never thought about rivers before, and this one, which looked a hundred times the size of Tuneyadevka's, was no joke. Indeed, Tuneyadevka was all Sendrel had to go by, and since he was not much on book knowledge, whatever he encountered for the first time seemed an unsurpassed marvel. Benjamin, on the other hand, being well-versed not only in the Seven Arts, but also in the four ancient rivers of Paradise, the three holy rivers of India, and any number of other flowing bodies, was not above managing a smile that said: "Yes, this is all very nice, but it's nothing compared to what's ahead . . ." The Fetidnelevka, he informed Sendrel, was a mere trickle next to the Jordan. Why, the Leviathan described in the Book of Job could swallow it in one gulp!

"Do you know what I've been thinking, Sendrel?" he asked one day, halting while deep in thought by the river's edge. "I've been thinking that we should continue our journey by water."

"God help you!" Sendrel gave a frightened start. "If our stream in Tuneyadevka, Benjamin, takes a life a year, just think of what this river must do. Have pity on us both, and on your wife and children!"

"It's not pity we should have, Sendrel, it's faith! Faith is the Jewish way. It was on faith that Jacob crossed the Jordan with but a stick, and it's on faith that a Jew opens a store with no stock. Not even the houses of Glupsk could stand without faith."

"But why must we have faith in water," asked Sendrel, "when we can just as well have faith on land?"

"For several reasons," answered Benjamin. "In the first place, because it's faster. The sooner we arrive, the better. For the moment you'll have to take my word for it, but every minute counts. Ah, Sendrel, I'm on fire to get there! It's all I think of—I'd give anything to be there already. If only I had wings and could fly . . . And in the second place, when Benjamin of Tudela set out on his voyage, he began by sailing down the Ebro. It says so in his book—and if that was the way to do it then, it's the way to do it now. He knew what he was about, I can promise you. When it comes to following the ancients, ours is not to reason why."

"Well now," said Sendrel, "that makes all the difference. As I'm a Jew, Benjamin, you explain it so well that I wouldn't stop at water. If your Benjamin of Tudela had ridden on a pitchfork, I'd choose pitchforks without thinking twice."

"And thirdly," Benjamin continued, "it won't hurt to start getting used to water now, before we have to cross the ocean. In fact, while we're finishing up our business in Glupsk it wouldn't be a bad idea to do some sailing. Look, there's a fellow over there with a fishing skiff! Hang it all, why don't we ask him to go for a spin?"

A few minutes later our two wanderers boldly boarded the skiff and embarked on the Fetidnelevka. At first they were rather nervous. Sendrel, indeed, trembled with fright; the boat had only to capsize and he would soon be at the bottom of the river with a real widow for a wife. Yet after a while he calmed down a bit, and as they sailed out into the current Benjamin said comfortingly:

"You're doing fine, Sendrel. Never mind if your head is spinning and you don't feel well. It's called seasickness and it's meant to happen on a first voyage. The second time will be better, you'll see. You won't feel a thing then."

From that day on our heroes often sailed on the river and came to enjoy it immensely. They grew so expert at it that crossing the ocean seemed like child's play. With Sendrel as his interpreter, Benjamin engaged the fisherman in conversation, drawing him out with overtures like: "Sendrel, ask the captain how far it is to the sea . . . Ask him if there are any islands on the way . . . Ask, Sendrel, what sort of people live on them . . . Now ask if there are Jews among them . . . What king do they pay tribute to? Are they ruled by Gentiles . . . ?" Or else he might begin: "Ask the goy, Sendrel, if he happens to have heard of Mount Nisbon and the heretic el-Torak . . . Ask him if he knows anything about the Ten Lost Tribes . . . Go ahead, maybe he does."

But although there was no end to Benjamin's queries, the smattering of Ukrainian that Sendrel had learned by his wife's side in the market was insufficient for such weighty matters. Haggling over onions, eggs, and potatoes was one thing; discussing learned subjects with a ship's captain was another; and as he squirmed, waved his hands, and worked himself into a sweat he was as sorry a sight as a dog trying to talk with its tail. God alone could have rescued him from the tight spot he was in, wedged between the fisherman, who spat and muttered angrily, and Benjamin, who kept peppering him with questions and staring at his mouth as if the answer were hiding there and needed only a good poke to come out.

*"Vin zahubleni zhidki vin pitaye?"* Sendrel might say, asking if their captain knew of any lost Jews.

*"Zahublenikh zhidkov ya zna Leibko, Shmulko,"* would come the answer, viz.: "Aye, two of them, lost and gone forever, Leibko and Shmulko."

*"Ni Leibko, ni, ni!"* Sendrel would expostulate. *"Zhidki* on Mount Nisbon."

"Explain to him what a mountain is, Sendrel," Benjamin would urge. "Go on, use your hands."

Sendrel would raise his hands and begin to draw a mountain; their captain would spit and wish them all the bad dreams in the world; and so they sailed on.

WRITING OF HIS voyages on the Fetidnelevka, Benjami
counted many wonders that have set the world astir. H
a few of them.

Once, while out on the river, Benjamin spied a gr
patch that he took to be a grassy island. He extended a leg a
was about to leap onto it when the fisherman grabbed him
from behind with a cry and flung him so powerfully back into
the skiff that he lay there in a stupor. Dimly he heard the boat
struggling to break free and slowly making headway. When he
recovered and asked what had happened, he was told that he
had been in great danger of drowning, because the green
patch was not an island but a glutinous sward put forth by the
Fetidnelevka. "Frankly," writes Benjamin, "I found this hard to
believe. True, there was a rank smell in the vicinity, but I had
never heard, or read in any book, of water sprouting a lawn.
Next it would be growing fruit trees! We had far more likely,
in my opinion, encountered the sea monster known as the
kraken, of which there is an excellent discussion in *The
Shadow of Eternity* that reads: 'This horrible great fish is covered all over with earth and grass and resembles a large island. Sailors catching sight of it have been known to mistake
it for a mountain on which they go ashore to cook their dinner; but feeling the heat from their fire, the kraken dives to
the nethermost depths and all aboard it are drowned.' In fact,
this constitutes a clear proof of the Glupskians' origins in
India, for the kraken is native to that land and must have mi-
grated to the Fetidnelevka in ancient times, its nature being to
swim after sailing ships."

Another time, as Benjamin stood gazing into the river, he
saw creatures with the faces of women. "For many years," he
says, "I had read about mermaids, always in ancient accounts
of unquestionable veracity. I had also heard of their joining
traveling circuses and being exhibited in peepshows, but this

was the first time that I had ever laid eyes on them myself. In my excitement, I pointed them out to our captain—who, however, turned around at that very moment and pointed to some washerwomen on a promontory above us. Over and over I pointed to the mermaids and over and over he pointed to the washerwomen, and since we did not understand each other's language I could not explain to him what I saw or get him to enlighten me."

Not far from shore and from Glupsk, Benjamin noticed a spot in the river where the water was oddly thick, in some places curdled like jelly and in others even more viscous. Large draughts of it were scooped by the water carriers, who went from house to house selling it. There it was mixed with ordinary barrel water and used to cook various dishes. "I tasted a number of these," relates Benjamin, "and more heavenly food I never have eaten. A simple pot roast thus prepared is a royal treat. I filled my pockets with this liquid and told Sendrel to save a bag of it, knowing that it would be useful when crossing the desert."

There came an afternoon that found our two heroes close to town and in a playful mood, laughing, joking, and regarding each as blissfully as a pair of newlyweds honeymooning in the country. What so gladdened their hearts? To what shall we ascribe the antic way they frolicked and sang as though deranged? The answer, dear reader, is that, if all went well, they were about to set out from Glupsk in the morning for the wide world.

Just then a wagon approached. In it were sitting two men, one holding the reins while the other lounged with his hat pushed back and a straw dangling from his mouth—always a sure sign that a Jewish brain is hard at work. The two Jews looked our merry pair over and stopped to chat. As usual, the first question was, "Well! Where might a Jew be from?" and the second, "And what might a Jew's name be?"

A long list of other queries followed, of the kind that Jews commonly put to each other upon being introduced. Our heroes only needed to be asked; in no time they were talking a blue streak. The two men exchanged smiles and whispers, and the straw chewer mused half aloud: "Yes, it just might work. And if it does, we'll clear a few coppers . . ."

The two turned to Sendrel and Benjamin. "You know what?" they said. "The town we come from would like a chance to host two fine fellows like you. Please, do us the honor—we won't take no for an answer! You have our word that you'll be wined, dined, and waited on hand and foot."

"Thank you kindly," replied Benjamin. "We would be only too happy to join you if we hadn't already made up our minds to head down the river."

"Begging your pardon," said the two Jews, "but we don't know what you're talking about. The Fetidnelevka a river? Why, it's nothing but a mudhole, a cesspool, a pisspot, a slops basin, a smelly, sticky, slimy, scurvy sewer! Our town is on the Dnieper, which runs right into the ocean. From there, God willing, you'll quickly reach your destination. Please don't be stubborn with us. Hop aboard and let's be off!"

"What do you think, Sendrel?" asked Benjamin. "Should we oblige these two gentlemen by accepting their offer of a ride?"

"What's it to me?" answered Sendrel. "If it's a ride you want, why should I care?"

Quicker than the shake of a lamb's tail our worthies were seated in the wagon, highly pleased to be so honored and promised such a fine reception. It was a jolly journey. The two Jews saw to Sendrel and Benjamin's every need, plying them

with food and drink as if they were new mothers in confine-
ment. It was more than either of them had ever dreamed of.
On the afternoon of the second day they arrived safely in
Dnieperovitsh. Their escorts brought them to lodgings in an
inn and ordered them a fine dinner.

"We can see that you're tired from your trip," they said.
"Get a good night's sleep, and tomorrow, God willing, you'll
rise feeling fresh. We'll bring you to some important people
and put in a good word for you. Once they take you under
their wing, you'll have nothing more to worry about; all your
needs will be provided. Good night!"

"Good night and sleep well!" answered our heroes. And
they quickly said their bedtime prayers, patted their full
stomachs, yawned, scratched themselves a bit, and fell into a
sweet slumber.

# 12

### IN WHICH OUR HEROES ARE TAKEN
### TO THE CLEANERS

"HELP! I WANT TO confess my sins before I die!" cried Sendrel
in his sleep, his strangled voice waking Benjamin.

Benjamin jumped blearily out of bed, splashed water over
his hands, quickly said the day's first blessing, and ran to see
what the matter was. Outside the dawn was breaking; the
only sounds were the snores in the room, each in its own reg-
ister. One blared like a trumpet, another skittered like a lute;
this one was short as a semiquaver, that one rose in three measures to a percussive snort; and still another performed a solo
nose concerto for the bedbugs of Dnieperovitsh, who were
banqueting on the sleepers. The little cannibals had come

from all over the city to pasture in this dowdy boardinghouse, where they were served all the Jewish blood they could suck.

Indeed, your Jew arriving in Dnieperovitsh did so with the knowledge that his only hope of departing again lay in bribing its bedbugs. "Step right up, you Dnieper cooties!" he all but called to them upon bedding down at night. "Dig in, drink up, and the Devil take you!"

"What are you screaming for, Sendrel?" asked Benjamin, going over to his friend. "Did a bug take a bite out of you? They kept me up all night. In fact, I just fell asleep."

"Ow! Quick, let's get out of here!" shouted Sendrel, still half-asleep.

"For goodness' sake, Sendrel, what's the matter? It's a bug, after all, not a man. How big a bite can it take?"

For a moment or two Sendrel stared at Benjamin bewilderedly. Then he rubbed his eyes and sighed:

"Ah, what a terrible dream I had! I only hope nothing comes of it."

"Tsk! What man doesn't dream?" replied Benjamin. "I had a dream too. In it an ogre galloped up to me and said: 'Are you Benjamin of Tuneyadevka? Please be so kind as to come with me, because Alexander the Great is camped nearby with his army and is eager to have a word with you.' The ogre took off on the run and I followed close behind. Suddenly I heard a voice call: 'Why, you're running like the wind! I can't catch up with you.' I turned around—and there was Alexander. 'Your Excellency!' I cried, seizing his hand and squeezing it as tight as I could. Just then there was such a horrible stink that I thought I was going to faint. I opened my eyes and in my hand was a crushed bedbug. Feh! Come, Sendrel, spit three times, I'm telling you, and forget your dream. What was it about?"

"Tfu! Tfu! Tfu!" spat the trusting Sendrel and began to relate his nightmare.

"I dreamed that I was walking down a long, long street. All of a sudden someone pounced on me from behind, threw me in a sack, and started to make off with me. I was carried a long ways until the sack was opened and I was given such a smack in the face that two of my teeth fell out. 'That's just the down payment,' I was told. 'The rest will come later.' I looked and saw my wife in a fur cap, foaming at the mouth and with hellfire in her eyes. 'You wait, my little man,' she said with a nasty laugh. 'I'm going to take the poker to you and teach you that there's a God.'

"Well, she went to get the poker, and I took to my heels and ran until I came to a tavern. It was dark and slippery inside, without a soul in sight, and I lay down in a corner, shut my eyes, and fell asleep. As I was sleeping, along came my great-grandfather Sendrel, may he rest in peace, looking sad and teary-eyed. 'Sendrel, my boy,' he said to me, 'get up. If you value your life, Sendrel, rise from your sleep, because wherever you look you're in danger!'

"I tried to get up, but I couldn't. It was as if I were being held down. I put my hands to my head—and there was a bonnet! I wasn't Sendrel anymore, I was a woman, without a trace of a beard, with a bodice over my middle . . . and the way it was hurting me there shouldn't happen to a Jew. 'You'll be all right,' I heard someone say. 'It's always hardest with a first child.' 'Mister, please!' I screamed. 'It's too much for me. I'm going to faint.' 'The best charm to help you get through this,' he said, 'is a good punch in the neck,' and he hauled off and gave me one, two, three rabbit punches, telling me: 'This is for what you've done! This is for what you're doing! This is for what you'll do!' Then he turned and disappeared.

"Afterwards, I lay there until, with God's help, I made myself rise and run to the door. The door was locked. I knocked and knocked but it did no good. And then all at once the door opened. I stepped out and was snatched by a band of thieves, who brought me to a cave and wanted to slit my throat with a slaughtering knife. That's when I yelled for help. There you have it, Benjamin, my whole dream. I only pray it doesn't come true."

"Spit again three times, Sendrel," Benjamin counseled, "and forget all about it. And you can get up now, because it's already day, and say a chapter of Psalms."

With another sigh Sendrel rose from his bed, washed his hands, said the blessing, put on his robe, and took out his Yiddish Psalter. Opening it to the Tenth Psalm, he began to recite in a doleful voice:

> Why hidest Thou, O Lord, from me,
> Far from my adversity?

The chant continued, growing more plaintive as it described the wicked oppressor:

> He lurketh in his ambuscade,
> From there the innocent to raid;
> Stalking with his eyes poor men,
> Like a lion in its den;
> Casting them into his net,
> Thinking that God doth forget.

By the time Sendrel was through, it was broad daylight and everyone had risen. A samovar as large as a cauldron was steaming on the table and all sat down to tea. After drinking a hot glass of it, Benjamin and Sendrel felt better. The same room that had been a dormitory and a refectory now became a chapel. Sleeves were rolled up and Jewish arms—hairy, smooth, thin, fat, swarthy, pale, all conceivable shades and

shapes of them—were bared for phylactery straps. Prayershawls were donned and everyone had a good pray, most of all
our heroes, who clamored and gestured like such woebegone
Jews entreating their Father in Heaven that they finished long
after the others. At the service's end there was strong grog
for everyone, guzzled with much smacking of the lips. Their
noses and cheeks as bright as red currants, all wished each
other a long and good life and invoked God's much-needed
mercy on His people. Eyes glittered; bosoms heaved; and
many a glass was drained in the conviction that the quicker its
descent, the nobler the swallower's.

One such Jewish aristocrat soon went off into town and
lingered there for several hours. When he returned beaming,
he was given a searching look by his sidekick and both seemed
highly content. They ordered dinner, washed their hands like
good Jews, and even checked to see if the kitchen was kosher
enough, and asked our heroes to join them for a bite. Their
high spirits continued at the table, where they praised the
innkeeper's wife for her cooking, which they consumed with
great relish while conversing about the Jewish Problem—it
being high time, they said, that the Jews take themselves in
hand and put an end to their sorry situation. Why, no people
was more gifted—there was no head like a Jew's—what
couldn't a Jew do if he put his mind to it! All of the world's
great inventions, such as the telegraph, the railroad, and other
such things had been discovered by Jews long ago . . . and yet
these were mere trifles, they were not the main thing at all,
which was—which was—the Jewish soul!

And with that Benjamin and Sendrel's companions began
lambasting the heretics, the modern Jewish intellectuals, blast
them all, and especially the new Jewish schools, in which children were taught every manner of abomination without even
a hat on their heads. Why, before long it would be easier to

find a Jew to write a business letter in Russian than to read a prayer in Hebrew. A fine world that would be!

From this the two Jews turned to our heroes' expedition. "We pray and hope," they said, "that God fulfill your endeavors, which are dear to our hearts." Benjamin was in seventh heaven, all the more so for being slightly sozzled. Neither fire nor water, he assured his listeners, could turn him back from his path.

The time came to rise from the table. "Listen here, Reb Benjamin, Reb Sendrel," the two men said heartily. "Simple folk like us have an old custom of lubricating our bones in a bathhouse at a journey's end. You can get a shave and a haircut there too—we promise you, you'll feel like new. Afterwards we'll attend to your business and you'll see it will all work out dandily. Oh, it's a bit old-fashioned, we know, a bathhouse is—the heretics don't think it's genteel—but we're not your la-di-da types. What was good enough for our grandfathers is good enough for us!"

What Jew can resist a bathhouse? Let the peasant have his tavern and the duck its pond; such attachments do not amount to the hundredth part of what is felt for his sweat-bath by a Jew. Here lies the source of his religion—the most sacred of his emotions—the secret of his intimate life. No Jewish soul would consider crawling into a womb without the prospect of a bath at birth. It is the omphalos, the infundibulum, linking heaven and earth, its stokers, scrubbers, and swabbers the midwives of this sublunary incarnation. Nor would that second soul, the Sabbath spirit, deign enter a Jew who is not steamed and rinsed once a week to keep him from going as stale as a crust of old bread. Regard him stepping out of the bathhouse on a Friday. He glows; looks years younger; has the Jewish spark back in his eyes; tingles with keen expectation; twitches his nose at the scent of the stuffed fish and carrot stew wafted mouthwateringly his way; sings, warbles, carols like a nightingale; basks like a pampered child; effervesces as though already halfway through heaven's gates. Truly, the bathhouse is the Jew's fatherland and in it alone does he inhabit a free country where every man has the right to his own thoughts and can reach the highest rung, that is, the uppermost bench. There, for a brief hour, his downtrodden soul casts off its burden of sorrows. Where would he be without it?

The idea of a bath, therefore, appealed to our heroes greatly, and without further ado they set out and soon arrived with their two new friends. Having imagined a bathhouse such as they were used to, a grimy, gloomy structure entered from the bottom of a dark alley by means of a rickety plank, they stared in wonderment at the handsome three-story building located on a main street. "Why, you're gaping like country boys," their hosts bantered. "Come on inside, it's even grander there."

Stepping into the lobby, our heroes were met by a gleaming floor covered with carpets. Convinced that they had entered a magic castle straight out of *The Arabian Nights,* they felt sure that a princess would soon appear to welcome them to a world of delight.

It was not, though, a princess that appeared but a bemedaled soldier, who politely asked them to undress. "Please do as he says," said the two Jews to Sendrel and Benjamin. "We'll go ahead and pay, and then we'll all enjoy a good sweat."

Our worthies took off their things and stood holding them with their packs, intending to steam them in the bath. They were not traveling with large wardrobes and had for weeks not changed their clothes, which naturally itched a great deal and needed a dry-cleaning. The soldier, however, insisted on taking these from them and ushering them into a bench-lined room with a table, around which sat several well-dressed men. Although they looked everywhere, neither Benjamin nor Sendrel could detect a hearth for the red-hot stones on which water was poured to make steam.

"Is this the *zhidovski banya?*" asked Sendrel, prompted by a hard jab from Benjamin.

A man rose from the table, went over to have a look at our naked heroes, who were all skin and bones, and addressed them in proper Russian.

"Come, Sendrel, what's he saying?" asked Benjamin.

"I'll be blamed if I understood a word," replied Sendrel with a shrug. "The Devil knows what language he thinks he's talking. All I could make out was something about a billet."

"You puddinghead!" exclaimed Benjamin. "A *bilyet* is a ticket in Russian. This man is the bathhouse attendant and won't let us in without one. Tell him our two friends have already paid."

"*Yak-zhe, pani, teya zhidki . . . ,*" began Sendrel, breaking off as helplessly in the middle as if he had lost his voice.

"*Bilyet, pani,* it's quite simple, two *zhidki,* they've gone ahead, *zaplatil,* we're all paid up!" said Benjamin, making things perfectly clear.

The man motioned with his hand and they were taken to another room, in which they were made to sweat indeed.

WHEN SENDREL AND Benjamin were led back out into the street, they truly looked like new men. Besides boasting shaves and haircuts that had sheared off their beards and ear- locks, they had great drops of perspiration on their foreheads, beady, vaporish expressions, and hot-and-cold flashes that made them shake all over. A detachment of soldiers surrounded them and the sky above them was darkened by clouds. Now and then lightning glittered, accompanied by rumbles of thunder that made the two of them shiver even harder. Soon a wild wind began to blow, carrying dust whirls, refuse, straw, dead leaves, and bits of paper that swirled higher and higher in a devilish dance. Herds of cattle, hastened back from pasture, ran nervously bellowing through the streets as if chased by a pack of hungry wolves. One might have thought that, fed up with the sinful earth, the Lord was casting His bolts of wrath on it.

Just then there was a frightful thunderclap and it began to pour, the torrents of rain quickly mingling with the sweat and bitter tears of our hapless heroes.

Alas, Benjamin and Sendrel had had no inkling that the greatest dangers are not those posed in the wilderness by snakes, scorpions, and other wild creatures, but those of civilization. And no civilized age has been more savage than our own, in which Jew hunts Jew,

> Stalking with his eyes poor men,
> Like a lion in its den,

and impressing helpless souls into the Czar's army so that others should not have to serve in it. Too late did our heroes realize that they were in the wilderness already, with beasts of prey all around them, none more cruel than the two ogres who had sold them into military service.

# 13

IN WHICH OUR HEROES BECOME SOLDIERS

THE DESPERATE PLIGHT of our poor heroes being easily imaginable, we shall forbear to describe it in detail. At first they were too confounded to grasp what had happened to them. Everything was totally strange—the soldiers, the barracks, the language, each single order they were given. Their greatcoats hung on them like sacks; their tunics bulged like bodices; their caps fell over their ears like bonnets. One might have thought one was watching two actors in a skit, mugging and mocking army life. Pity the poor rifle that fell into their hands, for it resembled an oven poker. The way they stumbled about the drill grounds was pure comedy.

And yet though our worthies were most reluctant soldiers, is there anything a man cannot get used to? Even the caged bird develops an appetite and begins to hop about and sing as if its little world were an expanse of fields and dales. Our Sendrel in particular adjusted to his condition. He watched the other soldiers at their drills and learned to ape them so successfully that it was a pleasure to see him snap to attention like a fiddle string, stick his neck out like a crane, and strut and puff his cheeks like a turkey until he finally tripped over his own feet.

Benjamin was another story. Like one of those migrating birds that take poorly to captivity, he stopped eating and drinking and thought only of escaping his bars. His expedition, which had gnawed away at him until he left wife and children for it, was by now such second nature that it fluttered and pecked incessantly inside him, crying: "Fly on, Benjamin! Fly on!"

And so the winter went by and our Benjamin chafed at the bit.

One sunny day after Passover, as Sendrel was practicing drilling, Benjamin approached him and said:

"I swear, Sendrel, what a baby you are, playing soldier like a schoolboy! What are you accomplishing? How can a married man, and a Jew to boot, spend all his time making right-faces and left-faces? What difference does it make?"

"How should I know?" answered Sendrel. "If it's right or left they want, let it be right or left. What's it to me?"

"And our expedition, you nit, I suppose you've forgotten all about it! Our expedition, our journey . . . basiliks, Minotaurs, rocs!"

"Hup! Hup! Hup! Hup!" said Sendrel, stamping his legs.

"Why, it's pathetic, Sendrel! You should be ashamed of yourself. Tell me, my soldier boy: are we going to travel on or not?"

"For my part," answered Sendrel, "we can start out the minute they let us."

"But what do I care about them? And what do they want with us?" exclaimed Benjamin. "I ask you, Sendrel, by all that's holy: if the enemy attacks, God forbid, are you and I going to stop him? Do you think that telling him a thousand times, 'You better go away or I'll say boo,' will make any impression? We'll be lucky to get out of it alive. The way I see it, the army should be happy to be rid of us. I myself heard our sergeant say that we're a nuisance he'd gladly send to the Devil. And really, what use to them are we? The fact is that it was a mismatch to begin with. The Jews who sold us down the river must have said that we were a pair of tough old troopers. Is it our fault if they tricked the army as rottenly as they tricked us? No, it's the fault of the low-down, lying Jews!"

"Well then, Benjamin," asked Sendrel, "what do you propose we do?"

"I propose," replied Benjamin, "that we push on with our expedition. A discharge, that's what I propose! There's neither rhyme nor reason to keep us here. And if you're afraid the army won't agree, I have a simple solution: we'll go without asking permission. Whose business is it anyway? There's no need for a formal farewell."

"I'm sure you're right," said Sendrel. "We didn't kiss anyone goodbye when we left home a year ago either."

Subsequently, our heroes turned their minds to their journey and began to plot their escape. Benjamin felt the call of the beyond: he was like a bird in spring that is impelled to reach its roosting grounds. So absorbed was he in his thoughts that he paid no attention to his whereabouts. He forgot to salute his officers, whose orders went in one ear and out the other, and winced no more at the blows given him than if they had landed on someone else. His expedition was the one thing on his mind, which had already flown far ahead of him.

Late one night, when the soldiers in the barracks were sound asleep, Benjamin tiptoed to Sendrel's cot and asked in a whisper:

"Sendrel, are you ready?"

Sendrel nodded, gripped Benjamin's coattails, and followed him noiselessly outside.

A warm breeze was blowing. Tufts of black and brownish-blue cloud floated overhead, one after another, like thousands of laden wagons on their way to some heavenly fair. The moon, like a busy caravan conductor, moved beside this long train, peering out from time to time to survey it before withdrawing again behind a cloudy, pitch-black curtain. Our heroes slipped across the dark yard and quietly reached the

fence, which was easily scaled with the help of a pile of logs.
Suddenly Sendrel gave himself a slap and whispered in his
friend's ear:

"Ah, Benjamin, I forgot the bag! We had better go back
for it."

"Not on your life!" declared Benjamin. "Turning back is
not for us. If God has decided to help us, He'll help us to a
new bag too."

"I now realize," Sendrel said, "what my great-grandfather,
may he rest in peace, meant when he warned me in my dream
of danger everywhere. I only hope his merit sees us through.
What a fine, no-nonsense Jew he was! My great-grandmother, may she rest in peace, used to say that he . . ."

But before Sendrel could tell Benjamin what his great-
grandmother said about his great-grandfather, they heard the
steps of a sentry. Holding their breaths, they lay hugging the
ground by the fence, beside which they looked like two large
rags.

The rags waited for all to be still again, came to life, and
crawled away from the fence on hands and legs, avoiding the
sentries and eventually reaching a street. There they rested,
regarding each other with bright eyes.

"My great-grandmother, may she rest in peace," continued
Sendrel when he had caught his breath, "used to say that my
great-grandfather always wanted to visit the Land of Israel.
On his deathbed he sat up and announced: 'If I haven't had the
good fortune, I'm sure that a child of mine will.' Something
tells me, Benjamin, that he meant me. May my words go
straight to God's ears!"

But these were not the ears they went to. They were
hardly out of Sendrel's mouth when a voice called out in
Russian: "Who goes there?" And no answer being forthcom-
ing, it came closer and asked again.

The foolish moon had chosen that exact moment to stick its head out from a cloud, casting its light on our worthies—who, their hearts in their boots, found themselves facing their sergeant. And a very angry sergeant he was, with an oath for each of their ancestors and a pair of hot-tempered hands.

A few minutes later our heroes were in the brig.

Words cannot describe their sufferings there. They grew so lean and haggard that they hardly looked like men. Sendrel at least was able to sleep and thus flee for a while from his sorrows, sometimes aided by pleasant dreams. His great-grandfather, indeed, took to appearing in them often and staying to chat. He always brought a gift with him: once a bow and arrow, another time a toy sword, still another a Purim rattle. Pinching Sendrel's cheeks, he would say with a smile: 'Here you are, you little rascal! Have yourself some fun. Go ahead, bing! bang! biff!' . . . Once he came with a Hanukkah top and sat down to play with his favorite grandchild. Sendrel played and played, won a whole farthing, and went about feeling good all that day. But it was only a dream, you say? And this world of ours, is it not a dream too?

Benjamin, however, did not sleep well at all. He was like a pot about to boil over. Through the window he could see the life-giving sun, the gloriously blossoming trees, the green grass growing all around. Men hurried back and forth and birds flew free in the sky. Now was the time for wandering! In his aggravation he could have jumped up and down, torn his hair, run around in circles crying bitterly: "Help! What have I done to them? And what do they want from me? Won't somebody—anybody—help?"

# 14

A FEW DAYS later a full complement of officers was gathered in regimental headquarters. The general was there with the colonel, while by the door stood two soldiers hanging their heads and looking like a pair of mice fished from a pitcher of sour milk. The officers took a minute to observe them and then conversed with faint smiles among themselves.

"Listen, Sendrel," whispered one of the soldiers while this confab was going on, "even if they kill me, I've got to tell them the whole truth. I can't keep it in any longer."

"For my part, Benjamin," replied the second soldier, "you can tell them whatever you like. If it's the truth you want, why should I care?"

"Are you the two men who were absent without leave from the barracks at night?" asked the general sternly. "Do you know what the punishment for such an infraction is?"

"Yes, sir, *vasha blagarodya*, sir!" answered Benjamin, launching his defense half in Yiddish and half in a broken Russian that would have made even Heikel the Stammerer of Tuneyadevka bury himself six feet deep.

With a wave of his hand, the general turned away to hide his laughter. The colonel relieved him and said:

"You two are guilty of a serious offense and deserve to be punished severely."

*"Vasha blagarodya!"* At long last the pot boiled over—and this time entirely in Yiddish. "I see that kidnapping men in broad daylight and selling them like chickens in the market is permitted, but that when the same men seek to free themselves, they're guilty of a crime! If that's the upside-down

world we live in, I don't know what right and wrong are. Suppose you were walking along one fine day and someone stuffed you into a sack, wouldn't you do all you could to get out of it? I tell you, this whole thing has been a cruel hoax. It's all the fault of those Jews and the bill of goods they sold you!

"We wish to make an official statement. Go ahead, Sendrel, speak up! Why are you standing there like a clod? Don't be afraid to tell them the truth, by God! We hereby declare, the two of us, that we are, have been, and always will be ignorant of all military matters; that we are, God be praised, married men with other things on our minds than your affairs, which are totally alien to us; and that we cannot possibly be of any use to you, who have every reason to discharge us!"

Benjamin was speaking the plain truth. Discharging him and Sendrel had long been the army's ambition. The way our heroes talked, gawked, squawked, and walked had made the officers of the regiment, who more than once were reduced by them to stitches, realize from the start what manner of men they were. The whole purpose of the present court-martial, indeed, was to have them medically reexamined. This, with God's help, they were, with results that caused much hilarity. "Well?" asked the general after the doctor had finished talking with our Tuneyadevkans. The doctor put a finger to his head and twisted it in a time-honored gesture.

The officers conferred, filled out a piece of paper, and handed our two heroes their discharge. "And now be off," they told them, "and let this be the last of you."

Benjamin bowed smartly and turned to go. Sendrel clicked his heels like a soldier and marched after him in perfect step.

## An Epilogue by Mendele the Book Peddler

While I was engaged in bringing to the public the adventures of Benjamin the Third, of which I have thus far, with God's help, issued this first volume, it was reported in the newspapers that our Benjamin has set out once more with a body of explorers for the far climes and archipelagos beyond the Mountains of Darkness. The details are as follows.

Recently, a treatise entitled *The Torah Upheld* (Right Mind Press, Jerusalem) appeared in the Holy Land. In it the authors declared:

"The Almighty having lately chosen to reveal to us the source of the Sambatyon; and this precious river, which by ceasing its torrential flow on the Sabbath proves the divine origin of the Day of Rest, now lying within reach; it behooves us to hasten to the defense of God's brazenly mocked Law . . . by founding the Torah Exploration Society to mount an expedition thither and back. We therefore appeal to all fellow God-fearers to assist the Society's efforts by either joining the expedition or helping to defray its costs, every man as he sees fit. The expenses are great: travel documents must be obtained; provisions must be purchased; and arrangements must be made for daily prayers to be said on the travelers' behalf. The expedition is open to ten volunteers."

No sooner did this notice come to his attention than Benjamin took Dame Sendrel, his prayershawl, his phylacteries, his walking stick, and his knapsack and hastened to join the right-minded explorers. At present he is marching at their head through a fearful wilderness and doing battle with basilisks, cockatrices, and the despotic Prester John and el-Torek.

He has my heartfelt blessings. May God bring him safely home again so that I may publish the tidings of his second journey for all the tribes of Israel to read.

# GLOSSARY

## Part I: Translations of Ukrainian and Russian Phrases

315/ *Nu, zhidka, a shtsho, troshki lipshi?* "Well, Jew, are you a little bit better?"

316/ *Troshki tebi lipshi?* "Do you feel a bit better?"

316/ *Lipshi.* "Better."

316/ *Ribi moi.* Exclamation that is roughly equivalent to "Oh, my God."

316/ *Izvidko ti, zhidka?* "Where are you from, Jew?"

316/ *Ti iz Tuneyadevki? Kazhi-zhe shtsho ti vitarashtshil na meni otshi i glyanish yak shilani. Alye mozshe ti take i shilani. Trastse tvoi materi.* "You're from Tuneyadevka? Do tell me why you're staring at me like a madman. Or maybe you *are* crazy. Damn it!"

316/ *Ya ub Tuneyadevka.* "I'm from Tuneyadevka" [garbled].

316/ *Tsharka vodka.* A small glass of vodka.

316/ *Zhidki hallah.* "Jewish challah" [i.e., braided bread].

316/ *Ti iz dobri zhidka.* "You're one of the good Jews."

316/ *Tshoyesh skilke khotshes za pivan? Za tsibuli?* "Listen, how much do you want for the rooster? For the onions?"

316/ *Mozshe mayesh kartofli, yaytsi?* "Maybe you have potatoes, eggs?"

334/ *Dobry dyen! Kozhi no tshelovitsche kudi dorogi Eretz-Yisro'eyl?* "Good afternoon. Can you tell me the way to the Land of Israel?"

334/ *Shtsho? . . . "Yaki Yisro'eyl? Nye batshil ya Yisro'eyl."* "What? . . . What Israel? I've never seen Israel."

334/ *Nye, nye.* "No, No."

334/ *Kudi dorogi Errrretz-Yisro'eyl.* "What's the way to the Laaaand of Israel?"

370/ *Vin zahubleni zhidki vin pitaye?* "Do you know of any lost Jews?"

370/ *Zahublenikh zhidkov ya zna Leibko, Shmulko.* "I know the Jews who were lost, Leib and Shmuel."

370/ *Ni Leibko, ni, ni!* "Not Leib, no, no!"

381/ *Zhidovski banya.* Jewish bathhouse.

381/ *Yak-zhe, pani, teya zhidki . . .* "Well, sir, those Jews . . ."

388/ *Vasha blagarodya.* "Your Honor."

## Part II: Definitions of Terms

**Afikoman:** the matzo that is eaten at the end of the Passover seder.

**Akdomes:** Hymn recited by Ashkenazic Jews on the first day of Shavuos.

**Bershad-wove "Four-corner" weskit:** See *Talis kotn.*

**Breviaries (tekhines):** Women's prayerbooks, written in Yiddish.

**Bubba's Book o' Wives' Tales (bobe mayses):** Fairy tales, often confused with the sixteenth-century Yiddish *Bovo bukh.*

**Challah:** Braided bread traditionally prepared for Sabbath eve.

**Crimean War:** Fought chiefly in the Crimea, 1853–56; Britain, France, Turkey, and Sardinia defeated Russia.

**Cymbal:** Hammer dulcimer played in Jewish folk music.

**Days of Awe:** The period from Rosh Hashanah to Yom Kippur.

**East-wall representation (mizrach):** Decorated wall-plaque or tapestry hung on the east wall of a house, inscribed with the Hebrew word *mizrach.*

**Fastday lamentations (kinot):** Lamenting elegies, read on the Ninth of Av (see *Tisha b'Av*), in addition to the Book of Lamentations, mourning the destruction of the Temple in Jerusalem.

**Fast of Av:** Fast on the Ninth of Av (see *Tisha b'Av*).

**Fast of Tammuz:** Fast on the seventeenth day of Tammuz, commemorating the capture of Jerusalem by the Babylonians and beginning a somber three-week period prior to the Ninth of Av.

**Feast of Tabernacles** See *Sukkoth.*

**First Candle:** See *Hanukkah.*

**Feast of Weeks:** See *Shavuos.*

**Four Questions:** The Four Questions asked early in the Passover seder.

**Glupsk:** Fictional place bearing a name that suggests it is a Town of Fools; based on the actual town of Berdichev, where Abramovitsh resided in the 1860s.

**Golem:** Artificial human being, created out of clay and magically brought to life.

**Goniff:** Thief.

**Goodspells (heyelekh, kameyelekh):** Amulets, charms.

**Haggada:** Narrative of the exodus from Egypt, read at home during the seder ceremony on Passover Eve.

**Hanukkah:** Holiday commemorating the victory of the Hasmoneans over the Greeks and the rededication of the Temple in 165 B.C.E.

**Heder:** Traditional Jewish school for young boys, prior to study at a yeshiva.

**Hoshanna Rabbah:** Seventh day of the holiday Sukkoth.

**Jethro's Portion:** Exodus 18-20. The Torah portion read in the synagogue in the month of Shevat, corresponding to February.

**Kabtsansk:** Fictional place with a name that derives from the Hebrew word *kabtsan,* meaning "beggar"; hence, Town of Beggars or Paupersville.

**Kaddish:** Prayer recited at different points in synagogue service; traditionally spoken by sons in memory of deceased parents.

**Kitl:** Man's white linen robe, traditionally worn on the Days of Awe, on Passover Eve, and on other occasions.

**Kosher meat tax:** Tax levied by a Jewish community to cover the cost of rabbinical supervision in the ritual slaughter of animals.

**Mezuzah:** Ritual container affixed to the doorposts of Jewish houses, containing the "Shema" prayer, "Hear, O Israel . . ."

**Mikve** (Yiddish) or **mikveh** (Hebrew): Ritual bath.

**Month of Elul Penitences:** Penitential prayers in anticipation of the Days of Awe during the following month.

**Ninth of Av (Tisha b'Av):** Fast day commemorating the destruction of the Temple in Jerusalem.

**Parish Corporation (kahal):** Jewish community, as guided by its leading citizens.

**Penitential prayers (selichot):** Verses based on biblical poetry that are recited on fast days, asking forgiveness for sins.

**Pentateuch:** The Five Books of Moses.

**Phylacteries (tefillin):** Small leather cases, containing a parchment inscribed with biblical verses, traditionally affixed to the forehead and left arm of men during weekday morning prayers.

**Pievke:** Fictional town's name resembling the Russian word for "leech."

**Poser** (*kashia,* Aramaic; *kashe,* Yiddish): A difficulty in a Talmudic passage; by extension, in Yiddish, a question.

**Prayershawl (talis):** Four-cornered garment traditionally worn by Jewish men during morning prayers.

**Purim:** Holiday that celebrates the rescue of the Jews from the Persian Haman.

**Ram's horn (shofar):** Horn that is sounded on Rosh Hashanah and Yom Kippur.

**Rashi script:** Hebrew typeface used in the printing of the biblical commentary by Rashi, Rabbi Solomon ben Isaac (1040–1105).

**Reb:** Term conveying respect, similar to the English "Mr."

**Rebbe:** Hasidic leader, as distinguished from a non-Hasidic rabbi (**rov**); in other contexts, a teacher.

**River Sambatyon:** Mythical river that flows somewhere beyond the "Mountains of Darkness."

**Scripboxes:** Black leather boxes containing portions of the Pentateuch written on parchment. Fastened to leather straps, they are bound on the arm and the head during the morning prayer; on the Ninth Day of Av, during the afternoon prayer.

**Shammes:** Sexton; synagogue caretaker.

**Shavuos** (Yiddish) or **shavuoth** (Hebrew): Feast of Weeks, or Pentecost, celebrating the wheat harvest. Traditionally associated with the giving of the Torah on Mount Sinai.

**Shema:** Prayer that begins, "Hear, O Israel, the Lord our God, the Lord is one." Declaration of God's unity and providence.

**Sheol:** Biblical phrase referring to the realm of the dead.

**Shorabor:** Legendary wild ox to be eaten by the righteous after the coming of the Messiah.

**Shul:** Synagogue.

**Simchas Torah** (*Simhath torah,* Hebrew, or *simkhes toyre,* Yiddish): Holiday after Sukkoth, celebrating the completion of the annual cycle of Torah readings.

**Standing benediction (amidah):** Eighteen blessings recited silently at each of the daily synagogue services.

**Sukkah:** A booth in which Jews are traditionally expected to dwell and eat their meals during the week of Sukkoth.

**Sukkoth:** Festival of Booths, commemorating the tabernacles inhabited by the Israelites in the wilderness, after the Exodus.

**Talis:** Prayer shawl, with knotted fringes on the four corners, traditionally worn by Jewish men during morning prayers.

**Talis kotn** ("small talis"): A rectangular cloth traditionally worn by Jewish men under the shirt, with knotted fringes on the four corners.

**Tekhines:** Women's prayerbooks, written in Yiddish.

**Third Feast** (*shaleshudes,* Yiddish): Late-afternoon meal on the Sabbath.

**Tisha b'Av:** Fast day commemorating the destruction of the Temple in Jerusalem.

**Tsviyachich:** Fictional town bearing a name that suggests it is a place of hypocrisy.

**Tu b'Shevat:** Festival of trees on the fifteenth day in the month of Shevat, six weeks after Hanukkah.

**Tuneyadevka** (from Russian *tuneyadetz,* "parasite"): Abramovitsh's fictional Town of Idlers, Parasitesville.

**Yosifon's history:** Popular chronicle of Jewish history ascribed to Joseph Ben Gurion, thought to have been compiled in the 8th century. Based on Josephus, it traces Jewish history from the return from the Babylonian exile to the destruction of the Second Temple by the Romans in 70 CE.